Praise for *Crave*

'*Crave* is about to become fandom's new favourite vampire romance obsession'
Hypable

'*Crave* sucked me into its dangerous – but oh so delicious – world. Suffice it to say: I have a new book boyfriend!'
Pintip Dunn, *New York Times* bestselling author of *Malice*

'*Crave* is this generation's *Twilight*'
Lynn Rush, *New York Times* bestselling author of the Touch of Frost series

'I'm having the BEST book hangover. Filled with danger, humour, and heart, *Crave* proves that vampires are definitely back!'
J. Kenner, *New York Times* bestselling author of *Release Me*

'Intricately crafted, deeply romantic, and with an ending that blew me away. I can't wait for the next instalment'
Victoria Scott, author of the Fire & Flood series

'Funny, smart, and compelling – Tracy Wolff's *Crave* is an addictive masterpiece!'
Emily McKay, author of *Storybound*

'Full of intrigue and mystery and with a sizzling romance, *Crave* is my new paranormal obsession!'
Mary Lindsey, author of *Haven*

About the Author

NYT and *USA Today* bestselling author Tracy Wolff wrote her first short story – something with a rainbow and a prince – in second grade. By ten she'd read everything in the young adult and classics sections of her local bookstore, so in desperation her mom started her on romance novels. And from the first page of the first book, Tracy knew she'd found her life-long love. A one-time English professor with over fifty novels to her name, she now devotes most of her time to writing romance and dreaming up heroes. She lives in Austin, Texas, with her family.

crave

TRACY WOLFF

HODDER &
STOUGHTON

First published in Great Britain in 2020 by Hodder & Stoughton
An Hachette UK company

20

This edition published by arrangement with Entangled Publishing LLC through RightsMix LLC.

This edition edited by Liz Pelletier.

A CIP catalogue record for this title is available from the British Library

Paperback ISBN 978 1 529 35555 0
eBook ISBN 978 1 529 35556 7

Printed and bound in Great Britain by Clays Ltd, Elcograf S.p.A.

Hodder & Stoughton policy is to use papers that are natural, renewable and recyclable products and made from wood grown in sustainable forests. The logging and manufacturing processes are expected to conform to the environmental regulations of the country of origin.

Hodder & Stoughton Ltd
Carmelite House
50 Victoria Embankment
London EC4Y 0DZ

www.hodder.co.uk

For my boys,
who have always believed in me
and
for Stephanie,
who helped me believe in myself again.

1

Landing Is Just Throwing Yourself at the Ground and Hoping You Don't Miss

"There she is," Philip says as we clear the peaks of several mountains, taking one hand off the steering column to point to a small collection of buildings in the distance. "Healy, Alaska. Home sweet home."

"Oh, wow. It looks..." Tiny. It looks really, really tiny. Way smaller than just my neighborhood in San Diego, let alone the whole city.

Then again, it's pretty hard to see much of anything from up here. Not because of the mountains that loom over the area like long-forgotten monsters but because we're in the middle of a weird kind of haze that Philip refers to as "civil twilight" even though it's barely five o'clock. Still, I can see well enough to make out that the so-called town he's pointing at is full of mismatched buildings randomly grouped together.

I finally settle on, "Interesting. It looks...interesting."

It's not the first description that popped into my head—no, that was the old cliché that hell has actually frozen over—but it is the most polite one as Philip drops even lower, preparing for what I'm pretty sure will be yet another harrowing incident in the list of harrowing incidents that have plagued me since I got on the first of three planes ten hours ago.

Sure enough, I've only just spotted what passes for an airport in this one-thousand-person town (thank you, Google) when Philip says, "Hang on, Grace. It's a short runway because it's hard to keep a long one clear of snow or ice for any amount of time out here. It's going to be a quick landing."

I have no idea what a "quick landing" means, but it doesn't sound good. So I grab the bar on the plane door, which I'm pretty sure exists for just this very reason, and hold on tight as we drop lower and lower.

"Okay, kid. Here goes nothing!" Philip tells me. Which, by the way, definitely makes the top five things you don't *ever* want to hear your pilot say while you're still in the air.

The ground looms white and unyielding below us, and I squeeze my eyes shut.

Seconds later, I feel the wheels skip across the ground. Then Philip hits the brakes hard enough to slam me forward so fast that my seat belt is the only thing keeping my head from meeting the control panel. The plane whines—not sure what part of it is making that horrendous noise or if it's a collective death knell—so I choose not to focus on it.

Especially when we start skidding to the left.

I bite my lip, keep my eyes squeezed firmly shut even as my heart threatens to burst out of my chest. If this is the end, I don't need to see it coming.

The thought distracts me, has me wondering just what my mom and dad might have seen coming, and by the time I shut down that line of thinking, Philip has the plane sliding to a shaky, shuddering halt.

I know exactly how it feels. Right now, even my toes are trembling.

I peel my eyes open slowly, resisting the urge to pat myself down to make sure I really am still in one piece. But Philip just laughs and says, "Textbook landing."

Maybe if that textbook is a horror novel. One he's reading upside down and backward.

I don't say anything, though. Just give him the best smile I can manage and grab my backpack from under my feet. I pull out the pair of gloves Uncle Finn sent me and put them on. Then I push open the plane door and jump down, praying the whole time that my knees will support me when I hit the ground.

They do, just barely.

After taking a few seconds to make sure I'm not going to crumble—and to pull my brand-new coat more tightly around me because it's literally about eight degrees out here—I head to the back of the plane to get the three suitcases that are all that is left of my life.

I feel a pang looking at them, but I don't let myself dwell on everything I had to leave behind, any more than I let myself dwell on the idea of strangers living in the house I grew up in. After all, who cares about a house or art supplies or a drum kit when I've lost so much more?

Instead, I grab a bag out of what passes for the tiny airplane's cargo hold and wrestle it to the ground. Before I can reach for the second, Philip is there, lifting my other two suitcases like they're filled with pillows instead of everything I own in the world.

"Come on, Grace. Let's go before you start to turn blue out here." He nods toward a parking lot—not even a *building*, just a parking lot—about two hundred yards away, and I want to groan. It's so cold out that now I'm shaking for a whole different reason. How can anyone live like this? It's unreal, especially considering it was seventy degrees where I woke up this morning.

There's nothing to do but nod, though, so I do. Then grab onto the handle of my suitcase and start dragging it toward a small patch of concrete that I'm pretty sure passes for an airport in Healy. It's a far cry from San Diego's bustling terminals.

Philip overtakes me easily, a large suitcase dangling from each hand. I start to tell him that he can pull the handles out and roll them, but the second I step off the runway and onto the snowy ground that surrounds it in all directions, I figure out why he's carrying them—it's pretty much impossible to roll a heavy suitcase over snow.

I'm near frozen by the time we make it halfway to the (thankfully still plowed) parking lot, despite my heavy jacket and synthetic fur–lined gloves. I'm not sure what I'm supposed to do from here, how I'm supposed to get to the boarding school my uncle is headmaster of, so I turn to ask Philip if Uber is even a thing up here. But before I can get a word out, someone steps from behind one of the pickup trucks in the lot and rushes straight toward me.

I think it's my cousin, Macy, but it's hard to tell, considering she's covered from head to toe in protective weather gear.

"You're here!" the moving pile of hats, scarves, and jackets says, and I was right—it's definitely Macy.

"I'm here," I agree dryly, wondering if it's too late to reconsider foster care. Or emancipation. Any living situation in San Diego has got to be better than living in a town whose airport consists of one runway and a tiny parking lot. Heather is going to die when I text her.

"Finally!" Macy says, reaching out for a hug. It's a little awkward, partly because of all the clothes she's wearing and partly because—despite being a year younger than my own seventeen years—she's about eight inches taller than I am. "I've been waiting for more than an hour."

I hug her back but let go quickly as I answer. "Sorry, my plane was late from Seattle. The storm there made it hard to take off."

"Yeah, we hear that a lot," she tells me with a grimace. "Pretty sure their weather is even worse than ours."

I want to argue—miles of snow and enough protective gear to give astronauts pause seem pretty freaking awful to me. But I don't know Macy all that well, despite the fact that we're cousins, and the last thing I want to do is offend her. Besides Uncle Finn and now Philip, she is the only other person I know in this place.

Not to mention the only family I have left.

Which is why, in the end, I just shrug.

It must be a good enough answer, though, because she grins back at me before turning to Philip, who is still carrying my suitcases. "Thanks so much for picking her up, Uncle Philip. Dad says to tell you he owes you a case of beer."

"No worries, Mace. Had to run a few errands in Fairbanks anyway." He says it so casually, like hopping in a plane for a couple-hundred-mile round-trip journey is no big deal. Then again, out here where there's nothing but mountains and snow in all directions, maybe it's not. After all, according to Wikipedia, Healy has only one major road in and out of it, and in the winter sometimes even that gets closed down.

I've spent the last month trying to imagine what that looks like. What it *is* like.

I guess I'm about to find out.

"Still, he says he'll be around Friday with that beer so you guys can watch the game in true bro-mance style." She turns to me. "My dad's really upset he couldn't make it out to pick you up, Grace. There was an emergency at the school that no one else could deal with. But he told me to get him the second we make it back."

"No worries," I tell her. Because what else am I supposed to say? Besides, if I've learned anything in the month since my parents died, it's just how little most things matter.

Who cares who picks me up as long as I get to the school?

Who cares where I live if it's not going to be with my mom and dad?

Philip walks us to the edge of the cleared parking lot before finally letting go of my suitcases. Macy gives him a quick hug goodbye, and I shake his hand, murmur, "Thanks for coming to get me."

"Not a problem at all. Any time you need a flight, I'm your man." He winks, then heads back to the tarmac to deal with his plane.

We watch him go for a couple of seconds before Macy grabs the handles on both suitcases and starts rolling them across the tiny parking lot. She gestures for me to do the same with the one I'm holding on to, so I do, even though a part of me wants nothing more than to run back onto the tarmac with Philip, climb back into that tiny plane, and demand to be flown back to Fairbanks. Or, even better, back home to San Diego.

It's a feeling that only gets worse when Macy says, "Do you need to pee? It's a good ninety-minute ride to the school from here."

Ninety minutes? That doesn't seem possible when the whole town looks like we could drive it in fifteen, maybe twenty minutes at the most. Then again, when we were flying over, I didn't see any building remotely big enough to be a boarding school for close to four hundred teenagers, so maybe the school isn't actually in Healy.

I can't help but think of the mountains and rivers that surround this town in all directions and wonder where on earth I'm going to end up before this day is through. And where exactly she expects me to pee out here anyway.

"I'm okay," I answer after a minute, even as my stomach somersaults and pitches nervously.

This whole day has been about getting here, and that was bad enough. But as we roll my suitcases through the semi-darkness, the well-below-freezing air slapping at me with each step we take, everything gets superreal, superfast. Especially when Macy walks through the entire parking lot to the *snowmobile* parked just beyond the edge of the pavement.

At first, I think she's joking around, but then she starts loading my suitcases onto the attached sled and it occurs to me that this is really happening. I'm really about to ride a snowmobile in the near dark through *Alaska* in weather that is more than *twenty degrees below freezing*, if the app on my phone can be believed.

All that's missing is the wicked witch cackling that she's going to get me and my little dog, too. Then again, at this point, that would probably be redundant.

I watch with a kind of horrified fascination as Macy straps my suitcases to the sled. I should probably offer to help, but I wouldn't even know where to begin. And since the last thing I want is for the few belongings I have left in the world to be strewn across the side of a mountain, I figure if there was ever a time to leave things to the experts, this is it.

"Here, you're going to need these," Macy tells me, opening up the small bag that was already strapped to the sled when we got out here. She rummages around for a second before pulling out a pair of heavy snow pants and a thick wool scarf. They are both hot pink, my favorite color when I was a kid but not so much now. Still, it's obvious Macy remembered that from the last time I saw her, and I can't help being touched as she holds them out to me.

"Thanks." I give her the closest thing to a smile I can manage.

After a few false starts, I manage to pull the pants on over the thermal underwear and fleece pajama pants with emojis on them (the only kind of fleece pants I own) that I put on at my uncle's instruction before boarding the plane in Seattle. Then I take a long look at the way Macy's rainbow-colored scarf is wrapped around her neck and face and do the same thing with mine.

It's harder than it looks, especially trying to get it positioned well enough to keep it from sliding down my nose the second I move.

Eventually, I manage it, though, and that's when Macy reaches for one of the helmets draped over the snowmobile's handles.

"The helmet is insulated, so it will help keep you warm as well as protect your head in case of a crash," she instructs. "Plus, it's got a shield to protect your eyes from the cold air."

"My eyes can freeze?" I ask, more than a little traumatized, as I take the helmet from her and try to ignore how hard it is to breathe with the scarf over my nose.

"Eyes don't freeze," Macy answers with a little laugh, like she can't help herself. "But the shield will keep them from watering and make you more comfortable."

"Oh, right." I duck my head as my cheeks heat up. "I'm an idiot."

"No you're not." Macy wraps an arm around my shoulders and squeezes tight. "Alaska is a lot. Everyone who comes here has a learning curve. You'll figure it all out soon enough."

I'm not holding my breath on that one—I can't imagine that this cold, foreign place will ever feel familiar to me—but I don't say anything. Not when Macy has already done so much to try and make me feel welcome.

"I'm really sorry you had to come here, Grace," she continues after a second. "I mean, I'm really excited that you're here. I just wish it wasn't because..." Her voice drifts off before she finishes the sentence. But I'm used to that by now. After weeks of having my friends and teachers tiptoe around me, I've learned that no one wants to say the words.

Still, I'm too exhausted to fill in the blanks. Instead, I slip my head in the helmet and secure it the way Macy showed me.

"Ready?" she asks once I've got my face and head as protected as they're going to get.

The answer hasn't changed since Philip asked me that same question in Fairbanks. *Not even close.* "Yeah. Absolutely."

I wait for Macy to climb on the snowmobile before getting on behind her.

"Hold on to my waist!" she shouts as she turns it on, so I do. Seconds later, we're speeding into the darkness that stretches endlessly in front of us.

I've never been more terrified in my life.

2

Just Because You Live in a Tower Doesn't Make You a Prince

The ride isn't as bad as I thought it would be.

I mean, it's not good, but that has more to do with the fact that I've been traveling all day and I just want to get someplace—anyplace—where I can stay longer than a layover. Or a really long snowmobile ride.

And if that place also happens to be warm and devoid of the local wildlife I can hear howling in the distance, then I'm all about it. Especially since everything south of my waist seems to have fallen asleep...

I'm in the middle of trying to figure out how to wake up my very numb butt when we suddenly veer off the trail (and I mean "trail" in the loosest sense of the word) we've been following and onto a kind of plateau on the side of the mountain. It's as we wind our way through yet another copse of trees that I finally see lights up ahead.

"Is that Katmere Academy?" I shout.

"Yeah." Macy lays off the speed a little, steering around trees like we're on a giant slalom course. "We should be there in about five minutes."

Thank God. Much longer out here and I might actually lose

a toe or three, even with my doubled-up wool socks. I mean, everyone knows Alaska is cold, but can I just say—it's freaking *cold*, and I was *not* prepared.

Yet another roar sounds in the distance, but as we finally clear the thicket of trees, it's hard to pay attention to anything but the huge building looming in front of us, growing closer with every second that passes.

Or should I say the huge *castle* looming in front of us, because the dwelling I'm looking at is nothing like a modern building. And absolutely nothing like any school I have *ever* seen. I tried to Google it before I got here, but apparently Katmere Academy is so elite even Google hasn't heard of it.

First of all, it's big. Like, really big...and sprawling. From here it looks like the brick wall in front of the castle stretches halfway around the mountain.

Second, it's elegant. Like, really, really elegant, with architecture I've only heard described in my art classes before. Vaulted arches, flying buttresses, and giant, ornate windows dominate the structure.

And third, as we get closer, I can't help wondering if my eyes are deceiving me or if there are gargoyles—*actual gargoyles*—protruding from the top of the castle walls. I know it's just my imagination, but I'd be lying if I said I didn't half expect to see Quasimodo waiting for us when we finally get there.

Macy pulls up to the huge gate at the front of the school and enters a code. Seconds later, the gate swings open. And we're on our way again.

The closer we get, the more surreal everything feels. Like I'm trapped in a horror movie or Salvador Dalí painting. *Katmere Academy may be a Gothic castle, but at least there's no moat*, I tell myself as we break through one last copse of trees. *And no fire-breathing dragon guarding the entrance*. Just a long, winding driveway that looks like every other prep school driveway I've ever seen on TV—except for the fact that it's covered in snow. Big shock. And leads right up to the school's huge, incredibly ornate front doors.

Antique doors.

Castle doors.

I shake my head to clear it. I mean, what even is my life right now?

"Told you it wouldn't be bad," Macy says as she pulls up to the front with a spray of snow. "We didn't even see a caribou, let alone a wolf."

She's right, so I just nod and pretend I'm not completely overwhelmed.

Pretend like my stomach isn't tied into knots and my whole world hasn't turned upside down for the second time in a month.

Pretend like I'm okay.

"Let's bring your suitcases up to your room and get you unpacked. It'll help you relax."

Macy climbs off the snowmobile, then takes off her helmet and her hat. It's the first time I've seen her without all the cold-weather gear, and I can't help smiling at her rainbow-colored hair. It's cut in a short, choppy style that should be smooshed and plastered to her head after three hours in a helmet, but instead it looks like she just walked out of a salon.

Which matches the rest of her, now that I think about it, considering her whole coordinating jacket, boots, and snow pants look kind of shouts cover model for some Alaskan wilderness fashion magazine.

On the other hand, I'm pretty sure my look says I've gone a couple of rounds with a pissed-off caribou. And lost. Badly. Which seems fair, since that's about how I feel.

Macy makes quick work of unloading my suitcases, and this

time I grab two of them. But I only make it a few steps up the very long walk to the castle's imposing front doors before I'm struggling to breathe.

"It's the altitude," Macy says as she takes one of the suitcases out of my hand. "We climbed pretty fast and, since you're coming from sea level, it's going to take a few days for you to get used to how thin the air is up here."

Just the idea of not being able to breathe sets off the beginnings of the panic attack I've barely kept at bay all day. Closing my eyes, I take a deep breath—or as deep as I can out here—and try to fight it back.

In, hold for five seconds, out. In, hold for ten seconds, out. In, hold for five seconds, out. Just like Heather's mom taught me. Dr. Blake is a therapist, and she's been giving me tips on how to deal with the anxiety I've been having since my parents died. But I'm not sure her tips are up to combatting all this any more than I am.

Still, I can't stand here frozen forever, like one of the gargoyles staring down at me. Especially not when I can feel Macy's concern even with my eyes closed.

I take one more deep breath and open my eyes again, shooting my cousin a smile I'm far from feeling. "Fake it till you make it is still a thing, right?"

"It's going to be okay," she tells me, her own eyes wide with sympathy. "Just stand there and catch your breath. I'll carry your suitcases up to the door."

"I can do it."

"Seriously, it's okay. Just chill for a minute." She holds up her hand in the universal *stop* gesture. "We're not in any hurry."

Her tone begs me not to argue, so I don't. Especially since the panic attack I'm trying to fend off is only making it harder to breathe. Instead, I nod and watch as she carries my suitcases—

one at a time—up to the school's front door.

As I do, a flash of color way above us catches my eye.

It's there and gone so fast that even as I scan for it, I can't be sure it ever really existed to begin with. Except—there it is again. A flash of red in the lit window of the tallest tower.

I don't know who it is or why they even matter, but I stop where I am. Watching. Waiting. Wondering if whoever it is will make another appearance.

It isn't long before they do.

I can't see clearly—distance, darkness, and the distorted glass of the windows cover up a lot—but I get the impression of a strong jaw, shaggy dark hair, a red jacket against a background of light.

It's not much, and there's no reason for it to have caught my attention—certainly no reason for it to have *held* my attention—and yet I find myself staring up at the window so long that Macy has all three of my suitcases at the top of the stairs before I even realize it.

"Ready to try again?" she calls down from her spot near the front doors.

"Oh, yeah. Of course." I start up the last thirty or so steps, ignoring the way my head is spinning. Altitude sickness—one more thing I never had to worry about in San Diego.

Fantastic.

I glance up at the window one last time, not surprised at all to find that whoever was looking down at me is long gone. Still, an inexplicable shiver of disappointment works its way through me. It makes no sense, though, so I shrug it off. I have bigger things to worry about right now.

"This place is unbelievable," I tell my cousin as she pushes open one of the doors and we walk inside.

And holy crap—I thought the whole castle thing with its

pointed archways and elaborate stonework was imposing from the outside. Now that I've seen the inside… Now that I've seen the inside, I'm pretty sure I should be curtsying right about now. Or at least bowing and scraping. I mean, wow. Just…wow.

I don't know where to look first—at the high ceiling with its elaborate black crystal chandelier or the roaring fireplace that dominates the whole right wall of the foyer.

In the end I go with the fireplace, because *heat*. And because it's freaking gorgeous, the mantel around it an intricate pattern of stone and stained glass that reflects the light of the flames through the whole room.

"Pretty cool, huh?" Macy says with a grin as she comes up behind me.

"Totally cool," I agree. "This place is…"

"Magic. I know." She wiggles her brows at me. "Want to see some more?"

I really do. I'm still far from sold on the Alaskan boarding school thing, but that doesn't mean I don't want to check out the castle. I mean, it's a *castle*, complete with stone walls and elaborate tapestries I can't help but want to stop and look at as we make our way through the entryway into some kind of common room.

The only problem is that the deeper we move into the school, the more students we come across. Some are standing around in scattered clumps, talking and laughing, while others are seated at several of the room's scarred wooden tables, leaning over books or phones or laptop screens. In the back corner of one room, sprawled out on several antique-looking couches in varying hues of red and gold, is a group of six guys playing Xbox on a huge TV, while a few other students crowd around to watch.

Only, as we get closer, I realize they aren't watching the video game. Or their books. Or even their phones. Instead, they're all looking at *me* as Macy leads—and by leads, I mean parades—me through the center of the room.

My stomach clenches, and I duck my head to hide my very obvious discomfort. I get that everyone wants to check out the new girl—especially when she's the headmaster's niece—but understanding doesn't make it any easier to bear the scrutiny from a bunch of strangers. Especially since I'm pretty sure I have the worst case of helmet hair ever recorded.

I'm too busy avoiding eye contact and regulating my breathing to talk as we make our way through the room, but as we exit into a long, winding hallway, I finally tell Macy, "I can't believe you go to school here."

"We *both* go to school here," she reminds me with a quick grin.

"Yeah, but…" I just got here. And I've never felt more out of place in my life.

"But?" she repeats, eyebrows arched.

"It's a lot." I eye the gorgeous stained glass windows that run along the exterior wall and the elaborate carved molding that decorates the arched ceiling.

"It is." She slows down until I catch up. "But it's home."

"Your home," I whisper, doing my best not to think of the house I left behind, where my mother's front porch wind chimes and whirligigs were the most wild-and-crazy thing about it.

"*Our* home," she answers as she pulls out her phone and sends a quick text. "You'll see. Speaking of which, my dad wants me to give you a choice about what kind of room situation you want."

"Room situation?" I repeat, glancing around the castle while images of ghosts and animated suits of armor slide through my head.

"Well, all the single rooms have been assigned for this term. Dad told me we could move some people around to get you one, but I really hoped you might want to room with me instead."

She smiles hopefully for a second, but it quickly fades as she continues. “I mean, I totally get that you might need some space to yourself right now after…”

And there’s that fade-out again. It gets to me, just like it does every time. Usually, I ignore it, but this time I can’t stop myself from asking, “After what?”

Just this once, I want someone else to say it. Maybe then it will feel more real and less like a nightmare.

Except as Macy gasps and turns the color of the snow outside, I realize it’s not going to be her. And that it’s unfair of me to expect it to be.

“I’m sorry,” she whispers, and now it almost looks like she’s going to cry, which, no. Just no. We’re not going to go there. Not when the only thing currently holding me together is a snarky attitude and my ability to compartmentalize.

No way am I going to risk losing my grip on either. Not here, in front of my cousin and anybody else who might happen to pass by. And not now, when it’s obvious from all the stares that I’m totally the newest attraction at the zoo.

So instead of melting into Macy for the hug I so desperately need, instead of letting myself think about how much I miss home and my parents and my *life*, I pull back and give her the best smile I can manage. “Why don’t you show me to *our* room?”

The concern in her eyes doesn’t diminish, but the sunshine definitely makes another appearance. “*Our* room? Really?”

I sigh deep inside and kiss my dream of a little peaceful solitude goodbye. It’s not as hard as it should be, but then I’ve lost a lot more in the last month than my own space. “Really. Rooming with you sounds perfect.”

I’ve already upset her once, which is so not my style. Neither is getting someone kicked out of their room. Besides being rude and smacking of nepotism, it also seems like a surefire way to piss people off—something that is definitely not on my to-do list right now.

"Awesome!" Macy grins and throws her arms around me for a fast but powerful hug. Then she glances at her phone with a roll of her eyes. "Dad still hasn't answered my text—he's the worst about checking his phone. Why don't you hang out here, and I'll go get him? I know he wanted to see you as soon as we arrived."

"I can come with you—"

"Please just sit, Grace." She points at the ornate French-provincial-style chairs that flank a small chess table in an alcove to the right of the staircase. "I'm sure you're exhausted and I've got this, honest. Relax a minute while I get Dad."

Because she's right—my head is aching and my chest still feels tight—I just nod and plop down in the closest chair. I'm beyond tired and want nothing more than to lean my head back against the chair and close my eyes for a minute. But I'm afraid I'll fall asleep if I do. And no way am I running the risk of being the girl caught drooling all over herself in the hallway on her very first day...or ever, for that matter.

More to keep myself from drifting off than out of actual interest, I pick up one of the chess pieces in front of me. It's made of intricately carved stone, and my eyes widen as I realize what I'm looking at. A perfect rendition of a vampire, right down to the black cape, frightening snarl, and bared fangs. It matches the Gothic castle vibe so well that I can't help being amused. Plus, it's gorgeously crafted.

Intrigued now, I reach for a piece from the other side. And nearly laugh out loud when I realize it's a dragon—fierce, regal, with giant wings. It's absolutely beautiful.

The whole set is.

I put the piece down only to pick up another dragon. This one is less fierce, but with its sleepy eyes and folded wings, it's even more intricate. I look it over carefully, fascinated with the level of detail in the piece—everything from the perfect points on the wings to the careful curl of each talon reflects just how much care the artist put into the piece. I've never been a chess girl, but this set just might change my mind about the game.

When I put down this dragon piece, I go to the other side of the board and pick up the vampire queen. She's beautiful, with long, flowing hair and an elaborately decorated cape.

"I'd be careful with that one if I were you. She's got a nasty bite." The words are low and rumbly and so close that I nearly fall out of my chair. Instead, I jump up, plopping the chess piece down with a clatter, then whirl around—heart pounding—only to find myself face-to-face with the most intimidating guy I've ever seen. And not just because he's hot...although he's definitely that.

Still, there's something more to him, something different and powerful and overwhelming, though I don't have a clue what it is. I mean, sure. He has the kind of face nineteenth-century poets loved to write about—too intense to be beautiful and too striking to be anything else.

Skyscraper cheekbones.

Full red lips.

A jaw so sharp it could cut stone.

Smooth, alabaster skin.

And his eyes...a bottomless obsidian that see everything and show nothing, surrounded by the longest, most obscene lashes I've ever seen.

And even worse, those all-knowing eyes are laser-focused on me right now, and I'm suddenly terrified that he can see all the things I've worked so hard and so long to hide. I try to duck my head, try to yank my gaze from his, but I can't. I'm trapped by his stare, hypnotized by the sheer magnetism rolling off him in waves.

I swallow hard to catch my breath.

It doesn't work.

And now he's grinning, one corner of his mouth turning up in a crooked little smile that I feel in every single cell. Which only makes it worse, because that smirk says he knows exactly what kind of effect he's having on me. And, worse, that he's enjoying it.

Annoyance flashes through me at the realization, melting the numbness that's surrounded me since my parents' deaths. Waking me from the stupor that's the only thing that's kept me from screaming all day, every day, at the unfairness of it all. At the pain and horror and helplessness that have taken over my whole life.

It's not a good feeling. And the fact that it's this guy—with the smirk and the face and the cold eyes that refuse to relinquish their hold on me even as they demand that I don't look too closely—just pisses me off more.

It's that anger that finally gives me the strength to break free of his gaze. I rip my eyes away, then search desperately for something else—anything else—to focus on.

Unfortunately, he's standing right in front of me, so close that he's blocking my view of anything else.

Determined to avoid his eyes, I look anywhere but. And land instead on his long, lean body. Then really wish I hadn't, because the black jeans and T-shirt he's wearing only emphasize his flat stomach and hard, well-defined biceps. Not to mention the double-wide shoulders that are absolutely responsible for blocking my view in the first place.

Add in the thick, dark hair that's worn a little too long, so that it falls forward into his face and skims low across his insane cheekbones, and there's nothing to do but give in. Nothing to do but admit that—obnoxious smirk or not—this boy is sexy as hell.

A little wicked, a lot wild, and *all* dangerous.

What little oxygen I've been able to pull into my lungs in this high altitude completely disappears with the realization. Which only makes me madder. Because, seriously. When exactly did I become the heroine in some YA romance? The new girl swooning over the hottest, most unattainable boy in school?

Gross. And so not happening.

Determined to nip whatever this is in the bud, I force myself to look at his face again. This time, as our gazes meet and clash, I realize that it doesn't matter if I'm acting like some giant romantic cliché.

Because he isn't.

One glance and I know that this dark boy with the closed-off eyes and the fuck-you attitude isn't the hero of anyone's story. Least of all mine.

3

Vampire Queens Aren't the Only Ones with a Nasty Bite

Determined not to let this staring contest that feels a little like a show of dominance go on any longer, I cast around for something to break the tension. And settle on a response to the only thing he's actually said to me so far.

"*Who's* got a nasty bite?"

He reaches past me and picks up the piece I dropped, holds the queen for me to see. "She's really not very nice."

I stare at him. "She's a chess piece."

His obsidian eyes gleam back. "Your point?"

"My point is, she's a *chess* piece. She's made of *marble*. She can't bite anyone."

He inclines his head in a *you never know* gesture. "'There are more things in heaven and hell, Horatio, / Than are dreamt of in your philosophy.'"

"Earth," I correct before I can think better of it.

He crooks one midnight-black brow in question, so I continue. "The quote is, 'There are more things in heaven and *earth*, Horatio.'"

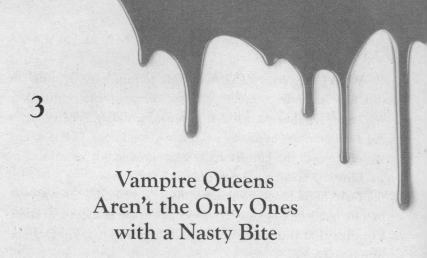

"Is it now?" His face doesn't change, but there's something mocking in his tone that wasn't there before, like I'm the one who made the mistake, not him. But I know I'm right—my AP English class just finished reading *Hamlet* last month, and my teacher spent forever on that quote. "I think I like my version better."

"Even though it's wrong?"

"Especially because it's wrong."

I have no idea what I'm supposed to say to that, so I just shake my head. And wonder how lost I'll get if I go looking for Macy and Uncle Finn right now. Probably very, considering the size of this place, but I'm beginning to think I should risk it. Because the longer I stand here, the more I realize this guy is as terrifying as he is intriguing.

I'm not sure which is worse. And I'm growing less sure by the second that I want to find out.

"I need to go." I force the words past a jaw I didn't even know I'd been clenching.

"Yeah, you do." He takes a small step back, nods toward the common room Macy and I just walked through. "The door's that way."

It's not the response I'm expecting, and it throws me off guard. "So what, I shouldn't let it hit me on the way out?"

He shrugs. "As long as you leave this school, it doesn't matter to me if it hits you or not. I warned your uncle you wouldn't be safe here, but he obviously doesn't like you much."

Anger flashes through me at his words, burning away the last of the numbness that has plagued me. "Who exactly are you supposed to be anyway? Katmere's very own unwelcome wagon?"

"*Un*welcome wagon?" His tone is as obnoxious as his face. "Believe me, this is the nicest greeting you're going to get here."

"This is it, huh?" I raise my brows, spread my arms out wide. "The big welcome to Alaska?"

"More like, welcome to hell. Now get the fuck out."

The last is said in a snarl that yanks my heart into my throat.

But it also slams my temper straight into the stratosphere. "Is it that stick up your ass that makes you such a jerk?" I demand. "Or is this just your regular, charming personality?"

The words come out fast and furious, before I even know I'm going to say them. But once they're out, I don't regret them. How can I when shock flits across his face, finally erasing that annoying smirk of his?

At least for a minute. Then he fires back, "I've got to say, if that's the best you've got, I give you about an hour."

I know I shouldn't ask, but he looks so smug, I can't help myself. "Before what?"

"Before something eats you." He doesn't say it, but the *obviously* is definitely implied. Which only pisses me off more.

"Seriously? That's what you decided to go with?" I roll my eyes. "Bite me, dude."

"Nah, I don't think so." He looks me up and down. "I'm pretty sure you wouldn't even make an appetizer."

But then he's stepping closer, leaning down until he's all but whispering in my ear. "Maybe a quick snack, though." His teeth close with a loud, sharp snap that makes me jump and shiver all at the same time.

Which I hate…so, so much.

I glance around us, curious if anyone else is witnessing this mess. But where everyone only had eyes for me earlier, they seem to be going out of their way not to glance in my direction now. One lanky boy with thick red hair even keeps his head so awkwardly turned to the side while walking across the room that he almost runs into another student.

Which tells me everything I need to know about this guy.

Determined to regain control of the situation—and myself—I take a big step back. Then, ignoring my pounding heart and the pterodactyls flapping around in my stomach, I demand, "What is *wrong* with you?" I mean, seriously. He's got the manners of a rabid polar bear.

"Got a century or three?" His smirk is back—he's obviously proud of getting to me—and for a moment, just a moment, I think about how satisfying it would be to punch him right in the center of that annoying mouth of his.

"You know what? You really don't have to be such a—"

"Don't tell me what I have to be. Not when you don't have a clue what you've wandered into here."

"Oh no!" I do a mock-afraid face. "Is this the part of the story where you tell me about the big, bad monsters out here in the big, bad Alaskan wilderness?"

"No, this is the part of the story where I show you the big, bad monsters right here in this castle." He steps forward, closing the small distance I managed to put between us.

And there goes my heart again, beating like a caged bird desperate to escape.

I hate it.

I hate that he's bested me, and I hate that being this close to him makes me feel a bunch of things I shouldn't for a guy who has been a total jerk to me. I hate even more that the look in his eyes says he knows exactly how I'm feeling.

The fact that I'm reacting so strongly to him when all he seems to feel for me is contempt is humiliating, so I take one trembling step back. Then I take another. And another.

But he follows suit, moving one step forward for every step I take backward, until I'm caught between him and the chess table pressing into the back of my thighs. And even though there's nowhere to go, even though I'm stuck right here in front of him, he leans closer still, *gets* closer still, until I can feel his warm breath on my cheek and the brush of his silky black hair against my skin.

"What are—?" What little breath I've managed to recover

catches in my throat. "What are you doing?" I demand as he reaches past me.

He doesn't answer at first. But when he pulls away, he's got one of the dragon pieces in his hand. He holds it up for me to see, that single eyebrow of his arched provocatively, and answers. "You're the one who wanted to see the monsters."

This one is fierce, eyes narrowed, talons raised, mouth open to show off sharp, jagged teeth. But it's still just a chess piece. "I'm not afraid of a three-inch dragon."

"Yeah, well, you should be."

"Yeah, well, I'm *not.*" The words come out more strangled than I intend, because he may have taken a step back, but he's still standing too close. So close that I can feel his breath on my cheek and the warmth radiating from his body. So close that one deep breath will end with my chest pressing against his.

The thought sets off a whole new kaleidoscope of butterflies deep inside me. I can't move back any farther, but I can *lean* back over the table a little. Which I do—all while those dark, fathomless eyes of his watch my every move.

Silence stretches between us for one…ten…twenty-five seconds before he finally asks, "So if you aren't afraid of things that go bump in the night, what *are* you afraid of?"

Images of my parents' mangled car flash through my brain, followed by pictures of their battered bodies. I was the only family they had in San Diego—or anywhere, really, except for Finn and Macy—so I'm the one who had to go to the morgue. I'm the one who had to identify their bodies. Who had to see them all bruised and bloody and broken before the funeral home had a chance to put them back together again.

The familiar anguish wells up inside me, but I do what I've been doing for weeks now. I shove it back down. Pretend it doesn't exist. "Not much," I tell him as flippantly as I can manage. “There’s not much to be afraid of when you’ve already lost everything that matters.”

He freezes at my words, his whole body tensing up so much that it feels like he might shatter. Even his eyes change, the wildness disappearing between one blink and the next until only stillness remains.

Stillness and an agony so deep I can barely see it behind the layers and layers of defenses he’s erected.

But I *can* see it. More, I can *feel* it calling to my own pain.

It’s an awful and awe-inspiring feeling at the same time. So awful I can barely stand it. So awe-inspiring that I can’t stop it.

So I don’t. And neither does he.

Instead, we stand there, frozen. Devasted. Connected in a way I can feel but can’t comprehend by our very separate horrors.

I don’t know how long we stay like that, staring into each other’s eyes. Acknowledging each other’s pain because we can’t acknowledge our own.

Long enough for the animosity to drain right out of me.

Long enough for me to see the silver flecks in the midnight of his eyes—distant stars shining through the darkness he makes no attempt to hide.

More than long enough for me to get my rampaging heart under control. At least until he reaches out and gently takes hold of one of my million curls.

And just that easily, I forget how to breathe again.

Heat slams through me as he stretches out the curl, warming me up for the first time since I opened the door of Philip’s plane in Healy. It’s confusing and overwhelming and I don’t have a clue what to do about it.

Five minutes ago, this guy was being a total douche to me. And now…now I don’t know anything. Except that I need space. And to sleep. And a chance to just breathe for a few minutes.

With that in mind, I bring my hands up and push at his shoulders in an effort to get him to give me a little room. But it's like pushing a wall of granite. He doesn't budge.

At least not until I whisper, "Please."

He waits a second longer, maybe two or three—until my head is muddled and my hands are shaking—before he finally takes a step back and lets the curl go.

As he does, he sweeps a hand through his dark hair. His longish bangs part just enough to reveal a jagged scar from the center of his left eyebrow to the left corner of his mouth. It's thin and white, barely noticeable against the paleness of his skin, but it's there nonetheless—especially if you look at the wicked vee it causes at the end of his dark eyebrow.

It should make him less attractive, should do something—anything—to negate the incredible power of his looks. But somehow the scar only emphasizes the danger, turning him from just another pretty boy with angelic looks into someone a million times more compelling. A fallen angel with a bad-boy vibe for miles...and a million stories to back that vibe up.

Combined with the anguish I just felt inside him, it makes him more...human. More relatable and more devastating, despite the darkness that rolls off him in waves. A scar like this only comes from an unimaginable injury. Hundreds of stitches, multiple operations, months—maybe even years—of recovery. I hate that he suffered like that, wouldn't wish it on anyone, let alone this boy who frustrates and terrifies and excites me all at the same time.

He knows I noticed the scar—I can see it in the way his eyes narrow. In the way his shoulders stiffen and his hands clench into fists. In the way he ducks his head so that his hair falls over his cheek again.

I hate that, hate that he thinks he has to hide something that he should wear as a badge of honor. It takes a lot of strength to get through something like this, a lot of strength to come out the other side of it, and he should be proud of that strength. Not ashamed of the mark it's left.

I reach out before I make a conscious decision to do so, cup his scarred cheek in my hand.

His dark eyes blaze, and I think he's going to shove me away. But in the end, he doesn't. He just stands there and lets me stroke my thumb back and forth across his cheek—across his scar—for several long moments.

"I'm sorry," I whisper when I can finally get my voice past the painful lump of sympathy in my throat. "This must have hurt horribly."

He doesn't answer. Instead, he closes his eyes, sinks into my palm, takes one long, shuddering breath.

Then he's pulling back, stepping away, putting real distance between us for the first time since he snuck up behind me, which suddenly feels like a lifetime ago.

"I don't understand you," he tells me suddenly, his black-magic voice so quiet that I have to strain to hear him.

"'There are more things in heaven and hell, Horatio, / Than are dreamt of in your philosophy,'" I answer, deliberately using his earlier misquote.

He shakes his head as if trying to clear it. Takes a deep breath, then blows it out slowly. "If you won't leave—"

"I *can't* leave," I interject. "I have nowhere else to go. My parents—"

"Are dead. I know." He smiles grimly. "Fine. If you're not going to leave, then you need to listen to me very, very carefully."

"What do you—?"

"Keep your head down. Don't look too closely at anyone or anything." He leans forward, his voice dropping to a low rumble as he finishes. "And always, *always* watch your back."

4

Shining Armor Is So Last Century

"Grace!" My uncle Finn's voice booms down the hallway, and I turn toward him instinctively. I smile and give him a little wave even though there's a part of me that feels frozen in place after being on the receiving end of what sounds an awful lot like a warning.

I turn back to confront Mr. Tall, Dark, and Surly, to figure out exactly what it is he thinks I need to be so afraid of—but he's gone.

I glance around, determined to figure out where he went, but before I can spot him, Uncle Finn is wrapping me in a huge bear hug and lifting me off my feet. I hang on for dear life, letting the comforting scent of him—the same woodsy scent my dad used to have—wash over me.

"I'm so sorry I couldn't meet you at the airport. A couple of kids got hurt, and I had to take care of things here."

"Don't worry about it. Are they okay?"

"They're fine." He shakes his head. "Just a couple of idiots being idiots. You know how boys are."

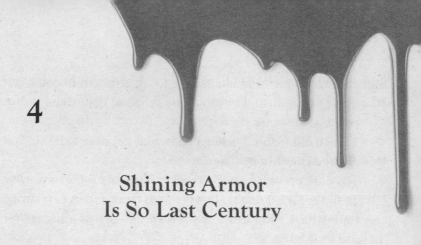

I start to tell him that I have no idea how boys are—my last encounter is proof of that—but some weird instinct I don't understand warns me not to bring up the guy I was just talking to. So I don't. Instead, I laugh and nod along.

"Enough about the duties of a headmaster," he says, pulling me in for another, quicker hug before leaning back to study my face. "How was your trip? And more importantly, how are you?"

"It was long," I tell him. "But it was fine. And I'm okay." The phrase of the day.

"I'm pretty sure 'okay' is a bit of an overstatement." He sighs. "I can only imagine how hard the last few weeks have been for you. I wish I could have stayed longer after the funeral."

"It's fine. The estate company you called took care of almost everything. And Heather and her mom took care of the rest. I swear."

It's obvious that he wants to say more but just as obvious that he doesn't want to get into anything too deep in the middle of the hallway. So in the end, he just nods and says, "Okay, then. I'll leave you to settle in with Macy. But come see me tomorrow morning, and we'll talk about your schedule. Plus, I'll introduce you to our counselor, Dr. Wainwright. I think you'll like her."

Right. Dr. Wainwright. The school counselor who is also a therapist, according to Heather's mom. And not just any therapist. *My* therapist, apparently, since she and my uncle both think I need one. I would argue, but since I've had to work really hard not to cry in the shower every morning for the last month, I figure they might be on to something.

"Okay, sure."

"Are you hungry? I'll have dinner sent up, since you missed it. And there's something we really need to discuss." He narrows his eyes at me, looks me over. "Although…how are you doing with the altitude?"

"I'm okay. Not great, but okay."

"Yeah." He looks me up and down, then harrumphs

sympathetically before turning to Macy. "Make sure she takes a couple of Advil when she gets to your room. And that she drinks plenty of water. I'll send up some soup and ginger ale. Let's keep things light tonight, see how you're doing in the morning."

"Light" sounds perfect, since even the thought of eating right now makes me want to throw up. "Okay, sure."

"I'm glad you're here, Grace. And I promise, things will get easier."

I nod, because what else am I going to do? I'm not glad I'm here—Alaska feels like the moon right now—but I'm all for things getting easier. I just want to go one day without feeling like shit.

I was hoping tomorrow would be it, but since I met Tall, Dark, and Surly, all I can think about is the way he looked when he told me to leave Katmere. And the way he glowered when I refused. So...probably not.

Figuring we're done here, I reach for the handle of one of my suitcases. But my uncle says, "Don't worry about those. I'll get one of the guys to—" He breaks off and calls down the hallway. "Hey, Flint! Come here and give me a hand, will you?"

Macy makes a sound halfway between a groan and a death rattle as her father starts down the corridor, presumably trying to catch up with this Flint person.

"Come on, let's go before Dad chases him down." She grabs two of my suitcases and practically runs for the stairs.

"What's wrong with Flint?" I ask as I grab my last remaining suitcase and try to keep up with her.

"Nothing! He's great. Amazing. Also, superhot. He doesn't need to see us like this."

I can see how she could think he doesn't need to see *me* like this, since I'm pretty sure I look half dead. But, "You look great."

"Um, no. No, I don't. Now, come on. Let's get out of—"

"Hey, Mace. Don't worry about those suitcases. I'll get them for you." A deep voice booms from several steps below us, and I turn around just in time to see a guy in ripped jeans and a white T-shirt charging toward me. He's tall—like, nearly as tall as Tall, Dark, and Surly—and just as muscular. But that's where the resemblance ends, because everywhere that other guy was dark and cold, this one is light and fire.

Bright-amber eyes that seem to burn from within.

Warm brown skin.

Black afro that looks amazing on him.

And perhaps most interesting of all, there's a smile in his eyes that is as different from the other guy's iciness as the stars just outside the windows are from the endless midnight blue of the sky.

"We've got them," Macy says, but he ignores her, bounding up the stairs three at a time.

He stops next to me first, gently eases the handle of my suitcase from the near death grip I've got on it. "Hey there, New Girl. How are you?"

"I'm okay, just..."

"She's sick, Flint," my uncle calls from below. "The altitude is getting to her."

"Oh, right." His eyes blaze with sympathy. "That sucks."

"A little bit, yeah."

"Well, come on then, New Girl. Climb on my back. I'll give you a ride up the stairs."

Just the idea has my stomach revolting even more. "Uh, what? N-No, that's okay." I back away from him a little. "I can walk—"

"Come on." He bends his knees to make it easier for me to grab on to his super-broad shoulders. "You've got a long three flights ahead of you."

They *are* a long three flights, and still I would seriously rather die than climb on a random stranger's back. "Pretty sure they'll be longer for you if you're carrying me."

"Nah. You're so little, I won't even notice. Now, are you going to get on or am I going to pick you up and toss you over my shoulder?"

"You wouldn't," I tell him.

"Try me," he says with an endearing grin that makes me laugh.

But I'm still not getting on his back. No way is one of the hottest guys at the school going to carry me up these stairs—on his back or over his shoulder. No. Freaking. Way. I don't care how much the altitude is bothering me.

"Thanks for the offer. Really." I give him the best smile I can manage right now. "But I think I'm just going to walk slowly. I'll be fine."

Flint shakes his head. "Stubborn much?" But he doesn't push the issue the way I'm afraid he will. Instead, he asks, "Can I at least help you up the stairs? I'd hate to see you fall down a flight or two on your very first day."

"Help how?" Suspicion has me narrowing my eyes at him.

"Like this." He slides his arm around my waist.

I stiffen at the unexpected contact. "What are you—?"

"This way you can at least lean on me if the steps get to be too much. Deal?"

I start to say *absolutely no deal*, but the laughter in his bright-amber eyes as he looks down at me—expecting me to do just that—has me changing my mind. Well, that and the fact that Uncle Finn and Macy both seem totally fine with the whole thing.

"Okay, fine. Deal," I say with a sigh as the room starts to spin around me. "I'm Grace, by the way."

"Yeah, I know. Foster told us you were coming." He heads toward the stairs, propelling me along with his right arm across my back. "And I'm Flint."

He pauses at the foot of the stairs for a moment, reaching for my bags.

"Oh, don't worry about the suitcases," Macy says, her voice about three octaves higher than it normally is. "I can get them."

"No doubt, Mace." He winks at her. "But you might as well use me if I'm volunteering." Then he grabs two of the bags in his left hand and heads up the stairs.

We start out going slowly, thankfully, as I'm struggling to breathe after only a few steps. But before long, we're moving fast—not because I've gotten used to the altitude but because Flint has taken on most of my weight and is basically carrying me up the stairs with an arm around my waist.

I know he's strong—all those muscles under his shirt definitely aren't for show—but I can't believe he's *this* strong. I mean, he's carrying two heavy bags *and* me up the stairs, and he isn't even breathing hard.

We end up beating Macy, who is huffing and puffing her way up the final few steps with my last bag, to the top.

"You can let me down now," I tell him as I start to squirm away. "Since you pretty much carried me anyway."

"Just trying to help," he says with a wiggle of his eyebrows that has me laughing despite my embarrassment.

He lets me down, and I expect him to pull away when my feet are finally back on the ground. Instead, he keeps his arm around my waist and moves me across the landing.

"You can let go," I say again. "I'm fine now." But my knees wobble as I say it, another wave of dizziness moving through me.

I try to hide it, but I must do a bad job because the look Flint is giving me goes from amused to concerned in the space of two seconds flat. Then he shakes his head. "Yeah, until you pass out and pitch over the railing. Nope, Headmaster Foster put me in charge of getting you to your room safely and that is what I'm going to do."

I start to argue, but I'm feeling just unsteady enough that I decide accepting his help might actually be the better part of valor. So I just nod as he turns around and calls to my cousin, "You okay there, Mace?"

"Just great," she gasps, all but dragging my suitcase across the landing.

"Told you I could have taken it," Flint says to her.

"It's not the weight of the suitcase," she snipes back. "It's how fast I had to carry it."

"I've got longer legs." He glances around. "So, which hallway am I taking her to?"

"We're in the North wing," Macy says, pointing to the hallway directly to our left. "Follow me."

Despite all her huffing and puffing, she takes off at a near run, with Flint and me hot on her heels. As we race across the landing, I can't help but be grateful for the supporting arm he's still lending me. I've always thought I was in pretty good shape, but life in Alaska obviously takes fit to a whole new level.

There are four sets of double doors surrounding the landing—all heavy, carved wood—and Macy stops at the set marked North. But before she can reach for the handle, the door flies open so fast that she barely manages to jump back before it hits her.

"Hey, what was that ab—" She breaks off when four guys walk through the door like she's not even there. All four are brooding and sexy as all get out, but I've only got eyes for one of them.

The one from downstairs.

He doesn't have eyes for me, though. Instead, he walks right by—face blank and gaze glacier cold—like I'm not even here.

Like he doesn't even see me, even though he has to skirt me to get by.

Like he didn't just spend fifteen minutes talking to me earlier.

Except…except, as he passes, his shoulder brushes against the side of my arm. Even after everything we said to each other, heat sizzles through me at the contact. And though logic tells me the touch was accidental, I can't shake the idea that he did it on purpose. Any more than I can stop myself from turning to watch him walk away.

Just because I'm angry, I assure myself. Just because I want the chance to tell him off for having disappeared like that.

Macy doesn't say anything to him, or the other guys, and neither does Flint. Instead, they wait for them to be out of the way and then head down the hallway like nothing happened. Like we didn't just get blatantly snubbed.

Flint tightens his warm arm around my waist, and I can't help but wonder why the guy with ice in his veins makes my skin tingle and the one literally lending me his warmth leaves me cold. Looks like my messed-up life is totally messing with my brain as well…

I want to ask who they are—want to ask who *he* is so I finally have a name to go with his insane body and even more insane face—but now doesn't feel like the time. So I keep my mouth shut and concentrate on looking around instead of obsessing over some guy I don't even like.

The North hallway is lined with heavy wooden doors on both sides, most with some kind of decoration hanging on them. Dried roses in the shape of an *X* on one, what looks to be an elaborate set of wind chimes on another, and a ton of bat stickers all over a third. I can't decide if the person living there has dreams of being a chiropterologist or if they are simply a fan of Batman.

Either way, I'm absurdly fascinated by all the decorations—especially the wind chimes, as I can't imagine there's much wind in an indoor hallway—and not at all surprised when Macy stops at the most elaborately adorned door of them all. A garland of fresh flowers winds its way around the doorframe, and lines of threaded, multicolored crystals fall from the top of the door to the bottom in a fancy kind of beaded curtain.

"Here we are," Macy says as she throws the door open with a flourish. "Home sweet home."

Before I can take a step over the threshold, another hot guy dressed entirely in black passes by. And though he pays us no more attention than any of the others did at the North hallway door, the hair on the back of my neck stands up. Because even though I'm sure I'm imagining things, it suddenly feels an awful lot like I'm being watched.

5

Things Hot Pink and Harry Styles Have in Common

"Which bed is hers?" Flint asks as he propels me over the threshold.

"The one on the right," Macy answers. Her voice is back to sounding funny, so I glance over my shoulder to make sure she's okay.

She looks fine, but her eyes are huge, and they keep darting from Flint to the rest of the room and back again. I give her a *what's up* look, but she just shakes her head in the universal sign for *don't say ANYTHING*. So I don't.

Instead, I look around the room I'm going to share with my cousin for the next several months. It takes only a couple of seconds for me to figure out that no matter what she said about being okay with me having my own room, she had planned on me rooming with her all along.

For starters, all her possessions are arranged neatly on one rainbow-colored side of the room. And for another, the spare bed is already made up in—of course—hot-pink sheets and a hot-pink comforter with huge white hibiscus flowers all over it.

"I know you like surfing," she says, watching me eye the blindingly bright comforter. "I thought you might like something that reminds you of home."

That shade of pink reminds me of surfer Barbie more than it reminds me of home, but no way am I going to say that to her. Not when it's obvious she's gone out of her way to make me feel comfortable. I appreciate she cared enough to try. "Thanks. It's really nice."

"It's definitely cheerful," Flint says as he helps me to the bed. The look he gives me is totally tongue-in-cheek, but that only makes me like him more. The fact that he realizes how absurd Macy's decorating choices are but is way too nice to say anything that might hurt her feelings totally works for me. If I'm lucky, maybe I've made another friend.

He drops my suitcases at the foot of the bed, then steps back as I sink onto my mattress, my head still spinning a little.

"Do you guys need anything else before I head out?" Flint asks after we are completely disentangled.

"I'm good," I tell him. "Thanks for the help."

"Any time, New Girl." He flashes me a ten-thousand-kilowatt smile. "Anytime."

I'm pretty sure Macy whimpers a little at the sight of that grin, but she doesn't say anything. Just kind of walks to the door and smiles weakly as she waits for him to leave. Which he does with a little wave for me and a fist bump for her on his way out.

The second the door is closed, and locked, behind him, I say, "You've got a crush on Flint."

"I don't!" she answers, looking wildly at the door, like he can hear us through the thick wood.

"Oh yeah? Then what was all that about?"

"All what?" Her voice is about three octaves too high.

"You know." I wring my hands, bat my lashes, give a halfway-decent imitation of the sounds she's been making since her father flagged down Flint for help.

"I don't sound like that."

"You totally sound like that," I tell her. "But I don't get it. If you like him, why didn't you try to talk to him more? I mean, it was, like, a perfect opportunity,"

"I don't *like* him like him. I don't!" she insists with a laugh when I give her a look. "I mean, yeah, he's gorgeous and nice and supersmart, but I've got a boyfriend who I really care about. It's just, Flint is so...*Flint.* You know? And he was in our *room*, *next to your bed.*" She sighs. "The mind boggles."

"Don't you mean swoons?" I tease.

"Whatever." She rolls her eyes. "It's not a real crush. It's more like..."

"More like the aura surrounding the most popular boy in school?"

"Yes, that! Exactly that. Except Flint's not quite that high on the list. Jaxon and his group have the top positions pretty much sewn up."

"Jaxon?" I ask, trying to sound casual even as my whole body goes on high alert. I don't know how I know she's talking about *him*, but I do. "Who's Jaxon?"

"Jaxon Vega." She fake swoons. "I have *no* idea how to explain Jaxon, except... Oh, wait! You saw him."

"I did?" I try to ignore the way flying dinosaurs have once again taken up residence in my stomach.

"Yeah, on the way to our room. He was one of the guys who nearly hit me in the face with the door. The really hot one out in front."

I play dumb even though my heart is suddenly beating way too fast. "You mean the ones who completely ignored us?"

"Yeah." She laughs. "Don't take it personally, though. That's just the way Jaxon is. He's...angsty."

He's a lot more than angsty, if our conversation a little while ago is anything to go by. But I'm not about to bring up what happened to Macy when I don't even know how I feel about it yet.

So I do the only thing I can do. I change the subject. "Thanks so much for setting up the room for me. I appreciate it."

"Oh, don't worry about it." She waves it away. "It was no big deal."

"I'm pretty sure it *was* a big deal. I don't know that many companies that deliver ninety minutes outside of Healy, Alaska."

She blushes a little and looks away, like she doesn't want me to know just how much trouble she's gone through to make me feel at home. But then she shrugs and says, "Yeah, well, my dad knows all the ones that do. It wasn't a problem."

"Still, you're totally my favorite cousin."

She rolls her eyes. "I'm your only cousin."

"Doesn't mean you aren't also my favorite."

"My dad uses that line."

"That you're his favorite cousin?" I tease.

"You know what I mean." She sighs in obvious exasperation. "You're a dork; you know that, right?"

"I absolutely do, yes."

She laughs, even as she crosses to the mini fridge next to her desk. "Here, drink this," she says as she pulls out a large bottle of water and tosses it to me. "And I'll show you the rest."

"The rest?"

"Yeah. There's more." She crosses to one of the closets and pulls open the doors. "I figured your wardrobe wasn't exactly equipped for Alaska, so I supplemented a little."

"*A little* is an understatement, don't you think?"

Lined up inside the closet are several black skirts and pants, along with white and black blouses, a bunch of black or purple polo shirts, two black blazers, and two red and black plaid scarves. There are also a bunch of lined hoodies, a few thick sweaters, a heavy jacket, and two more pairs of snow pants—none of which is in hot pink, thankfully. On the floor are a few pairs of new shoes and snow boots, along with a large box of what looks like books and school supplies.

"There are socks and thermal underwear and some fleece shirts and pants in your dresser drawers. I figure moving here is hard enough. I didn't want you to have to worry about anything extra."

And just like that, she manages to knock down the first line of my defenses. Tears bloom in my eyes, and I look away, blinking quickly in an effort to hide what a disaster I am.

It obviously doesn't work, because Macy makes a small exclamation of dismay. She's across the room in the blink of an eye, pulling me into a coconut-scented hug that seems incongruous here at the center of Alaska. It's also strangely comforting.

"It sucks, Grace. The whole thing just totally sucks, and I wish I could make it better. I wish I could just wave a wand and put everything back the way it used to be."

I nod because there's a lump in my throat. And because there's nothing else to say. Except that I wish for that, too.

I wish that the last words my parents and I spoke weren't hurled at each other in a fight that seems so stupid now.

I wish that my dad hadn't lost control of the car two hours later and driven himself and my mother off a cliff, plunging hundreds of feet into the ocean.

Most of all, I wish that I could smell my mother's perfume or hear the deep rumble of my father's voice just one more time.

I let Macy hug me as long as I can stand it—which is only about five seconds or so—and then I pull away. I've never particularly liked being touched, and it's only gotten worse since my parents died.

"Thanks for—" I gesture to the bed and closet. "All of this."

"Of course. And I want you to know, if you ever need to talk or whatever, I'm here. I know it's not the same, because my mom left; she didn't die." She swallows hard, takes a deep breath before continuing. "But I know what it's like to feel alone. And I'm a good listener."

It's the first time she's actually used the word "die." The first time she's actually acknowledged what happened to my parents by name. The fact that she has makes it so much easier to say, "Thank you," and mean it, even as I remember that Jaxon didn't shy away from it, either. He might have been a jackass all the way around, but he called my parents' death what it was. And didn't treat me like I was going to shatter under the weight of one harsh word.

Maybe that's why I'm still thinking about him when I should be writing him off for the jerk he is.

She nods, watching me out of worried eyes that only make me feel worse.

"I should probably get unpacked." I look down at my suitcases with distaste. It feels like I just packed them. The last thing I want to do is empty them right now. Not when my electric-pink bed is calling me like a beacon.

"I can totally help with that." She points at a door across the room. "Why don't you go take a shower and get into your pajamas? I'll check on the soup my dad said he sent up. Then you can eat, take some Advil, and get some rest. Hopefully, when you wake up, you'll be better acclimated to the altitude."

"That sounds…" I really do feel crappy, and a shower sounds amazing. As does sleep, considering I've been so nervous about the move that I haven't gotten much in the last week or so.

"Perfect, right?" She fills in the blank.

"It really does, yeah."

"Good." She walks to her closet and pulls out a couple extra towels. "If you want to hop in the shower, I'll get you some warm soup and hopefully, in half an hour, this whole day will feel a lot better."

"Thanks, Macy." I turn to look at her. "I mean it."

A grin splits her face and lights up her eyes. "You're welcome."

Fifteen minutes later, I'm out of the shower and dressed in my favorite pair of pajamas—a Harry Styles T-shirt from his first solo tour and a pair of blue fleece pants with white and yellow daisies all over them—only to find Macy dancing around the room to "Watermelon Sugar."

Talk about kismet.

Macy oohs and aahs over the concert tee—as she should—but other than that, she pretty much leaves me alone. Except to make sure I drink an entire thirty-two-ounce bottle of water *and* take the Advil she left on my nightstand.

There's a bowl of chicken noodle soup on my nightstand, too, but right now I don't have the energy to eat. Instead, I climb into bed and pull the hot-pink covers over my head.

The last thing I think about before drifting off to sleep is that—despite everything—tonight is the first time I've taken a shower without struggling not to cry since my parents died.

6

No, I Really Don't Want to Build a Snowman

I wake up slowly, head fuzzy and body as heavy as stone. It takes me a second to remember where I am—Alaska—and that the light snores that fill the room belong to Macy and not Heather, whose room I crashed in for the last three weeks.

I sit up, trying to ignore the unfamiliar howls and roars—and even the occasional animalistic scream—in the distance. It's enough to freak anyone out, let alone a girl born and raised in the city, but I comfort myself by remembering there's a giant castle wall between me and all the animals making those noises...

Still, if I'm being honest, it isn't the utter foreignness of this place that has my brain racing overtime. Yes, being in Alaska is bizarre on what feels like every level. But once I banish thoughts of my old life, it isn't Alaska that woke me up at—I glance at the clock—3:23 in the morning. And it's not Alaska that's keeping me awake.

It's him.

Jaxon Vega.

I don't know anything more about him than I did when he left me standing in the hallway, angry and confused and hurting more than I want to admit—except that he's the most popular guy at Katmere Academy. And that he's angsty, which…no kidding. I didn't exactly need a crystal ball to guess that.

But seriously, nothing Macy told me matters, because I've decided I don't want to know any more about him.

More, I don't want to know *him*.

Yet when I close my eyes, I can still see him so perfectly. His clenched jaw. The thin scar that runs the length of his face. The black ice of his eyes that lets me see for a second—just a second—that he knows as much about pain as I do. Maybe more.

It's that pain I think of most as I sit here in the dark. That pain that makes me worry for him when I shouldn't give a damn one way or the other.

I wonder how he got that scar. However it happened, it had to have been awful. Terrifying. Traumatic. Devastating.

I figure that's probably why he was so cold to me. Why he tried to get me to leave and, when I wouldn't, ended up delivering that ridiculous and—I admit, mildly disconcerting—warning.

Macy said he was angsty…does that mean he treats everyone the way he treated me? And if so, why? Because he's just a jerk? Or because he's in so much pain that the only way he can handle it is to make everyone afraid of him so that he can keep them at a distance? Or do people see his scar and his scowl and decide to keep their distance all on their own?

It's an awful thought but one I can totally relate to. Not the *people being afraid of me* part but definitely the *people keeping their distance* part. Except for Heather, most of my old friends drifted away after my parents died. Heather's mom told me it was because my parents' deaths reminded them of their own mortality, reminded them that their parents could die at any time. And so could they.

Logically, I knew she was right, that they were just trying to protect themselves the only way they knew how. But that didn't make the distance any less painful. And it definitely didn't make the loneliness any easier to bear.

Reaching for my phone, I shoot off a couple of quick texts to Heather—which I should have done as soon as I got here last night—telling her that I'm safe and explaining about the altitude sickness.

Then I lay back down, try to will myself to go back to sleep. But I'm wide-awake now, thoughts of Alaska and school and Jaxon blurring together in my head until all I want is for them to just stop.

But they don't stop, and suddenly my heart is pounding, my skin prickling with awareness. I press a hand to my chest, take a couple of deep breaths, try to figure out what has me so alarmed that I can barely breathe.

And suddenly it's right there. All the thoughts I'd shoved aside for the past forty-eight hours, just to get through leaving. Just to get here. My parents, leaving San Diego and my friends, that ridiculous airplane ride into Healy. Macy's expectations for our friendship, the way Jaxon looked at me and then *didn't* look at me, the things he said to me. The ridiculous amount of clothes I have to wear here to keep warm. The fact that I'm essentially trapped in this castle by the cold…

It all kind of melds together into one great big carousel of fear and regret, whirling through my brain. No thoughts are clear, no images stand out from any of the others—only an overwhelming feeling of impending doom.

The last time I freaked out like this, Heather's mom told me that experiencing too powerful emotions is completely normal after a huge loss. The crushing weight on my chest, the swirling thoughts, the shaking hands, the feeling that the world is going to come crashing in on me—all completely normal. She's a therapist, so she should know, but it doesn't feel normal right now.

It feels terrifying.

I know I should stay where I am—this castle is gigantic, and I have no idea where anything is—but I'm smart enough to know if I stay here staring at the ceiling, I'm going to end up having a full-blown panic attack. So instead, I take a deep breath and heave myself out of bed. I slip my feet into my shoes and grab my hoodie on my way out the door.

Back home, I'd go for a run when I couldn't sleep, even if it was three in the morning. But here, that's out of the question. Not just because it's as cold as death outside but because God only knows what wild animal is waiting for me in the middle of the night. I haven't been lying in bed listening to the roars and howls for the last half an hour for nothing.

But it's a big castle with long hallways. I may not be able to run through them, but I can at least go exploring for a while. See what I find.

I carefully close the door behind me—the last thing I want to do is wake Macy up when she's been so nice to me—then head down the hallway toward the stairs.

It's creepier than I expect it to be. I would have thought the hallways would be lit up in the middle of the night, safety protocols and all that, but instead they're dim. Like *just enough light to see imaginary shadows sweeping along the corridors* dim.

For a second, I think about going back into my room and forgetting about the whole walk/explore-the-castle thing. But just the thought has the merry-go-round starting in my brain again, and that's the last thing I can handle right now.

I pull out my phone and angle its flashlight down the hall. Suddenly the shadows disappear, and it looks like any other hallway. If you discount the rough stone walls and old-fashioned tapestries, I mean.

I have no idea where I'm going, only that I want to get off the dorm floor. I can barely stand the thought of dealing with *Macy* right now—dealing with anyone else seems blatantly impossible.

I make it to the long, circular staircase without a problem and take the steps two at a time, all the way down to the ground floor. After my shower last night, Macy mentioned that's where the cafeteria is, along with the library and a number of the classrooms. There are other classrooms in buildings around the grounds, but most of the core classes are taught here, inside the castle, which I am all for. The less I have to be out in that weather, the better.

Down here, the hallways are lined with more tapestries, worn and faded with age. My favorite stretches for yards and is vividly colorful. Purples and pinks, greens and yellows, all woven together with no apparent rhyme or reason—except as I step back and shine my flashlight on a wider swath of it, I realize there *is* a pattern. This is an artistic rendering of the aurora borealis—the northern lights.

I've always wanted to see them, and somehow, in all the pain and worry about moving to Alaska, I totally forgot that I'll pretty much have a front-row seat out here.

It's that thought that galvanizes me, that has me walking back toward the entryway and the giant set of double doors that lead to the front courtyard. I'm not foolish enough to go traipsing around in the snow in my hoodie and pajama bottoms, but maybe I can stick my head out, see if I can find any lights in the sky.

It's probably a bad idea—I should just head back up to bed and save the aurora borealis for another night—but now that it's in my brain, I can't shake it. My dad used to tell me stories about the northern lights, and they've always been a bucket list item for me. Now that I'm this close, I can't *not* take a look.

I use my flashlight to negotiate my way back down the hall. Once there, I hold it up so I can unlock the doors, but before I can do more than locate the first one, both doors fly open. And in walk two guys wearing nothing but old-school concert T-shirts, jeans, and lace-up boots. No jackets, no sweaters, no hoodies, even. Just ripped jeans, Mötley Crüe, and Timberlands. It's the most ridiculous thing I've ever seen, and for a second, I can't help wondering if this castle—like Hogwarts—comes equipped with its very own ghosts. Ones who died at an eighties rock concert.

"Well, well, well. Looks like we made it back just in time," says the taller of the two guys. He's got warm copper skin, dark hair tied back in a ponytail, and a black nose ring right through his septum. "What are you doing out of bed, Grace?"

Something in his voice has nervous goose bumps prickling along my skin. "How do you know my name?"

He laughs. "You're the new girl, aren't you? Everybody knows *your* name. *Grace*." He takes a step closer, and I would swear he was sniffing me, which is completely bizarre. And also not ghostlike behavior at all. "Now, how about you answer my question? What are you doing out of bed?"

I don't tell him about the northern lights—especially since I get a glimpse of the sky before he closes the door and it's just the regular black sprinkled with stars you can see almost anywhere in the world. Just one more disappointment in a long string of them lately.

"I was thirsty," I lie badly, wrapping my arms around my waist in an effort to combat the cold gust of wind that came in with them and still lingers in the air around us. "Just wanted to get some water."

"And did you find any?" says the second guy. He's shorter than the first and stockier, too. His blond hair is shaved close against his scalp.

It seems like an innocuous enough question, except he's walking toward me as he asks it, getting into my personal space until I have to decide whether to stand my ground or back up.

I decide to back up, mostly because I don't like the way he's looking at me. And because each step I take gets me closer to the stairs and—hopefully—my room.

"I did, thanks," I lie again, trying to sound unconcerned. "I'm just going to head back to bed now."

"Before we even have a chance to get to know you? That doesn't seem very polite, does it, Marc?" the short-haired one asks.

"It doesn't, no," Marc answers, and now he's really close, too. "Especially since Foster's been up our asses about you for weeks now."

"What does that mean?" I demand, forgetting to be afraid for a second.

"It means we've had three different meetings about you, all warning us to be on our best behavior. It's annoying as hell. Right, Quinn?"

"Absolutely. If he's that worried about you being here, I don't know why he didn't just leave you wherever you came from." Quinn reaches out, yanks one of my curls—hard. I want to pull away, want to shove him back and yell at him to leave me alone.

But there's trouble here. I can feel it, just like I can feel the barely leashed violence rolling off these guys in waves. It's like they're desperate to hurt someone, desperate to rip someone apart. I don't want that someone to be me.

"What do you think, Grace?" Marc sneers. "You think you can handle Alaska? Because I'm pretty sure it's going to naturally unselect you pretty damn quick."

"I'm just…trying to get by until graduation. I don't want any trouble." I can barely force the words out of my tight throat.

"Trouble?" Quinn laughs, but the sound is completely devoid of humor. "Do we look like trouble to you?"

They look like the very definition of trouble.

Like, if I looked trouble up in the dictionary, their pictures would be right there, front and center, along with a giant warning stamp. I don't say that, though. I don't say anything, actually, as my brain races to figure a way out of this terrifying situation. Part of me thinks I must be dreaming, because this feels like a scene out of every teen movie ever, where the school bullies decide to gang up on the new kid just to show her who's boss.

But this is real life, not the movies, and I have no delusions that I'm the boss out here or anywhere. I want to tell them that, but right now answering feels like acquiescence, and that's the last thing you're supposed to do when dealing with a bully. The more you give them, the more they try to take.

"So tell me, Grace. Have you had a chance to see the snow yet?" Marc asks, and suddenly he's way too close for comfort. "I bet you've never even seen snow before."

"I saw plenty of snow on the way up here."

"On the back of a snowmobile? That doesn't count, does it, Quinn?"

"No." Quinn shakes his head with a snarl that shows an awful lot of teeth. "You definitely need to get closer. Show us what you can do."

"What I can do?" I have no idea what they're talking about.

"I mean, it's obvious you've got *something* going on." This time, when he breathes in, I'm sure Marc is smelling me. "I just can't quite figure out what it is, yet."

"Right?" Quinn agrees. "Me neither, but there's definitely something there. So let's see what you've got, *Grace*."

He shifts, braces himself, and that's when it hits me. What they're planning on doing. And just how much danger I'm really in.

7

Something Really Freaking Wicked This Way Comes

I whirl around, adrenaline pumping, and make a break for the stairs. But Marc reaches out and grabs me before I make it more than a few feet. He yanks me hard against him—my back to his front—and wraps his arms around me as I start to struggle in earnest.

"Let me go!" I shout, bringing my heel back to kick him in the knees. But I don't have much leverage, and he doesn't so much as wince.

I think about stomping on his feet, but my Converse aren't going to do much damage to his boots, let alone his feet inside them. "Let me go or I'll scream!" I tell him, trying—and failing—not to sound scared.

"Go ahead," he tells me as he wrestles me toward the front door Quinn is conveniently holding open for him. "No one will care."

I throw my head back, slam it against his chin, and he curses, jerks one of his arms up to try to hold my head in place. Which infuriates me as much as it terrifies me. Bending down, I bite his arm as hard as I can.

He yelps and jerks, and his forearm slams against my mouth.

It hurts, has the metallic taste of blood pooling in my mouth. Which only pisses me off more.

"Stop!" I shout, bucking and kicking against him as hard as I can. I can't let them get me out the door; I *can't*. I'm dressed in nothing but a hoodie and a pair of fleece pants, and it's no more than ten degrees out there. With my thin California blood, I won't last more than fifteen minutes without getting frostbite or hypothermia—if I'm lucky.

But he still doesn't let go, his arms like bands of steel around me.

"Get your hands off me!" I yell, this time not caring who I wake up. In fact, hoping that I wake up someone. Anyone. Everyone. At the same time, I slam my head back with as much force as I can, aiming to break his nose.

I must hit something, because he lets me go with a curse. I hit the ground, hard, my legs buckling so that I end up on my knees just in time to see Marc go flying across the entryway, eyes wide as he slams into the farthest wall.

I don't have time to think about how that happened, though, because it takes only a second for him to recover, and then he's charging back across the foyer, straight at me. I turn to flee, fists up in an attempt to ward off Quinn if he tries to stop me, but suddenly he's flying across the foyer, too. He crashes into a bookshelf instead of a wall, and a vase falls off the top shelf and shatters against his head.

I turn around, looking for a way out, but Marc moves fast—really fast—and suddenly he's standing there, between the staircase and me. I twist to the right, trying to decide my best bet to get away, and that's when I run straight into a solid wall of muscle.

Shit. There are three of them now? Panic races through me, and I reach out, try to shove whoever it is backward. But like

Marc, this guy doesn't move. At least not until he wraps his hand around my wrist and tugs me forward hard enough to lift me straight off the ground.

It's as he's pulling me toward him that I get my first good look at his face and realize that it's Jaxon.

I don't know whether I should be relieved or even more afraid.

At least not until he yanks me behind him, putting himself between the others and me as he faces them down.

Mark and Quinn skid to a halt, the uneasiness on their faces turning to fear

"Is there a problem here?" Jaxon asks. His voice is lower than before and more gravelly. It's also colder than the snowdrifts right outside the front door.

"No problem," Marc says with a forced chuckle. "We were just getting to know the new girl."

"Is that what they call attempted murder these days? Getting to know someone?" He doesn't raise his voice, doesn't do anything the least bit threatening. And still all three of us wince as we wait for the other shoe to drop.

"We wouldn't have hurt her, man," Quinn pipes up for the first time. He sounds a lot whinier than he did a few minutes ago, when it was just them and me. But he's not slurring his words or anything, so I guess the vase must not have done him too much damage. "We were just going to toss her outside for a few minutes."

"Yeah," Marc adds. "It was just a joke. No big deal."

"Is that what you're calling this mess?" Jaxon inquires, and somehow his voice has turned even colder. "You know the rules."

I'm not sure what rules he's talking about—or why he sounds like he's personally in charge of enforcing them—but his words have Quinn and Marc cowering that much more. Not to mention looking a little sick to their stomachs.

"We're sorry, Jaxon. We just came in off a run, and things got a little out of hand."

"I'm not the one you should be apologizing to." He half turns, holds out a hand to me.

I shouldn't take it. Every ounce of self-defense training I've ever had says I should run. That I should take the reprieve he—Jaxon—is offering and make a mad dash for my room.

But there's a look of such intense rage simmering beneath his obsidian gaze, and I instinctively know he's turned to offer me his hand in an effort to keep the guys from seeing it. I don't know why; I just know he doesn't want them to realize how upset he is. Or maybe it's that he doesn't want them figuring out how upset he is on my behalf.

Either way, he saved me tonight, and I owe him. I hold his gaze, telling him with a look that I'll keep his secret.

And then I do what he is silently asking and step forward. I don't take his hand—that's a little too much after what he said and did earlier—but I move forward, knowing that Jaxon won't let Marc or Quinn do anything else to me.

I must get too close for his liking, however, because he shifts himself partially in front of me again, even as he shoots Quinn and Marc a cold look that warns them to behave. The warning might be unnecessary, though, because they're both looking pretty shamefaced already.

"We're sorry, Grace." Marc speaks first. "That was totally uncool of us. We didn't mean to scare you."

I don't say anything, because I'm sure as hell not going to tell them what they did to me was okay. And I'm not brave enough to tell them to go to hell, even with Jaxon acting as my shield. So I do the only thing I can do. I stare stonily at them and will their farce of an apology to be over so I can finally go back to my room.

"Yeah, you know." Quinn waves a hand at the ceiling. "The moon is doing its thing, so…"

That's the best they've got? *The moon is doing its thing*? I have no idea what that means, and honestly, I don't care. I'm so over this place and everyone in it. Except Macy and Uncle Finn and—maybe, just maybe—Jaxon.

"I'm going to bed." I turn to leave, but Jaxon's hand is back on my wrist.

"Wait." It's the first word he's spoken to me since the whole debacle from earlier, and it halts me in my tracks more surely than his hand around my wrist.

"Why?" I ask.

He doesn't answer. Instead, he turns back to Marc and Quinn and says, "This isn't over."

They nod, but they don't say anything else. His words must be a dismissal as well as a threat, though, because they take off down the hall, running faster than I've ever seen anyone move.

We both watch them go, and then Jaxon turns to me. For long seconds, he doesn't say anything, just looks me over from head to toe, his dark eyes cataloging every inch of me. Not going to lie. It makes me a little uncomfortable. Not in the same way that Quinn and Marc made me uncomfortable, like they were looking for a weakness to exploit. It's more a wow, did it suddenly get hot in here and why oh why am I wearing my oldest, most raggedy pair of pajama bottoms kind of uncomfortable.

Too bad I have no idea how I feel about feeling like that.

"Are you okay?" he asks quietly, his fingers finally releasing their hold on my wrist.

"I'm fine," I answer, even though I'm not sure it's true. What kind of place is this where people try to shove you outside to die as a *prank*?

"You don't look fine."

That stings a little, even though I know he's not wrong. "Yeah, well, it's been a crappy couple of days."

"I bet." His eyes are serious as he looks at me, his expression grave. "You don't have to worry about Marc and Quinn. They won't bother you again." The *I'll make sure of it* part of that statement goes unspoken, but I hear it all the same.

"Thank you," I blurt out. "For helping me, I mean. I appreciate it."

His brows go up and, if possible, his eyes go even darker in the dim light. "Is that what you think I did?"

"Isn't it?"

He shakes his head, gives a little laugh that has my heart stuttering in my chest. "You have no idea, do you?"

"No idea of what?"

"That I just made you a pawn in a game you can't begin to understand."

"You think this is a game?" I ask, incredulous.

"I know exactly what this is. Do you?"

I wait for him to say something else, to explain his cryptic comments, but he doesn't. Instead, he just stares at me until I can't help but squirm a little. I've never had anyone look at me the way he is right now, like he can't decide if he made a mistake rescuing me from imminent death.

Or maybe it's just that he can't decide what to say next. In which case, join the freaking club.

In the end, though, all that brooding silence is for nothing, because he simply says, "You're bleeding."

"I am?" My hand goes to my cheek, which aches from where Marc's shoulder banged into it when I was trying to get away from him.

"Not there." He lifts his hand to my mouth and gently—so gently I can barely feel him—brushes his thumb across my lower lip. "Here." He holds his thumb up, and in the dim light, I can just see the smear of blood glistening on his skin.

"Oh, gross!" I reach to wipe away the blood. "Let me—"

He laughs, cutting me off. Then brings his thumb to his lips and—holding my gaze with his own—sticks his thumb in his mouth and slowly sucks off the blood.

It's the sexiest thing I've ever seen, and I don't even know why. I mean, shouldn't this be totally creeping me out?

Maybe it's the way his eyes heat up the second he tastes my blood.

Maybe it's the little noise he makes as he swallows.

Or maybe it's the fact that that swipe of his thumb across my lips, followed by that lift of it to his own lips feels more intimate than any kiss I've ever shared with another boy.

"You should go." The words sound like they're being torn out of him.

"Now?"

"Yeah, now." His expression feels intentionally vacant. Like he's trying too hard not to share with me what he's really thinking. Or feeling. "And I strongly suggest that after midnight, you stay in your room where you belong."

"Stay in my—" I bristle at what he's implying. "Are you saying I'm responsible for what happened tonight?"

"Don't be ridiculous. Of course I'm not. They should both have better control."

It's a weird way of saying they shouldn't go around trying to murder people, and I start to ask him about it. But he continues before I can figure out how to phrase it. "But I warned you before that you need to be careful here. This isn't like your old high school."

"How do you know what my old high school was like?"

"I don't," he says with a smirk. "But I can guarantee it's

nothing like Katmere Academy."

Jaxon's right—of course he's right—but I'm not about to back down now. "You don't know that."

He leans forward then, as if he can't help himself, until his face, and his lips, are barely an inch from mine. And just like earlier, I know it should make me uncomfortable. But it doesn't. It just makes me burn. And this time, when my knees shake, it has nothing to do with fear.

My lips part, my breath hitches in my chest, my heart beats faster. He feels it—I can see it in his blown-out pupils, in the way he goes wary and watchful. Can hear it in the sudden harshness of his own breath, sense it in the slight tremble of his body against my own. For a second, just a second, I think he's going to kiss me. But then he leans in farther, past my mouth, until his lips are all but pressed up against my ear. And I get the strange sense that he's smelling me just like Marc and Quinn had, although it has an entirely different effect on me.

"You have no idea what I know," he says softly.

The warmth of his breath has me gasping, melting, my whole body sagging against his of its own volition.

He lets it happen for one second, two, his hands on my waist, his shoulders curving down and into me. And then, just as suddenly, he's gone, stepping back so fast, I nearly fall without the support of his body.

"You need to go," he repeats, voice even lower, rougher than before.

"Now?" I demand, incredulous.

"Right now." He nods to the staircase, and somehow I find myself moving toward it, though I never make a conscious decision to do so. "Go straight to your room and lock the door."

"I thought you said I don't have to worry about Marc or Quinn anymore?" I ask over my shoulder.

"You don't."

"Well then, why do I need to—?" I break off when I realize that I'm talking to myself. Because again, Jaxon is gone.

And I'm left wondering when I'll see him again. And why it matters so much that I do.

8

Live and Let Die

Not going to lie. I'm a little shell-shocked when I finally make it back to my room. It's nearly five a.m., and the last thing I want to do is crawl back into bed and stare at the ceiling until Macy wakes up. But it's not like I feel safe wandering the school anymore, either, considering I could be dead by now if Jaxon hadn't shown up when he did.

And since the last thing I can do—and the last thing I want to do—is count on him to save me if I end up in another bizarre situation like that, I think my best bet is to hang in my room until Macy wakes up and I can get her opinion on what just happened. Although, if her opinion is anything other than OMG, WTF?!?! I'm taking my unpacked suitcases and heading back to San Diego. Freeloading off Heather's family for the next eight months is better than dying. Or at least that's my story and I'm sticking to it.

Especially since I don't get altitude sickness in San Diego.

The nausea hits me as I'm tiptoeing across the room, and I barely make it back to my bed with a soft groan.

Macy must have heard me because she tells me, "I promise the altitude sickness won't last forever."

"It's not just the altitude sickness. It's everything."

"I bet," is all she says, and silence stretches between us. I'm pretty sure it's because she's giving me the space to sort through my thoughts and decide if I want to share any.

I stare at the gray stone ceiling above my bed pressing down on me, then take a deep breath. "It's just... Alaska's like a foreign planet, you know? Like everything about this place is so different than home that it's hard to get used to it." Normally I don't dump my stuff on people I don't know really well—it's easier to just keep everything inside—but Macy is the closest friend I have here. And there's a part of me that feels like I'll explode if I don't talk to someone.

"I totally get that. I've lived here my whole life, and some days it feels bizarre to me, too. But you've only been in the state about twelve hours, and you've been feeling gross for most of those. Why don't you give it a few days, wait till the altitude sickness wears off and you've gone to a couple classes? Maybe things won't seem as strange once you get into a routine."

"I know you're right. And I wasn't even feeling that terrible about things when I woke up, until—" I break off, trying to think of the best way to tell her about what just happened.

"Until what?" She throws back her covers and climbs out of bed.

"I know it's a pretty big school, but do you know two guys named Marc and Quinn?" I ask.

"That depends. Does one of them have a septum piercing?"

"Yes. It's a big black ring." I hold my fingers to my nose to demonstrate.

"Then yeah, I know them. They're juniors like me. And good guys, really funny. In fact, there was this one time—" I must not have a poker face, because she stops abruptly. Narrows her eyes. "Then again, I'm beginning to think the question I should be asking is how do *you* know them?"

"Maybe they were just fooling around, but...I'm pretty sure they tried to kill me tonight. Or at least scare me to death."

"They tried to *what*?" she squawks, nearly dropping the bottle of water she had gotten out of the fridge for me. "Tell me what happened right now. And don't leave *anything* out."

She seems adamant, so I faithfully recite the events until I get to the point where Jaxon saved me. I'm not sure how I feel about that—or how I feel about him—and I'm not quite ready to talk about it yet. And I'm certainly not ready to listen to Macy talk about it. Plus, I'd sort of silently agreed to keep something about the interaction a secret, although admittedly now, back in my room, I wonder if I'd imagined that silent exchange or not.

"So what happened?" she asks when I don't say anything else. "How did you get away from them?"

"Someone heard the fight and came to investigate. Once the boys realized there was a witness, they chilled out pretty quickly."

"I bet they did, the jerks. The last thing they'd want is to be reported to my dad. But they should have thought of that before they put their hands on you. I swear, I'm going to murder them myself."

She looks, and sounds, mad enough to do just that even before she continues. "What were they thinking? They don't even know you, so why do this?" She gets up, starts pacing. "You totally could have gotten hypothermia if they'd left you outside for too long, let alone what could have happened if they'd kept you out there more than ten minutes. You seriously could have died. Which makes no sense. They're always a little wild, super high energy. But I've never seen them be malicious before."

"The whole thing doesn't make sense. I'm beginning to think they were high or something, because there's no other explanation as to why they would have been outside in only jeans and T-shirts. I mean, how did *they* avoid getting hypothermia?"

"I don't know," Macy says. But she looks uncomfortable, like maybe she knows for a fact that they do drugs. Or like she thinks I'm delusional for even suggesting that they were outside without any protective clothing on. But I know what I saw. Those two guys were definitely not wearing any kind of cold-weather gear.

"Maybe they were only outside for a minute or two," she suggests eventually, handing me two Advil. "Either way, whatever's going on with them, I'm sure my father will figure it out."

There's a part of me that wants to ask her not to tell Uncle Finn, because it's hard enough being the new girl without also being a snitch. But every time I think about what might have happened—what *would* have happened if Jaxon hadn't come along—I know Uncle Finn has to be told. Otherwise, what's to stop them from doing it again to somebody else?

"In the meantime, you probably need to get some more sleep. Unless you're hungry?"

Since just the thought of food has my stomach spinning in protest, I tell her, "I think I'm going to pass on that. But I'm not sure I can sleep, either. Maybe I should unpack my suitcases, get stuff ready for tomorrow."

"Don't worry about your suitcases. I already did them."

"You did? When?"

"After you fell asleep last night. I figured if you didn't like where I put things, you could change it. But at least this way, all your stuff is within easy reach."

"You didn't have to do that, Macy."

"I know I didn't have to. But you're not feeling great, so I figured a little help couldn't hurt. Besides, we have a party to go to this evening and you need to be able to find your makeup and hair stuff."

I'm not sure what amuses me more, the way Macy just casually drops in the fact that she expects me to attend a party with her today or the fact that she actually expects me to wear makeup to it, when mascara and a couple of tubes of lip gloss are pretty much all I own.

Considering she had a full face of makeup on yesterday when she was riding a snowmobile through the Alaskan wilderness, I can only imagine what her party look will be.

"So what kind of party is this exactly?" I ask as I curl up under the hot-pink comforter that is rapidly growing on me—maybe because it's the softest, most comfortable one I've ever owned.

"It's a welcome to Katmere Academy party—for you."

"What?" I sit up so fast that my head starts to throb all over again. "A welcome party? For me? Are you *serious*?"

"Well, to be fair, the school hosts a kind of high tea one afternoon a month to promote student unity. We just decided to make today's tea a little more festive in your honor."

"Oh, yes. Because the students have all been *so* welcoming so far." I bury my face in my pillow and groan.

"I swear we're not all bad. Look at Flint. He's great, right?"

"He really was." I can't help smiling as I think of the way he teased me, called me New Girl.

"Most of the people you meet here are going to be like him, not like Marc and Quinn. I promise." She sighs. "But I can cancel if you want. Tell everybody that your altitude sickness is too bad. Which, at the rate you're going, might not even be a lie."

She's trying so hard not to sound disappointed, but I can hear it, even with a pillow over my face.

"No, don't cancel," I tell her. "As long as I'm not puking, I'll go."

I've got to face these prep school kids en masse sooner or later. Might as well get it over with today when they're all under adult supervision and presumably on their best behavior. So much less chance of me being tossed into the snow or out a window that way... I shiver. Too soon for that joke.

"Awesome!" She plops down on the bed beside me, holds out the water bottle she'd given me earlier. "Don't forget, water is your friend right now," she says with a wink.

"I don't want to," I whine playfully.

"Yeah, well, I'd do it anyway. Altitude sickness requires lots and lots of hydration. I mean, if you don't want to get pulmonary or cerebral edema, which, you know, could kill you almost as fast as hypothermia."

"Seriously?" I roll my eyes at her, but I take the bottle of water and drink half of it in one go. "Has anyone ever told you you're a lot tougher than you look?"

"My boyfriend. But I think he secretly likes it."

"Good for him." I take another long swallow of water. "Do you have Netflix?"

"Are you kidding?" She gives me a look. "I live on a mountain in the middle of Alaska. I'd die without Netflix."

"Point taken. How about *Legacies*? My best friend, Heather, and I just started watching it last week."

Macy's eyes go huge. "*Legacies*?"

"Yeah. It's this really cool show about a bunch of teenage vampires, witches, and werewolves all living together at a boarding school. I know it sounds a little silly, but it's fun to imagine."

"It doesn't sound silly at all," Macy says with a cough. "And count me in. I mean, who can resist a hot vampire?"

"My sentiments exactly."

We start the show back at the first episode so Macy can catch up. And as we watch the main character's foster brother become a werewolf, I can't help thinking about what Marc and Quinn said about the moon. I mean, I know it's just that they needed the brightness of the moon to illuminate the dark wilderness around here.

Of course I know that.

Still, after going two rounds with Jaxon—both of which ended with him warning me off—it's hard not to wonder exactly what I've gotten myself into here.

9

Even Hell Has its Factions

"Stop fidgeting!" Macy tells me several hours later, smacking at my hands as we get ready to head to the party. "You look amazing."

"Are you sure?" I open my closet door, look in the full-length mirror for at least the tenth time since I got dressed.

"I'm positive. That dress is amazing on you. The color is perfect."

I roll my eyes. "It's not the color I'm worried about."

"So what *are* you worried about?"

"Oh, I don't know." I tug on the neckline a little, try to pull it up an inch or three. "My boobs falling out, maybe? *So* not the first impression I'm going for here."

She laughs. "Oh my God. The dress is gorgeous. And you look gorgeous in it."

"The dress *is* gorgeous," I agree. Because it is. And it probably looks perfectly respectable on Macy's tall, willowy figure. My big boobs make things a little trickier, though. "Maybe if I don't take a deep breath for the whole night, things will be okay."

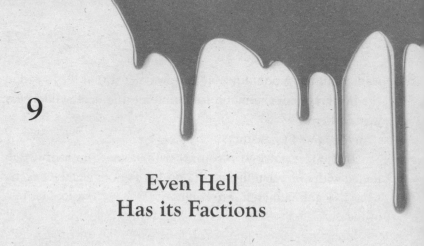

"Look, maybe you should wear the jeans you originally planned." Macy crosses to my bed and holds them up. "I don't want you to be uncomfortable."

It's tempting, so tempting. But… "Are any of the other girls going to be in jeans?"

"Who cares what the other girls are wearing."

"I take it that's a no." I tug on the neckline one more time, then give up and shut the closet door. "Come on, let's get going before I decide to stay in and binge-watch Netflix for the rest of the evening."

Macy gives me a hug. "You look really beautiful. So let's go have fun."

I roll my eyes at her a second time, because "beautiful" is a bit more than a stretch—with my curly auburn hair, plain brown eyes, and the random groupings of freckles on my nose and cheeks, I'm pretty much the opposite of beautiful.

On a good day, I'm cute. Standing next to Macy, who *is* freaking gorgeous, I'm wallpaper. The bland, boring kind.

"Come on," she continues, grabbing my forearm and tugging me toward the door. "If we wait much longer, we're going to be more than fashionably late to your welcome party."

"We could just skip it altogether," I say even as I let her pull me out the door. "Be fashionably absent."

"Too late," she answers with a deliberately obnoxious grin. "Everyone's waiting for us."

"Oh, yay." Despite the sarcasm, I head out. The sooner we get there, the sooner I'll get the hard part over with.

But as I start to weave my way through the crystal beads outside our door, Macy says, "Here, let me hold those for you. Don't want them to shock you. Sorry I didn't think about that yesterday."

"*Shock* me? What do you mean?"

"They shock everybody." She tilts her head to the side, gives me a funny look. "Didn't you feel it when you went downstairs last night?"

"Um, no." I reach out and close my fist around several strands of beads, trying to figure out what she's talking about.

"You really don't feel anything?" Macy asks after a second.

"I really don't." I look down at my favorite pair of rose-tattoo Chucks. "Maybe it's the shoes."

"Maybe." She looks doubtful. "Come on, let's go."

She closes the door, then brushes her hands through the beads several times, like she's *trying* to get shocked. Which, I know, makes absolutely no sense, but that's definitely what it looks like.

"So," I ask as she finally gives up on whatever she's doing. "Why would you deliberately keep a beaded curtain around that builds up static electricity and shocks everyone who comes in contact with it?"

"Not everyone," she answers with a pointed look. "And because it's pretty. Obviously."

"Obviously."

As we make our way down the hall, I can't help but notice the crown molding on the walls. Decorated with black shot through with thorny gold flowers, it's elaborate and beautiful and just a little creepy. Not as creepy as the lights that line the ceiling, however, which look a lot like trios of weeping black flowers connected by crooked, thorny stems. Gold light bulbs hang from the center of the flowers, partially obscured by their downturned petals.

The whole effect is eerie but beautiful and, while I definitely wouldn't choose to decorate my room like this, I have to admit it's stunning.

So stunning that I almost don't notice that, by the time we make it to the second floor, my stomach has calmed down. More like the pterodactyls have become butterflies, but I'm not going to complain, considering it's a definite step up. I've still got a low-grade headache from the altitude, but for now the Advil has everything under control.

I just hope it stays that way.

I know Macy says this is supposed to be a welcome party, but I'm kind of hoping the tea just goes on as usual. My goal is to be as invisible as possible this year, and a party where I'm the main attraction kind of messes with that plan. Or, you know, totally obliterates it.

As we approach the door, I grab Macy's wrist. "You aren't going to make me stand up in front of everyone, are you? We're just going to kind of mingle and walk around, right?"

"Totally. I mean, I think Dad is planning on giving a little welcome speech, but it won't be any big deal."

Of course he is. I mean, why wouldn't he? After all, who doesn't think painting a target on the new girl's back is a good idea? FML.

"Hey, don't look so worried." Macy stops in front of an ornately carved set of double doors and throws her arms around me. "Everything is going to be okay. I swear."

"I'm willing to settle for *not catastrophic*," I tell her, but even as I say it, I'm not holding my breath. Not when it feels like there's a weight pressing down on me. Making me smaller. Turning me into nothing.

It's not the school's fault—I've felt like this for the last month. Still, being here in this place—in Alaska—somehow makes it all worse.

"You'll settle for *amazing*," she corrects as she grabs my arm and wraps hers through it. Then she's leaning forward, sending the double doors flying in both directions as she walks in like she owns the place.

And maybe she does. From the way everyone in the room turns to look at her, I can believe it. At least until I realize my worst nightmares have come true and they're all looking at me. And none of them seem impressed.

So I decide to focus on the décor instead, which is amazing. I don't know where to look first, so I look everywhere, taking in the crimson and black velvet baroque wallpaper, the three-tiered iron chandeliers with black crystals dripping from each elaborately carved arm, the fancy red chairs and black cloth-covered tables that take up the back half of the large room.

Every five feet or so, there are dark wall sconces with what look like actual lit candles in them. I step closer to check them out and find myself completely charmed by the fact that each wall sconce is carved into the shape of a different dragon. One with its wings spread wide in front of a fancy Celtic cross, another curled up around the top of a castle, a third obviously in mid-flight. In all the dragons, the candle flame is lined up to flicker in their wide-open mouths, and as I get even closer, I realize that yes, the flame is real.

I can't imagine how my uncle gets away with that—no fire marshal in the country would be okay with letting a school have unattended candles around students. Then again, this is the middle of nowhere, Alaska, and I also can't imagine a fire marshal actually paying Katmere an unscheduled visit.

Macy tugs at my arm, and reluctantly I let her pull me away from the dragons and farther into the room. That's when I glance up and realize the ceiling is also painted red, with more of that black molding lining the top edges of the walls.

"Are you going to spend the entire party staring at the decor?" Macy teases in a low whisper.

"Maybe." Reluctantly, I take my eyes off the ceiling and focus them on the large buffet tables that run the length of the front wall, loaded down with cheese trays, pastries, sandwiches, and drinks.

No one is at the buffet table, though, and almost no one is seated at the other tables, either. Instead, students are grouped together in various areas of the room. This self-imposed isolation might be the only thing here that feels familiar. Guess it doesn't matter if you go to a regular high school in San Diego or a high-end boarding school in Alaska—cliques are everywhere.

And apparently—if you are at a high-end boarding school—those cliques are about a thousand times snobbier-looking and more unapproachable than normal.

Lucky, lucky me.

As Macy and I step farther into the room, I find myself eyeing the different...factions, for lack of a better word.

Energy—and disdain—permeate the air around the students near the window as they look me over. There are about thirty-five of them, and they're all huddled into one large group, like a team going over plays right before they take the field. The guys are all wearing jeans and the girls are in tiny little dresses, both of which show off strong, powerful bodies with some major muscle definition.

Curiosity and a healthy dose of contempt cover the faces of my new classmates at the back of the room. Dressed mostly in long, flowing dresses or button-up shirts in luxurious patterns and fabrics that fit the room perfectly, they're a lot more delicate-looking than the group near the windows, and even before Macy waves excitedly at them, I know that this is her group.

She starts moving toward them, and I follow, disguising my sudden nervousness with a smile I'm far from feeling.

On our way, we pass another large clump of students, and I swear I can feel heat radiating from them in waves. Every single person in this group is tall—even the girls are close to six feet—and the fact that they're watching me with varying degrees of scorn and suspicion makes walking past them distinctly uncomfortable. Basketball, anyone?

At least until I see Flint in the center of the group, grinning and wiggling his eyebrows at me so wildly that I can't help but giggle. Like every other guy in his group, he's dressed in jeans and a tight T-shirt that shows off his chest and biceps. He looks good. Really good. Then again, so do most of his friends. He sticks his tongue out at me right before I turn away, and this time I full-on laugh.

"What's funny?" Macy demands, but then she sees Flint and just rolls her eyes. "You know how long I spent trying to get his attention—and being totally ignored—before I gave up? If we weren't cousins who are also destined to be best friends, I would resent you."

"Pretty sure Flint and I are destined to be friends, too," I tell her as I hustle to keep up with her ridiculously long stride. "I don't think guys cross their eyes like that at girls they're interested in."

"Yeah, well, you never know. Dra—" She breaks off on a violent cough, like she's just choked on her own saliva or something.

"You okay?" I pat her back a little.

"I'm fine." She coughs again, looks a little nervous as she tugs at one of her flowy sleeves. "Drastic."

"Drastic?" I repeat, more than a little puzzled at this point.

"In case you were wondering." She shoots me an assessing look. "Before. I was going to say drastic. Like, sometimes guys go to drastic measures to get girls they like to notice them. That's what I was going to say. *Drastic.*"

"Oooookay." I don't say anything else because now I'm just confused. Not so much by what she's saying as by how emphatic she's being. Then again, she got weird around Flint yesterday, too. Maybe it's being this close to him that turns her all tongue-tied.

Macy doesn't say anything else as we finally make it to the center of the huge, ornately decorated room. Not that I blame her, because the group we're passing now is filled with the most intimidating people in the place—by far. And that's saying something, considering nearly everyone in this room is unnerving as fuck.

But these people take it to a whole new level. Dressed entirely in monochromatic shades of black or white—designer shirts, dresses, trousers, shoes, *jewelry*—they all but drip money...along with a careless kind of power that it's impossible to miss. Though they are as obvious a clique as any of the others in the room, there's a kind of formality among them that the other groups lack, a sense that they have one another's backs against anyone else in the room but that the alliance ends there.

As we walk by them, I realize there is another big difference between the other groups and them. Not one of them has so much as glanced my way.

I can't help being grateful for that fact, considering my knees wobble a little more with each step I take toward Macy's friends. I'm completely overwhelmed—not just by the number of people at the party who are looking at me but by how ridiculously tight most of the groups are. Like, seriously, there's zero crossover—no guy dressed all in black hanging with a girl in a long, flowy dress. No super-tall girl making eyes at one of the sporty-looking guys, or girls, near the window.

No, everyone here at Katmere Academy seems to be staying firmly in their own lanes. And judging by the looks on their faces, it's not fear keeping them there. It's disdain for everyone else in the room.

Fun times. Seriously. I mean, I've always known prep schools are exclusive and snobby—who doesn't? But I wasn't expecting it to this degree. How much money, status, and attitude can one group of people have, anyway?

Guess it's a good thing I'm related to the headmaster or I'd never make the cut. Nepotism for the win…or loss, depending on how this little soiree goes.

I can't imagine *why* I was nervous to come to this thing…

Only pride keeps me from fleeing as we get close to her friends. Well, that and the fact that acting like prey right now seems like a particularly bad idea. I mean, if I don't want to spend the rest of my senior year dodging every mean girl in the place.

"I can't wait for you to meet my friends," Macy tells me as we finally reach the group in the back. Up close, they're even more spectacular, different gemstones gleaming in their hair and against their skin. Earrings, pendants, hair clips, plus eyebrow, lip, and nose rings, all bedecked with colorful stones.

I've never felt plainer in my life, and it takes every ounce of self-control I have not to once again tug on the neckline of my borrowed dress.

"Hey, guys! This is my cousin, Gr—"

"Grace!" a beautiful redhead with a giant amethyst pendant interrupts. "Welcome to Katmere! We've heard soooo much about you." Her voice is enthusiastic to the point of being mocking, but I'm not sure who she's making fun of—Macy or me. At least until I look into her eyes, which are viciously cold—and focused entirely on me.

Big surprise.

I'm not sure how I'm supposed to answer her—being polite is one thing. Participating while she makes fun of me is something else entirely. Thankfully, before I can decide what to do, a girl with thick, curly dark hair and perfect cupid's bow lips does it for me.

"Knock it off, Simone," she tells her before turning to me with what appears (I hope) to be a genuine smile. "Hi, Grace. I'm Lily."

Her soft brown eyes seem friendly and her black hair is worn in locks woven through with sparkling ribbons that beautifully frame her rich brown skin. "And that's Gwen."

She nods toward an East Asian girl in a beautiful purple dress who grins and says, "It really is nice to meet you."

"Um, it's nice to meet you, too." I'm trying, I really am. But my tone must sound as doubtful as the rest of me feels, because her eyes grow cloudy.

"Don't pay any attention to Simone," she says, all but hissing the redhead's name. "She's just bitter because all the guys are looking at you. She doesn't like the competition."

"Oh, I'm not—" I break off as Simone snorts.

"Yeah, that's totally why I'm bitter. I'm worried about the competition. It has nothing to do with the fact that Foster brought a—"

"Why don't we go get something to drink?" Macy interrupts her loudly.

I start to tell her I'm not thirsty—the low-grade nausea is back—but she doesn't wait for my answer before she slips her hand in mine and draws me across the room to the buffet tables.

At one end, there are two huge teapots and an arrangement of teacups along with two open coolers filled with icy water bottles and cans of soda.

I start to reach for a cup—I've been freezing since I first landed in this state. But then I notice several orange and white five-gallon sports thermoses set up on a separate table. "What are those?" I ask, because I'm curious. And because there seem to be an awful lot of drinks for the number of people in this room. I really, really hope this doesn't mean that a bunch more students are going to be showing up. We're already over my comfort level with the number who are already here.

"Oh, those are just water," Macy says breezily. "We always

keep a bunch on hand in case the temperature drops suddenly and the pipes freeze. Better safe than sorry."

It seems to me that they'd have special pipes and extra insulation for places in Alaska to make sure that doesn't happen. But what do I know? I mean, it's only November and it's already below freezing outside. And that's *normal.* It makes sense that a particularly harsh winter could really mess things up here.

Before I can ask anything else, Macy bends down, pulls a Dr Pepper out of the cooler, and holds it out to me. "I made sure Dad told them to order Dr Pepper for the party—and the cafeteria. It's still your favorite, right?"

It *is* my favorite. I thought I was in the mood for tea, but there's something about that maroon can that gets to me. That reminds me of home and my parents and the life I used to have. Homesickness wells up inside me, and I take the drink, desperate for something—anything—familiar.

Macy smiles at me, nods encouragingly, and I realize that she knows what I'm feeling. Gratitude helps chase away the homesickness. "Thanks. That's really cool of you."

"It's nothing." She knocks her shoulder against mine. "So, who do you want to meet next?" She nods to two guys lounging in red velvet armchairs near the back of the room. They're dressed in the richly patterned button-ups that mark them as members of Macy's group. "That's Cam and his best friend."

"Cam?" She said the name as though I should recognize it, but I don't.

"My boyfriend. He's been dying to meet you. Come on."

Pretty hard to say no to that, so I don't even try, though I know Cam and anyone else who is "dying to meet" the new girl are destined to be disappointed. I'm just not that interesting.

"Cam! This is the cousin I was telling you about!" Macy squeals before we even get next to her boyfriend.

He stands and holds out a hand. "Grace, right?"

"Yes." I shake his hand, and as I do, I can't help noticing how pasty his skin is. "It's good to meet you."

"Good to meet you, too. Macy's been talking about you coming for weeks now." He grins at me. "Hope you like snow, surfer girl."

I don't bother to tell him that I'm not much of a surfer. God knows I'm guilty of stereotyping, too—before I got here, I was half certain I'd be living in an igloo.

"I don't know if I do or not," I tell him. "Yesterday was the first time I've ever seen it."

That gets his attention—and his friend's, too. "You've *never* seen snow?" the other guy asks incredulously. "Ever?"

"Nope."

"She's from San Diego, James." Macy looks, and sounds, exasperated. "Is that really so hard to believe?"

"I guess not." He shrugs and sends me a grin that I can tell is meant to be charming but grossly misses the mark. I've always hated guys who look at girls like they're food meant to be gobbled up. "Hi, Grace."

He doesn't extend his hand, and I definitely don't extend mine. "Hi."

"So what do you think of Alaska so far?" Cam asks as he loops an arm around Macy's waist. He doesn't wait for an answer before he sits back down, pulling my cousin onto his lap as he does.

Before I can answer, he's got his face buried in Macy's neck and she's giggling, her hands threading their way through his sleek brown hair as she burrows into him.

Which is pretty much my cue to leave, as things suddenly get really awkward. Especially since James continues to stare at me like he's waiting to see if I'm going to plop myself down on *his* lap—which, for the record, I most definitely am not.

"I, uh, need another drink," I tell him, awkwardly holding up my still mostly full can of Dr Pepper.

"I can get it for you," he offers, starting forward, but I take a big step back.

"You don't have to."

"You okay, Grace?" Macy breaks off her giggling long enough to ask, completely serious.

"Yeah, of course. I'm fine. I'm just—" Once again, I hold up my Dr Pepper. "I'll be back in a minute."

Cam must do something super sexy to her, because Macy's laugh changes, gets lower, about the same time I lose all her attention.

I don't wait for James to offer again—or worse, insist. Instead, I take off across the room like a shot. But I barely make it to the drinks table before two very large, very warm hands land on my shoulders.

10

Turns Out the Devil Wears Gucci

I freeze, my heart running wild as *NotJames NotJames NotJames* runs through my head like a mantra on overdrive. I mean, seriously. Don't I have enough on my plate right now? Do I really need some jerk trying to make me his afternoon snack as well?

But before I can figure out what to say, the guy leans forward and—in a low, rich voice—asks, "Want a piggyback ride?"

And just like that, the tension dissolves, leaving nothing but a cautious joy in its place. "Flint!" I whirl around to find him grinning at me, amber eyes dancing wickedly.

"Hey there, New Girl," he drawls. "Having fun?"

"Absolutely." I hold up my Dr Pepper. "Doesn't it look like I'm having a good time?"

"It looks like someone can't take a hint, so I thought I'd lend a hand." As one, we shift to watch James—who, as it turns out, did follow me to the drink table—sulkily make his way back to Cam and Macy, who are still wrapped up in each other.

"Thanks for that. I appreciate it."

"Gratitude is so last year." He says it in a fake, high-pitched voice that sounds remarkably like every mean girl everywhere.

The voice, along with the ridiculous hand gesture he uses to accompany it, has me laughing so hard, I nearly snort. And that's when I realize that half the room is still staring at me—while the other half is very deliberately *not* staring at me. Their disregard would be a relief *if* I didn't know they were doing it to make sure I understand how insignificant I really am to them.

Which, duh.

"So do you want to grab something to eat?" Flint asks, nodding behind us.

Before I can answer, both of the room's heavy wooden doors fly open. They slam against the wall with a *bang* that makes everyone in the room jump. And then turn to look.

On the plus side, that means no one is paying attention to me anymore. Because they're all looking at him. At *Jaxon*. And really, who could blame them when he walks in like he owns the place—and everybody in it.

Dressed all in Gucci black—silk V-neck sweater, wool pinstripe pants, shiny leather dress shoes—with his scarred eyebrow furrowed and his dark gaze as cold as the snow-covered ground outside, he shouldn't look sexy at all. But he does. God, he really, really does.

On the negative side, all that coldness—all that darkness—is focused directly on me. And Flint, whose arm has somehow found its way around my shoulders.

I try to glance away, but it's impossible. Try not to look Jaxon in the eyes. But he's just as captivating—just as mesmerizing—today as he was last night. And that's before he starts to move, all languid grace, all rolling shoulders and leading hips and legs that go on for freaking ever.

It's overwhelming.

He's overwhelming.

He's just a guy, I remind myself even as my mouth turns

desert dry. *Just a regular guy like everyone else here.* But even as I tell myself that, I know it's a lie. Jaxon is anything but regular. Anything but ordinary, even here, among the blatantly extraordinary.

Next to me, Flint chuckles a little, and I want to ask him what's so funny when I notice Jaxon heading straight toward us, with an icy blankness in his eyes that makes a shiver run straight through me. But I can't get the words out, can't get anything out of a throat that has closed up tight.

I take a strangled breath, hoping it will chill me out a little. It doesn't work, but then I never really thought it would.

Not when all I can see is how he looked last night, sucking my blood off his thumb.

Not when all I can hear is his voice—low, wicked, wild—warning me to lock my door.

Not when all I can think about is kissing that mouth, running my tongue along the perfect bow of his upper lip, dragging his lower lip between my teeth and biting down just a little bit.

I don't know where the thoughts are coming from—this isn't like me. I've never thought about a guy like this before, not even my old boyfriend from back home. Even before we went out, I never stood around imagining what it would be like to kiss him.

To wrap my arms around him.

To press my body tightly against his.

Because I can almost feel him—almost taste him. I try to make myself think of anything else. Snow. Tomorrow's classes. My uncle, who is supposed to be here but is currently MIA.

None of it works, because all I can see is *him*.

My skin heats up under his gaze, my cheeks burning with embarrassment at the thoughts flitting through my head. And at the way he's looking at me, like he can read every single one of them.

It's impossible; I know it is. But the idea terrifies me enough that I jerk my gaze from his and lift my Dr Pepper to my mouth, trying hard to look unconcerned.

All of which leads to the carbonated drink going straight down the wrong pipe.

My abused lungs revolt as I cover my mouth and cough hard, eyes watering and humiliation burning in my belly. I pretend he isn't watching, pretend Flint isn't pounding on my back, pretend that I don't even notice the weight of all those cold stares as my new classmates watch me trying to suck air into lungs that just won't cooperate.

I need to get away from Flint's overzealous help, from Jaxon's threatening, all-encompassing gaze. At least if I find the nearest restroom, I can die in peace.

I start to move—I think I saw a bathroom marked in the hallway a couple of doors down—but I've taken only a few steps when Jaxon's suddenly right next to me. He doesn't acknowledge me, doesn't even look at me as he passes, but just like at the top of the stairs yesterday, our shoulders brush as he walks by.

My choking fit disappears as quickly as it started. Fresh air floods my lungs.

If I didn't know it was impossible, I would think he had something to do with it. Not just the choking but the stopping of it, as well.

But he didn't. Of course he didn't. The whole idea is absurd.

Knowing that doesn't keep me from turning around and watching him walk away, even though it's the worst thing I can do—for my sanity and my reputation—if the snark and giggles behind me are any indication.

He doesn't look back. In fact, he doesn't look at anyone as he walks along the edges of the buffet table, surveying its bounty. Doesn't so much as glance up as he eventually swipes one large, perfect strawberry from a bowl.

I expect him to pop it in his mouth then and there, but he doesn't.

Instead, he walks to the center of the room—and the huge red velvet wingback chair positioned under the chandelier like a throne, with several other chairs in a half circle in front of it. Once there, he slouches down into the chair, legs spread out in front of him as he says something to the five guys—all dark, all gorgeous, all stunning—sitting in the other chairs.

It's the first time I realize there's anyone in those chairs.

By now, nearly everyone in the room is watching Jaxon, trying to catch his eye. But he ignores them all, deliberately studying the strawberry he is pinching between his thumb and index finger.

Eventually he lifts his gaze and looks straight at me. Then he raises the strawberry to his lips—and bites it clean in half.

It's a warning if I've ever seen one—and a violent one at that—as a drop of red juice hangs for a second on his bottom lip.

I know I should stay, know I should face him down. But as his tongue darts out and licks up the strawberry juice in a very obvious *screw you* to Flint and me and everyone else in the room, I do the only thing I can.

I turn to Flint and blurt out, "I'm sorry. I have to go."

And then I head for the doors in as close to a run as I can manage without looking even more pathetic, desperate to get away before I shatter beneath the weight of Jaxon's obvious contempt.

Because one thing is certain—that little show was meant to underscore just how insignificant I really am to every single person in that room. I just wish I knew why...

11

In the Library, No One Can Hear You Scream

Once I get outside the room, I start to run, desperate to put as much space between Jaxon and myself as I can manage. I have no idea where I'm running, and I don't think it would matter even if I did. Not when I don't have a clue where anything is in this place.

I take a left at the end of the hallway, operating on pure instinct. On my complete desperation to be anywhere but at that party.

I have no idea what I did to make Jaxon so mad, have no idea why he blows so hot and cold with me. I've run into him four times since I got to this frozen hellhole, and each time has been a different experience. Douchey the first time, blank the second, intense the third, and furious the fourth. His moods change more quickly than my bestie's Insta feed.

I get to another dead end, and this time I take a right. Seconds later, I come upon a staircase, this one as plain and un-fantastic as the main one is grand and ornate. I race down one flight and then another and another to the second floor. Once there, I take another right and don't stop until I run out of hallway.

I'm also out of breath and a little queasy, thanks to the

altitude sickness that I just can't seem to shake. I stop a minute and let myself breathe. As I do, the embarrassment finally recedes enough that my rational mind can take over.

Suddenly, I feel like a total moron for freaking out and an even bigger one for running away from Jaxon, who performed the very scary act of biting into a strawberry while looking at me.

Deep inside, I know it's more than that. It's the look on his face, the indolence of his body language, the very obvious *fuck you* in his eyes as he stared directly at me. But still, fleeing the way I did seems absurd now.

Not absurd enough to make me go back to that ridiculously uncomfortable party, but more than absurd enough to make me embarrassed by my actions.

As I straighten and try to figure out what I'm going to do—heading back to my dorm room for more Advil and then some sleep is pretty much top of the list—I realize I'm standing in front of the school's library. And since I've never met a library I didn't like, I can't resist opening the door and walking inside.

The moment I do, I get hit with the oddest feeling. Dread pools in my stomach, and everything inside tells me to turn around, to go back the way I came. It's the strangest feeling I've ever had in my life, and for a second I think about giving in to it. But I've already done more than enough running for the day, so I ignore the pressure in my lungs and the uneasy churning in my stomach and keep walking forward until I'm standing in front of the checkout desk.

Once there, I take a few minutes to just stand and look around the library. It only takes a second for the feeling of dread to dissipate and for absolute wonder to take its place. Because whoever runs this library is my kind of people. Part of it is the sheer number of books—tens of thousands of them at least, lined up in bookcase after bookcase. But there are other things, too.

Gargoyles perched on random bookshelves, looking down as if guarding the books.

A few dozen shimmering crystals, interspersed with sparkling ribbons, hanging from the ceiling in what appears to be randomly spaced intervals.

All the room's open spaces have been turned into study alcoves, filled with beanbags and overstuffed chairs and even a few well-worn leather couches where there's room for them.

But the pièce de résistance, the thing that has me dying to meet the librarian, is the stickers plastered everywhere. On the walls, on the bookshelves, on the desks and chairs and computers. Everywhere. Big stickers, little stickers, funny stickers, encouraging stickers, brand-name stickers, emoji stickers, sarcastic stickers... The list goes on and on, and there's a part of me that wants to wander the library until I read or look at every single one.

But there are too many for one tour—too many for a dozen tours, if I'm honest—so I decide to start this one by checking out the stickers I run across when following the gargoyles.

Because after seeing the rest of the library, I don't believe for one second that the statues are randomly placed. Which means I desperately want to know what the librarian wants to show me.

The first gargoyle—a fierce-looking thing with bat wings and a furious snarl—stands guard over a shelf of horror novels. The bookshelf itself is decorated with Ghostbusters stickers, and I can't help but laugh as I trace the spines of everyone from John Webster to Mary Shelley, from Edgar Allan Poe to Joe Hill. The fact that there's a special homage to Victor Hugo only makes it better, especially the tongue-in-cheek placement of three copies of *The Hunchback of Notre-Dame* right in the gargoyle's line of sight.

The second gargoyle—a squat fellow resting on his haunches

on a pile of skulls—presides over a bookcase filled with textbooks on human anatomy.

The fantasy bookshelf, complete with beautifully covered books about dragons and witches, is home to the third gargoyle statue, who has really fantastical wings and big claws curling around the miniature book she's reading. Unlike the others, both of whom look ferocious, this girl looks mischievous, like she knows she's going to get in trouble for being up way past her bedtime, but she just can't put the story down.

I decide instantly that she's my favorite and pick out a book from her shelf to read tonight in case I can't sleep. Then nearly laugh out loud as I trace my finger around the edges of a sticker that reads, "I'm not a damsel in distress; I'm a dragon in a dress."

I continue wandering from statue to statue, from a small shelf on Gothic architecture to a whole bookcase devoted to ghost stories. On and on it goes, and the longer I'm in here, the more convinced I am that the head librarian here is the coolest person ever—and has fantastic taste in books.

I make it to the end of the trail and turn the corner around the last bookshelf in search of the final gargoyle, only to find him pointing straight toward a half-open door. There's a huge sign on it that reads students must have permission to access this room, and—of course—that only makes me more curious. Especially since the light is on and there's some weird kind of music playing.

I try to place it, but as I get closer, I realize it's not so much music as it is chanting in a language I don't recognize and certainly can't understand. Instantly, my curiosity turns to excitement.

When I was researching Alaska, I learned that there are twenty different languages spoken here by the state's native peoples, and I can't help but wonder if that's what I'm hearing. I hope so—I've totally been wanting a chance to listen to one of the native languages spoken. Especially since so many of them are threatened, including a couple that have less than four thousand speakers in the entire world. That these native languages are dying out is one of the saddest things I've ever heard.

Maybe if I'm lucky, I can kill two birds with one stone here. I can meet the very cool librarian responsible for this library *and* get a lesson from her (because the voice is definitely female) on one of the native languages. Even one of those options makes for a much better night than standing around being stared at at a party that was supposedly thrown to welcome me.

But when I step up to the door, ready to introduce myself, I find that the person doing the chanting isn't the librarian at all. She's a girl about my age, with long, silky dark hair and one of the most beautiful faces I've ever seen. Maybe *the* most beautiful.

She's holding open a book and reading from it, which explains the chanting I heard. I want to ask what language it is, since I can't see the cover, but the way her head snaps up when I step over the threshold has the words drying up in my throat.

Whoever she is, she looks fierce, cheeks flushed, and mouth open wide to let out the unique sounds of whatever language she is speaking. She stops mid-word, with what looks an awful lot like fury burning in her swirling black eyes.

12

It's All Fun and Games Until Someone Loses Their Life

I fumble for an apology—or at least an excuse—but before I can come up with one, the rage in her eyes is gone. In fact, it dissipates so quickly, I can't be sure I didn't imagine it. Especially since the anger, or whatever it was, turns to welcome as she walks toward me.

"You must be Grace," she says in slightly accented English as she comes to a stop about a foot in front of me. "I've been looking forward to meeting you." She extends a hand forward and I take it, bemused, as she continues. "I'm Lia, and I have a feeling we're going to be really good friends."

It's not the strangest greeting I've ever gotten—that honor still belongs to Brant Hayward, whose version of *nice to meet you* was wiping his boogers all over my first-day-of-school dress when we were both in kindergarten—but it's a close second. Still, there's an infectiousness about her smile that has me grinning back.

"I *am* Grace," I agree. "It's nice to meet you."

"Oh, don't be so formal," she tells me, gently steering me out of the room before I can mention that I want to look around. Seconds later, she's got the lights off and the door closed behind us, all in the most efficient way possible.

"What language was that you were speaking? Was it native to Alaska? It was beautiful," I say as we start walking back toward the center of the library.

"Oh, no." She laughs, a light, tinkling sound that perfectly matches the rest of her. "It's actually a language I came across in my research. I've never heard it spoken out loud, so I'm not even sure I'm pronouncing it correctly."

"Well, it sounded amazing. What kind of book was it in?" Now I wish more than ever that I'd gotten a look at the cover.

"A boring one," she answers with a wave of her hand. "I swear this research project is going to kill me. Now, come on, let's go get some tea, and you can tell me all about yourself. Plenty of time to talk about classes when you're actually stuck *in* them."

I decide not to mention that starting new classes is pretty much the only thing I've been looking forward to about the move to Alaska. I mean, my public school definitely didn't offer Witch Hunts in the Atlantic World for a history credit. Besides, tea sounds wonderful, especially considering what just happened when I tried a Dr Pepper. So does the idea of making a friend at this place where everyone looks at me like I have three heads… or like I'm nothing at all.

"Are you sure you aren't busy? I didn't mean to interrupt. I just wanted to explore the library a little bit. I love the gargoyle theme. Very Gothic."

"It is, right? Ms. Royce is cool like that."

"Oh, yeah? Let me guess. Flannel shirts and a hipster vibe? That kind of thing?"

"You would think. But she's actually more a *hippie skirt and flower crown* kind of woman."

"Now I want to meet her even more." We're on the other side of the library from where I came in and we pass through a sitting area with a bunch of black couches, each one dotted with purple throw pillows bearing different quotes from classic horror movies. My favorite is Norman Bates's famous line from *Psycho*: "We all go a little mad sometimes." Although I'm also partial to the pillow next to it: "Be afraid. Be very afraid," from *The Fly*.

"Ms. Royce is big on Halloween," Lia says with a laugh. "I don't think she's put everything away yet."

Oh, right. Halloween was three days ago. I've been so focused on everything else that I just about forgot about it completely this year, even though Heather spent months making her costume from scratch.

I put the book I picked up earlier down on the nearest table—I'll come back for it when the librarian is here— Lia pushes the main door open and gestures for me to precede her. I wait while she turns off the lights, then locks the door. "The library is usually closed on Sunday nights, but I'm doing an independent study this semester, so Ms. Royce lets me work late sometimes."

"I'm sorry. I didn't realize—"

"No need to apologize, Grace." She shoots me a vaguely exasperated look. "How were you supposed to know? I'm just telling you why I have to lock things back up."

"Good point," I admit, a little surprised at how nice she's being.

She starts down the hallway. "So I'm assuming, since you aren't at the party Macy organized for you, that your first full day at our illustrious school hasn't been as smooth as your cousin hoped it'd be?"

She's got that right, but I'm not going to admit it when that would sound like I'm throwing Macy under the bus. Especially since Macy isn't the problem. Everything else is, but not her. "The party was good. I've just had a really long day. I needed a break for a few minutes."

"I bet. Unless you're coming from Vancouver or something, getting here is never easy."

"Yeah, I'm definitely not from Vancouver." I shiver a little as an unexpected wind whips through the hallway.

I glance around, looking for where it could be coming from, then get distracted as Lia raises her brows and says, "Alaska is a long way from California."

"How did you know I'm from California?" Maybe that's why everyone is staring at me—I must be wearing my not-from-here vibe like a parka.

"Foster must have mentioned it when he let us know you were coming," she answers. "And I've got to say, San Diego is pretty much the worst possible place to move here from."

"It's the worst possible place to move anywhere from," I agree. "But especially here."

"No doubt." She looks me up and down, then smirks. "So are you freezing in that dress?"

"Are you kidding? I've been freezing since I landed in Anchorage. Doesn't matter what I wear—even before Macy talked me into putting on this thing."

"Guess we better get you that tea, then." She nods to the staircase that's just come into view. "My room's on the fourth floor, if that's okay?"

"Oh, ours is, too. Mine and Macy's, I mean."

"Awesome."

Lia keeps talking as we make our way to the stairs, pointing out different rooms she thinks I need to know—the chem lab, the study lounge, the snack shop. Part of me wants to pull out my phone and take notes—or, better yet, draw a map, since I'm hopeless with directions. Maybe if I can figure out something as simple as the layout of the castle, other things will fall into place, too. And then I can start to feel safe again—something I haven't felt in a really long time.

We finally make it back to Lia's room—she's in what I'm assuming is the West hallway, judging by its location in relation to mine. I'm a little surprised when she stops in front of the one door on the hallway, maybe on the whole floor, that doesn't have some kind of decoration on it.

My surprise must show, because she says, "It's been a rough year. I just wasn't up to decorating when I got back here."

"That sucks. The rough-year part, I mean. Not the decorating part."

"I knew what you meant." She smiles sadly. "My boyfriend died several months ago, and everyone thinks I should be over it. But we were together a really long time. It's not that easy to just let him go. As I'm sure you know."

It's been a month since my parents died, and I still feel like I'm in shock half the time. "No, it's not."

Like I wake up every morning and for a minute, just a minute, I don't remember why I have that sinking feeling in my stomach.

I don't remember that they're gone and I'm never going to see them again.

I don't remember that I'm alone.

And then it hits me all over again, and so does the grief.

Getting on that first plane yesterday morning was the hardest thing I've ever done—besides identifying them—and I think it's because it made their deaths sink in just a little more.

Lia and I just kind of stand there in the middle of her dorm room for a second, two people who look fine on the outside but who are destroyed on the inside. We don't talk, don't say anything at all. Just stay where we are and absorb the fact that someone else hurts as much as we do.

It's a bizarre feeling. And an oddly comforting one.

Eventually, Lia moves over to her desk, where she has an

electric kettle plugged in. She pours some water into it from the pitcher she also has on her desk, then turns it on before opening a jar of what looks like potpourri and scooping it into two tea strainers.

"Can I help with anything?" I ask, even though she seems to have things under control. It's nice to see her go through the ritual of making tea from homemade leaves. It reminds me of my mom and all the hours we spent in the kitchen assembling all her different blends.

"I've got it." She nods to the second bed in the room, which she has set up as a kind of couch/daybed thing with a red comforter and a bunch of jewel-toned throw pillows. "Go ahead and sit down."

I do, wishing I was in yoga pants or joggers instead of this dress so I could sit like a normal person. Lia doesn't talk much as she makes the tea, and I don't, either. Kind of hard to know where to take the conversation now that we've covered everything from dying languages to dead loved ones.

The silence drags on, and I start to feel uncomfortable. But it doesn't take long for the teakettle to boil, thankfully, and then Lia's setting a cup of tea down in front of me. "It's my own special blend," she says, holding her cup up to her mouth and blowing softly. "I hope you like it."

"I'm sure it's awesome." I wrap my hands around my cup and nearly shudder with relief at finally being able to warm up my fingers. Even if it tastes terrible, it's worth it to have a chance at not being cold.

"These cups are beautiful," I tell her after taking a sip. "Are they Japanese?"

"Yes," Lia says with a smile. "From my favorite shop back home in Tokyo. My mom sends me a new set every semester. It helps with the homesickness."

"That's awesome." I think of my own mom and the way she always bought me a new tea mug every Christmas. Looks like Lia and I really do have a lot in common.

"So how did the party go? I assume not well, considering you ended up in the library, but did you at least get to meet some people?"

"I did, yeah. They seemed nice enough."

She laughs. "You're a really bad liar."

"Yeah, well, it seemed polite to try." I take a sip of the tea, which has a really powerful floral taste that I'm not sure I care for. But it's hot, and that's enough to have me taking another sip. "I've been told that before, though. The bad-liar part, I mean."

"You should probably work on that. At Katmere, knowing how to lie well is practically Survival 101."

It's my turn to laugh. "I guess I'm in serious trouble, then."

"I guess you are." There's no humor in her answer this time, and I realize suddenly that there was none in her original statement, either.

"Wait," I say, strangely discomfited by that fact. "What do you guys have to lie about that's so important?"

That's when Lia looks me straight in the eye and answers, "Everything."

13

Just Bite Me

I have no idea how to respond to that. I mean, what am I supposed to say? What am I supposed to think?

"Don't look so scandalized," she tells me after a few seconds of awkward silence. "I'm just teasing, Grace."

"Oh, right." I laugh along with her, because what else can I do? Still, it doesn't feel right. Maybe because of how serious she looked when she told me that she lies about everything. Or maybe because I can't help wondering if that was the truth and these are just lies... Either way, there's not much else for me to do but shrug and say, "I figured you were just messing with me."

"I totally was. You should have seen your face."

"I bet," I answer with a laugh.

She doesn't say anything for a few seconds and neither do I, until the silence starts to feel awkward. In self- defense, I finally blurt out, "What language were you reading earlier? It sounded so cool."

Lia looks at me for a second, like she's debating if she wants to answer or not. Finally, she answers, "Akkadian. It's the language that evolved from ancient Sumerian."

"Really? So it's three thousand years old?"

She looks surprised. "Something like that, yeah."

"That's incredible. I've always been so impressed with linguists and anthropologists who do that, you know? Like it's one thing to figure out what the different letters mean and the words they make." I shake my head in awe. "But to figure out what they sound like? It kind of blows my mind."

"Right?" Her eyes glow with excitement. "The foundation of language is so—"

My phone vibrates with several text messages in a row, cutting her off. I pull it out, figuring Macy finally got tired of waiting for me to come back. Sure enough, my home screen is a series of texts from my cousin, each one a little more frantic than the one before it. Looks like she's been texting me for a while but I had my ringer off.

Macy: Hey, where'd you go?
Macy: I keep waiting for you to come back
Macy: Hey, where are you????
Macy: I'm coming to find you
Macy: Are you okay????
Macy: Answer me!!!!!
Macy: What's going on?
Macy: Are. You. OK?????

I text her back a quick, *I'm good*, and my phone immediately buzzes again. A glance at my cousin's all-caps *WHERE ARE YOU?* and I know I'd better find her before she loses it completely.

"Sorry, Lia, but I've got to go. Macy's freaking out."

"Why? Because you left the party? She'll get over it."

"Yeah, but I think she's actually worried." I don't tell her about what happened with those guys last night, don't mention that that's probably why Macy is so upset that she can't find me. Instead, I focus on my phone and text back *Lia's room* before standing up. "Thanks for the tea."

"At least stay a couple more minutes, finish your drink." She looks half amused, half disappointed as she continues. "You don't want your cousin to think she can boss you around."

I carry my cup over to the bathroom sink. "She's not bossing me around. I think she's afraid I'm upset or something." It seems easier to give that explanation than to go into everything that happened with Marc and Quinn. "Besides, if I know her, she's on her way to your room right now."

"You're probably right. Macy does tend to be the hysterical type."

"I didn't say that—" A knock on the door cuts me off.

Lia just grins at me in an *I told you so* kind of way. "Don't worry about washing the cup," she says, taking it from my hands. "Just go show Macy that you're not crying your eyes out. And that I didn't murder you."

"She wouldn't think that. She's just worried about me." Still, I make a beeline for the door, then throw it open to reveal my cousin—as predicted—on the other side. "I'm right here," I tell her with a smile.

"Oh, thank God!" She throws her arms around me. "I thought something had happened to you."

"What could possibly happen to me when nearly everyone else is at the party? I just went for a walk," I try to joke.

"I don't know." She looks suddenly uncertain. "Lots of things…"

"I think Macy was worried you might have gone outside," Lia interjects. "If you had wandered out in that dress, you'd be close to dead by now."

"Yes, exactly!" Macy looks like she's seized on the excuse. "I didn't want you to freeze to death before your first full day in Alaska is over." It's a strange answer, especially considering she knows what almost happened to me last night and that I was terrified of being thrown outside for just that reason. But now isn't exactly the time to get into all that, so I turn to Lia instead. And say, "Thanks for everything."

"No worries." She grins at me. "Stop by again sometime. We'll do mani-pedis or facials or something."

"Sounds good. And I'd love to hear more about your research."

"Mani-pedis?" Macy repeats, sounding surprised. "Research?"

Lia rolls her eyes. "Obviously, you're invited, too." And then she closes the door in our faces.

Which...let's be honest, seems weird, considering how friendly she's been all night. Then again, the second Macy showed up, everything about Lia got a lot sharper. Maybe her abrupt good night has more to do with my cousin than it does with me.

And then Macy whispers, "I can't believe you got invited to do mani-pedis with Lia Tanaka. *After* being invited to her room."

She doesn't sound jealous, just confused. Like it's the strangest thing in the world for Lia and me to have something in common. "It wasn't hard. She seems really nice."

"'Nice' isn't the adjective I would normally use to describe her," Macy answers as we start down the hall. "She's the most popular girl in school and normally takes great pains to remind people of that. Although lately, she's been really reclusive."

"Yeah, well, after losing her boyfriend, I figure she's entitled."

Macy's eyes go huge. "She *told* you about that?"

"Yeah." A sickening thought occurs to me. "Is it a secret?"

"No. It's just... I've heard she doesn't talk about Hudson." Her voice is off when she says it, and suddenly she's looking anywhere but at me. I'm pretty sure it's because she's uncomfortable and not because the thousand-year-old tapestry she's currently looking at and has probably seen a million times is more interesting than our conversation. I just wish I knew why.

"That's not that surprising, is it?" I answer. "And she didn't really talk about him to me. Just told me that he died."

"Yeah. Almost a year ago. It kind of rattled the school." She's still not looking at me, which is growing weirder by the second.

"Was he a student here?"

"He was, but he graduated the year before he died. Still, it really freaked a lot of us out."

"I bet." I want to ask what happened, but she's so uncomfortable that it seems rude, so I let it go.

We walk in silence for a couple of minutes, giving the subject time to dissipate. Once it does, Macy bounces back to her normal self and asks, "Are you hungry? You didn't eat anything at the party."

I start to say yes—I haven't eaten since the bowl of Frosted Flakes Macy poured me this morning from her stash—but the altitude sickness must be back, because the mention of food has my stomach rumbling, and not in a good way. "You know, I think I'm just going to go to bed. I'm not feeling so great."

For the first time, Macy looks worried. "If you aren't feeling better in the morning, I think we'd better stop by the nurse. You've been here more than twenty-four hours now. You should be starting to get used to the altitude."

"When I googled it, it said twenty-four to forty-eight hours. If I'm not better after tomorrow's classes, I'll go. Okay?"

"If you're not better after tomorrow's classes, I'm pretty sure my dad will drag you there himself. He's been frantic about you since you asked him to leave you in San Diego to finish up your quarter."

Another awkward silence starts to descend, and honestly, I just can't take it right now. So it's my turn to change the subject when I say, "I can't believe how tired I am. What time is it anyway?"

Macy laughs. “It’s eight o’clock, party animal.”

“I’ll party next week. After I finally get some sleep…and after this gross altitude sickness goes away.” I put a hand to my stomach as the nausea from earlier returns with a vengeance.

“I’m such a jerk.” Macy rolls her eyes at herself. “Planning a party on your first couple of days here was a bad move on my part. I’m so sorry.”

“You’re not a jerk. You were just trying to help me meet people.”

“I was *trying* to show off my fabulous older cousin—”

“I’m older by, like, a year.”

“Older is older, isn’t it?” She grins at me. “Anyway, I was trying to show you off and help you get acclimated. I didn’t think about the fact that you might need a day or two to just breathe.”

We make it to our room, and Macy unlocks the door with a flourish. Just in time, too, because my stomach revolts about two seconds after I walk in the door. I barely make it to the bathroom before I throw up a noxious combination of tea and Dr Pepper.

Looks like Alaska really is trying to kill me after all.

14

Knock, Knock, Knocking on Death's Door

I spend the next fifteen minutes trying to throw up the inside of my stomach and hoping that if this godforsaken place *is* trying to kill me, it just gets it over with already.

When the nausea finally stops about half an hour later, I'm exhausted and the headache is back in full force.

"Should I get the nurse?" Macy asks, walking behind me, arms outstretched to catch me as I make my way to the bed. "I think I should get the nurse."

I groan as I climb under my cool sheets. "Let's give it a little while longer."

"I don't think—"

"Older-cousin prerogative." I shoot her a grin I'm far from feeling and snuggle onto my pillow. "If I'm not better in the morning, we'll call the nurse."

"Are you sure?" Macy dances from foot to foot as though unsure what to do.

"Considering I've had more than enough attention since I got to this school? Yes. Definitely."

She doesn't look happy by my refusal, but eventually she nods.

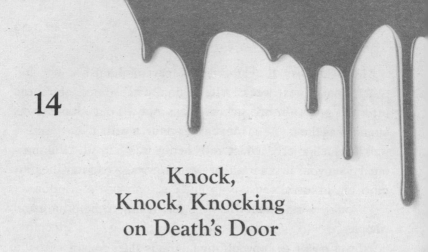

I drift in and out of sleep as my cousin washes her face and changes into her pajamas. But right around the time she turns off the light and crawls into bed, another wave of nausea rolls over me. I ride it out, trying to ignore how much I wish my mom were here to baby me a little, and eventually fall into a fitful sleep, one I don't wake from until an alarm blares at six thirty the next morning. It goes off just as abruptly as someone hits Snooze.

I wake up disoriented, trying to remember where I am and whose godawful alarm was beeping in my ear. Then it all comes flooding back. After one additional trip to the bathroom around three to dry heave my guts up, the nausea receded, which was a giant plus. And everything else feels okay now—my head has stopped spinning, and while my throat feels dry, it doesn't hurt, either.

Huh. Looks like the internet was right about the whole *twenty-four to forty-eight hours to acclimate* thing. I'm good as new.

At least until I sit up and realize the rest of my body is another story. Nearly every muscle I have aches like I've just climbed Denali—after running a marathon. I'm pretty sure it's just dehydration combined with how tense I was yesterday, but either way, I'm in no mood to get up. I'm certainly in no mood to put on a happy face for my first day of classes.

I lie back down and pull the covers over my head, trying to decide what I want to do. I'm still lying there ten minutes later when Macy wakes up with a grumble.

The first thing she does is slap at her alarm until it stops again—something I am eternally grateful for, considering she picked the most grating, annoying sound ever created to wake up to—but it takes her only a second to climb out of bed and come over to me.

"Grace?" she whispers softly, like she wants to check on me

but doesn't want to wake me up at the same time.

"I'm okay," I tell her. "Just sore."

"Yuck. That's probably dehydration." She crosses to the fridge in the corner of the room and pulls out a pitcher of water. She pours two glasses and then hands me one as she settles back onto her bed. She spends a minute texting—Cam, I figure—before tossing her phone aside and looking at me. "I have to go to my classes today—I've got tests in three of them—but I'll come back and check on you when I can."

I'm pretty much loving her assumption that I'm not going to class, so I don't argue. Except to say, "You don't have to go out of your way to check on me. I'm feeling much better."

"Good, then you can consider this a mental health day, of the *Holy crap, I just moved to Alaska!* variety."

"There's an actual mental health day for that?" I tease, moving around until I'm sitting up with my back against the wall.

Macy snorts. "There are whole mental health *months* for that. Alaska's not easy."

It's my turn to snort. "No kidding. I've been here less than forty-eight hours and I've already figured that out."

"That's just because you're afraid of wolves," she teases.

"And bears," I admit without a flicker of embarrassment. "As any sane person should be."

"You have a point." She grins. "You should take the day and do whatever you want. Read a book, watch some trash TV, eat my stash of junk food if your stomach feels up to it. Dad will let your teachers know you'll be starting tomorrow instead of today."

I hadn't even thought of Uncle Finn. "Will your dad be okay with me skipping class?"

"He's the one who suggested it."

"How does he know—?" I break off when a knock sounds at the door. "Who—?"

"My dad," Macy says as she crosses the room and throws open the door with a flourish. "Who else?"

Except it's not Uncle Finn at all. It's Flint, who takes one look at Macy in her tiny nightshirt and me in last night's dress and smeared makeup and starts grinning like a dork.

"Looking good, ladies." He gives a low whistle. "Guess you decided to take the tea party up a notch or four last night, huh?"

"Wouldn't you like to know," Macy taunts as she makes a beeline for the bathroom and the privacy it affords. I don't bother to answer, just stick my tongue out at him. He laughs and raises his eyebrows in response.

"I *would* like to know," Flint tells me as he crosses over to sit on the end of my bed. "Where'd you run off to? And why?"

Because telling him the whole reason involves trying to explain my bizarre reaction to Jaxon—not to mention everything that came after—I settle for part of the truth. "The altitude really started getting to me. I felt like I was going to throw up, so I came back to the room."

That wipes the smile off his face. "How are you now? Altitude sickness isn't anything to fool around with. Can you breathe okay?"

"I can breathe fine. I swear," I add when he doesn't look convinced. "I'm feeling almost normal today. Just had to get used to the mountains, I guess."

"Speaking of mountains." Flint's appealing grin is back. "That's why I came by. A bunch of us are having a snowball fight after dinner tonight. Thought you might want to join in… if you feel okay, I mean."

"A snowball fight?" I shake my head. "I don't think I should."

"Why not?"

"Because I don't even know how to make a snowball, let alone how to throw one."

He looks at me like I'm being silly. "You pick up snow, you pack it into a ball, and then you throw it at the nearest person." He uses his hands to mime his words. "It's not exactly hard."

I stare at him, unconvinced.

"Come on, New Girl. Give it a try. I promise it'll be fun."

"Careful, Grace." Macy comes out of the bathroom, her hair wrapped in a towel. "Never trust a..." She trails off when Flint turns to her, brows raised.

"They're having a snowball fight after class today," I tell her. "He wants us to join." He hadn't invited Macy in so many words, but there's no way I'm going without her. And from the sudden smile on her face, I'm guessing I made the right choice.

"Seriously? We have to go, Grace. Flint's snowball fights are legendary around here."

"That doesn't exactly raise my confidence level, considering I have no idea what I'm doing."

"It'll be fine," they both say at the same time.

It's my turn to raise my brows as I look back and forth between them.

"Trust me," Flint implores. "I'll take good care of you."

"Don't trust him," Macy tells me. "Put a snowball in that boy's hand and he's utterly diabolical. But that doesn't mean it won't be fun."

I still think it's a bad idea, but Flint and Macy are my only two actual friends at Katmere. Who knows what will happen with Lia, and as for Jaxon... Jaxon is a lot of things, but I definitely wouldn't call him a friend. Or even friendly, for that matter.

"Okay, fine," I give in gracefully. "But if I end up dying in the middle of the fight, I'm going to haunt both of you forever."

"I'm pretty sure you'll survive," Macy assures me.

Flint, on the other hand, just winks. "And if not, I can think of worse ways to spend eternity."

Before I can come up with a response to that, he leans over and drops a kiss on my cheek. "See you later, New Girl." And then he's gone, slipping out the door without a backward glance.

I'm left with a wide-eyed, openmouthed Macy, who is all but clapping her hands in delight over one little peck. And the sad knowledge that no matter how adorable Flint is, he doesn't make me feel anything close to what Jaxon does.

15

So Hell Actually *Can* Freeze Over

"Did he…" Macy gasps out after he shuts the door behind him.

"It's not a big deal," I assure her.

"Flint just…" Apparently the word is still failing her, because she taps her cheek in the same spot where Flint kissed mine.

"It's *not* a big deal," I say again. "It's not like he planted one on me or anything. He was just being friendly."

"He's never been friendly like that to *me*. Or anyone else I've seen."

"Yeah, well, you've got a boyfriend. He's probably afraid Cam will kick his ass."

Macy laughs. She actually laughs, which…okay. The idea of her thin, lanky boyfriend kicking Flint's ass does seem a little absurd. But still, shouldn't she at least *pretend* to defend him?

"You want me to talk to him?" I tease. "See if he'll kiss *you* next time?"

"Of course not! I'm very happy with Cam and his kisses, thank you. I'm just saying, Flint likes you." She grabs a brush, starts running it through her hair.

Despite her words, there's something in her tone that has me narrowing my eyes. "Wait. Do you have a crush on Flint *for real*?"

"Of course I don't. I love Cam." She avoids looking me in the eye as she grabs some product.

"Yeah, because that's real convincing." I roll my eyes. "Look, if you want to be with Flint, shouldn't you just break up with Cam and go for it?"

"I *don't* want to be with Flint."

"Mace—"

"I'm serious, Grace. Maybe I used to have a crush on him, way back in ninth grade or something. But that was a long time ago, and it doesn't matter anymore."

"Because of Cam." I watch her face closely in the mirror as she starts to style her short, colorful hair.

"Because I love Cam, yes," she says as she spikes up a few strands. "And also because it's not like that here."

"Not like what?"

"The different groups. They don't mix much."

"Yeah, I noticed that at the party. But just because they *don't* doesn't mean they *can't*, right? I mean, if you like Flint and he likes you—"

"I don't like Flint," she groans. "And he definitely doesn't like me. And if I did like him, it wouldn't matter anyway, because..."

"Because what? He's popular?"

She sighs, shakes her head. "It's more than that."

"More than *what*? I'm beginning to feel like I've fallen into *Mean Girls*, Alaska version or something."

A knock sounds on the door before she can answer.

"Exactly how many people stop by your room before seven thirty in the morning anyway?" I joke as I cross to the door. Macy doesn't answer, just kind of shrugs and grins as she starts on her makeup.

I pull open the door to find my uncle looking down at me

worriedly. "How are you feeling? Macy said you were throwing up last night."

"I'm better, Uncle Finn. The nausea's gone and so is the headache."

"You're sure?" He gestures for me to climb back into my bed, so I do—a little gratefully, if I'm being honest. I've gotten so little sleep the last two nights that I feel like I'm in a fog, even if the altitude sickness has finally gone away.

"Good." He puts a hand on my forehead, like he's testing if I have a fever.

I start to crack a joke about altitude sickness not being a virus, but as he follows the hand on my forehead with a kiss to the top of my head, I get choked up. Because right now, with his eyebrows furrowed and his mouth curled into a frown that only makes his dimples more apparent, Uncle Finn looks so much like my dad that it takes every ounce of willpower I have not to cry.

"I still think Macy's right," he continues, oblivious to how broken I suddenly feel. "You should spend the day resting and start class tomorrow. Losing your parents, the move, Katmere Academy, Alaska—it's a lot to get used to, even without altitude sickness."

I nod but look away before he can see the emotion in my eyes.

He must recognize my struggle, because he doesn't say anything else. Just pats my hand before wandering back to the built-in vanity where Macy is still getting ready.

They talk, but they keep their voices so low that I can't hear anything, so I just tune it all out. I crawl back into bed, pull my covers up to my chin. And wait for the pain of missing my parents to pass.

I don't plan to fall asleep, but I do anyway. The next time I wake up, it's after one, and my stomach is grumbling pretty much nonstop. This time, though, the discomfort is because it's been more than twenty-four hours since I've put anything that even resembles food into it.

There's a jar of peanut butter and a box of crackers on top of the fridge, and I glom onto both of them. A ton of peanut butter and an entire sleeve of crackers later and I finally feel human again.

I also feel trapped—inside this room and inside the school.

I try to ignore the restlessness, try to watch one of my favorite shows on Netflix or read the magazine I didn't finish on the plane. I even text Heather, though I know she's at school, hoping she can message back and forth with me for a while. Except—according to the one text she does manage to send back—she's about to take a calculus test, so definitely no distraction there.

Nothing else I try sticks, either, so finally I decide to just go for it. Maybe a walk around the Alaskan wilderness is exactly what I need to clear my head.

But deciding to go for a walk and actually getting ready for one are two very different things up here. I take a quick shower and then—because I'm a total newbie—I google how to dress for an Alaskan winter. Turns out the answer is *very* carefully, even when it's only November.

Once I pull up a site that looks reputable, the clothes Macy made sure I have make a lot more sense. I start with the wool tights she got me and one of my tank tops, then add a layer of long underwear—pants and shirt. After the underwear, I slip into fleece pants in hot pink (of course) and a fleece jacket in gray. The site gives me the option of another, heavier jacket to go over this one, but it's nowhere near as cold as it's going to get in a couple of months, so I decide to skip it and go straight for the hat, scarf, gloves, and two pairs of socks. Finally, I finish with the down-filled hooded parka my uncle got me and the pair of snow boots rated for Denali that are at the bottom of my closet.

A quick look in the mirror tells me I look as ridiculous as I feel.

But I figure I'll look even more ridiculous if I freeze to death on my second full day in Alaska, so I ignore the feeling. Besides, if I end up getting really warm during my walk, I can take off the fleece layer—or so the online guide suggests, as sweat is the enemy up here. Apparently walking around in wet clothes can lead to hypothermia. So…just like everything else in this state.

Instead of texting her and interrupting one of her tests, I leave Macy a note telling her I'm going to explore the school grounds—I'm not foolish enough to actually wander out past the wall into the wilderness, where there are wolves and bears and God only knows what else.

Then I head out. As I walk down the stairs, I ignore pretty much everyone I come across—which is almost nobody, since most of the school is in class right now. I should probably feel guilty that I'm not, but to be honest, I just feel relieved.

Once I'm on the ground floor, I take the first outside door I can find and then nearly change my mind as the wind and cold all but slap me in the face.

Maybe I should have put on that extra layer after all…

It's too late now, so I pull my hoodie up over my head and duck my scarf-covered face down into my parka's high collar. Then I set out across the yard, despite the fact that every instinct I have is screaming at me to go back inside.

But I've always heard you're supposed to start something how you plan to end it, and I am *not* going to be a prisoner inside the school for the next year. Over my dead freaking body.

I shove my hands in my pockets and begin to walk.

At first, I'm so miserable that all I can think about is the cold and how it feels against my skin, despite the fact that nearly every inch of me is covered in multiple layers.

But the more I walk, the warmer I become, so I up my pace and finally get the chance to start looking around. The sun rose about four hours ago—at nearly ten a.m.—so this is my first daylight look at the wilderness.

I'm struck by how beautiful everything is, even here on the campus grounds. We're on the side of a mountain, so everything is sloped, which means I'm constantly walking up or down one hill or another—not easy, considering the altitude, but at least I'm breathing a lot easier than I was two days ago.

There aren't a lot of different plants here right now, but there are a bunch of evergreens lining the various walkways and clustered at different points around campus. They're a beautiful green against the backdrop of white snow that covers nearly everything out here.

Curious what it feels like—but not ridiculous enough to take off my gloves—I bend down and scoop up a handful of snow, then let it slip through my fingers just to see how it falls. When my hand is empty, I bend down and scoop up some more, then do what Flint said earlier and pat it into a ball.

It's easier than I thought it would be, and it takes only a few seconds before I'm hurling the snow as hard as I can at the nearest tree on the left side of where the path forks ahead. I watch with satisfaction as it hits the trunk and explodes, before heading toward the path just beyond it.

But as I walk closer to the tree, I realize I've never seen anything like its dark, twisted roots. Huge and gray and gnarled together in a chaotic mess that looks like something out of a really bad nightmare, they all but scream for passersby to beware. Add in the broken branches and ripped-up bark off the trunk and the thing looks like it belongs in the middle of a horror movie instead of Katmere's otherwise pristine campus.

I'm not going to lie. It gives me pause. I know it's ridiculous to be repulsed by a tree, but the closer I get to it, the worse it looks—and the worse I feel about the trail it's guarding. Figuring I've already pushed my comfort zone enough for one day just being out here, I veer toward the sun-dappled path on the right instead.

Turns out, it's a good choice, because as soon as I make my way around the first bend, I can see a bunch of buildings. I pause to look at most of them from a safe distance, since class is in session and the last thing I want is to be caught trying to peek in through the windows like some kind of weirdo.

Besides, each cottage—and they do look like cottages—has a sign in front of it that names the building and says what it's used for.

I pause when I get to one of the larger ones. It's labeled Chinook: Art, and my heart speeds up a little just looking at it. I've been sketching and painting since I understood crayons can do more than color in coloring books—and part of me wants nothing more than to run up the snow-lined path and throw open the door, just to see what kind of art studio they have out here that I can work in.

I settle for pulling out my phone and taking a quick pic of the sign. I'll google the word "chinook" later. I know it means "wind" in at least one native Alaskan language, but it will be fun to figure out which one.

I kind of want to know what *all* the words mean, so as I continue walking past the different outlying buildings—some larger than others—I snap a picture of each sign so I can look up the words later. Plus, I figure it'll help me remember where everything is, since I don't have a clue what rooms my classes are in yet.

I'm actually a little concerned about having too many classes out here, because what am I supposed to do? Run back to my room and get all these clothes on in between classes? If so, exactly how long are the passing periods here at Katmere? Because the six minutes I got at my old school isn't exactly going to cut it.

When I reach the end of the scattered row of buildings, I find a stone-lined trail that seems to wind its way around the grounds to the other side of the castle. A weird sense that I should turn around settles across my shoulders—kind of like what I felt at the library last night—and I pause for a second.

But I know when I'm letting my imagination get the better of me—that tree back there really spooked me—so I shake off the feeling and head down the trail.

But the farther I get from the main building, the worse the wind gets, and I pick up my pace to try to stay warm. So much for getting too hot and taking off a layer like that website suggested. Pretty sure the threat of turning into a Grace-flavored Popsicle gets a little more real with every second that passes.

Still, I don't turn back. At this point, I think I've circled more than half the grounds, which means I'm closer to the main castle if I keep going forward instead of heading back the way I came. So I pull my scarf a little more tightly around my face, shove my hands deep into my coat pockets, and keep going.

I head by a few more clumps of trees, a pond that is completely frozen over that I would love to ice skate on if I can manage to balance with all these clothes on, and a couple more small buildings. One is labeled Shila: Shop and the other says Tanana: Dance Studio over the door.

The cottage names are cool, but the classes they house surprise me a little. I don't know what I expected of Katmere Academy, but I guess it wasn't that it would have everything a regular high school has and so much more.

Admittedly, my only knowledge of rich boarding schools comes from my mom's old DVD of *Dead Poets Society* she made me watch with her once a year. But in that movie, Welton Academy was super strict, super harsh, and super stuck-up. So far, Katmere Academy seems to be only one of the three.

The wind is getting worse, so once again I pick up my pace, following the trail past a bunch of larger trees. These aren't evergreens, their leaves long gone and their branches coated in frost and dripping with icicles. I pause to study a few of them because they're beautiful, and because the light refracting through them sends rainbows dancing on the ground at my feet.

I'm charmed by this little bit of whimsy, so much that I don't even mind the wind for a second because it's what's making the rainbows dance. Eventually, though, I get too cold to stand still and make my way out of the trees to find another frozen pond. This one is obviously meant as a place people can hang out, because there are a bunch of seats around it, along with a snow-topped gazebo several yards away.

I take a couple of steps toward the gazebo, thinking I might sit down and rest for a minute, before I realize that it's already occupied by Lia—and *Jaxon*.

16

Sometimes Keeping Your Enemies Close Is the Only Thing that Prevents Hypothermia

Damn it.

I swore to myself that I wouldn't go running like a scared rabbit the next time I saw Jaxon, but this doesn't exactly seem like the time to hang around. Not when everything about their conversation screams *intense*. And—more importantly—*private*.

The way his and Lia's bodies are angled toward each other but aren't actually touching.

The rigidness of their shoulders.

How they're both completely wrapped up in whatever the other one is saying.

There's a part of me that wishes I were closer, wishes I could hear what they're talking about even though it is *absolutely none of my business*. Still, any people who look as grim and angry as these two do obviously have some kind of problem, and I'd be lying if I said I didn't want to know what it is.

I'm not sure why it matters so much to me, except there's an intimacy to their fighting that makes my stomach hurt. Which is absurd, considering I barely know Jaxon. And considering that two of the four times we've run into each other, he's blown past me like I don't even exist.

That in and of itself is a pretty big hint that he wants nothing to do with me.

Except I keep remembering the look on his face when he chased those guys away from me the first night. The way his pupils were all blown out when he touched my face and wiped the drop of blood from my lips.

The way his body brushed against mine and it felt like everything inside me was holding its breath, just waiting for a chance to come alive.

We didn't feel like strangers then.

Which is probably why I keep watching him and Lia, against my better judgment.

They're arguing fiercely now, so much so that I can hear their raised voices, even as far away as I am. I'm not close enough to actually make out the words, but I don't need to know what they're saying to know just how furious they both are.

And that's before Lia lashes out at him, her open palm cracking against his scarred cheek hard enough to have Jaxon's head flying back. He doesn't hit her in return. In fact, he doesn't do anything at all until her palm comes flying at his face again.

This time, he catches her wrist in his hand and holds tight as she struggles to pull away. She's screaming full-out now, harsh sounds of rage and agony that claw their way inside me and bring tears to my eyes.

I know those sounds. I know the agony that causes them and the rage that makes it impossible to contain them. I know how they come from deep inside and how they leave your throat—and your soul—shredded in their wake.

Instinctively, I take a step toward her—toward them—galvanized by Lia's pain and the barely leashed violence that hangs in the air between them. But the wind picks up as I take that first step, and suddenly they're both turning and staring at me with flat black eyes that send a chill straight through me. A chill that has nothing to do with the cold and everything to do with Jaxon and Lia and the way they're looking at me.

Like they're the predators and I'm the prey they can't wait to sink their teeth into.

I tell myself that I'm just spooked, but it doesn't help me shake the weird feeling, even as I give them both a little wave. I thought Lia and I might be becoming friends yesterday—especially when she suggested doing mani-pedis together—but it's obvious that friendship doesn't extend to whatever is happening here. Which is fine. The last thing I want to do is get in the middle of a fight between two people who obviously have some kind of history together. But I also don't want to leave them alone if their fight has deteriorated to her hitting him and him grabbing her in self-defense.

All of which leaves me unsure of what I'm supposed to do now, stuck where I am, an awkward guard staring at both of them in an effort to prevent I-don't-know-what while they stare right back at me.

But when Jaxon drops Lia's wrist and takes a couple of steps toward me, the same panic that hit me yesterday at the party slams through me again. As does the same odd fascination I've had from the beginning. I don't know what it is about him, but every time I catch sight of him, I feel something tug at me I can't identify, something I have no ability to explain.

He advances a few more steps, and my heart kicks up another notch or fifty. Still, I stand my ground—I ran from Jaxon once. I'm not going to do it a second time.

But then Lia reaches out, grabbing *him*, holding *him* back, pulling *him* toward her. The dangerous look fades from her eyes (though not from his) until it's almost like it was never there, and she waves at me enthusiastically.

"Hi, Grace! Come join us."

Ummm, no thanks. Not in a million years. Not when every instinct I have is screaming at me to flee, even though I don't know why.

So instead of moving forward, I give her another little wave and call, "Actually, I've got to get back to my room before Macy sends out another search party. I just wanted to explore a little bit before I start classes tomorrow. Have a good afternoon!"

The last seems like major overkill, considering the fury I sense between them, but I tend to either clam up or babble when I'm nervous, so all in all, it's not a *terrible* performance. Or at least that's what I tell myself as I turn and start walking away as fast as I can without actually running.

Every step is a lesson in self-control as I have to force myself not to look back over my shoulder to see if Jaxon is still watching me. The prickle at the back of my neck says he is, but I ignore it.

Just like I ignore the weird feeling inside me that has shown up every time I've seen him. I assure myself it's nothing, that it doesn't matter. Because no way am I about to crush on a boy this complicated.

Still, the urge to turn around stays with me—right up until Jaxon appears by my side, eyes gleaming with interest and sexy-af hair blowing in the wind.

"What's the rush?" he asks, scooting in front of me so that he's directly in my path, walking backward so we're face-to-face and I'm forced to slow down or bump into him.

"Nothing." I look down so I don't have to look him in the eye. "I'm cold."

"So which is it? Nothing?" He stops walking, which forces me to do the same, then puts a finger under my chin and presses up until I relent and meet his gaze. He flashes me a crooked little smile that does unspeakable things to my heart—the whole reason I'd been trying not to look at him to begin with. Especially considering what I just saw between him and Lia. "Or the cold?"

If I look closely, I can still see the imprint of her hand on his scarred cheek. It pisses me off, more than it should considering I barely know the guy. Which is why I take a deliberate step to the side and say, "The cold. So if you'll excuse me…"

"You're wearing an awful lot of clothes," he tells me—confirming that I look as ridiculous as I feel—as he moves until he's once again in front of me. "You sure the cold's not just an excuse?"

"I don't need to make excuses to you." And yet I am—making excuses and trying to run away from him and what I just saw. Trying to run away from all the things he makes me feel when all I really want to do is grab on to him and hold on tight. It's an absurd thought, an absurd feeling, but that doesn't make it any less real.

He tilts his head, quirks a brow, and somehow has my heart beating that much faster because of it. "Don't you?"

This is the part where I should start walking. The part where I should do a lot of things, *any*thing, that doesn't involve throwing myself at Jaxon Vega like I'm the game-deciding pitch at the World Series. But I don't do that.

Instead, I stay where I am. Not because Jaxon is blocking my way—which he is—but because everything inside me is responding to everything inside him. Even the danger. *Especially* the danger, though I've never been that girl before, the one who takes risks just to see how they feel.

Maybe that's why—instead of moving around him and running back to the castle like I should—I look him straight in the eye and say, "No. I don't answer to you."

He laughs. He actually laughs, and it's the most arrogant

thing I've ever heard.

"Everyone answers to me…eventually."

Oh. My. God. What an *asshat.*

I roll my eyes and step around him, moving up the path with a stiff back and a fast pace that all but screams for him not to follow. Because when he says stuff like that, it doesn't matter how drawn to him I feel. I've got better things to do than waste my time on a guy who thinks he's God's gift to everyone.

Except Jaxon must not be as adept at reading body language as I thought—or he just doesn't care. Either way, he doesn't let me go like I expect. Instead, he starts walking right alongside me again, keeping pace no matter how hard and fast I push myself.

It's annoying as fuck, even without the obnoxious smirk he doesn't try to hide. Or the multiple sidelong glances that precede the words: "Hanging out with Flint Montgomery isn't exactly keeping your head down."

I ignore him, do my best Dory impression. *Just keep walking, just keep walking.*

"I'm only saying," he continues when I don't respond, "making friends with a dra—" He breaks off, clears his throat before trying again. "Making friends with a guy like Flint is…"

"What?" I turn on him, frustration racing through me. "Being friends with Flint is *what* exactly?"

"Like painting a target on your back," he answers, looking a little taken aback by my anger. "It's pretty much the opposite of keeping a low profile."

"Oh, really? So what exactly is hanging out with *you*, then?"

His face goes blank, and I don't think he's going to answer. But eventually, he says, "Utter and complete stupidity."

Not the answer I was expecting, especially from someone as arrogant and annoying as he can be. The blunt honesty of it slips past my defenses, though. Has me answering when I didn't think there was anything else to say. "Yet here you are."

"Yeah." His dark, bemused eyes search my face. "Here I am."

Silence echoes between us—dark, loaded, unfathomable—even as tension stretches taut as a circus high wire.

I should go.

He should go.

Neither of us moves. I'm not sure I even breathe.

Finally, Jaxon breaks the stillness—though not the tension—by taking a step closer to me. Then another and another, until the only thing that separates us is the bulky weight of my coat and the thinnest sliver of air.

Chills that have nothing to do with the cold and everything to do with Jaxon's proximity dance up and down my spine.

My heart pounds.

My head swims.

My mouth goes desert dry.

And the rest of me doesn't fare much better...especially when Jaxon reaches for my gloved hand, rubs his thumb back and forth across my palm.

"What were you and Flint talking about?" he asks after a second. "At the party?"

"I honestly don't remember." Which sounds like a cop-out answer, but it's really just the truth. With Jaxon touching me, I'm lucky to remember my own name.

He doesn't challenge my words. But the corners of his lips tip up in a very self-satisfied smile as he murmurs, "Good."

His smirk jump-starts my brain—finally—and then it's my turn to ask a question. "What were you and Lia fighting about?"

I don't know what I expect—his gaze to go flat again, probably, or for him to tell me that it's none of my business. Instead, he says, "My brother," in a tone that doesn't ask for sympathy and warns that he won't permit it.

It's not the answer I was expecting, but as the very few pieces I have start fitting themselves together in my head, my heart plummets. "Was…was Hudson your brother?"

For the first time, I see genuine surprise in his eyes. "Who told you about Hudson?"

"Lia did. Last night when we were having tea. She mentioned that—" I break off at the glacial coldness in his eyes.

"What did she tell you?" The words are quiet, but that only makes them hit harder. As does the way he drops my hand.

I swallow, then finish in a rush. "Just that her boyfriend died. She didn't say anything about you at all. I just took a guess that her boyfriend might also be…"

"My brother? Yeah, Hudson was my brother." The words drip ice, in an effort—I think—to keep me from knowing how much they hurt. But I've been there, have spent weeks doing the same thing, and he doesn't fool me.

"I'm sorry," I tell him, and this time I'm the one who reaches for him. The one whose fingers whisper over his wrist and the back of his hand. "I know it doesn't mean anything, that it doesn't touch the kind of grief you're feeling. But I truly am sorry you're hurting."

For long seconds, he doesn't say anything. Just watches me with those dark eyes that see so much and show so little. Finally, when I'm searching my brain for something else to say, he asks, "What makes you think I'm hurting?"

"Aren't you?" I challenge.

More silence. Then, "I don't know."

I shake my head. "I don't know what that means."

He shakes his head, then moves back several feet. My hand clenches, missing the feel of him under my fingers.

"I have to go."

"Wait." I know better, but I reach for him again. I can't help it. "Just like that?"

He lets me hold his hand for one second, two. Then he turns and walks back down the path to the pond so fast, it's nearly a run.

I don't even bother trying to keep up. If I've learned anything in the last couple of days, it's that when Jaxon Vega wants to disappear, he disappears, and there's nothing I can do about it. Instead, I turn in the other direction and head back to the castle.

Now that I have a set destination in mind, the walk seems much faster than my original wandering did. But I still can't shake the uncomfortable feeling that I'm being watched. Which is absurd, considering Jaxon went in the other direction and Lia disappeared right after her argument with him.

The feeling stays with me the whole time I'm outside. And something else is niggling at me, too, something I can't quite figure out. At least not until I reach the warmth and safety of the castle—and my room. It's as I'm peeling off all the layers I'm wearing that it finally hits me.

Neither Lia nor Jaxon was wearing a jacket.

17

It's Discretion, not Diamonds, That's a Girl's Best Friend

"You sure you're up for this?" Macy asks several hours later as I grab a sweatshirt from my closet.

Is she kidding? "Not even a little bit."

"That's what I figured." She heaves a huge sigh. "We could cancel if you want. Tell everyone you're still not over the altitude sickness."

"And have Flint think I'm chicken? No thank you." I actually couldn't care less if Flint thinks I'm afraid or not. But Macy has been so excited about this snowball fight that there's no way I'm going to take it away from her. The fact that she offered to cancel because she knows I'm not into it only makes me more determined to go. "We're doing this snowball fight and we're going to..."

"Kick some butt?"

"I was thinking more along the lines of not make complete and total fools of ourselves, but way to think positive."

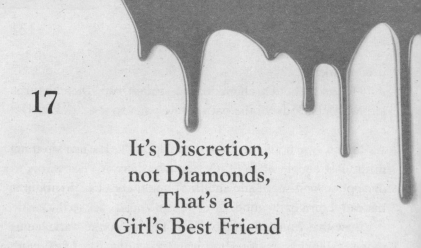

She laughs, as I intended her to, then bounds off the bed and starts layering up big-time. Which...finally, someone at this ridiculous school who has some sense. Between the jerks I met the first night and then Jaxon and Lia, I'm beginning to think everyone in this place has some bizarre immunity to cold. Like maybe they're aliens and I'm the ignorant and fragile human living among them.

After we both finish getting dressed in—I counted this time—six layers, she herds me toward the door. "Come on, we don't want to be late or we'll totally get ambushed."

"Ambushed. With snowballs. Sounds fantastic." San Diego has never looked so good.

"Just wait. You're going to love it. Plus, it'll give you a chance to meet all of Flint's friends." She checks her makeup one more time in the mirror by the door, then all but shoves me into the hallway.

"*All* of Flint's friends?" I ask as we make our way through the halls. "Exactly how many people are going to be at this thing?"

"I don't know. At least fifty."

"Fifty people? At a snowball fight?"

"Maybe more. Probably more."

"How does that even work?" I query.

"Does it matter?" she answers, brows raised.

"Yes, it matters. I mean, how can you possibly keep track of that many people trying to throw things at you?"

"I don't think you keep track of them so much as try to flatten everyone you come across without being flattened yourself."

"Maybe you're right. Maybe the altitude sickness is coming back."

"Too late." She links her arm through mine and grins. "We're almost there."

"So can you be a little more specific about who all is going to be there? Anyone I've already met—I mean, besides Flint?"

"I don't know if Lia will be there. Cam won't—he and Flint don't really get along. It's a…thing."

I think about asking exactly what kind of thing she's

referring to, but the truth is, I don't care if Lia shows up. Or Cam. There's only one person I'm trying to find out about, and since Macy isn't getting there herself, I guess I really am going to have to ask.

"How about Jaxon?" I keep my voice light even though, after our encounter earlier, my heart is pounding at the mere mention of his name. "Is he going to be there?"

"Jaxon Vega?" By the time she gets to the second syllable of Jaxon's name, her voice is little more than a squeak.

"He's the one we saw in the hall that first day, right?"

"Yeah. Um…yeah." Macy gives up any pretense of chill—and of walking, as it turns out. Instead, she turns to me, hands on her hips, and demands, "Why are you asking about Jaxon?"

"I don't know. We've met a couple of times, and I just wondered if he was into snowball fights."

"You've met *Jaxon Vega* a couple of times? How exactly did you meet, considering I've been with you almost all the time since you got here?"

"I don't know, just walking around the school. It was only a few times."

"A few times?" Her eyes almost bug out of her head. "That's more than a couple. Where? When? *How?*"

"Why are you being so weird about this?" I'm seriously beginning to regret bringing Jaxon up. I mean, she was freaked out over Flint, but it was a fun kind of freaked out. Right now, it looks more like she's going to blow a gasket. "He was in the hallway; I was in the hallway. It just kind of happened."

"Things don't *just happen* with Jaxon. He's not exactly known for being talkative with anyone outside of—" She stops abruptly.

"Outside of what?" I prompt.

"I don't know. Just…"

"Just?" I ask. She smiles a little sickly but doesn't say anything else, and it annoys me. Like, seriously annoys me. "Why do you keep doing that?"

"Doing what?"

"You start sentences and then never finish them. Or you start to say something and halfway through change what you were saying to something else entirely."

"I don't—"

"You do. All the time. And honestly, it's beginning to feel a little weird. Like there's some kind of secret I'm not supposed to know. What's going on?"

"That's ridiculous, Grace." She looks at me like I'm a few snowflakes short of a snowball. "Katmere is just, you know, full of all kinds of weird cliques and social rules. I didn't want to bore you with them all."

"Because you'd rather I commit social suicide?" I arch my brow at her.

She rolls her eyes. "Social suicide is the last thing you need to worry about here."

It's the first real thing she's said since we started this conversation, and I jump on it. "So what *do* I have to worry about, then?"

Macy sighs, low and long and just a little sad. But then she looks me in the eye and says, "All I was going to say is that Jaxon's not very friendly with people who aren't in the Order."

"*The Order?* What's that?"

"It's nothing, really." When I keep looking at her, silently pushing her to continue, she sighs again, then adds, "It's just a nickname we gave the most popular boys at school because they're always together."

I think about the guys Jaxon walked into the party with and the ones who were with him in the hall when Flint was carrying me to my room. At the time, I remember thinking that Jaxon looked like the leader, but I didn't think much of it. I was too busy trying not to stare at him.

Based on my recollections, Macy's explanation is reasonable. Still, there's something about the way she says it—and the way she's looking everywhere but in my eyes—that makes me think there's more to the story than she's letting on.

Although, standing in the middle of the hallway doesn't seem like the best place to keep pushing at her, especially since we really are going to be late if we don't get moving.

With that in mind, I start walking and Macy does, too, but she sticks close to my side. I give her a weird look, wondering what she's up to, at least until she asks in a kind of stage whisper, "Have you met the others, too?"

"The other guys in the Order?" I feel a little ridiculous just saying the name out loud. I mean, they're twelfth-grade students at a boarding school, not running a monastery in Tibet. "No. I've only met Jaxon."

"*Only?* You mean he was *alone*?" Now she doesn't just look worried; she looks downright sick.

"Yeah. So?"

"Oh God! What did he do? Are you okay? Did he hurt you?"

"Jaxon?" I can't keep the surprise from my voice.

"Of course Jaxon! That *is* who we're talking about, right?"

"No, he didn't *hurt* me. Why would you even think that?"

She throws her hands in the air, frustration and fear evident in every line of her body. "Because he's Jaxon. He's a one-man demolition crew. It's what he does!"

"He was..." I shake my head, try to think of the right word to describe our interactions. Then go with generic because I figure Macy won't get it anyway. "Most of the time he was actually kind of...interesting."

"Interesting?" This time she looks at me like I just said I

wanted to bodysurf the Alaskan tundra. "Okay, I'm confused. Are you sure we're talking about the same Jaxon?" She pulls me into the nearest alcove, then grabs my hands and squeezes them tightly. "Really tall, really gorgeous, *really scary*? Black hair, black eyes, black clothes, and a smoking-hot body? Plus the arrogance of a rock star...or the self-proclaimed dictator of a not-so-small country?"

I've got to admit, it's a pretty good description—especially the *arrogant* part. And the *really gorgeous* part, even if it doesn't take into account a lot of the things that make him so attractive. Like his eyes that see way too much and the way his voice gets all dark and growly when he expects things to go his way. Not to mention the thin scar that turns him from merely pretty to sexy. And also scary as hell. "Yeah, that's him."

"You know you don't have to lie, right? You can tell me what happened. I swear I won't tell anyone if you don't want me to."

"You won't tell anyone what?" I'm thoroughly confused now. Because while it might have been a stretch to call Jaxon interesting, I can't imagine why the fact that I've met him is eliciting this kind of response from my cousin.

"What he did to you?" She starts looking me over, like she's searching for some proof that I survived a rabid Jaxon attack.

"He didn't *do* anything, Macy." A little impatient now, I pull my hands from hers. "I mean, he wasn't Gandhi. But he helped me out when I needed it, and he sure as hell didn't hurt me. Why is that so hard to believe?"

"Because Jaxon Vega isn't helpful to anyone. Ever."

"I don't believe that."

"Well, you should." She enunciates each word in an obvious attempt to make sure I listen to—and understand—what she's saying. "Because he's dangerous, Grace. *Very* dangerous, and you should stay as far away from him as you possibly can."

I start to tell her that he's not the dangerous one, but then I remember the way Marc and Quinn fell right into line the second he showed up. It was hard to miss the fear on their faces, and not just because he'd sent them flying across the room.

Now that I think back on it, they *had* been scared of him. Like, really scared.

"I'm serious. You need to be careful of him. If he really was helpful to you, it's only because he wants something. And even that seems strange, because Jaxon takes what he wants. Always has, always will."

I've been here three days and even I know that's not true. Which is probably why I say, "Jaxon's the one who kept Marc and Quinn from throwing me out in the snow, Macy. I don't think he did it because he wanted something from me."

"Wait. *He's* the one?"

"Yes, he is. Why would he do that if he's such a bad guy?"

"I don't know." She looks stunned. "But just because he helped you once doesn't mean he'll do it again. So be careful with him, okay?"

"He's not the one who tried to kill me."

She snorts. "Yeah, well, you've only been here a few days. Give it time."

"That's…" For long seconds, I trip over my tongue as I try to find a comeback that will show her how absurd she sounds. But in the end, I can't get past the annoyance her words cause and end up saying exactly what I'm thinking. "A really awful thing to say."

"Just because it's awful doesn't make it any less true." She gives me a no-nonsense look that seems incongruous with her normally effervescent personality. "You need to trust me on this."

"Macy…"

"I'm serious. Don't worry about me being too harsh." She

narrows her eyes at me in obvious warning. "And don't worry about Jaxon Vega. Unless you're trying to figure out how to stay as far away from him as possible."

Behind her, something catches my eye, and my mouth goes dry. "Yeah, well, that might be a problem." I barely manage to get the words out past my suddenly tight throat.

"And why is that exactly?"

"Because I'm not going anywhere." Jaxon's low, amused voice cuts through my cousin's umbrage, has her eyes going wide and her skin draining of color. "And neither is Grace."

18

How Many Hot Guys Does it Take to Win a Snowball Fight?

Macy squeaks—she actually squeaks—but Jaxon just raises his brows at me. The look on his face is a little amused and a lot wicked and my heart starts beating like a metronome on high.

At least until Macy hisses, "Seriously? You couldn't tell me he was there?"

"I didn't—"

"She didn't know." He looks me over from top to bottom, and for a second, just a second, a smile touches the depths of those obsidian eyes of his. "Braving the snow twice in one day? I've got to admit I'm impressed."

"Don't be too impressed. I still have to make it through the snowball fight in one piece."

The smile drops—from his face and his eyes—as quickly as it came. "You're playing Flint's game?"

It sounds more like an accusation than a question, though I don't know why. "Isn't that why you're here?"

"For a *snowball* fight?" He shakes his head, makes a dismissive sound deep in his throat. "I don't think so."

"Oh, well..." That got awkward fast. "Um. We should probably..."

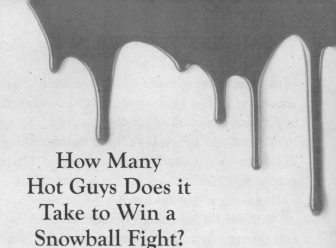

"Get going," Macy finishes.

Jaxon ignores her as he braces a hand on the wall behind me. Then he leans in and, in a voice so low I have to strain to hear him, murmurs, "You're determined not to listen to me, aren't you?"

"I don't know what you mean," I whisper back, but I can't look him in the face as I say it. Not when I'm lying—I know exactly what he's talking about—and not when his breath is so warm and soft against my ear that I can feel it everywhere, even deep inside.

"It really is for your own good," he tells me, still standing way too close. Heat slams through me—at his words and his proximity and the orange and dark-water scent of him currently wrapping itself around me.

"What—" My voice breaks, my throat so tight and dry, I can barely force the words through it when I try again. "What is?"

"You shouldn't go to that snowball fight with Flint." He pulls back, his gaze catching and holding mine. "And you sure as hell shouldn't be wandering around the school grounds on your own. You're not *safe* here."

It's not the first time he's implied that Katmere is dangerous for me. And I get it. I do. Alaska is no picnic for the uninitiated. But I'm with Macy, on school grounds. No way is she going to let anything happen to me.

"I'll be fine." It's easier to breathe now that Jaxon's mouth isn't a scant inch from my ear, but finding words is still harder than it should be under his watchful gaze. "I'm not planning on wandering off tonight. I'll be with the group the whole time."

"Yeah." He doesn't sound impressed. "That's what I'm worried about."

"What do you mean?" I clarify. "I thought you'd be relieved I'm not planning on tackling any wild animals with my bare hands."

"It's not the *wild* animals I'm concerned about."

Before I can ask him what *that* means, Macy interjects again. "We should get going. We don't want to be late."

"Well, whatever you're concerned about, you shouldn't be," I tell him, refusing to be pulled away before I'm ready. "I'm a big girl. I can take care of myself. But if you want, you can join us."

"Join you." His tone implies I just suggested that we fly to Mars under our own power.

But I refuse to be dissuaded. Not when Jaxon is standing so close to me instead of pulling his usual disappearing act. "It'll be fun. And I'm sure Flint won't mind."

"You're sure he won't mind." He repeats my words, and again it isn't a question. He's back to seeming amused, though—at least if you don't look too closely at his eyes. They're flat now, completely empty in a way I haven't seen since he looked through me at the party. "Because I've got to tell you, I'm pretty sure he will."

"Why would he? He invited a ton of people." I turn to look at Macy, who has gone absolutely sheet white.

I roll my eyes at her, annoyed she seems so freaked out at the idea of hanging with Jaxon, but before I can say anything, Flint walks up behind me and puts his hands on my shoulders. "Hey, Grace. Looks like you're ready to get your snowball on."

"I am, actually." I turn and end up grinning at him because it's impossible not to. He's just that fun *and* that charming. Not to mention the fact that he's wearing a snow hat in the shape of a fire-breathing dragon that looks absolutely ridiculous. "In fact, I was trying to talk Jaxon into joining us."

"Oh really?" Flint's eyes go a kind of burning amber as he looks from me to Jaxon. "What do you say, Vega? Wanna fight?"

Flint's smiling, but even I can tell it's not a friendly invitation… and that's before three other guys in all black join us, arranging themselves in a semicircle right behind Jaxon. For the first time, the phrase "got your back" makes sense to me, because it's very obvious that's why these guys are here. To have Jaxon's back. I just don't know from what.

These must be members of the infamous Order Macy was telling me about. And I can see why they got the nickname—there's a closeness among the four of these guys that even I can't miss. A bond that seems to be about a lot more than simple friendship.

Flint feels it, too. I can tell by the way he stiffens and the way he shifts his weight forward onto his toes, like he's just waiting for Jaxon to throw the first punch. More, like he's hoping for it.

Which…no. Just no. I don't care if there's suddenly enough testosterone in our little alcove to start the next world war; it's not going to happen. At least not while Macy and I are standing directly in the middle.

"Come on." I grab my cousin's arm. "Let's go figure out a way to win this snowball fight."

That gets both Jaxon's and Flint's attention. "Those are big words coming from someone who never saw snow before she got here three days ago," Flint teases, and while the tension isn't gone, it's way lower than it was a few seconds ago—exactly as I intended.

"Yeah, well, you know me. All about the bravado." I keep a firm grip on Macy's arm as I start to maneuver around Jaxon and his friends.

"Is that what you call it?" Jaxon murmurs in my ear as I slide past him. Once more, his warm breath is against the side of my neck, and a shiver that has nothing to do with the cold works its way down my spine.

Our eyes meet, and for a second, just a second, the whole world seems to drop away. Macy, Flint, the other students who are laughing and chattering as they move past us on their way to the door all disappear until it's just Jaxon and me and the electricity that arcs between us.

My breath catches in my throat, my whole body grows warm, and it takes real, physical effort to stop myself from reaching out and touching him.

I think he must be having the same problem, because his hand comes up, hovers in the air between us for one long, infinite moment.

"Grace." It's barely a whisper, but still I feel it all the way inside myself. I wait, breath held, for him to say something—anything—else, but before he can, the front door flies open, letting in a huge gust of freezing air.

It breaks the spell, and suddenly we're just two people standing in a crowded hallway again. Disappointment wells inside me, especially when Jaxon takes a step back, his face set once again in inscrutable lines.

I wait for him to say something, but he doesn't. Instead, he just watches as Flint herds Macy and me toward the open door. As we cross the threshold, I raise my hand in a small goodbye wave.

I don't expect him to return it, and he doesn't. But just as I turn away to take my first step outside, he says, "Don't forget to build an arsenal."

They're pretty much the last words I expect to hear from him…or anyone, for that matter. "An arsenal?"

"It's the most important part of winning a snowball fight. Find a base you can protect and concentrate on building up your arsenal. Only attack when you're sure you have enough ammunition to win."

Snowballs. Here I was, convinced we had just shared a moment, and he's thinking about snowballs. Fan-freaking-tastic.

"Ummm…thanks for the advice?" I give him a WTF look.

Jaxon responds with his regular, annoying blank face, but I swear his eyes are sparkling just a little. "It's good advice. You should take it."

"Why don't *you* take it? Join me and the two of us can build a bigger arsenal."

He lifts a brow. "And here I thought that's exactly what I have been doing."

"What does *that* mean?" I demand.

But he's already turning away, already *walking* away, and I'm left staring after him.

As usual.

Damn it.

Something tells me this boy—and his world-famous disappearing act—is going to be the death of me.

19

We Came, We Fought, I Froze

"Jaxon Vega, huh?" Flint asks as the cold slaps me in the face for the second time today.

"Don't start," I say, giving him the side eye.

"I'm not," he answers, holding both hands up in mock surrender. "I swear." He's silent for a minute or so as the three of us concentrate on trudging through the snow toward everyone else. And can I just say that I'm pretty sure Macy undersold the crowd when she said fifty people. Even in the weird civil twilight that surrounds us on all sides, it looks more like a hundred, maybe even the whole damn school—minus Jaxon and his friends, of course.

On the plus side, at least they're all wearing hats and scarves and coats…which I'm taking to mean that not everyone in this place is an actual alien. Thankfully.

"I just didn't know 'screwed-up and obnoxious' was your type, that's all."

I shoot him a glare. "I thought you weren't starting."

"I'm not. I'm just looking out for you. Jaxon is—"

"*Not* screwed up."

He laughs. "I notice you didn't even try to say he wasn't

obnoxious, though, did you? And no offense, Grace, but you're new here. You have no idea just how fucked-up he is."

"And you do?"

"Yeah. And so does Macy. Right, Mace?"

Macy doesn't answer, just keeps walking and pretends like she doesn't hear him. I'm beginning to wish I could do the same.

"All right, all right, I get it." Flint shakes his head. "I won't say anything else against the Chosen One. Except tell you to be careful."

"We're friends, Flint."

"Yeah, well, take it from someone who knows. Jaxon doesn't have friends."

I want to ask him what he means by that, considering Jaxon's got the Order, and they seem pretty damn close to me, but we've reached the first row of trees, where the others are gathered. Plus, I'm the one who just said I didn't want to talk about Jaxon. If I start asking questions, that gives Flint carte blanche to say whatever he wants, and that doesn't seem fair, since Jaxon isn't around to defend himself.

Flint walks into the middle of the group like he owns the place. Then again, judging from the way the others respond to him, maybe he does. It's not that they all come to attention, necessarily. It's just obvious that they all really want him to notice them...and they all really want to hear what he has to say.

I can't help wondering what that kind of popularity is like. I don't want it—would probably melt under the pressure of it in less than twenty-four hours. But I do wonder what it feels like. And how Flint feels about it.

I don't have long to dwell on my thoughts, though, because Flint gets started giving a quick rundown of the rules—starting with one that sounds an awful lot like *there are no rules*, except it's followed by the one that says if you get hit by five snowballs, you're out—and then disperses the crowd. As the five-minute countdown starts, he grabs Macy's and my hands and starts running with us toward a large thicket of evergreen and aspen trees several hundred yards away.

"We've got two minutes to find a good spot," he says. "Another two and a half to get things together. Then it's open season."

"But if everyone finds a spot, who will we have to throw sno—"

"They won't," Flint and Macy interrupt me at the exact same time.

"Don't worry," Flint tells me as we finally reach the trees. "There will be plenty of people to wage war on."

Wage war? I can barely breathe. It's a combination of the high altitude and cold air, I know, but I can't help feeling self-conscious about the way I'm huffing and puffing. Especially since he and Macy both sound like they just finished a leisurely garden stroll.

"So what do we do now?" I ask, even though it's fairly obvious, considering Flint is already scooping up snow and making it into balls.

"Build up our arsenal." He gives me a wicked grin. "Just because I think Jaxon is a jackass doesn't mean the guy doesn't know strategy."

We spend the next couple of minutes making as many snowballs as we possibly can. I half expect Macy and Flint to outpace me here, too, but it turns out all those years of making pastries and patting dough into balls with my mother paid off, because I am an *excellent* snowball maker. Totally kick-ass. And I'm twice as fast as they are.

"Coming up on five minutes," Macy says, her phone ringing with a fifteen-second warning.

"Move, move, move," Flint calls out, even as he shoos me behind the closest tree.

Just in time, too, because as soon as Macy's phone screeches out the five-minute mark, all hell breaks loose.

People drop from the trees all around us, snowballs flying fast and furious in every direction. Others run by at breakneck speeds, lobbing them kamikaze-style at anyone within range.

One snowball whizzes right past my ear, and I breathe a sigh of relief until another one slams into my side—even with the tree, and Flint, for cover.

"That's one," I hiss, jerking to the right to avoid another snowball flying straight at me. It hits Flint in the shoulder instead, and he mutters a low curse.

"Are we going to hide back here all day?" Macy demands from where she's crouched at the base of a nearby tree. "Or are we going to get in this thing?"

"By all means," Flint says, gesturing for her to go first.

She rolls her eyes at him, but it takes her only a few seconds to scoop snow into a couple of giant snowballs. Then she's letting her snowballs fly with a giant war whoop that practically shakes the snow off the nearby branches, before running toward our arsenal to reload.

I follow her into the fray, a snowball clutched in my gloved hands as I wait for a perfect opportunity to use it.

The opportunity presents itself when one of the large guys from Flint's group comes barreling toward me, snowballs hidden in the bottom of the jacket he's turned into a carrying pouch. He sends them flying at me, one after another, but I manage to dodge them all. Then I throw my snowball as hard as I can, straight at him. It hits him in his very surprised face.

We've built up about a hundred snowballs in our arsenal, and we use them all as more and more people pour through the forest, looking for a place to hide as they catch their breath and try to make a few extra snowballs of their own.

I'm a little surprised at how close-knit the groups are—and how alliances transcend snowball teams and seem to revert back to the factions I noticed at the party yesterday. Even though members of Flint's clique are divided into duos and trios, they all seem to come together and watch one another's backs when someone from one of the other factions—whether it's the slender group dressed in bright jewel tones or the more muscular group that Marc and Quinn are currently fighting with—threatens one of them.

I also notice that one group is missing—Jaxon's. Not just the Order, which is definitely not here, but the whole black-clothed designer faction that presided over the party with such obvious disdain. Guess Jaxon was right when he said Flint didn't want him here. Part of me wants to try to figure out what is up with that, but right now I'm too busy dodging snowball volleys to do more than give it a passing thought.

It's total guerrilla warfare out here—fast and brutal and winner takes all. It's also the most fun I've had since my parents died, and probably even longer than that.

We exhaust our supply of snowballs pretty quickly, and then we're just like everyone else, running through the trees, trying to find cover as we fling snow at whoever's within reach.

I laugh like a hyena the whole time. Macy and Flint look bemused at first, but soon they're laughing with me—especially when one or the other of us gets hit.

It's after an ambush that leads to Macy getting her fourth hit and Flint and me getting our third ones that we decide to get serious. We find the biggest two trees we can to hide behind, and we drop to our knees, packing snowballs as quickly as possible. After we've got about thirty made, Flint yanks off his hat and scarf and starts piling them inside.

"What are you doing?" I demand. "You're going to freeze to death out here."

"I'm fine," he tells me as he turns his scarf into a kind of carrying pack. "This is our chance to win."

"How?" I ask. There's chaos all around us, and though the others haven't found our hiding spot yet, it's only a matter of time—probably a minute or two—before they do. And while we've got ammunition, there's also a lot fewer of us than there is of them.

"By climbing the trees," Macy tells me.

Before I can express my utter incredulity at the thought of climbing one of the gigantic, leafless aspens—the lowest branches are more than fifteen feet off the ground—she runs straight at the trunk of the closest tree, then jumps and kicks out hard enough to send herself soaring up several feet at an angle, arms extended, to grab the branch of a neighboring tree. She hangs there for a few seconds, swinging back and forth to gain momentum, then thrusts herself up and onto a nearby branch.

The whole thing takes about ten seconds.

"Did she just do parkour against that tree?" I ask Flint before turning to Macy. "Did you just parkour that tree?"

"I did," she says with a laugh, then reaches down to catch the hat full of snowballs Flint sends flying her way.

"That's freaking awesome. But if you guys expect me to be able to do that, I think we're all going to be disappointed."

"Don't worry, Grace," Flint tells me as he thrusts his snowball-packed scarf into my arms. "Just hold on to these for me, will you?"

"Of course. What are you going to—?" I let out a screech as he grabs onto me and throws me over his shoulder.

"Quiet down or you're going to give away our hiding place," he tells me as he starts climbing the tree like some Alaskan version of Spider-Man, hands and feet practically sticking to the tree's bark as he carries me up the gigantic trunk. "And don't drop the snowballs."

"You should have thought of that before you decided to hang me upside down," I snark at him. But I tighten my grip on the scarf.

I don't know how he's doing it, and I wouldn't believe it if I wasn't witnessing—or should I say experiencing—it for myself. But thirty seconds later, I'm straddling a tree branch, snowballs in hand, as I wait to ambush the first people who come by.

Flint's on a branch several feet above mine. It's high enough off the ground to make me whimper just looking up at him, but he's standing there with a huge grin on his face, like balancing on a snow-packed tree branch is the easiest thing in the world.

Which, to be clear, it definitely is not. And I know that because I'm *sitting* on one and I still feel like I could slip off at any second.

"Someone's coming!" Macy hisses from one tree over.

I glance down at the ground and realize she's right—Quinn, Marc, and two other guys are heading our way. They're moving stealthily instead of quickly, almost like they know we're here. And maybe they do—it's not like I was exactly quiet while Flint hauled me up this tree.

Either way, it doesn't matter, because all we need is for them to get a few steps closer and—

Bam. Flint sends a snowball soaring straight into the leader's chest. Macy follows up with a one-two shot to the guy in the back. Which leaves Marc and Quinn. Which I'm definitely not going to complain about. I send a volley of snowballs straight at them, one after another. I hit Marc twice and Quinn at least four times, which—if their curse-laden complaints are anything to go by—knocks them completely out of the game. Something I'm also not going to complain about.

Flint is all but crowing in triumph as he dispatches a second group that made the mistake of coming this way, and Macy takes care of a couple of loners trying to sneak in from behind us. I restock from the thick snow on the branches and wait for whoever comes next.

Turns out it's a couple of girls dressed in teal and navy outerwear, who look like they're having about as much fun as I do at the dentist.

I think about pulling my punches—no reason to make them even more miserable—but I figure it's only putting off the inevitable. The faster I knock them out of the game, the faster they can head back to the castle. And the faster we can win this thing.

I reach for my last three snowballs and am just waiting for them to come within range when a powerful wind comes up and knocks me off balance. I make a grab for the tree trunk and manage to hold on while the wind shakes the whole tree.

Flint curses and makes a grab for the trunk, too. Then calls to me, "Hold on, Grace! I'll be there in a minute."

"Just stay there," I call back. "I'm fine."

Then I turn to look for Macy, worried my cousin might be in worse shape than I am. But just as I turn my head to look behind me, another gust of wind hits the tree, hard. It's an eerie sound, and as the trunk starts to sway under the wind's assault, I get more nervous. Especially when another gust comes through and hits me hard enough to threaten my grip on the tree.

Above me, Flint curses again, and Macy yells, "Hold on, Grace! Flint, go get her!"

"Wait!" I shout back to be heard over the wind. "Don't!"

But then Macy screams, and I whirl around, terrified I'm going to see her plunging to her death. And that's when the worst gust of wind yet hits, and I lose my grip on the tree completely.

I scramble to grab on to something—anything—but the wind is too strong. The branch I'm sitting on issues an ominous crack.

And then I'm falling.

20

There's Never a Parachute Around When You Need One

For one second, I have perfect clarity—I can hear Macy screaming, Flint calling my name, the wind roaring like a freight train—and then it's all drowned out in the panicked beat of my heart as terror races through me.

I brace myself for bone-crunching impact, but before I hit, Flint is grabbing me, pulling me against him, spinning us in midair. He hits the ground, back first, and I land on him, my face buried in the curve of his neck.

We hit hard enough that the breath is knocked out of me. For one second, two, three, I can't do anything but lay there on top of him, trying desperately to drag a breath into my abused lungs.

Flint's not moving either, and panic is a wild animal inside me as I struggle to get my weight off him. His eyes are closed, and I'm terrified that he's hurt—or worse. He took the brunt of the fall, deliberately spinning us so that he slammed into the hard, snow-packed ground while all I slammed into was him.

It's as I push up into a sitting position, knees on either side of his thighs, that I finally manage to pull in a huge gulp of air. It's also at that moment that all hell breaks loose.

Macy is screaming my name as she scrambles down her tree,

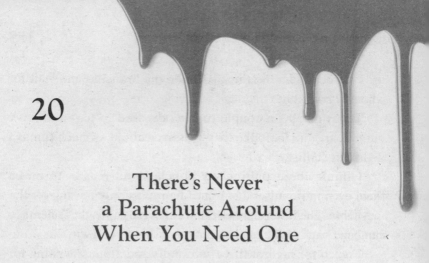

and people swarm us from all directions. I'm too busy shaking Flint and slapping at his cheeks—trying to get him to respond—to pay any attention to what anyone else is doing.

At least until he opens his eyes and drawls, "I'm beginning to think I should have let you fall."

"Oh my God! You're okay!" I scramble off him. "*Are* you okay?"

"I think so." He sits up with a little groan. "You're heavier than you look."

"You shouldn't move!" I try to shove him back down, but he just laughs.

"The snow broke my fall, Grace. I'm good." To prove it, he jackknifes to his feet in one lithe movement.

It's as he stands up that I realize he's telling the truth. There's a Flint-shaped indention in the snow from where he hit. For the first time since moving to this state, I'm grateful for its ridiculous climate. After all, when you're falling twenty feet, snow is so much softer than ground.

Still, if that's the case… "Why did you jump after me? You could have been hurt."

He doesn't answer, just kind of stands there watching me, a weird look in his eyes. It's not concern or annoyance or pride or any of the other expressions I'd expect him to be wearing right now. Instead, it looks an awful lot like…shame.

But that doesn't make sense. He just saved me from a concussion or a couple of broken bones—at least. What does he have to be ashamed of?

"What was the alternative?" Macy demands, voice shaking like she just got back the power of speech. "Let you be hurt?"

"You mean it's better for Flint to get hurt?" I ask bewildered.

"But he didn't, did he? And neither did you." She turns to him with a grateful look. "Thank you so much, Flint."

Her words make me realize that I've been too busy worrying about—and yelling at—Flint to do what I should have right away. "Thank you. I really appreciate it."

The words sound awkward after all my admonishments, but they are nothing compared to the look on Flint's face as he stares over my shoulder into the crowd. It alternates between looking like he's going to throw a punch and like he's dying to run away.

I figure it's because he's bad with gratitude—I'm terrible with it, so I get that—but as the talking in the crowd dies down and people start parting like a human Red Sea, I turn.

And nearly wither on the spot at the coldness in Jaxon's eyes. Only the fact that it's directed at Flint and not me keeps my knees from giving way completely. Because I only thought he was intimidating at the welcome party.

Right now, the look on his face is absolutely terrifying. And the five inscrutable guys at his back—I assume I'm seeing the whole of the infamous Order for the first time—only reinforce the fact that there's a problem.

A big problem.

I just wish I knew why.

Even Flint, who has never reacted to Jaxon in the past, turns a little sickly looking. And that's before Jaxon, in the coldest, most reasonable voice imaginable, asks him, "What the hell did you think you were doing?"

It's the tone even more than the look that has me moving, a frisson of fear working its way down my spine as I position myself between him and Flint before an all-out brawl can take place. I may not understand all the nuances of what's happening here, but it's obvious that Jaxon is livid—and more than ready to take it out on Flint. Which makes no sense, considering, "I fell, Jaxon. Flint saved me."

For the first time, he turns those cold eyes on me. "Did he?"

"Yes! The wind kicked up, and I lost my balance. I fell out of the tree, and Flint jumped after me." I shoot Flint a stare, telling him to back me up, but he's not looking at me.

He's not looking at Jaxon, either. Instead, he's gazing off into the distance, jaw and fists clenched.

"What's wrong?" I ask, reaching out to touch his shoulder. "Are you hurt after all?"

A fine tremor runs through the earth, a tiny little earthquake that rattles the tree branches a bit but doesn't do anything else. I've heard Alaska has them, so it doesn't surprise me when no one reacts. Even I don't get too excited. In San Diego, we'd have one or two of these tiny ones every couple of months. Flint doesn't even notice. He's too busy shrugging off my hand. "I'm fine, Grace."

"Then what's wrong?" I look back and forth between him and Jaxon. "I don't understand what's happening here."

Neither of them answers me, so I look to Macy for an explanation beyond my working hypothesis that Alaska brings out the worst in people. But she looks as confused as I do—and about a hundred times more terrified.

As for everybody else...they're riveted by the drama, eyes glued to Jaxon as he continues to watch Flint who continues to very obviously not watch him back. It's not the first time I've thought of Jaxon as a hunter, but it is the first time I've thought of Flint as prey. Other members of his group must agree, because in seconds they're moving, guys and girls alike, to flank him on either side.

Their obvious support of Flint only ups the tension between him and Jaxon, whose face has grown even more coldly amused.

I'm trying desperately to figure out how to break things up without bloodshed when Macy suddenly snaps out of whatever stupor she's been in and says, "We should go back to the room,

Grace. Make sure you're okay."

"I'm fine," I assure her. Like I'm going to leave Jaxon out here when he looks like he wants to rip Flint's throat out just for breathing. "I'm not going anywhere."

"Actually, that's the best idea I've heard all afternoon." Jaxon takes a step closer until he's right behind me. He doesn't touch me, doesn't even brush against me, but he's close enough that that doesn't matter. I can *feel* him. "I'll walk you back to your room."

The crowd recoils at this. Like, I actually see people drawing back, eyes wide, mouths open, faces slack with shock. I can't figure out what the big deal is unless it's that Jaxon is breaking up the showdown between the two most popular guys in school before it even begins. Not that it's even a real showdown, considering the way Flint's taken himself out of the whole thing by refusing to so much as acknowledge Jaxon's existence.

It's that uncharacteristic behavior more than anything else that has me stepping away from Jaxon and saying, "I need to stay with Flint. Make sure he's really—"

"I'm fine, Grace," Flint grates out from between clenched teeth. "Just go."

"Are you sure?" I reach out a hand to touch his shoulder again, but suddenly Jaxon's there between us, preventing my hand from landing. Then he's stepping forward, moving me slowly, inexorably away from Flint and back toward school.

It's the strangest thing I've ever seen. Definitely the strangest thing I've ever been a part of.

And still, I let it happen. Because this is Jaxon, and I can't seem to help myself.

"Come on, Macy," I say quietly to my cousin and reach for her hand. "Let's go."

She nods, and then we're walking back toward the castle—Macy, Jaxon, and me. I half expect the other members of the

Order to join us, but a quick glance behind me shows that they aren't moving.

No one is.

And can I just say, I'm beginning to feel an awful lot like Alice in Wonderland here—things keep getting "curiouser and curiouser." Maybe that last plane ride with Philip was really a trip down a really big rabbit hole.

We walk in silence for a minute or two, and with each step, I'm beginning to realize that maybe I didn't escape from the fall unscathed after all. Now that the adrenaline has worn off, my right ankle is hurting. A lot.

To keep my mind off the pain—and to keep Jaxon and Macy from noticing that I'm limping—I ask, "What are you doing out here anyway? I thought you weren't going to join the snowball fight."

"Good thing I *was* out here, considering the mess Flint got you into." Jaxon doesn't so much as glance my way.

"It really is no big deal," I tell him, despite the fact that my ankle is working its way up from painful to excruciating pretty quickly now. "Flint had me. He—"

"Flint very definitely did not have you," he snaps, his voice as hard and brittle as the ice all around us as he turns to face me for the first time. "In fact—" He stops, eyes narrowing. "What's wrong?"

"Besides not being able to figure out why you're so mad?"

He shrugs off the question as he looks me over from head to toe. "What's hurting you?"

"I'm fine."

"You're hurt, Grace?" Macy joins the conversation for the first time. The chicken.

"It's nothing." We've got a head start, but if we stop, the others are sure to catch up with us, and the last thing I need right now is to make an even bigger spectacle of myself. So much for fitting in…or even *blending* in. After tonight, I might as well be painted biohazard orange. Something I find particularly ironic, since Jaxon is the one who told me to keep my head down.

But seriously. It's just like San Diego all over again. There, I was the girl whose parents died. Here, I'm the girl who fell out of a tree and nearly caused World War III between the two hottest guys in school.

FML.

Determined to make it back to school and my room before the others head this way, I start walking again. Or, should I say, I try to start walking again, because I don't get very far before Jaxon is blocking my path.

"What hurts?" he asks again, and the look on his face tells me he's not going to let it go.

And since arguing with him wastes precious seconds, I finally give in. "My ankle. I must have twisted it when we hit the ground."

Jaxon's kneeling at my feet before I finish, gently probing at my foot and ankle through my boot. "I can't take this off out here or you'll get frostbite. But does it hurt when I do this?"

My gasp is the only answer he needs.

"Should I run ahead and get the snowmobile?" Macy asks. "I can be back before too long."

Oh my God, no. Talk about making a spectacle of myself. "I can walk. Honest. I'm okay."

Jaxon shoots both of us an incredulous look as he helps me to my feet. Then, without a word, he swoops me into his arms.

21

I Like Standing on My Own Two Feet, but Getting Swept Off Them Feels Surprisingly Good, Too

For long seconds, I can't move. I can't think. I can only stare up at him in a kind of openmouthed shock as my brain short-circuits. Because I'm not actually in Jaxon's arms, right? I mean, I can't be.

Except I am. And they feel really good around me. *Really* good. Plus, being in his arms, bride-style, gives me an up-close-and-personal view of his face. And can I just say how unfair it is that he's even hotter from an inch away? And he smells amazing, too.

His smell—like snow and orange—is what pushes me over the edge, what has me struggling against him like a madwoman in my effort to be put back down. Because if he carries me all the way to school looking and smelling and feeling like he does, I'm going to be a total incoherent mess.

"Can you please stop wiggling around so much?" he demands as I attempt to push myself out of his arms.

"Just let me down, then." I glance at Macy for support, but she's staring at us like she thinks she might be getting punked. Since she's clearly not going to be any help, I turn back to Jaxon. "You can't carry me all the way back to school!"

There isn't so much as a hitch in his stride. "Watch me."

"Jaxon, be reasonable. It's a long walk."

"What's your point?"

I squirm around some more, trying to force him to put me down, but that just makes him tighten his hold.

"My point is I'm too heavy."

Again with the incredulous look.

"I'm serious." I put my hands on his chest and use real effort to push. His arms don't budge from around me. If I'm being honest, I really don't want him to put me down. My ankle is full-on throbbing now, and walking on it is going to be a nightmare. But that doesn't mean I should let him damage himself trying to help me. "Put me down before you hurt yourself."

"Hurt myself?" The eyebrow arch I spent way too much time thinking about last night is back. "Are you *trying* to insult me?"

"I'm trying to get you to let go of me. You can't carry me all the way back to—"

"Grace?" he interrupts.

I wait for him to say something, but when he doesn't, I answer, "What?" in what could, perhaps, be described as not the nicest tone.

"Shut up."

Part of me is super insulted at his words, and the matter-of-fact way he says them, but the part of me that's actually in control of my tongue does exactly what he asks and shuts up. I mean, I suppose there are worse things in the world than being carried by a super-sexy guy instead of struggling along in terrible pain. Maybe.

With me in Jaxon's arms, we move three times as fast as we were when I was limping with every step. Before I know it, we're through the castle doors, striding up the stairs.

When we get to our room, Macy unlocks the door and holds

the weirdass beads back as she tells Jaxon to, "Go on in."

Seconds later, he deposits me on my bed and I think that's going to be the end of it. But then he reaches down and pulls off my boot.

"I can take it from here," I tell him. "Thanks for your help."

He shoots me a look that tells me to shut up again, this time without him ever having uttered the words. Which embarasses me so much that I try to pull my foot away from him and start peeling my sock off on my own.

"I sprained my ankle," I snark. "I'm not dying of consumption."

"Yeah, well, the night is young."

"Hey! What's that supposed to mean?" I glare at him.

"It means you've been here three days, and this is the second time I've had to get you out of trouble."

"Seriously? You're going to hold me responsible for a *windstorm* now?"

"I am." He wraps his hand around my calf and gently but firmly eases my leg over the edge of the bed so he can look at my ankle. "You didn't scc Macy falling out of *her* tree, did you?"

"It wasn't—" Macy starts, but no way am I going to let him get away with blaming me for this.

"*Her* branch didn't break!" I interrupt. "*Mine* did. What was I supposed to do? Grab on to the trunk and— Oww!" I try to yank my foot away as he probes at a particularly sore spot.

He ignores me, though his touch—already soft—gets even gentler. "There's no swelling and only a little bruising, so I don't think you broke anything."

"I already told you it was just sprained." I pull my leg away, but with much less force this time. Something about the feel of his hands on my leg, his skin against mine, has me especially unnerved. "You can go now."

This time, the look he gives me is half amused, half *don't push your luck*. And, despite that, also super sexy. Which is completely absurd, but that doesn't make it any less true. Heather would die if she saw me now—two small steps away from whimpering and *sighing* over some ridiculously commanding guy. It's gross, and normally I'd put him in his place. But the fact that he's all growly like this because he's worried about me and wanting to make sure I'm okay? I don't know. Somehow it makes a difference.

"Should I get ice?" Macy asks for the first time since Jaxon overrode her objection. She's currently standing near her bed, all but wringing her hands and trying not to show how freaked out she is that Jaxon is in our room.

I turn to answer—and hopefully reassure her—but realize she's talking to Jaxon. You know, the guy she spent ten minutes warning me about *before* the snowball fight. "Et tu, Brute?" I say with a roll of my eyes.

She shrugs, a little shamefaced, as Jaxon answers, "That'd be great." Then she all but runs to the door—at least until he smiles his thanks. Then she freezes. Like, actually *freezes* in the middle of walking, one foot off the floor. "Also," he adds, "do you happen to have an Ace bandage? I can wrap her foot before I go."

She doesn't answer.

"Macy?"

She still doesn't answer.

Jaxon glances at me, both brows raised, but I just roll my eyes. Then clap extra-loud to get her attention.

"Macy?"

"Oh yeah. Ice. I'm on it."

"So no bandage, then?" Jaxon asks.

"And a bandage. Yes. Absolutely. I have a few, actually." Suddenly she's stumbling over her words and her feet as she rushes to her bureau and starts wildly opening drawers.

She finally finds what she's looking for in the bottom drawer and spins around, a tightly wrapped hot-pink bandage in her hand. "Does this work, Jaxon?"

"It's perfect, thanks."

She glows under his praise, and it's all I can do not to make a teasing comment. But seriously, if she's not careful, she's going to turn into one of his minions. So much for *you can tell me how he hurt you.* Traitor.

I reach out to take the bandage from her, but Jaxon gets there first. "I really *can* do it, you know," I tell him.

"Maybe I want to do it for you."

As she heads for the door, Macy makes a sound like the melting is actually starting, and even I have to admit, it's a good line. Then again, convincing myself to like Jaxon has never been hard. I've been attracted to him from the very beginning, even when I was also supremely annoyed by him.

"What? No protests?" he asks a little sardonically.

"Are you going to wrap it or not?" I grouse, ignoring his question because answering it would be too embarrassing.

He ducks his head and gets to work, but not before I see the small grin he's got going on. His scar pulls on the very edges of his lips, but that just turns the smile into a crooked little smirk that is a million times hotter than it should be.

His fingers are cold as he wraps up my ankle, but his hands are so, so gentle. I find myself relaxing despite myself, my muscles going lax as he strokes a finger back and forth against my calf.

And when I say his name this time, even I can hear the yearning. His head snaps up, his dark, bottomless gaze locking with mine.

His hand on my leg becomes firmer, more insistent as he leans in just a little. His wildly sexy scent seems even stronger now than it did when he was carrying me. It fills my senses, makes my mouth water and my hands ache to touch him. Makes me want to press my face into the curve of his neck and just breathe him in.

I'm already on edge from his closeness, and these new longings he sets off in me have my breath catching in my throat. My heart goes wild and, as he leans in just a little farther, my whole body lights up like the aurora borealis I'm still dying to see.

"Grace." He says my name like it's a promise. It's the last straw, and I gasp, full-on melting commencing deep inside me. I'd say his name back, but I've lost control of my vocal cords. And pretty much the rest of my body, too.

His hand comes up to cup my cheek, and I close my eyes, lean into the caress. And then nearly jump out of my skin as the door crashes open and he yanks his hand back.

"I've got the ice," Macy says. "I even crushed it up and—" She stops cold, her eyes going wide as she senses the tension in the air. With the way Jaxon is leaning over me, it doesn't take a genius to figure out what she interrupted, and for a second, it looks like she's going to ease her way back out of the room.

But then the moment is gone, and Jaxon is standing up, heading toward thc door himsclf. "Put the ice on for twenty minutes and see how it feels. If it isn't better, ice it again in an hour. Got it?"

"Yeah, I've got it," I manage to croak out of my still-tight throat.

"Excellent." He risks giving Macy another smile, then shakes his head as she whimpers just a little. He doesn't say anything clsc until hc's about to walk out of my room. Then he turns around, hand on the doorknob, and says, "Stay away from Flint, Grace. He's not what you think."

The words chase away the last of my vocal paralysis—and goodwill. "Flint and I are friends. And you don't get to tell me what to do." I have just enough self-control not to add, *No matter how much you intrigue me.*

I expect him to fire back with something—God knows he's arrogant enough to believe he should be instantly obeyed—but instead he just tilts his head and watches me for several long seconds. Then he says, "Okay."

"Okay?" I narrow my eyes at his easy acquiescence. "That's it?"

"That's it." He turns to go.

"I didn't think it would be that easy."

He gives me his inscrutable look, the one I'm already coming to hate. "This is going to be a lot of things, Grace. Easy isn't one of them."

And then he's gone. As usual.

Double damn it.

22

Baby, It's Hot in Here...

For several seconds after Jaxon leaves, I wait for the other shoe to drop...in this case, a rainbow-colored Converse in the form of Macy demanding to know what's going on between us. Which I can already see is going to be a problem on a lot of levels, most obviously the one where I have *no idea about what's going on between us.* If anything.

Yes, Jaxon has sought me out twice today, but I have no idea what that means. Or even if it means anything.

And what was that parting shot about, anyway? *This is going to be a lot of things, Grace. Easy isn't one of them*? Who even says that? Was he saying that he's interested in me? Or that he isn't?

Ugh. Why do guys have to be so complicated?

Maybe he's just playing with me because he's bored or something. Because I'm fresh meat out here in the middle of nowhere. But he didn't look bored after the snowball fight—in fact, he looked pissed as hell at Flint. Which is ridiculous, considering Flint saved me from a concussion or a broken leg or worse.

But a guy who isn't interested doesn't act like Jaxon did, right? He doesn't have the kind of temper tantrum—and it was a tantrum, despite how cold it was—that Jaxon had in the middle of that forest because he thought Flint had put me at risk.

Does he?

I don't think so…but then, what do I know? I've only ever had one boyfriend, and the way I felt about Gabe was nothing like this. I mean, it was a decent relationship, I guess. We had been friends for years, and it just kind of drifted into something different for a while. We went places together, made out sometimes, did all the usual stuff. But it was easy with Gabe. He never made me feel like Jaxon does, never made my breath catch and my hands sweat and my stomach flip from just a look. I never spent hours obsessing over his every word, never found myself longing for his touch the way I do for Jaxon's.

I just wish I knew how *Jaxon* felt.

"Oh my God."

Apparently, Macy has finally snapped out of whatever weird Jaxon-induced coma she's been in for the last five minutes. I shoot her a look. "Don't start."

"Oh. My. God. OmigodOmigodOmigod. What just happened?"

"I fell out of a tree. Flint saved me from dying. Jaxon carried me back to the dorm because I sprained my ankle." I say it all very flippantly, hoping if I keep it casual, if I don't let Macy know how messed up my own head is, she'll let things drop.

"Those are just the details." She flops down on my bed, careful not to jostle my ankle as she does.

"I'm pretty sure the details are what's important here."

"Not right now they aren't! Right now, it's all about the big picture."

"And what exactly is the big picture?" I ask.

"That the two most popular boys in school are obsessed with you."

I nearly strangle myself on my sweatshirt as I try to get a look at her face to see if she's kidding or not. "I wouldn't say they're obsessed," I finally manage to get out once I untie my hoodie strings and stop strangling myself in the process. "And aren't you the one who was just warning me to stay as far away from Jaxon as I could get?"

"Yeah, but that was before."

"Before what?" I demand.

"Before I saw how he looks at you." She closes her eyes and makes a sound very close to the one she made when Jaxon smiled at her. "I wish Cam would look at me like that."

"You want your boyfriend to look at you like he's an arrogant prick used to getting his own way?"

"Yeah, he pretty much does that already," she says with a roll of her eyes. "I want him to look at me like it physically *hurts* him not to be touching me."

"Jaxon doesn't look at me like that." I'm beginning to think it's how I look at him, though.

Macy snorts. "Baby, if that boy wanted you any more, he would spontaneously combust."

Her words warm me, make me feel like *I* might spontaneously combust—especially if I spend much longer thinking about Jaxon. That guy is way too hot for his own good…or my own peace of mind. And if Macy's right, if he's thinking even a quarter of the things I'm thinking about him…

"Is it hot in here?" I start to shrug out of the million and three layers of clothing I'm currently wearing.

"After three days of watching you be miserable in the cold, I never thought I'd hear you say that," Macy teases as she grabs hold of my snow pants and starts tugging at them hard enough to pull me halfway down the bed. "Guess all it takes to warm you is getting up close and personal with the most dangerous boy at Katmere Academy."

I slap at her hands. "What are you doing?"

"Trying to help you. These things are hard to get out of if you can't stand." She yanks and tugs some more and still doesn't get much accomplished.

"It's okay; I can do it." I bat her hands away and stand up so that my weight is balanced on my unhurt leg as I slide off both the snow and fleece pants I'm wearing. Which leaves me in long underwear and wool socks, both of which are a million times more comfortable than the outerwear I'd been sweating in.

Macy strips off her own layers and doesn't say anything else until we're both settled back on my bed again. Then she looks me straight in the eye and says, "You've procrastinated long enough. Now spill."

"There's nothing to spill." I slip under the covers and lean my back up against the wall. "You're the one who said the different cliques never mix."

"Yeah, well, you don't have a *clique* yet, so apparently the rules don't apply to you. And as for having nothing to spill, I call bullshit on that. You've been here exactly seventy-two hours—and I've been with you most of those hours, by the way. Not all of them, obviously, because I had no idea the two hottest boys in school were going to have a massive pissing contest over you in front of half the senior class." She gives me an incredulous look. "When did this happen? *How* did this happen?"

"Nothing's happened, I swear. Flint and I are just friends—"

"Yeah, right."

"I'm serious. He's really nice, but he's never done anything even remotely un-friend-like."

Macy rolls her eyes. "You mean like carrying you up the staircase or going out of his way to invite you to a snowball fight?"

"You asked him to carry me up the stairs. Altitude sickness, remember?"

"Yeah, and did I also ask him to dive out of a tree to save your life?"

"I'm sure he thought you would have asked if there was time."

"Oh my God! You are so annoying." She flops back against the bed. "I can't decide if you're lying to yourself or if you're just this naive."

"I'm not lying. And I'm not naive." I give her my most sincere look. "I swear, Macy. There's nothing going on between Flint and me."

She studies me for a second, then nods. "Okay, fine. But I notice you didn't say the same thing about you and Jaxon."

"Jaxon and me… Jaxon is… I mean, we're… I don't…" I trail off, cheeks burning, because even I can tell how incoherent and ridiculous I sound. "Ugh."

"Wow." Now Macy's eyes are huge. "That serious, huh?"

I don't know what to say, so I almost don't say anything at all. Except Macy has gone to school here a lot longer than I have, which means she knows a lot more about Jaxon than I do, and I would really like to benefit from a little of that knowledge.

"It's complicated." I expect her to ask what's complicated about it, but she doesn't. Instead she just nods like, *of course it is.* "He's not really dangerous like you said, is he?"

Even as I ask the question, I know the answer…which is, *hell yeah, he is. And you should stay as far away from him as you possibly can.*

I mean, he's never been anything but gentle when he touched me, but it's as plain as the scar on his face that Jaxon isn't like the other boys I've known. Every single thing about him screams *danger*—of the dark and brutally wounded variety. It's in his eyes, in his voice, in the way he holds himself and the way he moves.

I recognize it, even acknowledge it. But when I'm near him, that doesn't matter. When I'm near him, *nothing* matters but getting closer, even though it's obvious he's been hurt before and just as obvious that he's determined to protect himself. Was it his brother's death that did this to him? Or is Hudson just one piece of a much bigger puzzle?

My instincts say it's the latter, but I haven't known him long enough to be sure.

Silence stretches between us for several long seconds. I watch Macy, who pretty much has the opposite of a poker face, as she tries to figure out what to say. It takes a little while, but finally she settles on, "He's not *Silence of the Lambs* dangerous. He's not going to drop you in a pit and starve you so he can make a dress out of your skin or anything."

I burst into incredulous laughter. "Seriously? That's the best you've got? He's not going to make a dress out of my skin?"

She shrugs. "I also said he wouldn't starve you in a pit."

"It's Alaska. You'd need a professional oil drill to make a pit in the frozen ground."

"Exactly." She holds her hands out in an obvious gesture. "See, told you he wouldn't do it."

"Are you trying to be reassuring here, or are you trying to scare the hell out of me?"

"Yes." She bats her eyes at me. "Is it working?"

"I have no freaking idea."

My phone buzzes, and I almost ignore it. But it has to be Heather—Macy's the only one at Katmere who's got my number—and right now, I could use a little of my best friend's brand of sanity.

Heather: How was your first day of classes?

Heather: Any hot guys in your English class?

Heather: Or hot girls? Asking for a friend...

She includes the dtf emoji in the last one, and I laugh despite myself. Then take a quick pic of Macy in her tank top and long underwear, who fakes a pouty pose when I say it's my best friend back home, and answer:

Me: ALL the hot girls.

Heather: Ugh. Mean

Heather: How was class?

Me: Altitude sickness kept me home. But I'm going tomorrow

And then, because Heather can go on forever and I want to finish this conversation about how Jaxon isn't an actual movie serial killer, I text:

Me: Busy right now

Me: ttys

Then I put my phone aside and turn back to my cousin, who is currently scrolling through her own phone. She quits as soon as she realizes I'm done texting and then says, "Tell me the truth, Grace. Do you like Jaxon?"

"Like" is too insipid a word for the emotions Jaxon stirs up in me. There's something about him that calls to me on a soul-deep level, something broken in him that somehow fits with what's broken in me.

I know Macy doesn't see it. She's too busy being afraid of his darkness and social status to pay attention to what's under the surface. But I see it—all the grief and pain and fear roiling around in him just beneath the blank face and empty eyes. I see *him* in a way I don't think anyone else at this school does.

I don't tell her any of that, though—it's not my place to share Jaxon's suffering. Instead, I answer, "What does it matter if I like him or not?"

"That's not an answer."

"Because I don't have an answer!" I groan. "I've been here three days, Mace. Three days! Everything feels upside down and backward, and I have no idea what I think about anything...or *anyone*. I mean, how am I supposed to know how I feel about a guy I barely know? Especially when he ignores me one minute and carries me home the next. He's different than anybody I've ever met and—"

Macy's snort interrupts my diatribe.

"What?" I beg. "Why do I get the feeling you know something you're not sharing?"

"I have no idea. Go ahead."

I narrow my eyes at her. "It sounds like you know something."

"Sorry." She holds her hands up in very obvious surrender. "I just…agree. Jaxon is definitely not like anyone you've ever met before."

"You say that like it's such a bad thing. I get that you don't want me to like him—"

"Hey, I told you to stay away from him because he's not an easy guy to be around. Or at least, he never was before. But with you…"

"What?"

"I don't know." She shrugs. "It sounds like every cliché in the book, but he's different when he's with you. He's somehow less intense but also *more* intense, if that makes sense."

"It doesn't. At all."

Macy huffs out a laugh. "I know. But you're the one who asked. I guess what I'm saying is that I'm wary about you and Jaxon doing whatever it is you're doing, but I'm not totally against it. Not like I would have been if I hadn't seen him with you today."

I want to push her on that, want to ask her exactly what she means. But there's a part of me that's sure I already have a pretty good idea. She's talking about the Jaxon I saw in the hall that first day, after Flint carried me up the stairs. Or the Jaxon I saw at the party, the one who looked so cold, so grim, that it sent me running in the opposite direction. Literally. If that's the only Jaxon she's ever seen, no wonder she felt the need to warn me off him.

"I still don't know what we're doing," I admit, slumping into my pillows. "Or even if we're doing anything. I just wish I knew what he thought about me, you know? Like, is he playing with me, or is he having some of the same thoughts I'm having?"

"What thoughts are you having?" She asks it so casually that I answer without thinking.

"I feel like I am obsessed with him. I think about him all the—" I break off when I realize what I'm saying. "You tricked me."

Her look is all mock innocence. "I just asked you a question. You didn't have to answer it."

"You knew I was preoccupied and wasn't thinking about guarding my words."

"Good. I'm glad you weren't censoring what you say. You don't have to do that with me." She reaches out and grabs my hand. "Seriously, Grace. Things are going to be weird here for you for a while. But *we're* not going to be weird." She gestures between the two of us. "Even if you can't trust anybody else, you can trust me to have your back—even with Jaxon. We're family."

Suddenly, there's a lump the size of Denali in my throat, and I swallow a couple of times, trying to clear it. I didn't know how badly I needed to hear those words until she said them, didn't realize how much I was missing having someone I can just count on—no questions asked—to be in my corner.

"You know that goes both ways, right, Macy? You can trust me, too."

She grins. "I already do. I just want to make sure you remember what I said. And that I'm here, no matter what, on your side."

There's something intense in the way she says it—and the

way she looks at me afterward. Like she's trying to warn me and reassure me at the same time. It's so bizarre that a frisson of unease runs down my spine, taking away the toasty warmth that comes with lying under my blanket and replacing it with a chill that has nothing to do with Alaska and everything to do with the feeling that I'm in way over my head here, even if I don't know it yet.

I try to ignore the feeling, tell myself I'm probably just being paranoid. I'm smart—and honest—enough to acknowledge that lately I tend to expect the worst in every situation.

But instead of dwelling on the discomfort, I just nod and say, "Good. I'm glad."

Macy grins. "Now that we've got that out of the way, there is something I want to talk to you about." She gets up, crosses to her mini fridge. "But I'm pretty sure you're not going to like it."

23

Never Bring an Ice Cream Scoop to a Gun Fight

I eye Macy warily as she opens up the fridge and rummages around. "Exactly how much am I not going to like it?"

She holds up a pint of Cherry Garcia with a triumphant sound.

My stomach drops. "It's so bad that we need Ben and Jerry's?"

"To be honest, I always need Ben and Jerry's." She pulls the top off thc brightly colored container, then grabs two spoons out of the bright-purple utensil cup on top of the fridge. "This just seems like a good time to indulge."

I take the spoon she holds out to me. "I didn't even know they sold Ben and Jerry's up here."

"It's ten bucks a pint at the closest store, but they sell it." She smiles at my look of horror.

"Wow. That's..."

She grins. "Welcome to Alaska."

"Guess what you have to talk about really is serious if it needs ten-dollar ice cream."

She doesn't say anything to my blatant fishing attempt, just holds out the open container so I can take a spoon of it. Which I do. She does, as well, and we do an ice-cream toast—mostly because toasting with the first bite of ice cream is a ritual we created the summer we spent together when we were five—before taking a bite.

I wait for Macy to tell me whatever's on her mind, but she just scoops up another spoonful of ice cream. Then a third and a fourth, until I give up and do the same.

We're about halfway done with the container before she finally says, "I need to warn you about something."

Okaaaaaay? "Haven't you already warned me about Jaxon? I thought that's what we just did."

"This isn't about him. Or, I mean, I guess it is, but not like you're thinking." I must look as confused as I feel, because she takes a deep breath and blurts out, "If you like Jaxon—and I'm cool with it if you do, honest. But if you like him, Grace, you can't keep hanging out with Flint, too. It won't work."

That's so far from where I expected her to go that it takes me a second to actually assimilate her words. And even after I decide I understand them, they still don't make any sense. "What do you mean, it won't *work*? I'm not actually dating either one of them right now, and even if I was...surely I can be friends with the other one?"

"No." She shakes her head emphatically. "You can't. That's what I'm trying to tell you."

I'm half convinced she's messing with me—because how could she not be?—but she looks so serious, I have to ask, "What do you mean I *can't*? What is this? *The Breakfast Club*?"

"Worse. Way worse."

"Obviously, because even in *The Breakfast Club*, they figured out it didn't matter what group you belong to."

"Isn't *The Breakfast Club* also the movie where Judd Nelson sexually harasses Molly Ringwald by reaching up her skirt when he's hiding under her desk?"

When she puts it that way… "Okay, so maybe it's not the best example."

She rolls her eyes. "You think?"

"Even so, this whole *Jaxon and Flint can't be civil to each other because they head up different groups* argument you're making is ridiculous. Do you know how many people have been nice to me since I got here?" I hold up four fingers and tick off the names as I say them. "You, Jaxon, Flint, and Lia. That's it. Four people. Which is why telling me that I can't talk to one of the four people in this entire place who doesn't treat me like I have the plague is total bullshit."

"Oh, Grace." She looks heartbroken. "Has it really been that bad?"

"Well, it hasn't exactly been a picnic—even without the near-death experiences." Still, she looks so distraught at my words that I can't help but walk them back a little. "Don't worry about it, Mace. I haven't even started classes yet. I'm sure people will loosen up and stop staring once they have a chance to get to know me."

She jumps on the walk-back. "They will, Grace. I swear. They just need to spend some time with you. We don't get a lot of new people here, and most of us have been together a long time, even before Katmere."

"I didn't realize that."

"Yeah. There's another school that most of us went to before this one, starting in fifth grade. So if we seem aloof, that's part of it, you know?"

"Yeah, but shouldn't knowing one another that long make it easier for all of you to get along and not harder?"

"It should. And for a while, even, it did. I don't know how to explain why things went bad, except to say that some awful stuff happened about a year ago and things got completely out of hand. I mean, on the surface it looks like everything's fine, but once you dig a little, the damage is all right there. And part of what happened makes it nearly impossible for Jaxon and Flint to be on the same side of…anything."

It's pretty much the vaguest explanation anyone has ever given me about anything. And still it has me thinking, trying to piece together the very few things I've learned since I've been here. "Is this about what happened to Hudson Vega?"

The question is out before I can think twice about it, and judging from the look on Macy's face, I definitely should have thought twice. "What do you know about Hudson?" she whispers so quietly that it feels like she's scared to say his name out loud.

"Lia told me that her boyfriend died, remember? But then Jaxon mentioned his brother, and I put two and two together after I saw them arguing."

"Did Jaxon tell you Hudson was dead?" I don't think she would look this shocked if I told her I was flying back to San Diego under my own power, and suddenly all kinds of doubts assail me.

"Isn't he?" If Jaxon was lying to me about something like that, I don't know what I'll do. I mean, what kind of person—?

"He is. Yes. It's just that he doesn't talk about it much. The whole thing almost destroyed him, and I just couldn't imagine him discussing it with…" She trails off.

"A total stranger?"

"Yeah." She looks a little guilty to be admitting it. "Not that you guys are strangers, I guess—"

"Sometimes it's easier," I interrupt. "Talking to your best friend about the worst thing that ever happened to you is excruciating. Talking to a stranger who doesn't have any kind of vested interest…sometimes it doesn't hurt so much." It sounds weird, but it's true. Just one of the things I've learned in the last month.

"That makes a strange kind of sense." She puts the ice cream down and leans over to hug me.

I hug her back for a few seconds—until I feel the tears that are never far from the surface start to well up in my eyes. Then I pull back and give her a grin that says I'm totally fine, even if I'm not. "Maybe that's why it seems like Jaxon is different with me. Because he knows I've lost someone, too."

"Maybe." She looks doubtful. "But if the attraction between you and Jaxon is because you've both lost someone… Just be careful, okay, Grace? The last thing you want is to become the chew toy in a game of tug-of-war between him and Flint. Because in the end, you're going to be the one who gets ripped apart."

I try to ignore her words—and do a pretty good job of it for the rest of the night. But once I'm in bed, with the lights out, I can't help but think about what Macy said…and how it feels more like a premonition than a warning.

A heaviness creeps into my bones at the thought, pushing me into the bed, weighing me down until the simple act of rolling over and curling into a protective ball feels impossible. I settle for wrapping my arms around my waist and telling myself that she's wrong. Even as a little voice inside me warns that she's not.

24

Waffles Are the Way to a Girl's Everything

I wake up slowly to the sound of a text coming in. I groan as I think about ignoring it, about staying wrapped up in my covers where it's warm and comfortable and *perfect*. But I've been slow in responding to Heather's texts since I got to Alaska, and that's not cool.

Except when I roll over and grab my phone, I realize two things. One, it's after ten in the morning, which means I slept right through first period. And two, the text isn't from Heather.

And it's not from Macy, either. Instead, it's from a number I don't recognize.

Unknown: How is your ankle?

Flint? I wonder as I brush my hair out of my eyes and sit up. *Or someone else?*

For a moment, Jaxon's eyes—deep, dark, fathomless—come to mind, but I can't believe it's him. Not when he's been so hot and cold the entire time we've known each other. And definitely not when he told me last night that we were going to do things the hard way—whatever that means.

Deciding to play it safe, I text back:

Me: Who is this?

There's a long pause. Then:

Unknown: Jaxon

It's only one word, and yet it somehow all but crackles with indignation. Like he can't imagine that I don't already have his number in my phone, just waiting for him to finally get around to texting me. I should be annoyed at the assumption, but I'm amused instead. So amused that I can't help answering:

Me: Jaxon who?

Jaxon: I don't know the punch line

Me: To what?

Jaxon: Whatever knock-knock joke you're setting up

I burst out laughing, because he's funny over text in a way he hasn't shown me in person.

Me: I'm terrible at knock-knock jokes

Jaxon: Finally some good news

Me: Hey!

Me: How many tickles does it take to make an octopus laugh?

There's a long pause, where I can totally imagine his face. Then:

Jaxon: I didn't realize octopi laughed

Yeah, that's pretty much the response I expected. I send an eye roll emoji, then:

Me: Come on. Play along.

Jaxon: I just wanted to know how your ankle was

Me: Take a guess and I'll tell you

Another long pause.

Jaxon: 17

Me: 17?!?!?!?!?!

Jaxon: Well, it's obviously not 8 or it wouldn't be a joke

Jaxon: And I don't have a clue otherwise, so why not 17?

I send him two more eye roll emojis.

Me: Let's try this again

Me: How many tickles does it take to make an octopus laugh?

This pause is so long that I've just about convinced myself that I've blown it and he isn't going to answer. But then:

Jaxon: How many?

I nearly drop my phone in excitement, and I'm grinning so hard that my cheeks hurt. Which is ridiculous, but I'm learning that when it comes to this boy, *I'm* ridiculous.

Me: Ten-tickles

Jaxon: That's…actually pretty good

Me: Wow. High praise

Jaxon: Don't let it go to your head

Me: Believe me, I won't

I end the text with three eye roll emojis, because he deserves it.

Jaxon: What do you get when you cross a vampire and a snowman?

What? A joke? From the perennially serious Jaxon Vega? I can't answer back fast enough.

Me: I have no idea.

Jaxon: Frostbite

I laugh out loud, because who is this Jaxon? And how do I keep him around?

Me: Halloween and Alaska all rolled into one, huh?

Me: Color me impressed

There's another long pause, but this time something tells me not to give up on Jaxon quite yet. That he isn't not texting because he's put down his phone but because he's trying to figure out what to say next. Which…can you say mind-boggling? I can barely imagine a Jaxon who doesn't know exactly what to do and say in any situation.

Finally my phone dings again.

Jaxon: You promised to tell me about your ankle

It's not a great segue from the fun conversation we were just having, but I go with it, because the alternative is not answering, and I don't want to do that. At least not yet.

Me: I don't know. I'm just waking up. My uncle must have decided I don't have to go to class again today.

Jaxon: I'd say lucky you, but…

Me: What, falling out of a tree not lucky enough for you?

Jaxon: Do you KNOW what lucky means?

The laugh hits me so unexpectedly that I nearly snort. Then slap a hand over my mouth in horrified amusement, even though there's no one around to hear.

Me: I walked away, didn't I?

Jaxon totally mimics me by sending an eye roll emoji.

Jaxon: Pretty sure I carried you away

Me: Oh. Right. Thanks again for that.

Jaxon's response is just a string of eye roll emojis.

Now that he's got me thinking about it, I'm curious how my ankle is, too. So I throw back the covers and try to climb out of bed—only to whimper the second I put any weight on my right foot. Well, that answers that. With the added problem that I really have to pee.

Jaxon: What are you going to do today?

Me: I think I'll lie in bed and feel sorry for myself

Jaxon: Good times

Me: Yeah, well, turns out the ankle hurts a little bit

Jaxon: You ok?

Me: Of course

Me: brb

I use the promise of Advil to propel myself across the room to the bathroom. When I'm done, I wash my hands and grab two of the little round pills and a bottle of water before hobbling back to my bed. I force myself to take the pills before I pick my phone back up again, but it's hard. I'm dying to know if Jaxon texted me back.

He didn't. Which is cool, I tell myself. I mean. I'm the one who cut our conversation off so abruptly.

Me: I'm back

No answer.

Me: Sorry that took so long.

Still no answer.

Ugh. I blew it.

I'm pissed at myself for stopping our conversation. And just as angry for being pissed off. Jaxon showed me more of himself in the last fifteen minutes than he has since I got here. What do I have to be annoyed about that he stopped texting?

Absolutely nothing. I mean, the boy does have to go to class, after all.

Somehow, telling myself that only makes everything worse. Well, that and the fact that I'm starving, and the peanut butter is all the way across the room. Of course.

I lie back against my pillows and fire off a couple of messages to Heather. Then I check Snapchat and Instagram and even play a couple of rounds of *Pac-Man*—all while telling myself that I'm absolutely, positively not waiting for Jaxon to text again.

But eventually my stomach starts growling, and I toss my phone aside. A girl can't live on peanut butter alone, even if right now I'm hungry enough to give it a try.

I start to hobble toward the fridge but get distracted halfway there by a knock on my door. For a second, just a second, I wonder if it might be Jaxon. Then common sense kicks in. It's probably Uncle Finn coming to check on me and my bum ankle.

Except when I answer the door, it's not Uncle Finn. And it's not Jaxon, either. Instead, it's a woman carrying a heavily loaded food tray.

"Grace?" she asks as I step aside to let her in.

"Yes." I smile at her. "Thank you so much. I'm *starving*."

"Anytime." She grins back. "Where do you want me to put it?"

"I can take it." I reach for the tray, but she shoots me a look that says to give her a break. "Um, the bed is fine, I guess." I gesture toward my side of the room.

She crosses to my bed and puts the tray down toward the foot of it. Then asks, "Is there anything else I can get you?"

I have no idea, considering the food is under two of those silver dome things to keep it warm. But since I'm hungry enough to eat almost anything—and I'm not in the habit of having anyone wait on me—I answer, "No, this is perfect. Thank you."

Trust Macy to think of me even when she's in class. My cousin is a goddess.

Except, as I settle back onto the bed, I realize there's a small black envelope on the tray. One that has my name written on the front in a masculine scrawl that definitely isn't Macy's.

Uncle Finn, I tell myself, even as my heart beats triple time.

Because it can't be Jaxon, I figure as I reach for the envelope with trembling fingers.

Can't be Jaxon, I think again as I slide out the simple black card.

Definitely can't be Jaxon, I tell myself one more time as I open up the card and search for a signature.

Except…except it *is* from Jaxon, and my heart is actually threatening to burst out of my chest.

I don't know what you like yet, but I figured you were hungry. Stay off that ankle.
Jaxon

Oh my God.

OmigodOmigodOmigod.

Oh. My. God.

I mean, it's not the *most* romantic note in the world, but that doesn't even matter. Because Jaxon sent me breakfast. *That's* why he didn't text me back. He was busy doing this.

I grab my phone and fire off a quick text to him.

Me: Thank you!!!!!!!!!!!! You really are a lifesaver

He doesn't answer right away, so I start poking around the tray, seeing what he had the cafeteria bring me. The answer is *everything.*

There's a cup of coffee and another one of tea. A bottle of sparkling water and a glass of orange juice. There's even an ice pack for my ankle.

I lift up the domes to find one plate loaded with eggs and sausage and a giant cinnamon roll that smells amazing. The other has a Belgian waffle on it, topped with strawberry compote and what looks to be freshly whipped cream…in the middle of Alaska. In *November.*

I'm so touched, I think I might cry. Or I would if I wasn't so hungry.

Still, there's no way I can eat all this, and I should feel bad about wasting the food. But right now, I'm too busy smiling to worry about anything else.

My stomach growls again, louder this time, and I dig in, starting with the waffle. Because whipped cream plus syrup plus strawberries equals nirvana.

I'm halfway through the whipped cream covered deliciousness when my phone finally dings again—and I nearly upend the whole tray trying to get to it.

Jaxon: Sorry, taking a test

Jaxon: Waffles or eggs?

Me: Waffles all the way

Jaxon: I figured

Jaxon: Use the ice pack

Me: Wow. Bossy much?

Me: I am using it. I can take care of myself, you know

Jaxon: Now who's being bossy?

I'm not sure if I should be offended or not by that latest crack. I probably should be, but a waffle this good gives the guy a little extra leeway. Plus, I maybe, possibly deserved it.

Me: How about you? Waffles or eggs?

Jaxon: Neither

Me: So what do you like to eat?

As soon as I hit Send, I realize what a bad idea that last text was and start freaking out. Because oh my God, that sounded way more suggestive than I meant it to be. Damn it. He's either going to think I'm a freak or he's going to respond with something really gross, and I don't want either of those things to happen.

It's been a long time since I've texted/flirted with a boy, and I'm not ready for it to end.

I'm ccrtainly not ready to stop talking to Jaxon, who's witty and sexy and makes me feel things no one else ever has. Plus, it's so much easier to talk to him like this than in person, when he's all dark and broody.

Several seconds pass without a response, and I contemplate throwing my phone across the room or drowning myself in the leftover maple syrup.

In the end, I do neither. I just wait impatiently for him to answer. And when he finally does, I hold my breath as I swipe open my screen. Then burst out laughing because:

Jaxon: I don't think we're there yet, but I'm sure you'll let me know when we are

Way. Right. Answer.

25

Truly, Madly, Deeply Bitten

I spend the rest of the morning lying around, waiting for Jaxon to text whenever he can. Which is so not a badass feminist move, but I've given up controlling my brain when it comes to this boy. Plus, it's not like there's anything else to do. I've read everything on my Kindle, and I can't watch any more episodes of *Legacies* without Macy. Add in my bum ankle and the fact that I can't go anywhere and that leaves…

Jaxon: What's your favorite movie?

Me: Atm? To All The Boys I've Loved Before

Me: Of all time? Some Kind of Wonderful

Me: Yours

Jaxon: Die Hard

Me: Seriously?

Jaxon: What's wrong with Die Hard?

Me: Nothing

Jaxon: Jk. It's Rogue One

Me: The Star Wars movie where everybody dies????

Jaxon: The Star Wars movie where people sacrifice themselves to save their galaxy

Jaxon: There are worse ways to die

It's not the answer I'm expecting, but now that he's said it, I can totally see how that movie would appeal to this guy who has gone out of his way to rescue me over and over again. Even *Die Hard* makes sense when I put it in that light. A main character who's willing to die if it means keeping other people safe.

There's a lot more to Jaxon than the person I met at the bottom of the stairs my first day here. I mean, he's still the jerk who told me not to let the door hit me on my way out. That's not something I'm likely to forget any time soon. But he's also the guy who saved me from Marc and Quinn. *And* the guy who carried me all the way back to my dorm room last night. That has to count for something, right?

Plus, I can't believe how different he is when there's no one else around. When it's just the two of us texting and he's not so busy trying to convince me that he wants nothing to do with me… and, more, that I should want nothing to do with him.

I wish I could ask the real Jaxon Vega to please stand up, but the truth is, I'm kind of hoping he's the guy who's been texting me for the last two hours. And if he's not…well, I guess I don't want to know that yet.

Me: Favorite ice cream flavor?

Jaxon: Don't have one

Me: Because you like them all???

Me: Which, btw, is the only acceptable answer to not having a favorite

Jaxon: I think we both know there are a million different reasons I'm unacceptable and ice cream choice barely makes the list

That line shouldn't make me swoon. *It shouldn't*, especially when it's so obviously a warning. But how can it not when it's delivered by the same boy who said *Rogue One* is his favorite movie?

It's pretty obvious Jaxon is the villain of his own story. I just wish I knew why.

Jaxon: Favorite song?

Me: OMG, I can't choose

Jaxon: What if I said you had to?

Me: I can't. There are too many

Me: You?

Jaxon: I asked you first

Me: Ugh. You suck

Jaxon: You have no idea how much

Me: Okay, fine

Me: Atm, Niall Horan's Put a Little Love on Me and anything by Maggie Rogers

Me: Of all time? Take Me to Church by Hozier or Umbrella from Rihanna

Me: You?

Jaxon: Savage Garden Truly, Madly, Deeply

Jaxon: Anything by Childish Gambino or Beethoven

Jaxon: Van Morrison's "Brown-Eyed Girl" is my new favorite, though

I drop my phone because…what do I say to that? How am I not supposed to swoon over this boy? Like, seriously? *How am I not supposed to swoon?* It's impossible.

I pick my phone back up with shaking hands. He hasn't texted anything else, but to be honest, I don't expect him to for a while. That was…a lot.

Instead, I swipe open my Spotify app. And play "Brown-Eyed Girl"…on repeat.

I'm still listening to it when Macy stops by around noon to check on me. "What are you listening to?" she queries, nose wrinkled.

"It's a long story."

She eyes me speculatively. "I bet. You should tell me all about—" She breaks off when she sees the remains of my very big breakfast. "Where did you get the waffle?" she demands, crossing the room so she can scoop a little of the leftover whipped cream out of its bowl and suck it off her finger. "It's not Thursday."

I stare at her, baffled. "I don't even know what that means."

"It means the cafeteria only makes waffles on Thursdays. And we only get whipped cream on special occasions." She dives back into the whipped-cream bowl, holds up a finger covered in the sweet, fluffy stuff. "Today is *not* a special occasion."

"Apparently, it is," I answer with a shrug, and I try to ignore the way her words warm me up all over. "At least for me."

Not going to lie, it *feels* like a special occasion. How can it not when I have texts on my phone from Jaxon right now telling me this is his favorite song?

"I can't believe my dad had them make you—" My face must give it away, because she breaks off mid-sentence. "This breakfast didn't come from my dad, did it?"

I don't know how to answer that. I mean, if I try to pretend it's from Uncle Finn, she'll just ask him about it and find out the truth. If I tell her it's from someone else, she's going to want to know who sent it, and I'm not sure I'm ready to tell her. I kind of like the idea of this Jaxon—the one who tells me vampire jokes and sends me waffles with fresh whipped cream—as my secret. At least for a little while.

But the look on Macy's face says she's not about to be put off. And that she's got a pretty good idea of where the food came from, even though I haven't answered her yet.

Which leaves me with only one option, really. A downplayed version of the truth. "It's really no big deal, okay? My ankle's bothering me, and he was trying to help."

"Flint?" she asks, eyes wide. "Or Jaxon?" She says the last

in a whisper.

"Does it matter?" I ask.

"Oh my God! It was Jaxon! He talked Chef Janie into making you waffles. I didn't even know that was possible—she's really tough. Then again, if anyone could do it, Jaxon could. I mean, the boy is terrifyingly efficient. And he always gets what he wants." She grins. "And I'm pretty sure what he wants right now is you."

A knock sounds from behind her, and I've never been more relieved to have someone come to my door in my life. "Can you get that? My ankle still hurts."

"Of course! I want first crack at interrogating Jaxon anyway."

"It's not going to be Jaxon," I tell her, but just the idea that it could be has my palms sweating a little. I sit up straighter, try desperately to fix the mess that is currently my hair as Macy opens the door.

Looks like the panic was for nothing, though, because it isn't Jaxon. It's a woman, carrying a large yellow envelope.

I tell myself I'm not disappointed, even as the sudden butterflies in my stomach kind of fall back down with a *thud*. At least until the woman, who Macy calls Roni, hands her the package. "I'm supposed to deliver this to Grace."

Macy whips her head around to look at me even as she takes the large envelope being thrust into her hands. Her eyes are huge, but I can't blame her. I'm sure mine are just as big.

I don't know what else Macy says to Roni to get her out of our room, because every ounce of my attention is focused on the envelope in her hands. And my name written on the front of it in the same bold scrawl that was on the earlier note.

"Give me!" I practically beg as I push myself to my feet. My ankle still hurts, but for this, I'm willing to suffer.

Except Macy is in full mother-hen mode, apparently. "Sit back down!" she squawks as she shoos me back to bed.

“Give me the envelope!” I make grabby hands at it.

“I’ll give it to you as soon as you’re back in bed with your ankle on that pillow.”

And then she glares at me, standing just out of reach, until I do what she says.

But the second I’m settled, the stern look goes away and the stars come back to her eyes. She thrusts the envelope at me and practically yells, “Open it, open it, open it!”

“That’s what I’m doing!” I tell her as I tear at the seal. It’s one of those plastic Bubble Wrap ones, so it’s harder than it should be, but eventually I get it open.

And out falls a large black library book.

“What is it?” Macy climbs on the bed next to me in an effort to get a better look.

“I don’t know,” I answer. But then I turn it over and…it’s totally the last book I ever would have expected him to send.

“*Twilight*? He sent me a copy of *Twilight*?” I turn to Macy in confusion.

Macy gasps as she stares from the book to me. And then she starts to laugh. And laugh. And laugh.

And I guess it’s kind of funny…the idea that a guy like Jaxon would send a girl a paranormal romance, but I don’t think it’s nearly as amusing as Macy is making it out to be. Plus, I’ve always kind of wanted to read it, to see what all the fuss was about all those years ago.

“I like it,” I tell her a little defiantly. Because I do—almost as much as I like the fact that Jaxon took the time to pick it out for me.

“I do, too,” Macy says around another fit of giggles. “I swear. It’s super…charming, actually.”

“I agree.” I open the front cover, and my heart stutters as I see the small Post-it note stuck to the cover page. In the scrawl

I'm rapidly coming to recognize as Jaxon's is this quote from the novel: "*I said it would be better if we weren't friends, not that I didn't want to be.*"

"Ooooooooh!" Macy clutches her hands to her chest and pretends to swoon. "If you don't kiss that boy soon, I'm going to disown you. Or I'm going to kiss him myself."

"I'm sure Cam would appreciate that." I trace my finger over the individual letters of every word he wrote, one after the other, even knowing it makes me look as starry-eyed as I feel.

"Hey, Cam's always talking about doing things for the greater good. Here's his chance to put his money where his mouth is."

"You kissing Jaxon is for the greater good?" I open the book to the first page.

"Me kissing Jaxon as your proxy is definitely for the greater good. Put you both out of your misery." She bats her eyelashes. "Though it definitely wouldn't be a sacrifice."

"How about we make a pact? You keep your lips off Jaxon and I'll keep mine off Cam?"

"Wooo!" Macy shouts so loud, it makes me jump. "I knew last night you were into him, with your babbling and your I-we-he stuff."

"I didn't say I was into him." But it's kind of hard not to fall for him at least a little after a morning like this one.

"You didn't say you weren't, either."

I roll my eyes. "Don't you have a class to go to?"

"Trying to get rid of me?" But she climbs off my bed, starts straightening her hair in the mirror over the dresser.

"I am, yes." I hold up the book. "I want to start reading."

"I bet you do." She makes kissy faces at me. "Oh, Edward, I love you so much! Whoops, I mean Jaxon."

I throw a pillow at her, but she just laughs and grabs her

backpack. Then she gives me a quick wave before heading out the door.

The second Macy's gone, I sink back onto the bed and hold *Twilight* to my chest. Jaxon sent me a love story. I mean, yeah, it's about a vampire, but it's still a love story. And that quote... I didn't want to show it in front of my cousin, but swoooooooon.

I grab my phone and fire off a text to Jaxon.

I hesitate then send a swoon emoji.

Jaxon: Don't get too starry-eyed

Jaxon: It's supposed to be a warning

But he punctuates his warning with a winky face/kiss emoji.

Me: Of what?

Jaxon: Things that go bump in the night

Jaxon: You never can be too careful

Me: I like scary stories

Jaxon: But do you like the monsters in them?

Me: I guess it depends on the monster

Jaxon: I guess we'll see, then, won't we?

Me: I don't know what that means

I start to text more—his mood is so different than it was earlier, and I want to get to the bottom of the change—but there's yet another knock on my door.

Me: Hey, did you send me something else????????

Jaxon: Why don't you open the door and find out?

Me: That sounds like a yes

Me: You don't have to do this, you know

Me: I mean, I appreciate it so much

Me: But it's not necessary

Jaxon: Grace

Jaxon: Open the door

I start making my way across the room to the door, thrilled that since the Advil kicked in, walking doesn't hurt as much, and my limp is a lot less pronounced. Then, right before I open the door, I text:

Me: How do you know I haven't already opened the door?

"Because I think I would have noticed," he answers from where he's standing on the other side of the beaded curtain.

"Jaxon!" I squeak out his name, my free hand going to my hair automatically in an effort to smooth down the mess. "You're here."

He lifts a brow. "You want me to go?"

"No, of course not! Come on in." I hold the door open as I step back.

"Thanks." He jerks a little as he steps over the threshold and Macy's beads brush against him.

"I don't know why Macy insists on keeping those up when they shock people on the regular," I say, swatting the annoying things out of the way so I can close the door. "Are you okay?"

"I have no idea." His eyes meet mine for the first time, and the happiness bubbling inside me dies down as I realize the blankness is back.

"Oh, well." I duck my head, suddenly way self-conscious around this guy who I've had no trouble talking to all day. "Thanks for the book."

He shakes his head, but at least he's smiling when he answers. "I thought it might give you something to do while you're resting your ankle." He looks at me pointedly.

"Hey, I was in bed. You're the one who knocked on my door."

His eyes widen a little at my mention of being in bed, and then we both do the only thing we can do in the situation—stare awkwardly at my rumpled hot-pink sheets and comforter.

"Do you, um—" I clear my suddenly clogged throat. "Do you want to sit down?"

He makes a face, then moves in a negative motion but

seconds later does the opposite and plops down at the end of my bed. All the way in the corner, like he's afraid I'm going to bite him—or jump him.

It's such an un-Jaxon-like move that for a second, I just kind of stare at him. And then decide, screw it. I'm not going to spend the next hour feeling awkward. I'm just not. So I flop down on the bed next to him and ask, "What did one bone say to the other bone?"

He eyes me warily, but his shoulders relax—and so does the rest of him. "I don't think I want to know."

I ignore him. "We have to stop meeting at this joint."

He groans. "That was..."

"Fabulous?" I tease.

He shakes his head. "Really, really awful." But he's smirking, and finally I can see something in the depths of his eyes—something real, instead of that terrible blankness.

Determined to keep it that way, I tell him, "It's kind of a specialty of mine."

"Bad jokes?"

"Terrible jokes. I inherited the talent from my mother."

He lifts a brow. "So terrible jokes run in the DNA?"

"Oh, it's totally a gene," I agree. "Right next to the ones for curly hair and long eyelashes." I bat my eyes at him to make a point, much the way Macy did to me a little while ago.

"Are you sure you didn't get it from both sides?" he asks, face totally innocent.

I narrow my eyes at him. "What's that supposed to mean?"

"Nothing." He holds his hands up in mock surrender. "Just that your jokes are *really* terrible."

"Hey! You said you liked my octopus joke."

"I didn't want to hurt your feelings." He reaches for my leg, drapes my foot and ankle over his lap. "It seemed rude to kick you when you were down and out."

"Hey! I may be down, but I'm not out." I try to pull my foot back, but Jaxon holds me in place, his long, elegant fingers instinctively finding the spots that hurt the most and massaging them.

I moan a little because the massage feels *really* good. And so does having his hands on me. "How are you so good at that?" I ask when I can finally speak again.

He shrugs, shoots me a little smirk. "Maybe I inherited it."

It's the first time he's mentioned any family except his one cryptic comment about his brother yesterday, and I jump on it. "Did you?"

He stops for a second—his hand, his breath, everything—and just looks at me with those eyes I try so hard to find emotion in. And then he says, "No."

His fingers start back on their massage like they never even stopped.

It frustrates me, but not enough to push when he has No Trespassing signs posted all over himself in huge black letters. Which says a lot more about him than he could possibly imagine.

We spend the next couple of minutes in silence as he massages my foot until the ache is almost completely gone. Only then, when his fingers finally still for good, does he say, "My eyes."

My gaze darts to his. "What do you mean?"

"That's what I got from my mother. My eyes."

"Oh." I lean forward until I can once again see the silver flecks against the darkness of his irises. "They're beautiful eyes." Especially when he's looking at me the way he is now—a little bemused, a little intrigued, a lot surprised. "Did you inherit anything else from your mother?" I ask softly.

"I hope not." His words are low, unguarded, and it's the first time he's ever been so open with me.

I search for something to say that won't break the mood, but it's too late. The second he registers what he said, Jaxon's entire face closes up.

"I need to go," he tells me, setting my foot gently on the bed before getting to his feet.

"Please don't." It's barely more than a whisper, but the sentiment comes from deep inside me. I feel like I'm seeing the real Jaxon for the first time up close and personal, and I don't want to lose that.

He pauses, and for a moment, I think he might actually listen to me. But then he's reaching inside the pocket of his designer jacket and pulling out a rolled-up piece of paper that's been fastened with a black satin ribbon.

He holds it out to me.

I take it with hands that I have to will to stay steady. "You didn't have to—"

"It made me think of you." He reaches up, takes a gentle hold of one of my curls, as has become his habit. But this time, he doesn't stretch it out and let it boing back into place. Instead, he simply worries it between his fingers.

Our eyes meet, and suddenly the room feels about twenty degrees hotter. My breath catches in my throat, and I bite my lower lip in an effort to keep myself from saying—or doing—something we're not ready for.

Except Jaxon looks like he might be ready for all kinds of things, with his gaze fastened on my mouth and his body swaying toward me just a little.

And then he's reaching out, pressing his thumb against my lip until I get the hint and stop biting it.

"Jaxon." I reach for him, but he's already across the room, his hand on the doorknob.

"Rest that ankle," he tells me as he opens the door. "If it feels better tomorrow, I'll take you to my favorite place."

"Which is?"

He quirks a brow, tilts his head. And doesn't say another word as he slips into the hall and closes the door behind him.

I stare after him, the scrolled-up piece of paper he gave me still in my hand. And wonder how on earth I'm going to keep this beautiful, broken boy from cracking my already battered heart wide open.

26

The Uniform Doesn't Make the Woman, But it Sure Does Bring Out the Insecurities

Pants or skirt?

I stare at my closet and all the clothes neatly lined up in it, courtesy of my cousin. I know I should have done this last night, but after a giant plate of nachos followed by three episodes of *Legacies* and a marathon gossip session over my jam-packed day, I didn't have the energy to do much more than lie in bed and think about Jaxon.

I turn toward my desk—and the paper Jaxon brought me yesterday, which is lying directly under the copy of *Twilight* he sent me. Not because I don't like it but because I like it too much, and I don't want to share it with anyone. Not even Macy or Heather.

It's a page ripped straight out of a copy of Anaïs Nin's journals—I don't know which one, because the heading doesn't say. I almost googled it yesterday to find out, but there's something special about not knowing, something intimate about having only this one page of her diary to go by. To have only these words that Jaxon wanted me to see.

Deep down, I am not different from you. I dreamed you, I wished for your existence.

The page has a lot more than that simple phrase on it, but as I read and reread it about a hundred times yesterday, these are the words that jumped out at me over and over again. Partly because they were so swoon-worthy and partly because I'm starting to feel the same way about him. About Jaxon, whose deepest thoughts and heart and pain seem to so closely echo mine.

It's a lot to take in at any time, let alone on my first day, when my mouth is dry and my stomach is churning with nerves.

Which is why I'm currently standing here, in front of my closet with absolutely no idea of what to wear. Because I obviously worried about the wrong first-day stuff...

Do the girls usually wear their uniform pants or skirts here? Or doesn't it matter? I try to remember what Macy wore the last couple of days, but it's all a blank besides the tropical-print snow pants she wore for the snowball fight.

"Skirt," Macy says as she walks out of the bathroom, a towel wrapped around her head. "There are wool tights to go with it in the bottom drawer of your dresser."

I close my eyes in relief. Thank God for cousins.

"Awesome, thanks." I slip one of the black skirts off the hanger and step into it, then add a white blouse and black blazer before going over to my dresser for a pair of black tights.

"If you wear the blouse, you've also got to wear the tie," Macy tells me as she opens one of my dresser drawers and pulls out a black tie with purple and silver stripes on it.

"Seriously?" I demand, looking from her to the tie and back again.

"Seriously." She drapes it around my neck. "Do you know how to tie one?"

"Not a clue." I head back toward the closet. "Maybe I should go for one of the polo shirts."

"Don't worry about it. I'll show you. It's a lot easier than it looks."

"If you say so."

She grins. "I do say so."

She starts by draping the tie unevenly around my neck and wrapping the longer end over the shorter end. A couple more wraps and a tuck and pull through—all narrated by my cousin—and I've got a perfectly tied tie around my neck...even if it is a little tight.

"Looks good," Macy says as she steps back to admire her handiwork. "I mean, the knot's not as fancy as some of the guys wear, but it gets the job done."

"Thanks. I'll look up a couple of videos on YouTube this afternoon, make sure I know what I'm doing before I have to tie it again tomorrow."

"It's pretty easy. You'll get the hang of it in no time. In fact—" She breaks off at the loud knock on our door.

"Are you expecting someone?" I ask as I move toward the door, motioning for her to move back toward the bathroom, as all she's currently wearing is a towel.

"No. I usually meet my friends in the cafeteria." Her eyes go wide. "Do you think it's Jaxon?" She whispers his name like she's afraid he'll hear it through the door.

"I didn't think so, no." But now that she's planted the idea in my head… Ugh. My already nervous stomach does a series of somersaults. "What do I do?" My own voice drops to a whisper without the conscious decision to do so on my part. He texted me last night before bed, but I haven't seen him since he came to my room yesterday around lunch, and after lying awake half the night thinking about him, I'm feeling hella awkward.

She looks at me like I'm missing the obvious. "Answer the door?"

"Right." I smooth my sweaty palms down the sides of my skirt and reach for the door handle. I have no idea what to do, what to say...although judging by how tight this ridiculous tie suddenly feels, I may not be able to say anything at all before it actually strangles me.

I glance back at Macy, who shoots me an encouraging thumbs-up one last time, then take as deep a breath as I can manage before pulling open the door.

All my nerves dissipate in the space from one strangled breath to the next, largely because the person standing at our door is most definitely *not* Jaxon Vega.

"Hi, Uncle Finn! How are you?"

"Hi, Gracey girl." He leans down and drops an absentminded kiss on the top of my head. "I just stopped by to check on your ankle and finally deliver your schedule." He holds a blue sheet of paper out to me. "And to wish you luck on your first day of class. You're going to do great!"

I'm not so sure about that, but I'm determined to think positive today, so I smile and say, "Thanks. I'm excited. And my ankle's sore, but okay."

"Good. I made sure you got into that art class you wanted and that you have our best history teacher, since that's your favorite subject. But check over your schedule, make sure you're not repeating any classes. I did my best, but mistakes happen."

He tweaks my cheek like I'm a five-year-old. It's such a Dad thing to do that my heart aches a little.

"I'm sure it's perfect," I tell him.

Macy snorts. "Don't bet on it. If Dad did it himself instead of letting Mrs. Haversham do it, no telling what he's got you signed up for."

"Mrs. Haversham did it," he tells her with a wink. "I just supervised. Brat." He walks over and gives her a one-armed shoulder hug and the same kiss on the top of her head that he gave me.

"Ready for that math test today?" he asks.

"Been ready for a week." She rolls her eyes.

"Good. And how's that English project going? Did you finish—?"

"This is a boarding school," Macy interrupts, smacking lightly at his arm. "That means parents don't get to give their kids the third degree over every assignment."

"That's because they don't know about every assignment. I, however, do. Which means I get to check up on you whenever I want."

"Lucky me," she deadpans.

He just grins. "Exactly."

"Are you going to get out of here so I can get dressed? Grace and I still need to hit the cafeteria before class. Breakfast *is* the most important meal of the day, after all."

"Not if you waste it on cherry Pop-Tarts."

"Cherry Pop-Tarts are their own food group." She glances my way. "Back me up here, Grace."

"Maybe two food groups, if you count the frosting," I agree. "So are the brown sugar ones."

"Exactly what I'm talking about!"

It's Uncle Finn's turn to roll his eyes. But he drops another kiss on her head before heading for the door. "Do your old man a favor and grab some fruit with those Pop-Tarts, will you?"

"Cherries are fruit," I tease him.

"Not that way, they aren't." He gives me a comforting shoulder squeeze. "Don't forget to stop by my office later. Now that you're feeling better, I want to talk to you about a few things and hear how your first day went."

"It'll be fine, Uncle Finn."

"I'm hoping it will be more than fine. But good or bad, come tell me about it. Okay?"

"Yeah, okay."

"Good. See you later, girls." He smiles at us, then disappears out the door.

Macy shakes her head as she grabs her own school uniform out of the closet. "Just ignore him. My dad's a total dork."

"Most good dads are dorks, aren't they?" I ask as I move to the mirror on my closet door so I can start fixing my hair. "Besides, he reminds me of my dad. It's kind of nice."

She doesn't say anything to that, and when I glance her way, it's to find her staring sadly at me—which is, bar none, the second worst thing about losing my parents. I hate the sympathy, hate the way everyone feels sorry for me and no one knows what to say.

"That was supposed to be a happy comment," I tell her. "You don't need to feel bad."

"I know. It's just that I'm so happy you're here and we have this time to get to know each other. And then it hits me all over again and I feel gross for being happy." She sighs. "Which sounds like I'm making this all about me, but I'm not. I just—"

"Hey, you." I break into what I'm learning could be a really, *really* long soliloquy. "I get it. And though how I got here sucks, I'm glad we have this time, too. Okay?"

A slow smile takes the place of her worried look. "Yeah, okay."

"Good. Now get dressed. I'm starving."

"On it!" she says, disappearing into the bathroom to do just that.

Twenty minutes later, we finally make it down the back stairs ("sooooo much less crowded," Macy swears) to the cafeteria, after winding our way past *no less* than seven suits of armor, four giant fireplaces, and more columns than existed in all of

Ancient Greece.

Okay, the last might be a slight exaggeration, but only slight. Plus, the fact that they're black instead of white gets them extra points in my book. And that's not even counting the gold filigree around the tops and bottoms of the columns.

I mean, the whole thing is a total head trip. Seriously. Going to school in Alaska is wild enough. Going to school in an actual castle, complete with halls whose bloodred ceilings are lined with Gothic lancet arches, is hella cool.

At least if you don't count all the people staring at me as we make our way through the halls. Macy dismisses it as "new-girl stuff" and tells me to ignore it. But it's pretty hard to do that when people are honest-to-God turning around to stare at me when I pass. I know Macy said they've all been together for a long time, but come on. I can't actually be the first new person to land here, can I? Just the idea is absurd. Schools get new kids all the time—even schools in Alaska.

Macy interrupts my inner diatribe with an excited "We're here!" as we stop in front of three sets of black-and-gold doors. The wood is carved, and I try to get a closer look at the designs, but my cousin is in too big of a hurry to show me the cafeteria. Which…seen one, seen them all, I figure.

But as she throws open one of the doors with all the pomp and flair of a game-show hostess showing me the car behind curtain number one, it's pretty obvious that I'm wrong. Again. Because this cafeteria—and it feels wrong to even refer to the room by such a mundane name—is like nothing I've ever seen before. Ever.

I'm pretty sure it even puts the library to shame.

To begin with, the room is huge, with long walls covered in different murals of dragons and wolves and I don't know what else. Crown molding in black and gold runs around the edges of the ceiling and down the walls, framing each mural like a regular painting. The artist in me is fascinated and wants to spend hours studying each one, but I've got class in half an hour, so it'll have to wait. Plus, there's so much else to see here that I don't know where to look first.

The ceiling is arched and an in-your-face, unapologetic bloodred, overlaid with curved black molding in elaborate geometric patterns. A huge crystal chandelier hangs from the center of each one, casting the whole room in a soft glow that only makes its grandeur more obvious.

There are no picnic-style tables here, no utilitarian trays or plastic silverware. Three long tables covered in tablecloths in shades of gold and black and cream run the length of the room. They are surrounded by tufted, high-backed chairs and set with real china and silverware.

Classical music floats through the room, dark and more than a little eerie. I don't know much about this kind of music, but I know creepy when I hear it, and this is definitely it.

So much so that I can't resist saying to Macy, "This music is very, um…interesting."

"'Danse Macabre' by Camille Saint-Saëns. Overkill, I know, but my dad has it playing in here every year for Halloween. Along with the score from *Jaws* and a few other classics. It just hasn't been changed over yet."

I think about Lia and how she said the same thing about the pillows in the library. In my old school, the Halloween spirit was pretty much exhausted by reading a scary story in English class and a costume contest on the quad at lunch. Katmere Academy takes the holiday to a whole new level.

"It's cool," I say as we make our way along one of the tables until we find a cluster of empty seats. "It's a lot, but Halloween has always been my dad's favorite holiday."

"Really? That's so weird, considering my dad hated it. I thought it must have been something that happened when he was a kid, but apparently not, if your dad goes all out for the holiday." I asked Dad once, a few years ago, why he disliked Halloween so much, and he said he would tell me when I was older.

Turns out the universe had other plans.

"Yeah, that is weird." Macy glances around. "But isn't this place cool? I've been dying for you to see it."

"Totally cool. I want to spend hours just looking at the murals."

"Well, you've got all year, so..." She gestures for me to sit. "What do you want to eat? Besides cherry Pop-Tarts, I mean."

"I can come with you."

"Next time. Right now you should get off your hurt ankle for a few minutes. Besides, I'm pretty sure today is going to be a little overwhelming. Let me help out where I can."

"It's pretty hard to say no to that," I tell her, because she's right. I'm already overwhelmed, and the day has barely started. I'm also touched by how hard Macy is working to make things easier for me. I smile my thanks at her.

"So don't say no." She pushes me playfully toward a chair. "Just tell me what you want to eat, or I'll bring you seal steak and eggs."

The horror must show on my face, because she bursts out laughing. "How about a pack of cherry Pop-Tarts and some yogurt with canned berries?"

"Canned berries?" I ask, doubtful.

"Yeah, Fiona, our chef, cans them herself when they're in season. Fresh fruit is pretty hard to come by up here once late fall hits. The display at the party the other day was a special treat."

"Oh, right." I feel silly. Of course there aren't any fresh berries in Alaska in November. If a pint of Ben and Jerry's costs ten bucks, I can't imagine what a pint of strawberries would be.

"That sounds great. Thanks."

"No problem." She grins at me. "Sit down and take a load off. I'll be right back."

I do as she directs and pick a chair that faces the wall—partly because I really do want to study the closest mural and partly because I'm sick of pretending I don't see people staring at me. At least with my back turned to most of the room, I won't be able to see them and they won't be able to see my face.

The negative is that I also won't be able to watch for Jaxon, and I was really hoping to see him this morning. Which sounds desperate, I know, but I can't stop thinking about everything that happened between us yesterday. I kind of hoped he'd text me this morning, but he hasn't so far.

I want to know what he meant by that journal page, want to know if it means he feels all the wild things I do. It's impossible to imagine that he does—I knew he was out of my league the first day I met him. But that doesn't keep me from wanting him, any more than Macy's warnings do. Or the air of darkness that he wears like a badge of honor…or a set of shackles. I haven't quite figured out which.

There's a part of me that wants to sneak a look behind me, just to see if I can catch a glimpse of him. But it seems way too obvious, at least with half the cafeteria watching me. And they *are* watching—I can feel their eyes even with my back turned. I know Macy says it's no big deal, that it's just new-girl stuff, but it feels like more than that.

I don't have time to dwell on it, though, because Macy's got a fully loaded tray in her hands and is heading straight for me.

"That looks like more than Pop-Tarts and yogurt," I tease as I help her set it down so she won't spill anything.

"I did fine on the food, but when I got to drinks, I didn't know if you wanted coffee or tea or juice or water or milk, so I brought one of each."

"Oh, wow. Um, the juice is great."

"Thank God." She holds out a glass of red liquid. "I was afraid you were going to say you wanted the coffee, and then I was going to *die*. Especially since Cam drinks tea, so I can't steal his when he gets here."

She flops dramatically into the chair across from me.

"I promise, the coffee's all yours," I tell her with a laugh. "And you picked the right juice—cranberry is my favorite."

"Good." She takes a long sip of the hot drink just to prove a point. "I thought all you California girls were Starbucks addicts."

"I guess Cam and I have something in common. It was always more about tea at my house. My mom was an amazing herbalist. She made her own tea blends, and they were fantastic." It's been a month, but I can still almost taste her lemon-thyme-verbena tea. I have a few bags of it in my carry-on, but I don't want to drink it. And truth be told, I'm afraid to even smell it in case I start crying and never stop.

"I can only imagine."

There's something in the way Macy says it that gets my attention, that has me trying to figure out what she means. I wait for her to say more, but then her eyes go wide, and she starts choking on a sip of coffee.

Before I can turn around to see what's got her so discombobulated, someone asks, "Is this seat taken?"

And then I don't have to turn around at all. Because I'd know that voice anywhere.

Jaxon Vega just asked to sit next to me. In front of everyone.

It really is a brave new world.

27

Ten-Degree Weather Gives a Whole New Meaning to the Cool Kids' Table

"Um, yeah. Sure. Of course." As I turn to look at him, the words pour out of my mouth without any rhyme or reason, making me sound—and feel—like a jerk.

Jaxon inclines his head, lifts a brow. "So it *is* taken, then?"

Forget sounding like a jerk. I *am* a jerk. "No! I mean, yes. I mean…" I stop, take a deep breath, and then blow it out slowly. "The seat isn't taken. You can sit down if you'd like."

"I *would* like." He grabs the chair and turns it around so that when he drops down into it, he's facing the back of the chair, one elbow draped negligently over the top.

It's a completely ridiculous way to sit, especially on a chair this elegant…but it's also superhot. And it's pretty much been my kryptonite since Moises de la Cruz did it at a pool party when we were in seventh grade.

What can I say? I'm weak.

Guess I'm not the only weak one, though, because Macy makes another choked sound as she stares behind me—this one worse than the last. I tear my eyes away from Jaxon long enough to make sure that sip of coffee isn't *actually* killing her. Thankfully, it's not, but the fact that the other members of the

Order are currently settling themselves down at the table with us just might.

"How's your ankle?" Jaxon asks, his dark gaze sliding over me in what I know is concern but what feels a little like a caress.

"Better. Thanks for…yesterday."

"Which part?" The crooked grin is back, and this time when he looks me over, it feels a *lot* like a caress.

But just because I'm flustered doesn't mean I'm a pushover. "The waffles. Obviously."

One of the members of the Order snorts at my answer, then darts a quick look at Jaxon as he tries to smother the sound. Jaxon just kind of rolls his eyes, though, and gives a little nod in his direction. Which makes the guy laugh again and has the added effect of relaxing all the other guys as well.

"Obviously." He shakes his head, looks away. But his smile doesn't fade. "So you're planning on going to class today."

It's not a question, but I answer anyway. "Yeah. It's time."

He nods like he knows what I'm talking about. "What's your first period?"

"I don't remember." I pull the blue schedule Uncle Finn gave me from my jacket pocket. "Looks like Brit Lit with Maclean."

"I'm in that class," says one of the other members of the Order. He's black, with friendly eyes and the hottest set of locks I've ever seen. "You'll like her. She's cool. I'm Mekhi, by the way, and I'm happy to walk you to class if you want, show you where it is."

Macy makes yet another choking sound—I'm beginning to think her death really is imminent—at the same time that Jaxon replies, "Yeah, that's going to happen."

The other guys laugh, but I don't get the joke. So I just kind of smile and say, "Thanks, Mekhi. I'd appreciate it, if you wouldn't mind."

That only makes them laugh harder.

I give Jaxon a WTF look, but he's just kind of shaking his head at them. Then he leans in and says, "I'll walk you to class, Grace."

He's so close that his breath tickles my ear, sending shivers down my spine that have nothing to do with Alaska and everything to do with the fact that I want this guy. That, despite all the warnings and bad behavior, I really do think I'm falling for Jaxon Vega.

"That would—" My voice breaks, and I have to clear my throat a couple of times before I can try again. "That would be nice, too."

"It *would* be nice." There's amusement in his voice, but when our eyes meet, there's no trace of laughter in his. There's also no trace of the coldness that's as much a part of him as the dark hair and long, lean body. Instead, there's a heat—an intensity—that has my hands shaking and my knees going weak.

"Should we head over now?" The question is ripped from my dry throat.

He looks pointedly at my tray. "You should eat now."

"You should eat, too." I reach for the silver package on my tray, hold it out to him.

He looks from me to the breakfast pastries and back again. "Pop-Tarts aren't what I'm hungry for."

This time, Macy's not the one making the choking sound. I look up, tracing it to its origin—the only member of the Order who looks like he might be Native Alaskan, a guy with bronze skin and long, dark hair tied into a neat ponytail at the nape of his neck.

"Something funny, Rafael?" Jaxon asks, eyes narrowed and tone silky smooth.

"Absolutely not," he answers but glances at me even as he says it, eyes brimming with mischief and delight. "I think I'm going to like you, Grace."

"And here the day was going so well."

He grins. "Yeah, definitely going to like you."

"Don't feel too flattered, Grace. Rafael's not exactly the most discerning guy around," says one of the others, a boy with twinkling blue eyes and gold hoop earrings.

"Like you are, Liam?" Rafael shoots back. "The last girl you dated was a barracuda."

"I'm pretty sure that's an insult to barracudas everywhere," chimes in another one of Jaxon's friends, his Spanish accent sexily rolling his *R*s.

"Luca knows what I'm talking about," Rafael says.

"Because Luca's dating history is so impressive?" Jaxon drawls, joining the conversation for the first time.

The quip is so unexpected—so what I'm used to from his texts but not in person—that I can't help staring at him. Then again, everything about this morning has been unexpected—especially the dynamic among the members of the Order. Every time I've seen them, they've appeared so tough and unapproachable. So unfeeling.

But sitting here with one another—and no one but Macy and me to witness it, since Cam and his group took one look at who was sitting with us and headed in the other direction—they're just like any other group of friends. Except funnier. And way, way hotter. Knowing he's got friends like this—and that he can *be* a friend like this—makes me like Jaxon even more.

Jaxon catches me staring and raises a questioning brow in my direction.

I just shrug at him like it's no big deal and reach for my glass. Then nearly choke at the look in his eyes as he watches me. Because there's a craving there, a dark and devastating desperation that has my breath stuttering in my chest and heat blooming deep inside me.

He holds my gaze for one second, two. Then he slowly blinks, and when he opens his eyes again, the emptiness is back.

And still, I watch him. Still, I can't look away. Because there's something just as beautiful—and just as devastating—in their emptiness as there is in their heat. Eventually, though, I force myself to look down. Mostly because if I don't, I'm afraid I'll do something foolish like throw myself at Jaxon in front of the entire school.

Turning away from him, I forcibly yank my attention back to the conversation at hand, just in time to hear Luca say, "Hey, now. How was I supposed to know Angie was a soul-sucking demon?"

"Ummm, because we told you so?" Mekhi answers.

"Yeah, but I thought you were biased. You didn't like her from the start."

"Because she was a soul-sucking demon," Liam repeats. "What part of that are you not getting?"

"What can I say?" Luca gives a careless shrug. "The heart wants what the heart wants."

"Until what the heart wants tries to kill you," Rafael teases.

"Sometimes even then." The words are quiet, spoken from the haunted-looking guy sitting to Macy's right.

"Seriously, Byron?" Mekhi grouses. "Why you always got to shut the conversation down?"

"I was just making an observation."

"Yeah, a depressing observation. You need to lighten up, man."

Byron just stares at him, lips twisted in a tiny little smile that makes him look like a modern-day embodiment of his poet namesake.

Mad, bad, and dangerous to know.

The famous quote from Lady Caroline Lamb goes through

my mind. But I'm not focused on Byron's wavy black hair and dimples when I think about her words. No, in my head, they're all about Jaxon, with his scarred face and cold eyes and smile that borders on cruel at least half the time.

Definitely bad. Definitely dangerous. As for mad…I don't know yet, but something tells me I'm going to find out.

When I think of him like that, I wonder what the hell I'm doing even contemplating feeling the way I do. After all, in San Diego, dark and dangerous wasn't exactly my type. Then again, maybe that's because I never ran into the genuine article back home. Here in Alaska… Well, all I'm saying is, there's a reason half the girls in the school are swooning over Jaxon.

Besides, there's more to him than meets the eye. No matter how angry he is, he's never been anything but gentle with me. Even that first day, when he was so obnoxious, he still never did anything that made me uncomfortable. And he's certainly never hurt me. To everyone else, he might be as dangerous as Macy warns. But to me, he seems more misunderstood than malicious, more broken than bad.

Besides, Byron called it when he implied the heart wants what the heart wants, even when it's bad. And no matter how many warnings I get about Jaxon, I'm pretty sure he's what my heart wants.

Suddenly, a weird kind of chiming sound cuts through Dvořák's "The Noonday Witch" (if I'm not mistaken) that's currently playing over the cafeteria's loudspeakers. "What is that?" I ask, looking around to see if we're suddenly being invaded by a bunch of triangle-playing guerrillas.

"The bell," Macy says. They're the first two words she's managed to choke out since the Order took up residence next to us, and all seven of us turn to her in surprise. Which just makes her flash a small little smile before shoving half a Pop-

Tart in her mouth.

"You still didn't eat," Jaxon says. And then he picks a Pop-Tart and hands it to me.

"Seriously?" I take it, because I know he's just going to stand there holding it until I do. But I'm still going to call him on it. Because I'm smart enough to know that if I let him get away with the small things, he'll try his best to steamroll me with everything else, too. "I'm pretty sure I can figure out for myself if I'm hungry or not."

He shrugs. "A girl's got to eat."

"A *girl* can decide that for herself. Especially since the guy sitting next to her didn't eat anything, either."

Mekhi lets out a little whoop. "That's right, Grace. Make sure he doesn't walk all over you."

Jaxon gives him a look that sends a chill right through me, but Mekhi just rolls his eyes, although I notice that he *does* shut his mouth for pretty much the first time since he sat down. Not that I blame him. If Jaxon looked at me like that, I think I might run for the hills.

"What classroom are you going to?" Jaxon asks as we maneuver our way through the suddenly bustling cafeteria. It's easier than it should be, considering the mad stampede toward the doors that is currently going on. But as long as Jaxon is in the lead, the sea of students does more than just part. It pretty much leaps out of the way.

I fumble for my schedule again, but before I can so much as pull it out, Mekhi answers, "A246," right before he disappears into the crowd.

"Apparently, A246," I repeat, tongue firmly in cheek.

"Apparently." He moves slightly ahead of me to push open the door. As he holds it for me, not one person darts through. Instead, they all wait patiently as I walk through, and I have the fleeting thought that this is more than just popularity, more than just fear.

This must be what royalty feels like.

It seems absurd to even think something so bizarre, but I make it through the door and down the hall without another body—besides Jaxon's—coming within five feet of me. And I don't care whether I'm in an elite boarding school in Alaska or a crowded public high school in San Diego, that is *not* normal.

I also realize that the same thing happened yesterday before the snowball fight. No matter how crowded the hall got or how much jostling went on, no one so much as touched Jaxon—or Macy and me, as long as he was standing with us. "So what do you do to deserve all this?" I ask as we move toward the staircase.

"Deserve all what?"

I roll my eyes at him, figuring he's messing with me. But the blank look he gives me says otherwise. "Come on, Jaxon. How do you not see what's going on here?"

He glances around, clearly mystified. "What's going on?"

Because I still can't decide if he's playing with me or if he really is this obtuse, I just shake my head and say, "Never mind." Then plow ahead and pretend that I don't notice everyone staring at me even as they scramble to get out of my way.

So yeah, that whole blending-in plan I hatched in San Diego? Officially dead on arrival.

28

"To Be or Not to Be" Is a Question, Not a Pickup Line

Jaxon walks me right up to my classroom door—which we get to in what I'm guessing is record time, considering there's no one else in the room, not even the teacher.

"Are you sure this is the right place?" I ask as we step inside.

"Yes."

"How do you know?" I glance at the clock. Class should start in less than three minutes, and still nobody's here. "Maybe we should check if it got—"

"They're waiting for me to either sit down or leave, Grace. Once one of those things happens, they'll come in."

"Sit down or—" I goggle at him. "So you *were* just messing with me in the hallway? You *do* notice how people treat you?"

"I'm not blind. And even if I was, it would still be hard to miss."

"It's madness!"

He nods. "It is."

"That's all you've got to say about it? If you know how bizarre it is, why don't you do something to stop it?"

"Like what?" He gives me that obnoxious smirk from the first day, the one that made me want to punch him. Or kiss him.

Just the thought has my stomach spinning and has me taking a cautious step back.

He doesn't like the added distance, at least not if his narrowed eyes can be believed. And the way he takes two steps toward me before continuing. "Stand up at the pep rally and reassure everyone that I'm not going to eat them if they get too close? Somehow I don't think they'll believe me."

"Personally, I think they're more worried about being thrown in high school jail than getting eaten—"

The smirk is back. "You might be surprised."

"Well, then, you *should* reassure them. Be friendly. You know, show them that you're harmless."

I feel ridiculous even before that left eyebrow of his goes up. "Is that what you think? That I'm *harmless*?"

Jaxon doesn't sound insulted so much as astonished, and really, I can't blame him. Because I've never met anyone *less* harmless in my life. Just looking at him feels perilous. Standing next to him feels like walking a hundred-foot-high tightrope without a net. And wanting him the way I do…wanting him feels like opening a vein just to watch myself bleed.

"I think you're just as dangerous as everyone gives you credit for. I also think—"

"Yo, Jaxon, at some point, class does need to start," Mekhi interrupts as he saunters into the room—apparently the only one in this class who isn't afraid of Jaxon. "You going to take off, or are you going to keep everyone standing around watching you try to woo this girl?"

Jaxon whips his head around to glare at Mekhi, who raises his arms defensively and takes a big step back. And that's before Jaxon's voice drops a full octave as he growls, "I'll leave when I'm ready."

"I think you should probably go now," I tell him, even though

I'm as reluctant to see him go as he apparently is to leave. "The teacher needs to start class. Besides, aren't you the one who told me to keep my head down and not draw attention to myself?"

"That was the old plan."

"The old plan?" I stare at him, bemused. "When did we get a new plan?"

He smiles at me. "Two nights ago. I told you it wasn't going to be easy."

"Wait a minute." My stomach drops. "Are you telling me the cafeteria, the walk to class… This was all because of *Flint*?" Just the thought makes me feel awful.

"Flint who?" he deadpans.

"Jaxon."

"It was all because of you," he tells me.

I'm not sure I believe him, but before I can probe any more, he reaches out and takes hold of one of my curls in that way he does. He rubs it between his fingers for a couple of seconds as he watches me with those unfathomable eyes of his. "I love the way your hair smells." Then he stretches out the curl before letting it go so it can boing back into place.

"You need to go," I tell him again, though the words are a lot more breathless this time around.

He doesn't look happy, but I stare him down.

It takes a few seconds, but eventually Jaxon nods. He steps back, a grudging look on his face, and it's only as he moves away that I realize my heart is beating like a heavy-metal drummer.

"Text me a pic of your schedule," he says as he moves toward the door.

"Why?"

"So I know where to meet you later." His face melts into a grin, and the butterflies I always feel when he's around take flight in my stomach.

"I have AP Physics right now, so I'm out in the physics lab and won't make it back before you have to go to your second period. But I'll catch up with you later. If I can't, I'll have one of the others walk you to class."

Yeah, because that will help me blend in. "You don't have to do that."

"It's not a problem, Grace."

I sigh. "What I mean is I don't want you to do that. I just want to get to class like everyone else. On my own."

"I get that. I do," he continues when I give him a disbelieving look. "But I meant it when I said you aren't safe here. At least let me watch out for you for a few days, until you learn the ropes."

"Jaxon—"

"Please, Grace."

It's the please that gets me, considering I'm pretty positive Jaxon isn't the kind of guy to ask for something when he can order it. And though I think he's overreacting, he seems really worried, and if this will set his mind at ease, I guess I can handle it for a few days.

A very few days.

"Fine." I tell him, giving in as gracefully as I can. "But only until the end of the week, okay? After that, I'm on my own."

"How about, we renegotiate at the end of the week and see—"

"Jaxon!"

"Okay, okay!" He puts his hands up. "Whatever you say, Grace."

"Yeah, right. That's a bunch of—" I break off because he's gone again. Because of course he is. Because that's the story of our lives. He disappears, and I get disappeared on.

One of these days, I'm *going* to turn the tables.

He's right, though. As soon as he leaves, the classroom floods with people. I try to stand to the side, waiting to see where there might be an empty seat, but Mekhi nods me over to the desk next to him in the second row.

I go, even though I don't know if a person normally sits there, because it's nice to have someone in this class to talk to. Especially since he's grinning at me while everyone else is doing the same old stare-and-glare.

The teacher—Ms. Maclean—bustles in after everyone has taken their seats. She's dressed in a flowing purple caftan, her wild red hair piled atop her head in a haphazard bun that looks like it's going to fall down at any second. She's not young, but she's not old, either—maybe forty or so—and she's got a huge smile on her face as she tells everyone to open their copies of *Hamlet* to Act II.

Half the class has books and the other half has laptops, so I pull out my phone and start looking for a public-domain copy, since I left my book in California. But I've barely typed "Hamlet" in the search bar before Ms. Maclean drops a dog-eared copy on my desk.

"Hello, Grace," she murmurs in a low voice. "You can borrow one of mine until you can find one of your own online. And since you look like the shy type—despite your association with Katmere's most notorious student—I won't make you stand up and introduce yourself to the class. But know that you're welcome here, and if you need anything, feel free to stop by my office hours. They're posted by the door."

"Thanks." I duck my head as my cheeks start to get warm. "I appreciate it."

"No worries." She gives my shoulder a comforting squeeze as she heads back to the front of the room. "We're excited to have you here."

Mekhi leans over as I pick up the book and says, "Act two, scene two."

Thanks, I mouth back just as Ms. Maclean claps her hands.

Then, in true drama queen–style, she throws her arms wide and says in a booming but perfect iambic pentameter:

"Something have you heard
Of Hamlet's transformation; so call it,
Sith nor the exterior nor the inward man
Resembles that it was."

We spend the rest of the class discussing Hamlet's shift from perfect prince to total downer. With Ms. Maclean doing her drama thing in the front of the room and Mekhi making sly comments in my ear every couple of minutes, it's a lot more fun than it sounds. Mekhi may look intimidating, but he's way more chill than Jaxon—and also really funny. It's easy to be around him, and I end up enjoying class a lot more than I expected to, especially considering I've already read the play once this year.

In fact, I enjoy it so much that I'm a little disappointed when the bell rings, at least until I remember that I've got art next. Art's been my favorite class pretty much since elementary school, and I'm excited to see what it's like here. But it means heading out to the art studio, and that means a detour to my room, where I can put on at least a couple more layers to protect myself from the cold.

It's only a ten-minute walk to the studio, so I don't need to put on everything I did the last two times I went outside. But I do need a heavy sweatshirt and a long coat—plus gloves and a hat—if I don't have any plans to get frostbite. Which I definitely don't.

I just hope I have enough time to make it to my room and out to the art studio before the next bell rings. Just in case, I speed up a little, hoping to make it to the main staircase before the masses.

"Hey! What's your rush, New Girl?"

I glance over at Flint with a grin as he comes up on my left side. "I have a name, you know."

"Oh, right." He pretends to think. "What is it again?"

"Bite me."

"That's an interesting first name…and a phrase you might want to be careful saying around here."

"And why is that exactly?" I lift a brow at him as we weave our way through the halls. Unlike earlier with Jaxon, the whole *parting of the halls* thing is currently nowhere in effect. In fact, traversing the school with Flint is an awful lot like playing this old video game my dad used to like, where you have to race to get the frog across the street before one of the eight million cars going by splats it on the pavement.

In other words, it's a normal high school hallway. I can feel myself relaxing a little more with each near-collision.

"You're actually going to pretend you don't know?"

"Know what?"

Flint studies me, then shakes his head when I look back at him, brows raised in a definite WTF. "My mistake. Never mind."

There's something about the way he says it that has an uneasy feeling sliding through me. It's the same feeling I got when I saw Jaxon and Lia outside without a jacket yesterday.

The same feeling I got when Flint fell out of that tree and walked away with only a few bruises.

The same feeling I got when Lia was chanting in tongues in the library, even though she had no idea what I was talking about when I mentioned several of the Alaskan languages.

"I'm not dense, you know. I am aware that something isn't quite right here, even if I don't know what it is yet."

It's the first time I've acknowledged my suspicions even to myself, and it feels good to give voice to it all, instead of letting the thoughts fester below the surface.

"Are you?" Suddenly Flint is right up in my face, his whole

body only inches away from mine. "Are you really?"

I don't back down, despite the sudden desperation in his voice. "I am. Now, do you want to tell me what it is?"

It takes a minute, but when he next speaks, the worry is gone. And so is everything else except the teasing drawl that's as much a part of him as his amber eyes and muscles. It's like the warning never happened, even before he says, "Where's the fun in that?"

"You've got an odd definition of fun."

"You have no idea." He wiggles his brows. "So what are you up to anyway?"

I stare at him. "Do you ever finish any conversation without starting another?"

"Never. It's part of my charm."

"Yeah, just keep telling yourself that."

"I will." He walks several more feet with me, happily bopping along to a song that's only in his head. "Where are you going? The classrooms are back that way."

"I've got to go to my room and grab some warmer clothes. I have art next, and I'll freeze if I go outside like this."

"Wait." He stops dead. "No one told you about the tunnels?"

"What tunnels?" I eye him suspiciously. "Are you messing with me again?"

"I'm not, I swear. There's a whole network of tunnels that run under the school and lead to the different outbuildings."

"Seriously? This is Alaska—how did they dig tunnels in the frozen ground?"

"I don't know. How do they drill in the frozen ground? Besides, summer is a thing." He gives me the best Boy Scout look in his repertoire. "I promise. The tunnels are real. I just can't believe the omnipotent Jaxon Vega forgot to mention them to you."

"Are you kidding me? You're going to start in on Jaxon now?"

"Of course not. I'm just saying, I'm the one telling you about the tunnels and keeping you from freezing off all the important parts of your anatomy. He could have mentioned them to you before sending you out into the cruel, cruel winter."

"It's fall." I roll my eyes. "And are we going to do this every time we talk about Jaxon?"

He holds his hands up in mock innocence. "As far as I'm concerned, we *never* have to talk about Jaxon."

"Funny claim coming from a guy who keeps bringing him up."

"Because I'm worried about you. I swear." He draws an *X* over his heart. "Jaxon's a complicated guy, Grace. You should stay away from him."

"I find it interesting that he says the exact same thing about you."

"Yeah, well, nothing says you have to listen to him." He makes a disgusted face.

"Nothing says I have to listen to you, either." I give him a shit-eating grin. "You see my conundrum, right?"

"Ooh. The new girl's got some claws after all. I like it."

I roll my eyes. "You're a total weirdo. You know that, right?"

"Know it? I own it, baby."

I can't help but laugh as he makes a ridiculous face at me, crossing his eyes and sticking out his tongue. "So are you going to show me these tunnels sometime this year, or am I going to have to do my best impression of the abominable snowwoman?"

"Definitely the tunnels. Turns out I'm headed that way myself. Come on."

He reaches for my hand and makes an abrupt left turn, tugging me down a narrow corridor that I don't think I would have even noticed if he hadn't dragged me into it.

It's long and winding and slopes down so gradually that it takes me a minute to notice we're descending. Flint keeps a firm grip on my hand as we pass a couple of students coming the other way.

The hallway is so narrow that all four of us have to press our backs up against the wall to keep from crashing into one another as we pass.

"How much farther is it?" I ask as we get back to walking normally. Or at least as normally as we can walk as the ceiling starts to get lower as well. If this keeps up, we'll be duck-walking through this thing like they had to do in the pyramids.

"Just another minute to the tunnel entrance and then a five-minute walk to the art studio."

"Okay, cool." I pull out my phone to check how we are on time—seven minutes—and see that Jaxon has texted me twice. The first one is just a string of question marks that I assume is a reminder about my schedule. And the second is the start of a joke:

Jaxon: What did the pirate say when he turned 80?

Oh my God. I've totally created a monster. And I love it.

I text him back a laughing emoji along with a string of question marks of my own. I also text a copy of my schedule—not because he demanded one earlier but because I want to see if he'll follow through and find me again. Once the texts are delivered, I shove my phone back in my pocket and try to tell myself that I don't care that much if he shows up or not. But it's a lie, and I am very well aware of that fact.

The light is getting dimmer and dimmer the farther we go down this corridor, and if I were with anyone but Flint (or Jaxon or Macy), I'd be getting nervous. Not because I think there's anything wrong necessarily, but because I can't help wondering: If the walkway to the tunnels is this creepy, what are the actual tunnels going to look like?

"Okay, here we go," Flint finally says as we come up against an old wooden door—one that's protected by an electronic keypad that has my eyebrows lifting to my hairline. Nothing in my life has ever looked as incongruous as that keypad in the middle of this musty, dusty corridor with a door that looks to be at least a hundred years old.

He punches in a five-digit code so fast that I don't see any number past the first three. It takes a second, but then the light above the door flashes green at the same time as the door unlocks.

Flint glances over his shoulder at me as he reaches to pull open the door. "You ready?"

"Yeah, of course." Another glance at my phone tells me we better hustle or I'm going to be late.

Flint holds the door for me, and I smile my thanks at him, but the second I take a step over the threshold, a little voice deep inside me starts screeching—telling me not to go any farther.

Telling me to run.

Telling me to get the hell away from these tunnels and never look back.

But Flint's waiting for me to go. Plus, if I don't get moving, I'll be seriously late to art. Definitely not the first impression I wanted to make on the teacher of my favorite class.

Besides, this is Flint. The guy who jumped out of a tree and took the brunt of a very nasty fall just to save me. It's ridiculous to think that I might have to run from *him* of all people, no matter what Jaxon says.

Which is why I shove all the new and bizarre misgivings I'm suddenly having back down where they belong. And walk straight across the threshold.

29

With Friends Like These, Everyone Needs Hard Hats

Flint follows me through, then lets the door close behind us with a solid *thump.*

The room is dim, even dimmer than the passageway here, and it takes a minute for my eyes to adjust.

"What is this place?" I demand once they do. "It doesn't look like a tunnel."

In fact, what it looks like is a prison. Or at least the holding area of a jail. There are several cells lining the wall in front of us, each one equipped with a bed—and, more importantly, two sets of shackles. Castle or not, Alaska or not, I am *not* okay with what I'm seeing. At all.

"I think we should go back," I tell him, pulling at the door handle, to no avail. "How do I get this door open?" There's no keypad on this side, nothing I can see that will get us out of here.

"You have to open it from the other side of this room," Flint tells me, looking amused. "Don't worry. We'll be through here in a second."

"I thought we were going to the tunnels. I've got to get to art, Flint."

"This *is* the way to the tunnels. Chill, Grace."

"What tunnels? This is a dungeon!" Alarm is racing through me at this point, my brain warning me that I don't know this guy that well. That anything could happen down here. That— I take a deep breath, try to shut down the panic tearing through me.

"Trust me." He puts a hand on my lower back, starts guiding me forward. I don't want to go, but at this point, it's not exactly like I've got a dozen alternatives. I can pound on the door, hoping that someone hears me, or I can trust Flint to do what he says and get me to the tunnel I need. Considering he's been nothing but kind to me since I got here, I let him propel me forward and pray I'm not making a mistake.

We walk all the way to the end of the room, past four separate cells, and I don't say a word of complaint. But when Flint stops in front of the fifth cell and tries to get me to go in, my trust and patience come to an abrupt end.

"What are you doing?" I demand. Or screech, depending on your point of view. "I'm not going in there."

He looks at me like I'm being completely irrational. "It's where the entrance to the tunnels is."

"I don't see an entrance," I snap at him. "All I see are bars. And shackles."

"It's not what it looks like, I swear. These are secret tunnels, and when they built the castle a hundred years ago, they did a really good job of disguising the entrance."

"A little too good a job, in my opinion. I want to go back up, Flint. I'll make up some excuse for my art teacher for being late, but I—"

"It's okay." For the first time, he looks concerned. "We use these tunnels all the time. I promise I won't let anything happen to you."

"Yeah, but—" I break off as the door at the other end of the room opens. And in walks Lia.

"Hey, hold the door!" I call to her, slipping out of Flint's loose hold and making a mad dash back toward the only obvious exit point in this hellhole of a room.

But she obviously doesn't hear me. The door slams shut behind her. Damn it.

"Grace!" She looks surprised to see me as she fishes a pair of earbuds out of her ears. "What are you doing here?"

"I'm taking her to the tunnels." Flint shoots me an exasperated look as he catches up to me. "She's got art."

"Oh yeah? With Kaufman?" Lia looks interested.

"Yeah."

"Cool. Me too." She gives Flint a cool glance. "I'll take it from here."

"No need for that," he answers. "I'm going that way, too."

"You don't have to bother."

"No bother. Right, Grace?" He grins at me, but this time he sure seems to be showing a lot of teeth.

Then again, who can blame him? He was trying to help me, and I freaked out on him for no reason. "If you're sure."

"Oh, I'm sure." He loops an arm through mine. "I would love to escort you ladies to class."

"Lucky us." Lia's own smile is saccharin sweet as she takes hold of my other arm and starts to walk us back toward the end of the room. As we move—both of them holding on to me—I can't help but feel a little like a ping-pong ball caught between them.

Lia doesn't let go until we reach the final cell. She marches inside and grabs hold of one of the arm shackles—exactly as Flint was aiming to do when I freaked out—and then pulls, hard.

The portion of the stone wall the shackles are attached to opens wide. She glances back at us, eyebrows raised. "Ready?"

Flint looks at me, tilts his head questioningly.

I feel myself blushing yet again, this time out of shame.

"Sorry. I freaked out when I shouldn't have."

He shrugs. "No worries. I guess I come down here so often, I forget how creepy it looks."

"*So* creepy," I tell him as we move into the cell. "And when you reached for that shackle—"

He laughs. "You didn't really think I was going to chain you up down here, did you?"

"Of course she did," Lia tells him as we walk through the trick door and she pulls it closed behind us. "I wouldn't trust you, either. You look like exactly the kind of pervert she should never be alone with."

"And what kind of pervert is that exactly?" he demands, glancing between the two of us.

Suddenly, I remember what Macy said about Jaxon when she was trying to warn me off him, and I can't resist. "You know, the kind who starves a girl so he can make a dress out of her skin."

They both stare at me like I've lost my mind completely. Lia looks taken aback but amused, and Flint...Flint looks more offended than anyone *ever*. It's totally inappropriate, but I can't help laughing. Because, come on. Who hasn't seen that movie—or at least heard of it?

"Excuse me?" he says after a second, more ice in those words than in the entire school grounds outside.

"From *Silence of the Lambs*? That's what the serial killer Jodie Foster is trying to catch does to his victims. It's why she needs Hannibal Lecter."

"Never saw the movie."

"Oh, well, he would kidnap girls and—"

"Yeah, I got it." He lets go of my arm for the first time since Lia showed up. "For the record, clothes made of skin, not so much my style."

"Obviously. That's why I made the joke." When he doesn't

respond, I bump my shoulder against his. "Come on, Flint. Don't be mad. I was just playing."

"Don't waste your breath," Lia tells me as we make our way farther into the tunnels. "He's a total drag—"

"Bite me," Flint growls.

She eyes him scornfully. "You wish."

"I wish you'd try." He returns her look with interest.

Wow, this devolved quickly.

"Don't we need to get to class?" I ask, determined to interrupt whatever this is before it gets even worse. "The bell's going to ring in a minute."

"Don't worry about it," Lia tells me. "Kaufman knows it's a pain to get to her class, so she doesn't sweat it."

But she does pick up the pace—after giving Flint one last look that's a cross between a snarl and a smirk.

I follow her, leaving Flint to bring up the rear, as I figure we'll all do better with me as a buffer between them. For the first time since last night, when Macy tried to explain that I can't be friends with both Jaxon *and* Flint, I actually start to believe her. Lia's obviously Team Jaxon despite whatever I witnessed between them the other day, and look how well this little excursion is going.

We're moving fast through the tunnels now, so I don't get to check them out the way I really want to. Still, the recessed lighting, dim as it might be, gives me at least a decent view of where I'm walking. And I have to say, terrifying entrance notwithstanding, these things are freaking *cool.*

The walls are made entirely of different-colored stones—mostly white and black, but there are colored stones, too. They gleam red and blue and green even in the faint light, and I can't help reaching out to touch one of the bigger ones, just to see what it feels like. Cool, obviously, but also smooth, polished, like a gemstone. For a second, I wonder if that's what they are.

But then I dismiss it as ridiculous, because what school (even a fancy, rich one like Katmere Academy) has the money to embed gemstones in the walls?

The floor is made of white brick, as are a bunch of the columns we pass as we walk. But what really gets me is the art that is down here—bone-like sculptures embedded in the walls, hanging from the ceiling, even resting on pedestals in various alcoves along the way.

It's an obvious homage to the Paris catacombs, where seven million skeletons are laid to rest—or used for macabre decorations throughout. And I can't help wondering if the school's art classes added the "bone" sculptures to the tunnels here. I also want to know what art supplies the bones are really made of.

But trying to figure that out has to wait, too, if I have any hope of making it to art class even close to on time.

As we follow the tunnel, we get to a kind of rotunda-type room that pretty much has my eyes bugging out of my head. It's obviously a main hub for the tunnels, because eleven other tunnels feed into it as well. But that's not what has my eyes going wide, even though I have no idea which of the other tunnels we should take.

No, what has my mouth falling open and my eyes pretty much bugging out of my head is the giant chandelier hanging in the center of the room, unlit candles at the end of each arm. But it's not the size of the chandelier or the fact that there are actual candles in it that catches my attention (although, fire code, anyone?). It's the fact that the chandelier, like so many of the other decorations down here, looks to be made entirely of human bones.

I know it's just art, and the bones are made of plastic or whatever, but they sure look realistic hanging off the chandelier—so much so that a chill creeps down my spine. This is more than an homage to the catacombs. It's like someone actually tried to re-create them.

"Why are you stopping?" Flint asks, following my gaze.

"This is bizarre. You know that, right?"

He grins. "A little bit. But it's also cool, isn't it?"

"Totally cool." I step farther into the room to get a better look. "I wonder how long it took. I mean, it had to be a class art project, right? Not just one student."

"Art project?" Flint looks confused.

"We don't know," Lia interjects. "It was done years before we got here—years before your uncle or any of the other current teachers got here, too. But yeah, it had to be a class project. No way one artist could do all this in a semester or even a year."

"It's amazing. I mean, so elaborate and lifelike. Or…you know what I mean."

She nods. "Yeah."

There are more bones above each of the tunnels, as well as plaques bearing inscriptions in a language I don't recognize. One of the Alaskan languages, I'm sure, but I want to know which one. So I take out my phone and snap a pic of the closest plaque, figuring I'll google it along with the cottage names.

"We need to go," Flint says as I start to take a second pic. "Class is starting."

"Oh, right. Sorry." I glance around as I shove my phone back in my blazer pocket. "Which tunnel are we taking?"

"The third one to the left," Lia says.

We head that way, but just as we're about to reach it, a low-grade tremor rips through the room. At first, I think I'm imagining it, but as the bones in the chandelier start to clink together in the eeriest sound imaginable, I realize there's nothing imaginary about it.

We're standing in the middle of a musty, crumbling old tunnel just as the earth begins to shake for real this time.

30

You Make the Earth Shake Under My Feet... and Everywhere Else, Too

Lia's eyes go wide as the chandelier sways above us. "We need to get out of this room."

"We need to get out of these tunnels!" I answer. "How sturdy do you think they are?"

"They won't collapse," she assures me, but she starts moving toward the tunnel that's supposed to lead to the art studio pretty damn quickly.

Not that I blame her—Flint and I are moving fast, too.

It's not a big earthquake, at least not the kind that Alaska is known for. But it's not like the small tremors that I've felt since coming here, either. Based on what I've experienced back home, this one is an easy seven on the Richter scale.

Lia and Flint must realize that at the same time I do, because once we hit the new tunnel, our fast walk becomes a run.

"How far to the exit?" I demand. My phone is vibrating in my pocket, a series of texts coming in fast and furious. I ignore them as the ground continues to move.

"Maybe another couple hundred yards," Flint tells me.

"Are we going to make it?"

"Absolutely. We—" He breaks off as a loud rumbling sound

comes from the ground, followed closely by a violent shift that turns the quake from rolling to shaking.

My legs turn to rubber, and I start to stumble. Flint grabs me above the elbow to steady me, then uses his grip to propel me through the tunnel so fast that I'm not sure my feet are even touching the ground anymore. Unlike on the stairs a few days ago, this time I'm not complaining.

Lia's in front of us, running even more quickly, though I don't know how that's possible, considering just how fast Flint has us moving.

Finally, the ground starts to slant upward, and relief sweeps through me. We're almost there, almost out of this place, and so far the tunnels have held. Twenty more seconds and a door looms ahead of us. Unlike the one we originally came through, this one is covered in drawings of dragons and wolves and witches and what I'm pretty sure is a vampire on a snowboard.

It's all done graffiti-style, using every color imaginable. And it is totally badass. Another day—when the earth isn't literally moving under my feet—I'll stop to admire the artwork. For now, I wait for Lia to punch in the code—59678 (I watch carefully this time)—and then the three of us burst through the door and into what is obviously a very large art supply closet.

The earthquake stops just as the door closes behind us. I exhale in relief as Flint drops my arm, then bend over and try to catch my breath. He might have been doing most of the work to get us here, but I was moving my legs as fast as I could.

Several seconds pass before I can breathe without feeling like my lungs are going to explode. When I can, I stand back up—and notice a few things all at the same time. One, this closet is really well stocked. Two, the door into the art classroom is wide open. And three, Jaxon is standing in the doorway, face wiped completely blank of expression.

My stomach drops at my first glimpse of his clenched fists and the wild fury burning in the depths of his eyes—not because I'm afraid but because it's obvious that he was.

For long seconds, no one says or does anything, except for Lia, who glances between Jaxon and me with a look that seems just a little bit sly. Then she tells him, "Don't worry, Jaxon darling; *I'm* fine." She pats him on his unscarred cheek as she walks right by him into the art classroom and closes the door behind her.

He doesn't even glance her way. His eyes, flat and black, are pinned to Flint. Who rolls his own eyes as he says, "They're both fine. You're welcome."

For long seconds, Jaxon doesn't respond. He doesn't even make a sound. But it turns out I only *thought* Jaxon was pissed before. Because after Flint's comment, he looks like he's one very small step away from an aneurysm. Or mass murder.

"Get out of here," he growls.

"I wasn't planning on sticking around." Flint doesn't move, though. Instead, he stays in front of me, staring Jaxon down.

And that's it. That's just it. "Move," I order, and when Flint doesn't move fast enough, I shove past him.

For a second, it looks like he's going to stop me, but a low snarl from Jaxon has him stepping back. Which only pisses me off more. I get that he was afraid for me, but that doesn't give him the right to act like a psychopath.

"Are you really okay?" Jaxon demands as I step forward.

"I'm fine." I try to shove past him, too, but unlike Flint, Jaxon doesn't move. He just stands there, in my way, eyes dark and still filled with anger...and something I can't quite put my finger on as he stares down at me. Whatever it is, it makes me feel all fizzy inside, like a carbonated drink that's been shaken way too much. Or it would if I let it. Right now, I'm too busy concentrating on the anger to get sidetracked by the rest of it.

"I tell you to stay away from Flint, so you go into the *tunnels* with him?" he demands.

It's the way wrong thing to say to me right now, when adrenaline is still coursing through me from the quake. And the run. And the terror. But just because I was scared out of my mind a few minutes ago doesn't mean I'm going to put up with Jaxon demanding anything from me. Any more than I'm going to put up with him telling me what to do.

"I'm not talking to you about this right now," I answer. "I'm late for a class that I really didn't want to be late for, and the last thing I have time for is all this bizarre posturing from the two of you." I include Flint in my anger.

"There's no posturing, Grace." Jaxon reaches for me, but I yank my hand away before he can take hold of it.

"Whatever you want to call it. It's boring and annoying and I'm over it. So get out of my way and let me go to class before I forget I'm a pacifist and punch you in the face."

I'm not sure which word shocks him more—the "punch" or the "pacifist." Before either of us can figure it out, though, Flint jumps in with a, "You go, Grace. Tell him to back the fuck off."

This time, Jaxon's snarl is terrifying as fuck. It's also loud enough to have the class on the other side of this closet going completely silent—even the teacher. Which, terrific. Just freaking terrific.

I whirl on Flint. "You shut up, or I'll think of something really terrible to do to you, too." I turn back to Jaxon. "As for you, get the hell out of my way or I'm never talking to you again."

At first, Jaxon doesn't move. But I think that has more to do with complete and utter astonishment (if his face is anything to go by) rather than a deliberate attempt to push back at me.

In the end, though, he lifts his hands and steps out of my

way, exactly as I'd demanded.

"Thank you," I tell him much more quietly. "And I appreciate your concern. I really do. But this is my first day of school, and I just want to go to class."

And then, without waiting for him to answer, I sweep past him and into a classroom where everyone—even Lia and the teacher—is staring at me.

Big. Freaking. Surprise.

31

Big Girls Don't Cry (Unless They Want To)

"Grace! Look out!"

I turn toward my cousin's voice—the first girl to speak to me since I went off on Jaxon and Flint five hours ago—just in time to see a basketball flying toward my head. I swat it away, then press my lips together to keep from crying out as pain radiates up my hand.

It's ridiculous that the act of deflecting a basketball could hurt this much, but whoever threw it threw it hard. My whole arm aches from the jolt of coming into contact with it, and I didn't even know that was possible.

"What the hell?" Macy asks the gym at large as she jogs over to me. "Who threw that?"

No one answers.

"Seriously?" My cousin puts her hands on her hips and glares at a group of girls standing by the locker room door. "Did you do this?"

"Don't worry about it," I tell her. "It doesn't matter."

"Doesn't matter? I heard how hard that ball hit your hand. If it had gotten your head, you could have had a concussion!"

"But it didn't. And I'm fine." It's a bit of a stretch, considering

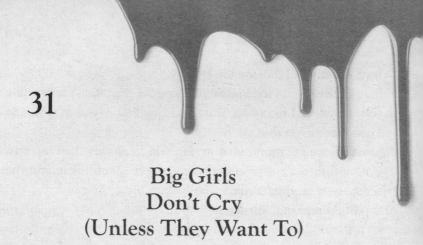

I'm still in pain, but I've made a big enough spectacle of myself today, thank you very much. No way am I going to start whining about a few mean girls.

Or a lot of mean girls, for that matter, one of whom apparently has a future in professional basketball.

I mean, yeah, I'm not denying it's been a weird day. I haven't seen Jaxon or Flint since I went off on them this morning. But even though Jaxon hasn't shown up at any more of my classes, Byron was waiting outside my art class with an extra parka when it let out—so I wouldn't have to go through the spooky-as-hell tunnels again, thank God. Rafael sat with Macy and me at lunch plus walked us to AP Spanish, the one class we share. And Liam walked me from Spanish to PE.

None of which went unnoticed by the other students and none of which has exactly worked in my favor. I mean, I wasn't looking to make a bunch of friends here, but I also don't want to have to dodge flying basketballs every second of the day, either.

"You sure you're okay?" Macy asks, frowning at the way I'm wiggling my fingers and shaking my hand.

I stop immediately. "I'm sure. I'm fine." The last thing I want is for Macy to make a big deal out of something that could have been a lot worse.

She shakes her head but doesn't say anything else about the basketball. And if I catch her glaring at some of my classmates, I'm not going to call her out on it. I'd be pissed if someone was messing with her, too.

Still, it's past time to change the subject, so I ask, "What's all this?" gesturing to the black leotard, tights, and sequined skirt she's wearing.

"Dance team," she answers with a proud little grin. "I've got one of the solos at Friday's pep rally."

"Seriously? That's amazing!" I squeal, even though I've never been a big dance team enthusiast. But Macy obviously loves it, and that's enough for me.

"Yeah. I'm dancing to—" She breaks off as the coach blows a whistle.

"What does that mean?" I ask.

"It means the period's over. And since this is the last one, it also means you're free." Macy grins. "I've got practice for two hours after school, but I'll find you when I'm done, and we can go to dinner together. *If* there's not another earthquake, that is."

"Right?" There have been several more tremors this afternoon—nothing big, just aftershocks, but they've definitely set most of the students, me included, on edge. "Who knew I'd experience more earthquakes in four days at the center of Alaska than I did my whole life living on the coast in California?"

"It's weird," she agrees, looking baffled. "Sure, we have a quake every once in a while, but we haven't had this many in a row in a long time. Maybe ever. You must have brought them with you."

"Sorry about that," I joke. "I'll try to tone it down."

"You do that," she answers with a grin. "See you after practice."

"See you."

I shoot her a little wave before heading back toward the locker room. No one bothers me as I change, but no one talks to me, either. And I gave up trying to talk to people somewhere around lunchtime. I can only take so many cold shoulders before I get the message.

I get dressed in record time, then grab my backpack and head out. I probably should go back to my room and get started on my homework, but I'm not used to being cooped up in one room all the time.

Back home, I was always outside—in the pool, at the beach,

running through the park. I even did my homework on the front porch swing, watching the sun set over the water.

Going from that to being stuck inside almost all the time is more than a little rough.

I think about heading to my room and changing into all those outdoor clothes so I can go for a walk. But nothing about me is particularly thrilled at the idea of putting on half my closet just to brave the subfreezing temperatures, either, so in the end, I decide on a compromise. I'll wander around the castle, getting to know it better, since there are huge portions I haven't set foot in yet, even with my classes taking me all over the place today.

For a second, Jaxon's warning from the first night flits through my head, but that was for late at night. Just because the sun outside the castle has been down for a couple of hours already doesn't mean the halls aren't safe now, while everyone is awake and going from one activity to another. Also, I'm not going to spend the next year and a half afraid of the people I go to school with. Those guys the other night were assholes, no doubt about it, but they caught me unprepared. No way am I going to let it happen again. And no way am I going to become a prisoner in my own school.

Thoughts of Jaxon have me pulling out my phone and opening my message app. There are six text messages waiting for me from Jaxon—all sent during the earthquake. I haven't opened them yet because at first I was too mad to want to know what he had to say. Then I didn't want to be around anyone when I opened them. I tend to wear my emotions on my sleeve, and the last thing I want is for someone watching me to see how I feel about Jaxon—especially when I currently have no idea what, if anything, is going to happen between us.

The first message came in a few minutes after Brit Lit got out.

Jaxon: Hey, thought I'd catch you at art, but you aren't here.

Are you lost? ;)

A few more minutes had passed before the second message came in.

Jaxon: Need a search and rescue? o_O

The third message came in pretty fast after the second one, followed in quick succession by the next three.

Jaxon: Sorry to bug you, just want to make sure you aren't in any trouble. Quinn and Marc aren't bothering you, are they?

Jaxon: Hey, you okay?

Jaxon: Getting worried over here. Just looking for a heads-up that those jerks haven't found you again. You good?

Jaxon: Grace?

I remember the messages coming in during the earthquake and not paying any attention to them. But now that I've read them, I feel like a total jerk. Not for not answering them right away, because—earthquake!

And yeah, I definitely don't have to answer him just because he wants me to. But I do feel guilty for laying into him the way I did in the art studio when he was obviously just worried about me. And for not answering him for so long when he actually apologized in his texts—something—like please—I'm pretty sure the great Jaxon Vega almost never does.

All I was thinking about in that art closet was how embarrassed I was that he was there, arguing with Flint and making a spectacle of me. I didn't think about the fact that he was there because he was concerned about me and that the fight with Flint happened because he was so on edge.

In my old school, it would be absurd, and probably even a little freaky, to have a guy get so worried about me. But I can't really blame Jaxon for being legitimately concerned, not when he's already had to rescue me twice. And not when his last texts came in the middle of a freaking earthquake, which got people so worked up that every teacher I had for the rest of the day took ten minutes out of class time to go over earthquake safety.

If everyone else is freaked out by the quake, it's hard to be upset at Jaxon for feeling the same way.

Because I feel bad for making him wait so long for a response, I fire off a couple of texts in quick succession.

Me: Sorry, been busy and haven't checked my phone

Me: You busy? Want to explore the castle with me?

Me: And hey, you never told me the punch line to the joke

When he doesn't answer right away, I shove my phone in my blazer pocket and wander into one of the side hallways with no real destination in mind for my exploration.

I pass a room where two people are fencing, complete with white uniforms and head masks, and pause to watch for a little while. Then I wander down to the music hall, where a curly-haired boy is playing the saxophone. I recognize the tune as "Autumn Leaves," and just the sound of it nearly brings me to my knees.

Cannonball Adderley cut an album in 1958 called *Somethin' Else*. Miles Davis and Art Blakey played on it, and it was my father's favorite—especially the song "Autumn Leaves." He used to play it over and over when he was working around the house, and he made me listen to it with him at least a hundred times, where he described every single note, explaining over and over how and why Adderley was such a genius.

The last month since my parents died is probably the longest I've gone without hearing that song in my entire life, and to run across it here, now, feels like a sign. Not to mention a punch to the gut.

Tears flood my eyes, and all I can think about is getting away. I turn and run, not caring where I'm going, knowing only that I need to escape.

I take the back stairs and climb up and up and up, until I arrive at the highest tower. Most of it is taken up by whatever room lies behind the closed door, but there's a tiny alcove right off the stairs with a huge window—the first one in the castle that I've actually seen with the curtains open—that looks out over the front of the school. It's dark out right now, but the view is still gorgeous: the snow lit up by lampposts and the midnight-blue sky filled with stars as far as the eye can see.

The room itself has built-in bookshelves that go all the way around it and a couple of comfy, overstuffed chairs to lounge in. It's obviously a reading nook—everything from the classics to modern-day Stephen King fill up the shelves—but I'm not here to read, no matter how much I usually love it.

Instead, I sink down on one of the chairs and finally, finally let the tears come.

There are a lot of them—I haven't cried, really cried, since the funeral, and now that I've started, I'm not sure I'll ever stop. Grief is a wild thing within me, a rabid animal tearing at my insides and making everything hurt.

I'm trying to be quiet—the last thing I want is to draw more attention to myself—but it's hard when it hurts this much. In self-defense, I wrap my arms around myself and start to rock, desperate to ease the pain. Even more desperate to find a way to hold myself together when everything inside me feels like it's falling apart.

It doesn't work. Nothing does, and the tears just keep coming, as do the harsh, wrenching sobs tearing from my chest.

I don't know how long I stay here, battling the pain and loneliness that comes from losing my parents in the blink of an eye and then everything familiar in my life less than a month later, but it's long enough for the sky to turn from the dark blue of civil twilight to pitch black.

Long enough for my chest to hurt.

More than long enough for the tears to run dry.

Somehow, running out of tears only makes everything hurt worse.

But sitting here isn't going to change that. Nothing is, which means I might as well get up. Macy should be done with dance practice soon, and the last thing I want is for her to come looking for me.

Having her see me like this—having *anyone* see me like this—is the threat that finally galvanizes me. Except that when I climb to my feet and turn around, it's to find that someone already has.

Jaxon.

32

It's Not a Coincidence that Denali and Denial Use All the Same Letters

Jaxon's standing at the head of the stairs, face blank but eyes searching as he stares at me.

Embarrassment slams through me, makes my face hot and my breath stutter. I start to ask him how long he's been there, but it doesn't really matter. He's been there long enough.

I wait for him to say something, to ask if I'm okay again or to tell me to stop whining or to say one of the million and three things that fall somewhere in between those two reactions.

He doesn't, though.

Instead, he just stands there, watching me with those black-magic eyes of his until I lose my breath again…this time for a whole different reason.

"I-I'm sorry," I finally stumble out. "I should go."

He doesn't respond, so I move toward the stairs, but he keeps blocking them. And keeps watching me, head tilted just a little, like he's trying to figure something out while I pray for the ground to open up and swallow me.

Now would be a perfect time for another one of those earthquakes, is all I'm saying.

When he finally speaks, his voice sounds a little rusty. "Why?"

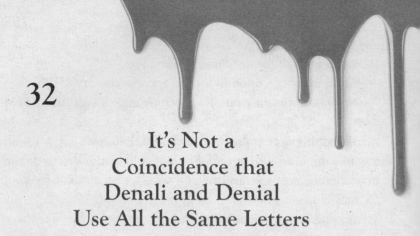

"Why should I leave? Or why was I crying?"

"Neither."

"I...have no idea what I'm supposed to say to that." I blow out a long breath. "Look, I'm sorry I threatened to hit you in the art studio today. You're just...a lot sometimes."

He lifts a brow, but other than that, his blank expression doesn't change. "So are you."

"Yeah." I give a watery laugh, gesture to my still-wet cheeks. "Yeah, I can see why you might think that."

I'm only a few steps from him, but he closes the gap, moving in until he's only inches away from me. My mouth goes desert dry.

I wait for him to say something, but he doesn't. I wait for him to touch me, but he doesn't do that, either. Instead, he just stands there, so close that I can feel his breath on my cheek. So close that I'm sure he can feel my breath on his.

And still his eyes are dark, empty, blank.

More seconds that feel like minutes tick by until finally, *finally* he whispers, "What's it like?"

"What's what like?" I'm baffled, and a little afraid that I'm setting myself up to be the punch line of some joke.

"What's it like to just be able to let go like that?"

"Like what? My crying jag?" Embarrassment swamps me again, and I wipe at my cheeks, trying to disappear even the remnants of my tears. "I'm sorry. I didn't mean for anyone to see me. I—"

"Not just that. I mean, what's it like to be able to show what you feel and how you feel, whenever you want, without having to worry about..." He trails off.

"What?" I ask. "Without having to worry about what?"

For long seconds, he just looks at me. Then he kind of shakes his head and says, "Never mind." He walks past me, opens the door to the room that lays just beyond the alcove, and walks inside.

I stare after him, not sure what I'm supposed to do. It feels like our conversation is over, like he just dismissed me, but he left his door open in what looks like an invitation.

I stand there for another minute or so, undecided, before he finally sticks his head back out the door. "Coming?" he asks.

I follow him inside—of course I do. But I'm completely unprepared for what I find when I walk into the room, a room I can't help thinking of as my own private wonderland.

Books are everywhere, stacked haphazardly on nearly every available surface.

There are three guitars in the corner, along with a drum kit that has my mouth watering and my fingers itching to touch it. To play it, like I used to play mine back when I still had one.

Back when I still had a lot of things.

In the center of the room is a giant black leather couch, covered with piles of thick, soft pillows that all but beg to be napped on.

I want to touch everything, want to run my hands over the drum kit just so I can feel its soul. I have just enough self-control left not to follow my impulses, but it's hard. So hard that I can't help but tuck my hands in my blazer pockets, just to be on the safe side.

Because I've only just now realized that this is Jaxon's dorm room, and to say it's unexpected is pretty much the understatement of the century.

Jaxon seems completely uninterested in his surroundings, which seems bizarre to me even though I know it's because this is his stuff. He sees and touches and uses it every day. But there's a part of me that still wants to know how he can just ignore the pile of art books by the couch or the giant purple crystal on his desk. It's the same part of me all but screaming that, no matter what Jaxon thinks, I'm nowhere near cool enough to be in here with him.

Since he's not talking, I turn to look at the art on the wall, big, wild paintings with bold colors and strokes that excite all kinds of ideas inside me. And hanging next to his desk—even more unbelievably—is a small pencil sketch of a woman with wild hair and sly eyes, dressed in a voluminous kimono.

I recognize it, or at least I think I do, so I walk closer, trying to get a better look. And sure enough—

"This is a Klimt!" I tell him.

"Yes," he affirms.

"That wasn't a question." It's under glass, so I reach out and tap the artist's signature in the bottom right corner. "This is an original Klimt, not a reproduction."

This time he doesn't say anything, not even *yes*.

"So you're just going to stand there with your hands in your pockets?" I demand. "You're not even going to answer me?"

"You just told me you weren't asking questions."

"I'm not. But that doesn't mean I don't want to hear the story."

He shrugs. "There's no story."

"You have an original Klimt hanging next to your desk. Believe me, there's a story there." My hands are shaking as I trace the lines through the glass once again. I've never been this close to one of his pieces before.

"I liked it. It reminded me of someone. I bought it."

"That's it? That's your story?" I stare at him incredulously.

"I told you there wasn't a story. You insisted there was." He cocks his head to the side, watches me through narrowed eyes. "Did you want me to lie?"

"I want you to…" I shake my head, blow out another long breath. "I don't know what I want you to do."

At that, he lets out a small laugh—the very first sign of emotion he's shown since that one frantic *are you okay* in the art room. "I know the feeling."

He's halfway across the room, and there's a part of me that wishes he were closer. That wishes we were touching right now.

Of course, there's another part of me that's still terrified of touching him, even more terrified of having him touch me. Being in his room is too much. Looking at him worry his lower lip in the first show of nerves I've ever seen from him is too much.

Being touched by him, held by him, kissed by him, would be so, so, *so* too much that I'm afraid I'll implode at the first brush of his lips against mine. Afraid I'll just burn up where I'm standing. No warning, no chance to stop it. Just a brush of his hand against mine and poof, I'm a goner. I swear it almost happened when he carried me back to my room the other night, and that was before he sent me waffles and walked me to class and charmed me with his text messages. Way before I saw this place.

I wonder if he's afraid of the same thing, because instead of answering, he turns around and enters what I assume is his bedroom. At least until he realizes I'm still staring at the Klimt—and every other fabulous thing in the room—to be following him.

He kind of rolls his eyes, but then he comes back and gently herds me toward his bedroom, all without laying a finger on me.

"Come on. There's something I want you to see."

I follow him without question. With Flint earlier, I had moments of concern, of worry that it wasn't safe to be alone with him. Everything inside me warns that Jaxon is a million times more dangerous than Flint, and still I have not an ounce of trepidation when it comes to being alone in his bedroom with him. When it comes to being anywhere, or doing anything, with him.

I don't know if that makes me foolish or a good judge of character. Not that it really matters, because it is what it is.

Jaxon stops near the edge of his bed and picks up the heavy

red blanket folded across the edge of it. Then he reaches into his top dresser drawer and pulls out a pair of faux fur–lined gloves and tosses them to me. "Put those on and come on."

"Come on where?" I ask, baffled. But I do as he asks and slide my hands into the gloves.

He opens the window, and frigid air rushes in.

"You can't be serious. No way am I going out there. I'll freeze."

He looks over his shoulder at me and winks. He *winks*.

"What was that?" I demand. "Since when do you wink?"

He doesn't answer beyond a quick twist of his lips. And then climbs out the window and drops three feet onto the parapet just below the tower.

I should ignore him, should simply turn around and walk out of this room, away from any boy who thinks I'm dumb enough to hang out on an Alaskan roof in November with nothing more than a blazer to keep me warm. That's what I *should* do.

Of course, just because I should do it doesn't mean I will.

Because, apparently, when I'm with this boy, I lose all common sense. And part of losing that common sense means doing exactly what I shouldn't—in this case, following Jaxon straight out the window and onto the parapet.

33

Madonna's Not the Only One with a Lucky Star

The second I drop down beside him—or should I say the second he helps me down, being super careful of my still tender ankle—Jaxon wraps the blanket around me, head and all, so that only my eyes stick out. And I have to say, I'm not sure what the blanket is made of, but the moment it's wrapped around me, I stop shivering. I'm not exactly warm, but I'm definitely not going to be dying of hypothermia anytime soon, either.

"What about you?" I ask when I realize he's wearing only his hoodie. It's a heavy hoodie, the same one he was wearing when I saw him outside yesterday with Lia, but still, nowhere near enough protection for the weather. "We can share the blanket."

I break off when he laughs. "I'm fine. You don't need to worry about me."

"Of course I'm going to worry about you. The weather is frigid."

He shrugs. "I'm used to it."

"That's it. I have to ask."

Everything about him turns wary. "Ask what?"

"Are you an alien?"

Both his brows go up this time, all the way to his hairline.

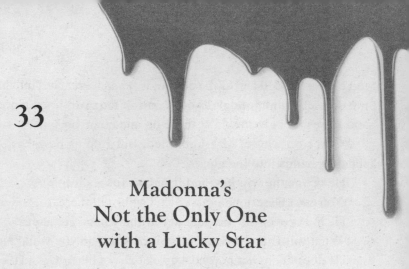

"Excuse me?"

"Are. You. An. Alien? I can't believe it's that shocking of a question. I mean, look at you." I wave an arm up and down under the blanket, my way of encompassing everything that is Jaxon in one fell swoop.

"I can't look at myself." For the first time, he sounds amused.

"You know what I mean."

"I really don't." He leans down so there's only a couple of inches separating our faces. "You're going to have to explain it to me."

"Like you don't already know you're pretty much the hottest person alive."

He rears back like I've struck him, and I don't think he even realizes that he touches his scar as he says, "Yeah, right."

Which…come on. "You have to know that scar makes you sexy as hell, right?"

"No." It's a short answer. Simple. Succinct, even. And yet it reveals so much more than he'd ever want anyone to see.

"Well, it does. Sexy. As. Hell," I repeat. "Plus, there's the way everyone pretty much kisses your ass *all* the time."

"Not everyone." He gives me a pointed look.

"*Almost* everyone. And you never get cold."

"I get cold." He burrows a hand inside the blanket, presses his fingers to my arm. And he's right; he is cold. But he's also nowhere close to being frostbitten, which is what I would be if I'd stood out here this long in just a hoodie.

I give him a look and try to pretend that, despite the chill, his hand on my arm doesn't flood every cell of my body with heat. "You know what I mean."

"So let me get this straight. Because I: one, am the hottest person alive"—he smirks as he says it—"two, make everyone genuflect, and three, don't get cold very often, you've decided

I'm an alien."

"Do you have a better explanation?"

He pauses, considers. "I do, actually."

"And it is *what* exactly?"

"I could tell you…"

"But then you'd have to kill me?" I roll my eyes. "Seriously? We've reverted to tired old *Top Gun* lines?"

"That's not what I was going to say."

"Oh yeah?" It's my turn to cock my head to the side. "So what were you going to say?"

"*I* was going to say, 'You can't handle the truth.'"

He totally deadpans it, but I burst out laughing anyway. Because how can I not when he's quoting *A Few Good Men* to me? "So you're an old-movie buff? Or just an old-Tom Cruise-movie buff?"

"Ugh." He makes a face. "Definitely not the second. As for old movies, I've seen a few."

"So if I mentioned starving women and making a dress out of their skin, you'd know I meant—"

"Buffalo Bill from *Silence of the Lambs*? Yeah."

I grin at him. "So maybe not an alien after all."

"*Definitely* not an alien."

Silence stretches between us for a while. It's not awkward. In fact, it's kind of nice to just be able to *be* for a little while. But eventually the cold works its way through his magic blanket. I pull it more closely around myself and ask, "Are you going to tell me what we're doing out here?"

"I told you I was going to show you my favorite place today."

"*This* is your favorite place?" I look around with new eyes, determined to figure out what he likes about it.

"I can see for miles up here, and no one ever bothers me. Plus…" He glances at his phone, then very deliberately looks up at the sky. "You'll figure it out in about three minutes."

"Is it the aurora borealis?" I ask, trepidation replaced instantly by excitement. "I've been dying to see it."

"Sorry. You've got to be up in the middle of the night to get a look at the northern lights."

"So then what—?" I break off as what appears to be a giant fireball streaks its way across the sky. Seconds later, another one follows it.

"What's going on?" I wonder aloud.

"A meteor shower. We don't get many up here because they tend to take place in the summer, when we've got daylight most of the time and can't see them. But when we do have one in the winter, it's pretty spectacular."

I gasp as another three meteors fly by, leaving long, glowing tails in their wake. "That's an understatement. This is incredible."

"I thought you might like it."

"I do. I really do." I glance at him, suddenly shy, though I don't know why. "Thank you."

He doesn't answer, but then I'm not expecting him to.

We stand out on the parapet for a good half an hour, not talking, not even looking at each other much, just watching the most brilliant show I've ever seen light up the sky. And I love every second of it.

It's weird, but something about being out here, looking at the vast night sky overlooking the vast, snowy mountains…it puts things in perspective. Reminds me of how tiny I really am in the grand scheme of things, of how fleeting my problems and my grief are, no matter how painful and all-encompassing they feel right now.

Maybe that's what Jaxon intended when he brought me out here.

When the shower ends, it comes with a burst of seven or eight comets in a row. I can't help oohing and aahing as they burn their way across the sky. When it's over, I expect to feel let down—like what happens at the end of a really good movie or fireworks show. That little pang of disappointment that something so wonderful is over forever.

But with the meteor shower, I feel…as close to peaceful as I have in a very long time.

"We should go in," Jaxon says eventually. "It's getting colder."

"I'm okay. I just want another minute or two, if that's all right."

He inclines his head in an *of course* kind of gesture.

There's so much I want to say to him, so many things he's done for me in the very short time we've known each other. But whenever I try to come up with the words, they don't sound right in my head. So eventually, I settle for "Thank you."

He laughs, but it's a sound completely devoid of humor. I don't understand why until I look in his eyes and realize they are completely blank again. I don't like it at all.

"Why do you laugh when I thank you?" I demand.

"Because you don't ever have to thank me, Grace."

"Why not? You did something really nice for me—"

"No I didn't."

"Um, yeah you did." Under the blanket, I hold my arms out in the universal gesture of look-at-all-this. "Why don't you just admit it? Take the compliment and move on."

"Because I don't deserve the compliment." The words seems to burst straight out of him without his permission, and now that they're hanging there, he looks a little sick. "I'm just doing my…"

"Your what? Your *job*?" I ask, my stomach clenching at the thought. "Did my uncle ask you to be nice to me or something?"

He laughs, but there's still no amusement in the sound. No joy. Just a soul-deep cynicism that has my eyes watering all over again but for very different reasons. "I'm the last person Foster would ever ask to be friends with you."

If I were more polite and less concerned about him, I'd be inclined to drop the subject entirely. But politeness has never been one of my virtues—I've got too much curiosity for that—so instead, I call him on his shit. "And why is that exactly?"

"It means I'm not a nice person. I don't do *nice* things. Ever. So it's ridiculous to compliment me on your perception of what I do."

"Really?" I shoot him a skeptical look. "Because I hate to be the one to break it to you, but cheering up a sad girl is a *nice* thing to do. So is carrying her back to her dorm when she hurts her ankle and chasing off guys who think pranks that can kill people are funny. So is charming the cook into making an injured girl waffles. All nice things, Jaxon."

For the first time, he looks uncomfortable, but he still won't back down. "I didn't do it for you."

"Oh yeah? Then who did you do it for?"

He doesn't have an answer. Of course he doesn't.

"That's what I thought." I grin up at him, all cocky and obnoxious because, on this, I can be. "Looks to me like you're just going to have to accept the fact that you did something sweet. You won't burn at the stake, I promise."

"They only burn witches."

He sounds so serious that I can't stop myself from laughing. "Well, I'm pretty sure we're safe, then."

"Don't be too sure about that."

I start to ask him what he means, but a violent shiver racks me at the same time—blanket or no blanket, it's freaking cold out here—and Jaxon takes the decision into his own hands. "Come on. Time to get you inside."

Hard to argue when my teeth are about a minute away from chattering. But when I glance up at the window we came out of,

I can't help wondering, "How exactly are we going to get back in? And by we, I mean me." Dropping three feet out of a window is one thing. Boosting myself back up is another thing entirely.

But Jaxon just shakes his head. "Don't worry. I've got you, Grace."

Before I can figure out why those words sizzle through me like a lightning bolt, he's grabbing onto the windowsill and swinging himself inside. The whole move takes about one point four seconds, and I have to admit, I'm impressed. Then again, nearly everything Jaxon does impresses me, whether he means it to or not. *He* impresses me.

More, he makes me feel not so alone at a time when I've never been lonelier.

He's back in moments, poking his head and upper body out of the window. "Give me your hands."

I lift my arms up without a second thought, and he grabs onto my forearms, right below the elbow, and pulls. Seconds later, I'm back through the window and standing an inch, maybe two, from Jaxon.

And for once, his eyes aren't dead. They're on fire.

And they're focused directly. On. Me.

34

All's Fair in Love and Earthquakes

I stare back at him, not sure what to expect…or what to do. There's a part of me that thinks he's going to back up and a part of me that really hopes he doesn't. A part of me that wonders what it would feel like to kiss him and a part of me that thinks I should run for the hills, because Jaxon might not be an alien, but he's not like any boy I've ever met, either. And I am more than honest enough to admit that, much as I may want him, there's no way I can actually handle him.

In the end, he doesn't kiss me. But he doesn't back up, either. And neither do I. So we stand there for I don't know how long, him looking down, me looking up, the air between us loaded, heavy, electric.

I'm in it now, captivated by everything Jaxon is and everything he isn't, despite my misgivings. I wait for him to make a move, but he doesn't. He just keeps looking at me with those midnight eyes of his, emotion he rarely shows seething right below the surface. It makes me ache for him. Makes me physically hurt as I remember the question he asked earlier, the one that started all this.

I finally have the words—or in this case, the word—to answer him. “Overwhelming,” I say just as he starts to slide the blanket from my shoulders.

He freezes, the blanket, and his hands, hovering somewhere around the middle of my back. “What are you talking about?”

“You asked me what it was like to just let go and purge my emotions the way I did. It feels overwhelming sometimes, even a little terrifying. But what you just did for me…made me feel safe in a way I haven’t in quite a while. So thank you. Seriously.”

“Grace…”

I take one step closer, until my breasts are just brushing against his chest. I don’t know what I’m doing here. I’ve never made a move on a guy in my life, and Jaxon isn’t just any guy. I’m flying blind, but that doesn’t matter now. Nothing does except touching him somehow.

I want him to feel the strength of my arms around him, the softness of my body against his. And I want to feel the warm power of him against my own.

Except he’s not warm at all, that hoodie of his obviously no defense against the weather, despite what he said.

“Jaxon, you’re freezing!” I pull the blanket from his hands and throw it around his shoulders before wrapping it all the way around him. Then I rub my hands up and down his blanket-covered arms, trying to chafe some warmth back into him.

“I’m fine,” he says, trying to back away.

“You’re obviously not fine. I’ve never felt anyone as cold as you are right now.”

“I’m fine,” he insists again, and this time he does take a step back. Several steps, in fact.

Everything inside me stops. “I’m sorry. I didn’t mean to invade your personal space…” I break off, because I don’t know what else to say. I don’t know what I’ve done that is so wrong.

“Grace…” His voice trails off, too. And in that moment, he

looks different than all the other times. He isn't confident, isn't amused, isn't even stoically silent as he was when I was yelling at him in the art studio.

No, right now he just looks...vulnerable.

There's a desire in his eyes, a craving that has nothing to do with wanting me and everything to do with needing me. Needing my comfort. Needing my touch.

I can no more deny him than I can jump off this tower and fly under my own power. So I follow his retreat, taking the steps that bring my body back into contact with the hardness of his. Then I cup his face in my hands, stroke my thumbs over his ridiculous cheekbones and my fingers over the jagged edges of his scar.

His breath catches—I hear it in his chest, feel it against me. And though my heart is beating faster than triple time, I don't back away. I can't. I'm dazzled, mesmerized, enthralled.

All I can think about is him.

All I can see is him.

All I can smell and hear and taste is him.

And nothing has ever felt so right.

"Can I ask you a question?" I move even closer to him, unable to stop myself. *Unwilling* to stop myself.

For a second, I think he's going to take a step back, but he doesn't. Instead, he opens up the blanket and wraps it around me, too, so that his arms are around my waist and we're both sheltered within it. "Of course."

"Who did that Klimt sketch remind you of when you bought it?"

"You." The answer comes fast and honest. "I just didn't know it yet."

And just like that I melt. Just like that, this boy—this dark, damaged, devastating boy—touches a part of me I wasn't even sure existed anymore. A part of me that wants to believe. Wants to hope. Wants to love.

I want to reach for him, want to grab on—want to hold on—but I can't. I'm frozen, terrified of wanting too much. Needing too much, in a world where things can just disappear between one moment and the next.

"Grace." He says my name softly, half whisper, half prayer, as he waits patiently for me to look at him.

But I can't. Not now. Not yet. "Have you ever—" My voice breaks and I take a deep breath, blow it slowly out. Take another one, and blow that one out, too. Then try again. "Have you ever wanted something so much that you were afraid to take it?"

"Yes." He nods.

"Like it's right there, waiting for you to just reach out and grab it, but you're so terrified of what will happen when you lose it that you never make the reach?"

"Yes," he says again, his voice low and deep and comforting in a way that burrows inside me.

I tilt my head up until our eyes meet, and then I whisper, "What did you do?"

For long seconds, he doesn't say anything. He doesn't do anything. He just stares back at me with a look in his eyes as scarred and broken as the rest of him. And says, "I decided to take it anyway."

Then he leans down and presses his lips to mine.

It's not a passionate kiss, not a hard kiss, definitely not a wild kiss. It's just the brush of one mouth against another, as soft as a snowflake, as delicate as the permafrost that stretches in all directions.

But for me, at least, it's just as powerful. Maybe more.

And then—suddenly—his hands are on my upper arms, holding me in place. His fingers squeezing tightly, pulling me against him as his mouth goes crazy on mine.

Lips, tongue, teeth, it's a cacophony of sensations—a riot of pleasure, desperation, need all wrapped into one—as he takes me. As he takes and takes and takes…and gives back even more.

It's a good thing he's holding on to me because my head spins and my knees go weak at the first swipe of his tongue along mine—just like one of those heroines from a novel. I've been kissed before. But no kiss ever made me feel like this. I strain against him, try to slide my arms up around his neck, but his hands are vises on my biceps, holding me in place. Holding me still, so that all I can do is take what he gives me.

And he gives a lot, head tilting, mouth moving on mine. My head gets lighter, my knees get weaker, and I swear I feel the ground trembling beneath my feet. And still the kiss goes on.

The trembling gets worse, and it hits me a second before my knees buckle. It's not just our kiss. The earth is actually shaking again.

"Earthquake!" I manage to squeak out, wrenching my mouth from his.

Jaxon doesn't listen at first, just follows my lips with his like he wants to keep on kissing me forever. And I almost let it go, almost melt back into him—I'm a California girl, after all. If it were a bad one, things would already be falling off the walls.

But it must hit Jaxon at the same time I'm about to forget about it, because not only does he let me go, but he's halfway across the room between one breath and the next.

I watch as he clenches his fists by his sides, as he takes a long, slow, deep breath…and then another and another as the earth continues to shake.

"It's okay," I tell him. "It's just a small quake, nowhere near as bad as the one this morning. It'll be over in a second."

"You have to go."

"What?" I couldn't have heard him right. He couldn't have

been kissing me like he wanted to devour me a few seconds ago and now be demanding that I leave in a voice as cold as the air outside. "It's fine."

"It's not fine," he snaps out, and it's the only sign of emotion from him now that his face and eyes are blank again. "You. Need. To. *Go!*"

"Jaxon." I can't stop myself from reaching for him. "Please—"

All of a sudden, his bedroom window shatters, glass flying in all directions. It sounds like an explosion, and I let out a strangled scream as shards of glass hit me above my eyebrow and on my neck, my cheek, my shoulder.

"Go!" Jaxon shouts, and this time there's no defying him. Not when he looks and sounds so out of control.

He advances on me then, fingers flexing and eyes burning like black coals in a face livid with rage.

I turn and run as fast as my weak knees will carry me, determined to get to the staircase, to freedom, before this strange, monstrous version of Jaxon overtakes me.

I don't make it.

35

Baked Alaska Is More than Just a Yummy Dessert

I wake up in my bedroom with bandages on my neck and face and shoulder—and absolutely no memory of how I got here.

Macy is sitting cross-legged on the end of my bed, my uncle is standing by the door, and a woman I assume is the school nurse is hovering over me. With her waist-length black hair, bloodred nails, and stern face, she looks nothing like any nurse I've ever seen, but she's got a stethoscope around her neck and a roll of bandages in her hand.

"See, Finn, here she is. I told you the sedative wouldn't knock her out for long." She smiles at me and, though it is open and inviting, she still manages to look intimidating. I think it's the long, beak-like nose, but it could also be the medicine she said she gave me. I'm awake, but I still feel really fuzzy, like nothing is quite as it appears.

"How are you feeling, Grace?" she asks.

"I'm okay," I answer, because nothing hurts. In fact, everything feels warm and floaty right now.

"Yeah?" She leans over me. "How many fingers am I holding up?"

"Three."

"What day is it?"

"Tuesday."

"Where are you?"

"In Alaska."

"Good enough." She turns to my uncle. "See, I told you she was going to be okay. She lost some blood, but—"

"Jaxon!" The warm, floaty feeling melts away as I struggle to sit up. I don't know how I could have forgotten. "Is he okay? He was..." I stop when I realize I don't have a clue what to say next. Because I don't have a clue what actually happened up in that tower.

I remember Jaxon kissing me...and probably will for the rest of my life.

I remember the earthquake.

I remember running, though I don't know why.

And I remember blood. I know there was blood, but I can't figure out why.

"Don't push so hard," the nurse tells me with a pat to the back of my hand. "It'll come if you don't try to force it."

It doesn't feel like it will come. It feels like everything's a blur, like my synapses just aren't connecting the way they should.

Exactly what kind of sedative did this nurse give me anyway?

"Macy?" I turn to my cousin. "I—"

"Jaxon's fine," she assures me.

"He saved you," my uncle tells me. "He got you to the nurse, Marise, before you could bleed out."

"Bleed out?"

Marise is the one who answers. "When the window shattered, flying glass nicked an artery in your neck. You lost a lot of blood."

"My artery?" My hand flies to my neck as terror sets in for the first time. That's how my mother died. An arterial bleed-out before the ambulance could arrive.

"You're fine," my uncle says, his voice low and soothing. He reaches for my hand, pats it a few times. "Thankfully Jaxon was there. He slowed the bleeding and got you to Marise's office before..."

"Before I died." I say what he won't.

My uncle turns white. "Don't think about that now, Grace. You're fine."

Because Jaxon saved me. Again. "I want to see him."

"Of course," Uncle Finn agrees. "Once you're up and about."

"No, I'd really like to see him now." I start kicking at my covers, which feel like they weigh a thousand pounds. "I need to make sure he's okay. I need..." I trail off. I don't know what I need, except to see Jaxon. To see his face, to touch him, to feel him breathe and know that he's really okay.

And also because I'll go out of my mind if I don't find out how he feels about the kiss we shared. Soon.

"Whoa, now." Marise puts a firm hand on my shoulder and pushes me back down against the bed. "You can see Jaxon tomorrow. For now, you need to stay here and rest."

"I don't want to rest. I want—"

"I know what you want, but that's not possible right now. You're weak." The stern look is back, and it has multiplied times ten. "I don't think you realize how serious this injury is. You need to recuperate."

"I know exactly how serious an arterial bleed is," I insist, my mother's face floating behind my eyes for a few seconds before I manage to blink it away. "I'm not planning on snowboarding down the side of Denali. I just want to see my..."

I break off because I was about to call Jaxon my boyfriend and no, just no. One kiss does not a boyfriend make, even if it was the best kiss of my life. Maybe even the best kiss in the history of the world. I mean, until the glass started flying.

I try to play it off by picking at my comforter, but Macy's wide eyes tell me I'm not doing a very good job of it.

All of a sudden, Marise and Uncle Finn are studying me a lot more closely, too, though neither of them makes a comment about my slipup. Instead, Marise simply pulls my comforter back over me and says, "Behave or I'll give you another sedative. And this time I'll make sure it knocks you out for several hours."

The threat is real—I can see it in her eyes—so I don't push to see Jaxon any more. Instead, I settle back against my pillows and do my best impression of a good little patient.

"I'll behave," I promise. "You don't need to give me a sedative."

"We'll see," she harrumphs. "You need rest, and it's my job to make sure you get it. How that happens is completely up to you."

"He's okay," Macy reassures me when I don't say anything else. "I promise, Grace. He's just busy right now cleaning up the mess in the tower."

Oh, right. Arterial bleeds aren't exactly tidy. "Is it bad?" I know it's ridiculous, but I'm embarrassed that I bled all over Jaxon's tower, that I caused all this fuss for so many people. "Does he need help?"

"I've got it covered," Uncle Finn assures me dryly. "Thankfully the earthquake only caused minimal damage throughout the rest of the castle, so all my people are up in Jaxon's room."

"You're sure?" It's a question for Macy, not Uncle Finn. I don't know why I'm being so insistent, except there's this feeling deep inside me that something isn't quite right. That Jaxon is in trouble somehow. It's probably just the medicine messing with my head, but I can't seem to shake it. I need to know for sure that he's all right.

"I swear, Grace." She reaches over from her spot at the end of the bed and squeezes my hand. "Everything is under control with Jaxon. He's fine, his rooms will be fine soon enough, and no one else was hurt in the earthquake. You can relax."

It's hard to imagine relaxing when fear is still a tight ball in the pit of my stomach. But it's not like I have a choice with everyone hovering over me.

Though it's the last thing I want to do right now, I relax back against my pillows. Maybe if I start being more compliant, Marise and Uncle Finn will leave me alone for a while.

"Are you thirsty, Grace?" Marise asks after a moment. "Do you want some juice?"

For the first time, I realize I *am* thirsty. Like, really, really thirsty. Like, can't remember the last time I needed a drink this badly thirsty. "Yes, please. Or water. Anything would be good."

"Let's start with a little cranapple juice. The sugar will be good for you, and then we'll go from there."

"Why do I need sugar?" I ask, even as I accept the small bottle she hands me. I drink it down in one gulp and pretend I don't see the look she exchanges with Uncle Finn.

"Can I have another?"

"Of course." A second bottle appears in her hand, though I would swear she didn't even turn around. I'm too thirsty to care, though, so I take it with a murmured thank-you. I try to drink it more slowly but end up chugging this one, too.

When I'm finished, Uncle Finn takes the bottle from me. Then he strokes a hand over my hair in that way that always makes me think of my dad and says, "I'm sorry, Grace."

"For what?" I ask, confused by the words and the pained look on his face.

"First the altitude sickness, now an earthquake. I brought you to Alaska because I wanted you to feel safe, wanted to help you find a new home. Instead, you've been miserable since you got here."

"I'm not miserable," I tell him. When it looks like he doesn't believe me, I reach for his hand. "I mean, Alaska is about as different from San Diego as it can get, but that doesn't mean I hate it here. I thought I would, but I don't."

I start out meaning to reassure him, but the more I say, the more I realize I mean every word. Alaska does feel alien, but if I didn't come here, I wouldn't have met Jaxon. I wouldn't have had that incredible kiss. And I wouldn't be living with my cousin, working on a friendship that I'm pretty sure is going to last the rest of our lives.

"Besides, the altitude sickness is gone. And we have earthquakes back home, too, you know." I grin. "It's pretty much the one thing Southern California and Alaska have in common."

"Yeah, but I should have given you more of an introduction to Katmere Academy. I guess I thought ignorance would keep you safe."

"I don't think a tour of the school would have stopped me from getting hurt in an earthquake, Uncle Finn."

He smiles a little sadly. "That's not what I mean."

My radar, fuzzy as it is, goes off again. "What *do* you mean, then?"

"He means that, like any school, it takes a little time to learn the ropes here," Marise interjects, and the look she gives my uncle tells him now is not the time to discuss those ropes. "I'm sure Macy will help you out with a lot of it. Plus, you're a smart girl. I think you'll be fitting in here in no time."

I'm not so sure, but I'm not about to argue with her. Not when doing so will just keep her and my uncle here longer.

Instead, I change the subject, hoping covering the last of my medical stuff will move them along. "What about my other cuts?" My hand goes to my cheek and the bandage there. "Are they bad?"

"No, not at all. They'll be healed in no time, and none of them was deep enough to leave a scar."

"Except on my neck."

"Yes." She sounds reluctant to admit it. "You will have a small scar on your neck."

"Better than the alternative, I guess." I smile at her. "Thanks for taking care of me. I appreciate it."

"Of course, Grace. You're a model patient."

We'll see if she still thinks so after I sneak out of my room tonight to go to Jaxon's. I want to see him, want to make sure he wasn't hurt, too. And I want to know how he feels about our kiss, if he's still thinking about it—or if he's decided I'm just too much trouble.

I also want to know what happened between the glass breaking and me getting to the nurse's office, and he's the only one who can tell me. I hate that I can't remember anything. It makes me feel completely out of control, and I can't stand that feeling. It gets my anxiety up, so much so that I'm sure I'd be on the verge of a panic attack if it weren't for the sedative.

"Is it okay that I'm still so sleepy?" I ask, not because I actually want to take a nap but because I want everyone to stop hovering. Especially my uncle.

"Of course," Marise tells me. "It will probably be tomorrow morning before all the sedation wears off." She turns to my uncle. "Why don't we head out, Finn? Give Grace a chance to rest. I'll come back and check on her before bed and, in the meantime, I'm sure Macy will get us if there's any problem."

"Of course I will." Macy gives her father the most virtuous look I have ever seen on her face or any other. If I weren't so impressed, plus desperate for Uncle Finn to leave, I'd probably burst out laughing.

"How about you?" my uncle asks, stroking a hand over the

top of my head. "You okay with us leaving so you can get some sleep?"

"Of course. It feels rude to sleep while you're here, but I'm just so tired, Uncle Finn." Turns out Macy isn't the only one who can lay it on thick.

"Okay, then. I'll head out. Macy, why don't you come with me? You can grab some food for you and Grace from the dining room before Marise leaves." He looks at me. "You must be hungry."

I am, actually, now that he mentions it. Starved, actually. "I would love something to eat."

"Nothing too heavy," Marise warns. "Some soup and maybe a pudding to start with. If that stays down, we can talk about something a little more substantial."

"Of course." Macy sends me a reassuring look, then loops an arm through her father's. "Come on, Daddy. Let's go get Grace that food before she falls asleep."

My uncle walks out right behind her, and I tell myself I have to remember to do something really nice for Macy to pay her back for her help with him. Doing her laundry for a month, maybe, or cleaning the bathroom the next several times.

After they leave, I'm a little nervous about being left alone with the nurse, but she seems content to let me "doze," and I'm prepared to take full advantage of it. Now that the sedative has worn off some, I feel like I've been run over by a snowplow… twice. I'm sure it's just because of all the blood loss, so I'm not worried. But it still feels gross.

A few minutes go by in silence, but Marise must figure out I'm not actually napping because she asks, "Do you have any more questions about your condition, Grace?"

"No, I'm good," I answer. But then something occurs to me. "Actually, I was wondering how long before you take the stitches out?"

"Stitches?" She seems baffled at the question, which doesn't make any sense at all.

"For the arterial tear? You did stitch it up, right? Or is that just something they do on *Grey's Anatomy*?"

"Oh, right. Of course." Now she just looks uncomfortable. "The stitches I used on the artery will melt away, so no worries there."

"And the ones on the outside? That closed the wound?"

"They'll dissolve, too," she tells me.

Her answer strikes me as odd, but I'm not a nurse, so I'm willing to go with it. At least until she continues. "Keep that cut covered, by the way. Come to me tomorrow and I'll change the dressing for you, but don't uncover it on your own for at least a week."

"A week? What about when I take a shower?"

"I'll give you some waterproof film you can put over the bandage. It will keep it dry, even when you're washing your hair."

Seems like a lot of work for a wound that is supposed to heal normally, but I'm not going to call her on it. At least not yet. Instead, I simply say, "Thanks." And this time when I close my eyes, I actually try to fall asleep.

It doesn't work, though, because no matter how drowsy I am, something just doesn't feel right here, including the fact that a school nurse sewed up my artery...and then seemed shocked at the mere mention of stitches. Where I come from, doing stitches is a doctor's job, pure and simple.

Then again, this is Alaska, and we are ninety minutes from the closest hint of civilization. It probably stands to reason that the school nurse at Katmere can do a lot more than an average school nurse. Maybe she's a nurse practitioner and that's why she can prescribe sedatives and fix arteries.

Either way, I'm grateful when Macy finally gets back. I keep pretending to be asleep until Marise leaves, but as soon as the door closes behind her, I spring up in bed.

"What aren't you telling me?" I demand of my cousin, who screams and nearly drops the tray she's carrying.

"I thought you were asleep!"

"I wanted to make sure Marise left." I throw back my covers and swing my legs off the side of the bed so that my feet are on the floor.

"You need to lay back down," Macy admonishes.

"I *need* to find out what really happened to me," I counter. "I mean, what are the odds that the window would shatter like that during an earthquake and that the flying glass would actually nick my artery? It seems like a long shot. And then Marise told me not to look at the cut. What is that?"

"She probably just doesn't want you to freak out about it being ugly or something."

Macy sets the tray down on her desk, but she doesn't turn around to face me. Instead, she fusses with the dishes on the tray until I want to scream. After all, there's only so much prep a bowl of already heated soup needs.

Which is why I push to my feet, ignoring how light-headed I feel, and start to walk over to her. The room begins swaying before I'm halfway there, though, and I put a hand on the wall to steady myself.

Just a small nick, my ass. I'm in seriously bad shape here.

Macy turns around and shrieks all over again when she sees how unsteady I am. "Get back in bed!" she orders, grabbing my arm and throwing it over her shoulders. "Come on, I'll help you."

"Tell me the truth. Did my artery really just get nicked or is there something they're not telling me?" I ask, refusing to let her move me until I get some of my questions answered.

"Your artery was nicked. I saw the blood myself."

"That's not what I asked."

"Yeah, but that's all I know. I wasn't there when Jaxon brought you to the nurse, you know. I was at dance practice."

"Oh, right." I sigh, fighting the urge to pull out a chunk or two of my hair. "Sorry. I just feel like something is off about this whole story."

"I don't know, Grace. It makes sense to me. Although I do feel like you have the worst luck ever. That tree branch breaking and now the window. It's weird."

"It *is* weird. That's what I was thinking earlier. I mean, the odds are way skewed. I just don't know what to think about it."

"Right now? You don't have to think about anything that doesn't involve crawling back into your bed and getting some sleep. Marise would kill me if she saw you up wandering around the room."

"And what's up with that?" I demand, even as I let Macy help me to my bed. "She's, like, the scariest school nurse anywhere."

"She's not so bad. She's just…serious."

I snag the pencil bag off my desk on my way by. I've got a mirror inside, and I want to get a look at the damage. "Yeah, that's one way to describe her."

"What kind of soup do you want?" Macy asks as she settles me down into a bed whose sheets seem a lot smoother than when I climbed out of it. Which makes no sense, considering Macy has been across the room the whole time.

"Hey, did you fix this?"

"What?"

"My bed. It was a mess when I got out of it."

"Oh, yeah. I, uh…" She moves her hand horizontally in a kind of smoothing motion.

"When?" I must be more out of it than I think. I didn't even see her come over here.

"I did it when you were leaning against the wall. You had your eyes closed for a minute, and I didn't want to disturb you while you were getting your bearings."

Again, that doesn't seem right. I was sure she came directly over to me once she realized I was standing. Then again, I'm the one who's totally drugged while she's the one who has all her faculties about her. Besides, what does it matter anyway? It's not like my bed made itself.

"Well, I appreciate it," I say as I pull back the covers over me. "So thanks."

"No worries." Still, she looks a little white as she reaches for the food tray. "I brought potato, chicken noodle, and corn chowder. I didn't know what kind of soup you like."

"Honestly, I'm hungry enough that I'll eat anything. Pick what you want and give me whatever's left."

"Umm, no. You're the sick one."

"Exactly. I'm so drugged, it won't matter. Besides, tomato soup is pretty much the only kind I really don't like, so just give me something."

In the end, she hands me the corn chowder and a bowl of canned fruit—peaches this time.

I end up scarfing down half the bowl in three minutes flat. Macy eats at a more sedate pace, taking a couple of bites and then asking, "Hey, why exactly were you in Jaxon's room anyway? Last I heard, he was avoiding you."

The last thing I want to do is tell Macy about how I was crying. I don't want her to worry about me, and I definitely don't want her thinking that she hasn't been wonderful since I got here, because she has. "We were talking, and he offered to show me the meteor shower."

"The meteor shower? That's the best you've got?"

"It's the truth. It was gorgeous. I've never seen one so bright before."

She still looks skeptical. "And how exactly were you watching this meteor shower from inside his bedroom?"

"We were on the parapet *outside* his bedroom. We'd just crawled back through the window when the earthquake hit."

"The earthquake."

"Yeah, the earthquake. You know, that whole *ground shaking* thing that happened about five thirty this afternoon. It must have been an aftershock from this morning."

"Oh, I know about the earthquake. We all felt it."

"So why are you acting like I'm losing it?"

"I'm not. I was just thinking… I mean, it's probably silly. But what exactly were you and Jaxon doing when the earthquake hit?"

I freeze at the question, my gaze fastening on the wall directly behind her ear. But it doesn't really matter where I look, because I can feel my cheeks heating up.

"Oh my God. Were you—" Her voice drops. "Were you *hooking up* with him?"

"What? No! Of course not!" Pretty sure my cheeks just went from pink to bright red. "We were…"

"What?"

"Kissing. He was kissing me, okay?"

"That's it? Just kissing?"

"Of course that's it! I met the guy less than a week ago."

"Yeah, but…it seems like it would have to be more than that."

"What does? I mean, I'm not even sure he likes me."

Macy starts to say something but must think better of it, because in the end, she just shakes her head and stares down into her soup like it's suddenly the most interesting thing on the planet.

"Seriously?" I implore. "You don't get to do that. I answered all your questions. You need to answer mine!"

"I know. It's just—" She breaks off as a knock sounds at our door. Of course. "It's probably my dad wanting to check on you again," she says as she climbs to her feet. "He's not very good at waiting on the sidelines, especially when someone he cares about is sick."

I put what's left of my soup on my nightstand and burrow down under my covers. "Will it offend you if I pretend to be asleep? I'm really not up for talking to anyone else right now."

"Of course not. Fake sleep away. I'll let him get a good look at you, and then I'll kick him out."

"Best. Roomie. Ever."

I close my eyes and roll onto my side—face toward the wall—while Macy goes to answer the door. I can hear a deep murmur from whoever is on the other side of the doorway, but I can't understand the words.

It must be Macy's dad, though, because she answers, "She's fine. She just had some soup, and now she's sleeping."

More murmuring from that deep voice and then Macy offering, "Do you want to come in and see for yourself? Nurse Marise gave her a lot of medicine. She's still drugged to the gills."

There's a little more murmuring, not much. And then Macy closes the door.

"Coast clear," she says, but her voice sounds a little off.

"Hey, I'm sorry if I made you feel like you had to lie to your dad. If you want to call him back—"

"It wasn't my dad."

"Oh. Who was it, then? Cam?"

"No." She looks a little sick as she admits, "It was Jaxon."

I spring up in bed for the third time tonight. "Jaxon? He was here? Why didn't you let him in?" I throw back the covers and climb out of bed, searching the room for my Chucks, but they're nowhere to be found.

"I did invite him in. He's the one who declined."

"Because you told him I was sleeping." I give up on the shoe hunt and head for the door.

"Where are you going?" Macy squeaks.

"Where do you think?" I pull open the door. "After Jaxon."

36

No Harm, All Foul

I charge out of our room, figuring I'll catch Jaxon a few doors down. But the hallway is completely empty. Still, he couldn't have gone far, so I take off toward the main staircase. Worst-case scenario, I know where his room is, even if a cleaning crew is currently in there.

I finally find him on the stairs, taking them three at a time. He's not alone, though—Liam and Rafael are with him, and all three of them seem like they're in a really big hurry.

I should probably let them go, but he's the one who came to my room, not the other way around. Which means he wanted to see me.

It's that thought that galvanizes me, that has me calling out his name as I move to the top landing.

He stops on a dime. All three of them do, and then they're all staring at me out of the same blank eyes. I have a second to try to absorb the direct impact of all that male beauty and intensity—it's a lot—before Jaxon is bounding back up the stairs.

Liam and Rafael watch for a second, their faces locked in that expressionless look I'm coming to hate. But then they both give me a little wave, plus Rafael adds a thumbs-up, before they turn away and bound down the stairs.

"What are you doing out here?" Jaxon demands, and just that quickly, he's in front of me. Only his face isn't blank. It's livid with a mixture of self-loathing and regret, his eyes an incandescent black that has shivers sliding through me for all the wrong reasons.

"Macy said you were looking for me."

"I wasn't looking for you. I came to make sure you were okay."

"Oh." I hold out my arms, do a little self-deprecating shrug. "Well, as you can see, I'm fine."

He snorts. "Pretty sure that's a matter of opinion."

"What's that supposed to mean?"

"It means, you look like you're going to fall down any second. I don't know what you were thinking to come running down the halls after you nearly bled to death. Go back to bed."

"I don't want to go back to bed. I want to talk to you about what happened this afternoon."

"Blank" doesn't describe what happens to his face. It goes beyond blank, beyond empty, until there's absolutely nothing there. No sign at all of the Jaxon I watched the meteor shower with. Definitely no sign of the boy who kissed me until my knees buckled and my heart nearly exploded.

He looks like a stranger. A cold, emotionless stranger, one who has every intention of ignoring me. But then he finally answers. "You got hurt. That's what happened."

"That's not all that happened." I reach for his arm—I want to touch him, feel him—but he steps out of reach before my fingers can so much as brush against his shirt.

"It's the only thing that happened that matters."

Ouch. My heart falls straight to my feet as I struggle with the fact that he's grouping our kiss in with all the things he thinks *don't* matter.

For long seconds, I don't know what to say. But then I ask the one question that's been burning inside my brain since I woke up. "Are *you* all right?"

"I'm not the one you need to worry about."

"But I am worried about you." It's a lot to admit—especially when he's working so hard to shut down everything between us—but that doesn't make it any less true. "You look..."

His eyes meet mine. "What?"

"I don't know." I shrug. "Not okay."

He looks away. "I'm fine."

"Okay." It's obvious he doesn't want to talk to me right now, so I take a step back. "I guess I—"

"I'm sorry." It sounds like the words are dragged out of him.

"For what?" The apology astounds me.

"I didn't protect you."

"From an *earthquake*?"

His gaze swings back to mine, and for a second, just a second, I can see something in his eyes. Something powerful and terrible and all-consuming. But it's gone as quickly as it came and then he's back to showing nothing. "From a lot of things."

"From what I understand, you saved my life."

He snorts. "That's the point. You don't understand much. Which is why you should go back to your room and forget all about what happened earlier."

"Forget about the earthquake?" I ask. "Or forget about you kissing me?" I don't know where I got the guts to bring it up... except, truth is, it's not bravery so much as desperation. I have to know what Jaxon's thinking and why he's thinking it.

"Forget about it all," he answers.

"You know that's not going to happen." I reach for him once more, and this time he doesn't jerk away. Instead, he just watches me as I rest my hand on his shoulder, hoping the contact will remind him of what it was like to touch me. Hoping it will break through the barriers he's erected between us.

"Yeah, well, it needs to happen. You have no idea what we just did."

"We kissed, Jaxon. That's all we did." It felt momentous, important—it still feels that way to me—but in the grand scheme of things, it really was just a kiss.

"I keep telling you that it doesn't work like that here." He shoves a frustrated hand through his hair. "Don't you get that? You've been a pawn since you got here, a chess piece to move around the board to get the desired result. But now...now we've upped the stakes. This isn't just a game anymore."

He might mean his words as warnings, but they feel like body blows.

"I was a game to you?"

"You're not listening." His eyes glow incandescent with the effort of holding in emotions I can't even begin to decipher—no matter how much I wish I could. "From the moment I kissed you. From the moment you got hurt, everything changed. You were in danger before, but now—"

He breaks off, jaw clenching, throat working. Then says, "Now I've all but put a bull's eye in the middle of your back and dared someone to take a shot."

"I don't understand. You didn't *do* anything."

"I did *everything*." He moves then, swift as one of those shooting stars from last night, until his face is right up in mine. "Listen to me. You need to stay away from me. I *need* to stay *away* from you."

His words send a chill through me, make my mouth go dry and my palms sweat. And still I can't just walk away. Not when he's standing right here. "Jaxon, please. You're not making any sense."

"Only because you refuse to understand." He backs away. "I have to go."

The words hang in the air between us—dark and somber—but he doesn't go. He doesn't do anything but stand there, staring at me with tortured eyes.

So *I* do something. I step forward until our bodies are just barely brushing against each other.

It's not much, but it's enough to have heat pooling in my stomach and electricity crackling just below my skin. "Jaxon." I whisper his name because my vocal cords have forgotten how to work. He doesn't answer me, but he doesn't move away, either.

For one second, two, he just stands there looking down at me, his gaze locked with mine. His body pressing forward into mine.

I whisper his name again, and it's almost enough. I can see him waver, feel him lean more heavily against me.

But then he snaps out of it, his voice cutting like broken glass as he tells me, "Stay away from me, Grace." He turns away, takes the steps three at a time, and doesn't stop until he's on the landing ten feet below. Then, without turning around, he calls up to me. "It's the only way you're getting out of this school alive."

"Is that a threat?" I ask, more shaken than I want to admit—to him or to myself.

"I don't make threats." The *I don't have to* hangs in the air between us.

Before I can respond, he puts two hands on the iron banister and vaults straight over it. I let out a strangled scream, rush to the edge of the staircase, half afraid I'll see his mangled body down below. But not only is he not lying broken on the ground three stories below, he's nowhere to be seen at all. He's vanished, right into thin air.

37

Don't Ask the Question if You Can't Handle the Answer

I stand, staring down at where Jaxon should be but isn't for several seconds. He couldn't have just disappeared. It's impossible.

I start down after him—the sane way—but I've barely made it four steps before someone is calling behind me. "Hey, Grace! Where are you going?"

I turn to see Lia coming across the landing toward me. She's dressed in all black, as per usual, and looks totally badass in a chic, feminine way. Also as per usual.

"I wanted to talk to Jaxon, but he's too fast for me."

"No news there. When Jaxon doesn't want to be caught, he's too fast for everyone." She rests a hand lightly on my shoulder. "But, Grace, honey, are you okay? You don't look so good."

I'm pretty sure that's the understatement of the year, so I just kind of shake my head. "It's been a weird day. And a long one."

"It always is when Jaxon is involved," she tells me with a laugh. "What you need is a little more of my tea and some girl time. We should arrange that for later."

"Yeah, definitely."

"In the meantime, maybe you should go after Jaxon.

Otherwise who knows how long he'll brood."

I think about it, I really do. But I have no idea where he went—or even if he's still in the castle. And if he's not inside, it's not like I can exactly go chasing after him in my pajamas.

Which is why, in the end, I just kind of sigh and say, "I think I'm going to go back to my room for now. Maybe try to text him."

"Oh, yeah, of course you *could* do that." She sounds a little patronizing, but it could just be that I'm pissy. Which is why, when she says, "Here, let me help you back to your room. You look like you're going to collapse at any second," I try not to be annoyed.

I *feel* like I'm going to collapse at any second, but I figure that's no one's business but my own. Especially in this school, where physical weakness seems like a character flaw.

Which is why, instead of answering her, I cast one more look down the stairs after Jaxon—to no avail—before turning to walk back the way I came. Lia seems to think I'm going to fall at any moment, though, because she walks right next to me, hand up like she's prepared to catch me if I fall. Which I absolutely am not going to do. I've caused enough trouble this week to last a lifetime.

"So what's going on?" she asks as we slowly make our way back to my room. "I thought I'd see you at dinner, but you weren't there."

"Oh, yeah. I had a little...accident."

"I can see that." She eyes the bandages covering too many of my visible surfaces. "Anything serious? Because you look like you went three rounds with a polar bear. And lost."

I shake my head with a laugh. "A little flying glass from the earthquake earlier, no big deal."

"Oh, right. The earthquake." She studies me for a second. "You know, we've had more tremors since you got here than we've had in the last year. I'm beginning to think you brought them with you, California girl."

I snort. "Yeah, I've already had that discussion today. But I have to tell you, I never got hurt like this from a quake in California."

"Oh yeah? Well, you know what they say about Alaska."

"North to the Future?" I respond, quoting the state motto I found online when I was researching this state.

She laughs. "More like, everything here is designed to kill you in ten seconds or less."

"I thought that was Australia?"

"I'm pretty sure it works for any place that begins and ends with an A." She grins, but there's a bite to the words that reminds me just how bad things can get here. I may have fallen out of a tree and gotten cut by some glass since I got here, but Lia lost her boyfriend. And Jaxon lost his brother.

"How are you doing?" I ask as we get closer to my room.

"Me?" She looks startled. "You're the one who's all cut up."

"I didn't mean physically. I meant..." I take a deep breath, blow it out slowly. "About Hudson. How are you doing?"

For a second, just a second, rage flashes in her eyes. Towering, unadulterated, infinite. But then she blinks, and it's replaced with a bland, pleasant expression that is somehow a million times worse than the fury beneath it.

"I'm doing all right," she says with a strange little smile that makes me ache in sympathy. "I mean, I'm not good. I'll never be good. But I've figured out how to say no, so that's something."

"To say no?"

"Yeah, we talked about this before. Everyone wants me to just move on, and I can't. They tell me that nothing has to change, that Jaxon's a perfectly good replacement—"

"Jaxon?" My whole body tightens up at the mention of his

name linked with hers. She can't be serious…can she?

"I know. It's absurd. He and Hudson are nothing alike. And I don't care about politics or family dynasties even if he does. I just want Hudson back."

I'm reeling under the news that she and Jaxon are supposed to be together—and the implication that *he's* willing to go along with it. But she looks so small when she says it, so exposed, that my heart twists for her.

Besides, it doesn't make sense. Not with the way he held me earlier. Not with the way he kissed me. He didn't do either of those things like a guy who had another girl on his mind. He did them like a guy who was as desperate for me as I was for him.

Yeah, he tried to take it back on the stairs a few minutes ago, but you can't just take something like that back. Not when I've never felt anything close to it before in my whole life, and I would swear he never had, either.

So what's all this about, then? What's Lia getting at? And why is she talking about it to *me*, of all people?

I don't have answers to those questions and, more than likely, I'm not going to find them standing in the middle of the dorm hallway. Especially not when the combination of sedative and blood loss is still fogging up my brain, making me feel like half my body isn't even here.

On the plus side, we're finally back at my and Macy's room. I'm exhausted and more than ready to be back in my own bed. I'm also more than ready to be away from Lia, at least until I figure out if I'm being paranoid or if she's trying to subtly warn me off Jaxon because she considers him hers.

If that is what she's doing, it isn't going to work. Not when I already feel this connection to Jaxon. It's strange, I know, considering we've spent as much time sniping at each other as we have talking, but the more time I spend with him, the more time I want to spend. Like there's something pushing me toward him, making me want him. There's not a chance her subtle little speech about how everyone wants her and Jaxon to be together because of *family* reasons is going to change that.

I reach up to knock—I was in such a hurry to get to the incredible disappearing Jaxon Vega that I forgot my key—but the door flies open before my fist can so much as touch the wood.

"There you are!" Macy exclaims. "I was just about to come looking—"

She breaks off when she sees Lia standing behind me. "Oh, hi, Lia." She nervously smooths her hair down. "How are you?"

"Good," Lia tells her dismissively before turning back to me with a concerned look on her face. "Rest up, okay, Grace? I'll come by to check on you tomorrow. Bring you a special blend of tea that will help you feel better faster."

"You don't have to do that." I cross through the beaded curtain into my room. "But I appreciate you walking me back. Thanks."

"Of course. And the tea is no bother." She smiles sweetly. "Get some rest."

"I will. Thanks." I don't bother to smile.

"Thanks for bringing her back. I appreciate it," Macy tells her with a grateful smile that gets my back up.

Lia ignores her. "I can bring the tea by now if you want it, Grace."

"I'm good." I wave a dismissive hand at her as I flop down on my bed. "I think I'm just going to sleep."

To prove my point, I lie down on my freshly made bed (again) and turn so I'm facing the wall, my back to the door—*and* Lia. I know it's rude, but right now, I don't actually care. I'm *so* done with this conversation, and for the moment, I'm done with Lia, too. Not just because of the Jaxon thing but because I really don't like how she treats Macy. I can't stand how abrupt she is with her, like my cousin is some annoying puppy nipping at her shoes.

There's some soft murmuring from the door—my cousin apologizing to Lia for my churlish behavior, I'm sure—and then the door closes softly.

I roll over right away, and as I do, I come face-to-face with the bag of cookies and fresh glass of juice Macy has put on my nightstand.

"You really are the best cousin in the world," I tell her as I sit up. "You know that, right?"

"I do," she agrees, settling down on the bed next to me. "How are you feeling?"

"The truth?"

"Always."

"Awful. I should have listened to you." But it's ridiculous. And I hate it. All I did was run down the hall after Jaxon, and my body feels weak, exhausted.

"No shit." She reaches for the glass of juice and holds it out to me. "Drink up, buttercup."

For the first time, I can't help thinking about how much blood I must have actually lost.

It's that thought that has me taking the glass from her and downing the juice in a couple of swallows. It's what also has me eating a cookie even though my stomach is roiling and food is the last thing I want.

Macy watches me like a hawk, then smiles her approval when I manage to choke down a second cookie as well as a glass of water. Only then does she ask, "So are you going to tell me how you left here chasing Jaxon and came back with Lia?"

"Not much to tell. Jaxon did what he always does."

"And what's that?"

"He disappeared."

Macy nods. "Yeah."

I think about the look on Jaxon's face when I was trying to talk to him at the top of the stairs, then I think about what Lia just let "slip."

I think about the way Jaxon has managed to help me every time something bad happens to me. And I think about how he finds it so easy to walk away, time and time again.

It's enough to have my already addled brain begging for mercy.

"We should get some sleep," Macy says and, for the first time, I realize she's already in her pajamas. "It's after two."

"It's really that late? How long was I out?"

"Long enough." She gives me a hug before crawling off my bed. "Get some sleep. We'll talk more about the ins and outs of Jaxon Vega's brain tomorrow."

I nod and try to do as she suggests. But I can't stop thinking about how late it is. And about how much time I've lost. I must have been out a lot longer than I thought if it's really—I pick up my phone to check the time—2:31 in the morning.

There are a couple of messages from Heather—about how much Calculus sucks and how she wishes she could work up the nerve to talk to Veronica (her current crush). I shoot back a couple of texts of my own. Nothing about my most recent near-death experience, just encouragement about Veronica and Calculus. Plus a little whining of my own over Jaxon.

She doesn't answer—probably because it's the middle of the night. So I spend a few minutes scrolling through my Insta feed. As I stare blankly at the pics, I can't help thinking about this afternoon. Can't help wondering what happened in the time I was so out of it.

Was it exactly as Marise said? That Jaxon rushed me to her office and she drugged me so she could repair the "nick" in my artery? Or is there something more to the story, something that accounts for why my uncle was so nervous and Jaxon so determined to put distance between us?

It's these thoughts that have me staring at the ceiling until nearly three in the morning.

These thoughts that finally have me heading to the bathroom and closing the door between Macy and me.

And it's these thoughts that have me peeling back the bandage I promised I wouldn't lift for at least a few days and staring at the cut on my neck.

Or, more precisely, at the two perfectly round, perfectly spaced puncture marks about an inch below a jagged cut.

Nothing
“I Like Y
Like a Fang to th

Needless to say, there’s no going to sleep after that.

There’s no doing anything except checking and rechecking my throat about a thousand times in the next two hours as I wait for the last of the drugs—and what I’m hoping is some kind of bizarre hallucinogen—to wear off.

Because if this isn’t some drug-induced hallucination, then nicked arteries and aliens are the least of my concerns.

Part of me wants to get up and go for a walk to clear my head, but memories of what happened the other night are still fresh. After the day I’ve had, and what I just saw in the mirror, I’m pretty sure I’m going to lose my shit completely if anyone tries to hassle me tonight. Especially when a glance out the window reveals that the moon is still high in the sky.

Not that that should matter in a normal world, but “normal” has pretty much been a distant memory since I set foot in this place. Just the thought has me running my fingers over the bandage on my neck, my mind racing all over again as I try to figure out what could possibly have caused the puncture marks on my neck.

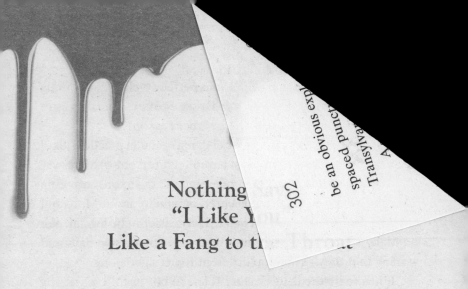

I mean, sure, if I was living in a horror novel, there would

anation for those perfectly placed, perfectly ures. But I'm not Bram Stoker, and this isn't ia, so there has to be another reason.

snake? Two shots to my neck? A really mean practical joke?

It has to be something. I just haven't figured out what it is yet.

The fact that I can't help but remember Jaxon's warning about the full moon and his sneered comment about Marc and Quinn being animals doesn't make it any easier to be logical. Nor do Macy's warnings that Flint and Jaxon come from different worlds, that they're just too different to ever get along.

It has to be the drugs, right? It has to be.

Because what's skating around the edges of my mind is totally absurd. Completely bonkers. There are no such things as monsters, just people who do monstrous things.

Like this.

If Marise didn't give me a couple of shots in the neck, then this *has* to be a practical joke. Jaxon *has* to be messing with me. He has to be. There is no other reasonable explanation.

This is the idea I hold on to all through the next couple of hours, the mantra I repeat to myself over and over and over again. And still, as soon as the clock on my phone hits six a.m., I'm up and in the shower—being careful, as instructed, not to get the bandage on my neck wet.

After all, what do I know about vampire bites? The last thing I need to do is aggravate the thing...

Not that this is a vampire bite or anything. I'm just saying, at this point I'm taking nothing for granted.

After I'm dressed in a black skirt, black tights, and purple polo shirt this time, I arrange my hair so it covers both my neck bandage and the cut on my cheek, grab my lined hoodie, and sneak out of the bedroom before Macy's alarm even goes off. Part of me wants to wake her up and ask her the question burning itself indelibly within my mind, but I don't want her to lie to me.

I'm also not sure I want her to tell me the truth.

Jaxon, on the other hand… If he lies to me, you'd better believe I'm going to stake him through his fangy black heart. And yes, I know that makes no sense. I just don't happen to care at this exact moment.

I march through the school like a woman on a mission. The fact that I'm also still a little dizzy—just how much blood did I *lose*, anyway?—makes things particularly interesting, but there's no way I'm lying around in bed, waiting to talk to him, for one second longer.

I make it up to the tower in about five minutes flat, which pretty much has to be some kind of record, considering it's all the way at the other end of the castle. But when I rush through the alcove to pound on Jaxon's door, there's no answer.

I keep pounding, and when that doesn't work, I text him. And call him. And then pound some more. Because this can't be happening right now. He can't really not be here when I most need answers from him.

Except apparently he can. Damn it.

Frustrated, pissed off, and more worried than I'd like to admit, I drop down on one of the overstuffed chairs in his reading alcove and stare at the now-boarded-up window that started all this so I can pretend not to notice that the rug that was here yesterday is now gone.

Then I lean back and prepare to wait Jaxon Vega out.

Fifteen minutes later and I'm pretty much climbing the walls. Half an hour later and I'm firing off more than a few obnoxious texts to the raging jackass. And forty-five minutes later, I'm contemplating burning down the whole freaking tower…at least until Mekhi walks in, sleepy-eyed and amused.

"What are you smiling at?" I demand none too politely.

"You look cute when you're grumpy."

"I am *not* grumpy."

"Oh, right. You're pissed off beyond belief and more than capable of ripping Jaxon's fat black heart out of his chest and stomping on it?" He quotes my most outrageous text back to me, I assume to embarrass me. But I am beyond being embarrassed. I mean, I have fang marks in my neck. *Fang marks.*

"Exactly," I answer with a glare. "Not to paraphrase Sylvia Plath or anything."

"Not to paraphrase her *badly*, don't you mean?"

"Keep it up and I'm going to get pissed off at you, too," I add. He smiles, but before he can say something that makes me want to punch him in his ridiculously pretty face, I demand, "Where's Jaxon? And why is he hiding from me? Or showing you my texts?"

"He's not hiding from you."

"Oh, really?" I walk over and ceremoniously knock on his door. Once again, there's no answer. "Pretty sure he is."

"Really? And why would he be hiding from you exactly?" Mekhi crosses his arms over his chest and grins at me, brows raised and head tilted.

"Because of this." I reach up and rip the bandage off my throat, turning my head so Mekhi can see what I saw.

I take a perverse kind of satisfaction in watching the grin drop from his face. In watching his eyes widen and his face go slack with shock. "What the hell! Who bit you?"

Oh God. My stomach revolts, and for a second, I think I'm going to throw up as nausea washes through me. He didn't deny someone bit me. He just asked *who* bit me, like it's perfectly normal that I have two puncture wounds on my neck.

Like it's perfectly normal that there might be someone or, judging by his question, a *lot* of someones at this school who walk around biting people.

Fear skitters up my spine at the implication, has the hair on my arms and the back of my neck standing straight up.

"Grace?" Mekhi prompts when I'm too busy trying not to hyperventilate to answer him. "Who bit you?"

"What do you mean, who?" I nearly choke on the words. "Jaxon bit me. Obviously."

"Jaxon?" He shakes his head, a little wild-eyed. "No, I'm pretty sure that's not how that went down."

"What do you mean? Of course it is. I was up here, got cut by glass, and Jaxon bit me. I'm sure of it."

"You remember that happening? Just like that? You remember him biting you?"

"Well, no." I'm pretty sure I'm as wild-eyed as he is at this point. "But if it *wasn't* him, then who the hell was it?"

"I have no idea." He pulls out his phone and fires off a series of texts.

My head is swimming. Because of everything he's said *and* everything he hasn't. The only things that bite people are animals and— No. I'm not ready to go there yet. Not ready to actually think the word. My brain might explode.

"I swear to God, if you're messing with me, Mekhi... If this is all just some great, big practical joke you guys cooked up, I'm going to *murder* you all. Like, disembowel you while you're still alive and feed your entrails to whatever poor, starving polar bear I can find. We're clear about that, right?"

"Crystal." His phone vibrates with several return texts, and his face gets even more grim as he reads them. "It definitely wasn't Jaxon."

The shiver along my spine turns into a violent chill, one that makes it hard for me to think. Hard for me to breathe. "How do you know he's not just saying that?"

"Because Jaxon doesn't lie to me. And because he is currently freaking the fuck out." His phone buzzes again, and he reads the newest messages before continuing. "He wants you to sit tight. He's on his way back. He'll be here in a few hours."

"On his way back?" My head is actually threatening to blow up. Like, it seriously might just explode right here, right now, and then it won't matter who made these marks on me or why. "Where exactly did he go?"

"The mountains."

"The mountains? You mean *Denali*?"

Mekhi doesn't look at me when he answers. "Farther than that."

"Farther than… How much farther are we talking about here?"

He shakes his head. "Don't worry about it."

"Don't you tell me not to worry about it." I poke him in the shoulder. "I'm the one with fang marks in my neck from some asshole's practical joke, and Jaxon is the last one who saw me besides the medical professional. So I'm going to worry until he gets back here and explains this to me. Okay?"

"Okay, okay!" He pretends to rub the spot I poked. "Jeez, woman. You definitely know how to make your point."

"Yeah, well, you might want to pass that along to your mountain-traversing friend. And by the way, why aren't you freaking out that I have fang marks in my neck?"

"I *am* freaking out! Jaxon's freaking out. We're all freaking out."

"Yeah, but you're freaking out because you don't know *who* bit me. You're not freaking out because—oh, I don't know—*someone bit me*!"

"Oh yeah." He shoves his hands in his pockets, looks anywhere but at me. "I think I'm going to leave that for Jaxon to explain."

"Because he's just so talkative."

I'm completely fed up with both of them at this point, not to mention the entire situation, so screw it. Just screw it. I push off the chair and head for the door.

Except Mekhi gets there before me—the boy sure can move fast when he wants to—and blocks my path. "Hey. Where are you going?"

"Back to my room to get my stuff. I have class." And a cousin who I am totally prepared to torture the truth out of if I have to. I move to go around him, but he shifts to block my path.

"I told you Jaxon wants you to stay put. Just…I don't know, grab a book and a blanket and curl up by the fire." He gestures to the empty fireplace.

"There's no fire."

"I'll build one. It'll take me five minutes, I promise."

"Mekhi." I speak slowly and in the most reasonable tone I can manage, but I can see that just makes him warier. Smart boy.

"Yes, Grace?"

"If Jaxon wants me to stay put, maybe he should have done the same. As it is, he's on some mountain God only knows where doing God only knows what, and I'm here with inexplicable *fang* marks in my neck that happened when I was *unconscious*." The terror is back, so I focus on the anger. It's so much easier to deal with. "I assume you can see why I don't actually give a *damn* what Jaxon wants right now."

"Um, yeah. I absolutely can see that." He gives me the grin that I'm sure normally gets him everything he wants in life and more, but I refuse to cave. Not now and not over this. "How about we compromise? You go back to your room and chill until Jaxon gets here. That way you'll be safe, and then you two can figure this out together."

"You really think I need to hide from some moron with a staple remover or a pet snake?"

"A staple remover didn't make those marks, Grace. And neither did a snake. I think you know that, or you wouldn't have been up here pounding on Jaxon's door at six in the morning."

His acknowledgment of the elephant in the room—or should I say the monster—has a kind of calmness washing over me from the top of my head to the tips of my toes. Maybe it's the medicine, maybe I'm going into shock, or maybe I'm just relieved to have someone finally being real with me.

Whatever it is, I take a deep breath and hold on to it with both hands as my very first conversation with Jaxon plays through my head. *There are more things in heaven and hell, Horatio, than are dreamt of in your philosophy.* And then I ask him—because I have to hear it out loud: "So what *did* make these marks?"

For long seconds, he doesn't answer. And then, just when I've given up on him speaking at all, he says, "The truth is, Grace, sometimes the most obvious answer really is the right one."

39

There's Never a Hallucinogen Around When You Need One

Mekhi and I don't have a lot to say after that charming revelation—except for him insisting on escorting me back to my room. I mean, there really isn't much to say, considering I can't decide if I should trust him or not. I don't know this guy. I mean, yeah, Jaxon trusts him, but Jaxon is currently MIA, so that's not exactly a ringing endorsement.

The fact that Jaxon's been blowing up my phone with text messages for the last fifteen minutes doesn't matter much to me, either. I texted him earlier, and the only response I got was him sending Mekhi. So now he can ask Mekhi what he wants to know about me, because I am *not* answering.

Childish? Maybe. Prudent? Absolutely. Because in the mood I'm in, I'm afraid I'm going to say something I'll regret. Better to calm down and talk to him in person when he gets back. And also, if he tries to lie to me right now, I'll burn whatever is growing between us straight to the freaking ground.

Mekhi tries to start conversations several times on the way back to my room, but I'm too shell-shocked to participate much. It's not that I'm ignoring him; it's just that my head is spinning. This has to be a nightmare. It's the only reasonable explanation.

Eventually, Mekhi gives up on the small talk. It should be a relief, but that just leaves silence to stretch between us.

Still, it might just be the most awkward silence of my life, so I expect him to cut and run the second he delivers me to my door. Instead, he waits until I get the door unlocked.

"I'm not inviting you in," I tell him without so much as bothering to turn my head to look at him.

"I don't expect you to." But the moment I get the door open, he slaps his palm flat against it to keep me from closing it. He doesn't step inside, though, just stands as close to the threshold as he can get without actually crossing over it. Which seems strange, considering the beads are probably shocking the hell out of him—at least until I remember one of the first rules of vampire lore.

That they can't come inside unless they're invited in.

Which only makes his behavior more upsetting and me more freaked out—even before it becomes obvious that he's going to prevent me from closing my door until he decides it's okay.

"Hey! What are you doing?" I grab his arm and start trying to tug him back through the door.

He just shrugs me off. "Don't worry. I'm not getting any closer." Then he grins at my cousin. "Hey, Macy."

"Hi, Mekhi." She's still bleary-eyed and in her pajamas, which probably accounts for why she doesn't notice the power struggle going on between us. The cup of coffee in her hand attests to the fact that we didn't wake her up, but I'm still glad she wasn't in her underwear or something. "What's up?"

"Nothing. He was just leaving." I shoot him a warning look.

He doesn't even pretend to look shamefaced when he says, "Jaxon doesn't want her going to class today."

"Okay." She doesn't even pause.

"Okay?" I demand. "Jaxon doesn't get to tell me—"

"My dad already told her teachers she wouldn't be there after what happened yesterday. Great minds and all that." She scowls at me. "You're supposed to be in bed."

"You going to stay with her?" Mekhi asks before I can defend myself.

"Yeah, absolutely. Why? What's going on?"

"I don't know yet. But I'm pretty sure that's what Jaxon aims to find out."

Macy's face tightens. "Is something wrong?"

"I don't know yet." Mekhi nods toward me. "I'll let her tell you about it."

"You know I'm standing right here in front of you, yeah? Which means you can talk *to* me instead of *over* me."

Mekhi's brows hit his forehead. "Oh, really? Because I'm pretty sure I already tried that."

"You know what? Bite me." I make an oops face. "Oh right, I forgot. Someone already did."

Macy whips her head around like it's on springs. "What did you say?"

"She knows, Mace."

If possible, my cousin turns even paler. "What exactly does she know, Mekhi?"

"You can go now," I tell him, grabbing on to the edge of the door and using it to back him off the threshold.

"Look, Grace, I'm really sorry," he says right before I get the door closed.

I pause. "Did you bite me?"

"What? No! Of course not."

"Then you've got nothing to apologize for." I sigh as some of the rage drains away. "I'm not mad at you personally, Mekhi. I'm just mad...and scared."

"I get that." He looks hesitant. "Does this mean you're not mad at Jaxon, either?"

"Oh, no. I've got *all* the anger stored up for Jaxon, so don't you dare go telling him otherwise."

"Believe me, I won't." Mekhi grins. "The last thing I'm interested in doing is getting in the middle of *that* argument. Besides, it might be time someone takes my boy down a peg or two."

"More like twelve," I answer with a snort. "Now go away. I have stuff to do."

With that, I close the door right in his face. And now that it's just Macy and me, everything suddenly gets a whole shit ton more real.

I take a second to gather my wits, to try to formulate what I want to say. But Macy jumps in before I can do much more than have an OMG moment.

"Grace, it's not—"

I turn to face her. "I'm going to ask you one question, Macy. Just one. And I want you to be totally honest with me. Because if you're not...if you're not, I'm going to pack up all my shit and go back to California. I'll stay with Heather; I'll file for emancipation; I'll do whatever I have to do. But I swear, you will never see or hear from me again. Got it?"

If it's possible, she grows even paler. Plus, if her eyes got any bigger, they'd take over her entire face. But that doesn't stop her from nodding and saying quietly, "Okay."

"Are you a vampire?" I can't even believe I'm asking the question.

"What?" She shakes her head vehemently. "No."

The answer has me sagging with relief...at least until I realize one question isn't going to cut it. I have *dozens*.

"Is your father a vampire?"

"No."

"Was *my* father a vampire?"

"Absolutely not." She reaches a hand out to me. "Oh, Grace, is that what you're afraid of?"

I blow out a long breath as the biggest, tightest knot in my stomach unwinds. "At this moment, I don't know what I'm afraid of, Macy. But since you're not acting like I'm losing my mind for asking these questions—and I have a perfect bite mark on my neck at this very moment—I assume that means vampires are real."

"They are, yes."

"And they go to this school."

She nods. "Yes."

"And Jaxon is a vampire." I hold my breath as I wait for her answer.

"I really think you should talk to him about that, Grace. I mean—"

"Macy." I drop the anger, let her see the fear and frustration that are riding me hard. "Please."

She just looks at me, her face miserable.

"I thought we were friends, not just family."

"We are. Of course we are."

"Then tell me the truth. Is. Jaxon. Vega. A. Vampire?"

Macy sighs. "Yes."

I was expecting it—I was—and still it explodes over me like a grenade. My knees go out from under me, and I hit the floor hard.

"Grace!" Macy's next to me in the space between one second and the next. "Are you okay?"

"I have no idea." I close my eyes, lean my head back against the door, which is conveniently close to where I dropped. "That's why he can be outside without a jacket."

"Yes."

"So that means Lia..."

"Yes."

I nod. "Flint?"

"No, no. Flint's definitely not a vamp."

I close my eyes as relief sweeps through me, at least until she continues. "He's a..."

"What?" I open one eye. "He's a what?"

"I'm not sure you're ready."

"Will I ever be ready? Finish the sentence, please. He's a..."

"Dragon."

Now I open both eyes. "Say that again?"

She sighs. "He's a dragon, Grace. Flint is a dragon."

"Of course he is. You mean he's got—" I hold my arms up and kind of flap them up and down.

"Yes, he's got wings."

"And...fire?" I answer my own question. "Of course he does. With a name like Flint, how could he not?"

My brain is imploding. I can feel it actually turning to mush and folding in on itself under the weight of all this new information. I mean, who needs LSD when you go to Monster High?

Even worse, something tells me we aren't done yet. Which is probably what leads me to snark, "And that makes you what? A fairy?"

"I'm not a fairy." She sounds insulted.

"Not a fairy, not a vampire, not a...dragon?"

Macy sighs. "I'm a witch, Grace."

I run her words back through my head another time or five, but still. They make the least amount of sense of anything I've heard this afternoon. "I'm sorry?"

"You heard me." Now she's smirking at me. "And you want to know something else?"

"At this point, no. I don't. Not even a little bit. I'm done. My brain is—"

"You should have been one, too."

40

Be Careful What You Witch For

Her words go off like a bomb inside me. They can't be right—*she* can't be right. I mean, the whole idea is absurd.

"I'm sorry, but you just blew it." Not for the first time in the last ten minutes, I stare at my cousin like she's a few pieces of straw short of a broomstick. Or, perhaps more appropriately, as if she's taken to riding a broom around our dorm room in a pointy black hat.

"Whatever prank this is, whatever weird-ass mass hallucination you have going on here, you took it one step too far with that claim. Because I may be a lot of things, but I am not, nor have I ever been, a witch."

I wave my hand in a magic-wand kind of gesture. "See, nothing happens. No glass dissolving and sending you tumbling into a snake pit. No ruby-red slippers to click together and take me home. No poisoned apple or magic mirror. So no, definitely not a witch."

Macy laughs. She actually laughs. "I'm not saying you *are* a witch. I'm just saying that if your dad hadn't fallen in love with your mom and lost his magic, you probably would be."

"Wait a minute. You're saying my dad *was* a witch?"

"A warlock, yeah. Just like my dad. And I'm a witch. It's a family thing."

I'm pretty sure my mind has stretched as far as it can go before just full-on caving in on itself. "I don't understand. How could my dad be a witch and I not know it?"

"Because he lost his powers when he fell for your mom. Witches aren't supposed to marry ordinary humans—weakens the bloodlines. So usually, when a witch falls in love with one, they...lose their powers."

"So my dad was a warlock, but then he wasn't. And that's why I'm not a witch?" Looks like I was wrong. My mind can still boggle.

"Pretty much. Yeah."

"Are you screwing with me, Macy?" I ask, because I have to. "I mean, you have to be messing with me, right?"

"I'm not messing with you, Grace."

"Are you sure? Like...really sure?"

She leans over and hugs me. "I'm really, really sure."

"Yeah, I was afraid of that." I just sit there for a minute, trying to absorb what she's telling me. "And my dad was okay with that? Losing all his powers?"

"From what my dad says, he really loved your mom. So yeah, he was."

"He did love her. They loved each other a ridiculous amount." I can't help but smile a little as I remember. "They were totally the parents who couldn't keep their hands off each other. I used to tell them how gross they were. But honestly, it was kind of nice, you know? To see that two people could love each other that much after so many years."

"I bet." Macy sighs wistfully.

"So," I say, trying to act like I'm okay with everything I've just learned. "I'm related to witches, huh?"

"Yeah. Bizarre, right?"

"A little bit." I eye her speculatively. "So…can you fly around the room or something?"

"To prove I'm not messing with you?" she asks with an arch of her brow.

"Maybe." Definitely.

"No, I can*not* fly around the room."

"Why not?" I ask, strangely disappointed.

"You know this is real life and not a book, right? Things like that don't actually happen."

"Well, what kind of witch are you if you can't do something an eleven-year-old kid can do?"

"The kind that doesn't come from J. K. Rowling's brilliant imagination." She waves a hand toward the electric teakettle that always sits on top of the fridge. It starts steaming and whistling instantly.

I try to tell myself that she had it turned on the whole time, but a quick glance reveals that it's not even plugged in. Because of course it isn't. Why would it be?

She doesn't stop with the teakettle, though. She waves her hand again, murmurs something under her breath, and I watch in fascination as she makes a cup of tea without ever leaving her spot on the floor.

"That's a real cup of tea?" I ask her as it comes floating across the room toward us.

"Of course it is." She snatches the cup out of midair, then holds it to me. "Want a sip?"

At this point, I'm pretty sure I'd rather drink rat poison. "I think I'll pass, thanks."

She shrugs, then lifts the tea to her own lips and blows a few times before taking a small sip.

"Why didn't you tell me about this when I got here? Why

didn't your dad?"

For the first time, she looks shamefaced. "I think he was planning to, but you kept getting hurt, and it never seemed like a good time."

"I'm not sure there's ever a good time to tell someone that monsters are real." I shake my head, try to remember how to breathe. "I can't believe this is happening. I just…can't believe it."

"Sure you can," she says with a sly smile. "Otherwise you wouldn't be so freaked out."

"I'm not freaked out. I mean, yeah, I'm on the floor and I can't feel my legs, but other than that, I think I'm handling the whole thing fairly well."

"Of course you are." She grins. "Except for the fact that every word that's come out of your mouth for the last ten minutes has squeaked."

"That's—" I pause and clear my throat because maybe, just maybe, I'm a little high-pitched. "What do you expect? You and Mekhi are trying to convince me that I'm living in the middle of a less bloody version of *Game of Thrones*. And winter is already here."

Macy laughs, then raises a brow. "You don't actually believe high school is a *less* bloody version of *Game of Thrones*, do you? I mean, how many times have you almost died since you got here?"

"Yeah, but those were accidents. I mean…they were accidents, right?"

"Probably." She inclines her head. "Yeah, they were. But Jaxon's freaking out, and he never freaks out, so…"

"He's freaking out because someone *bit* me! Someone who isn't him, I mean." I pull off the bandage for a second time and turn my head so she can see the puncture marks just below my cut.

"Oh! Is that what this is all about?" She sounds way too

relieved, considering I just told her some vampire sunk his or her teeth into me without my permission.

Then again, do they ever ask permission before they bite? And if so, who would be foolish enough to say yes? One more question to add to the tally of about a hundred or so I have waiting for Jaxon.

"I can explain everything," Macy adds flippantly.

"Oh, well, okay then." I make an expansive go-ahead gesture, then continue. "Please feel free. Explain away."

"Marise did that to you."

"The school nurse?" I don't know why that shocks me so much, but it really, really does. "Marise is a vampire, too?"

"She is. And she didn't have a choice. She had to bite you if she had any hope of repairing your arterial tear."

I narrow my eyes at her. "I thought it was a nick?"

"It was a tear. And you almost died. You would have died, in fact, if Jaxon hadn't been there and done what he did to save you."

"You mean running me to the nurse's office?" The squeak is back.

"I mean sealing your wound so you wouldn't bleed out while he got you to the nurse's office." She puts her cup of tea aside and reaches for my hands. Then, as she's squeezing tight, she continues. "Vampire venom has a lot of different properties, depending on what the vampire intends. Jaxon didn't bite you, but he did use his venom to seal your wound. And from what I understand, he was a little too thorough, and Marise couldn't get through it to actually suture the wound."

"So she bit me and got through that way?" I try not to shudder at the thought of her teeth sinking into my neck. When I believed it was Jaxon, it *freaked* me out but didn't *gross* me out. I can't say the same about having anyone else's teeth in me, though.

"She bit you and injected her own venom, using the

anticoagulant properties instead of the coagulant ones. It was enough to break down what Jaxon had done and let her heal you properly."

"So vampires can just do that? Just...override each other's venom?"

"Keep in mind, I'm not a vampire, but—"

"Right. You're just a witch."

She ignores my interruption. "I don't think they can. At least, not normally. But she's an older, more mature vampire and she's also a healer, which gives her extra abilities in times like that. It's why she's the school nurse. But from what my dad said, it still took a lot of skill and venom to undo what Jaxon had done. That boy was determined to save you."

Not going to lie, hearing that feels good. But I'm still mad at him, even though right now, I'm not sure why. Except... "So what you're saying is that I have two vampires' venom running through my blood right now?"

Macy settles back with a laugh and an eye roll. "Trust you to focus on that."

"I'm sorry, but it's pretty hard not to focus on it when every vampire movie I've ever seen is playing in the back of my head. I mean, I'm not going to..." I mime getting fangs.

She cracks up. Like full-on, rolling on the floor, laughing her ass off.

"That's not a no!" I whine.

She sits up, wiping tears from her eyes even as she continues to giggle. "No, Grace, you're not about to sprout fangs and start sucking people's blood. You're fine. In fact, the only reason you're alive is because a vampire was with you. And not just any vampire, but Jaxon. Most of the others would have had a really hard time stopping themselves from..."

"Drinking me dry?" I finish the thought she very obviously

didn't want to.

She rolls her eyes. "Yeah, that's not how I would have put it."

"Doesn't make it any less true, though, does it?"

Macy doesn't answer, just grabs her teacup and stands.

I follow her, unwilling to just let her walk away right now when I still have so many questions. About vampires. And witches. And dragons, for God's sake. How can *dragons* exist and the rest of the world not know about it?

Speaking of which... "There aren't any other creatures here that you forgot to mention, right? No zombies, no unicorns, no—"

"Werewolves."

"Exactly. No werewolves."

"I wasn't saying no, Grace. I was answering your question."

"Oh." I swallow. "So...vampires, dragons, witches, and werewolves."

"Well, if you're going to get technical, they're wolf shifters really, more than werewolves."

By all means, let's get technical at this late date. "And the difference is?"

"Werewolves need the full moon. Wolf shifters can shift anytime. Same with the dragons."

"So Flint can be a dragon anytime he wants?"

"Flint *is* a dragon, all the time. He can shift between his dragon and human form whenever he wants."

"I have so many questions." And most of them start and end with *how is this possible?*

"I know." She leans over and gives me another hug.

"Marc and Quinn?" I think about the guys who tried to throw me out in the snow the first night. "Wolf shifters?"

"Yeah. Who apparently do get a little extra wild around the full moon." She shakes her head, obviously still annoyed. "The jerks."

"No argument here. They really were douches." I pause as something occurs to me, then say, "But they listened to Jaxon, even though he's a vampire."

Macy snorts. "I'm sorry, but haven't you noticed? *Everyone* listens to Jaxon."

"Yeah." Like in my Brit Lit class yesterday, when no one would come in. "Why is that exactly?"

"It's a really long, really messed-up story, which I'm happy to tell you. But I'm seriously starving. Can I answer the rest of it over breakfast in the dining hall?"

"Yeah, of course. But I thought you told Mekhi we weren't going to leave the room until Jaxon gets here."

"I told him we weren't going to class. And if the bite on your neck is what's got their panties all wadded up, then it's no problem. We know where the bite came from, and we know that it's harmless. So we'll just go grab a quick breakfast and be back in the room before Jaxon even gets here."

She's right. I know she's right. Plus, it's not like I'm going to ask how high every time Jaxon expects me to jump. Everyone else at this school might listen to him, but I'm not some supernatural creature. I'm human, and now's as good a time as any for Jaxon to figure out I don't play by the same weird, convoluted, *terrifying* rules everyone else around this place does.

"Sounds good," I tell her. "Turns out, I'm suddenly really hungry, too."

"I bet. Massive blood loss will do that to a girl," Macy says as she disappears into the bathroom, a pair of school sweats and PE T-shirt in her hands.

She comes out two minutes later, and not only is she dressed, but her hair is slicked back in an adorable style, and her face looks like she spent half an hour putting on makeup in front of the mirror.

"What happened to you?" I demand.

"Oh, just a little glamour." She wiggles her fingers in front of her face. "And can I say how glad I am that you know now? My life is going to get so much easier."

"Apparently." Suddenly self-conscious, I grab my purse off my desk and pull out the peach lip gloss I always keep in the inside pocket. I swipe it over my lips as we head out the door. "So how exactly do you do that glamour thing?"

"Oh, it's just a little trick all witches know."

"Yeah, well, flying's still cooler," I tease.

"Maybe." She closes the door behind me. "But there's a lot I can do that you don't know about yet."

"Like what?" I ask, totally fascinated.

"Pretty sure that's for me to know and you to find out..."

41

Vampires, Dragons, and Werewolves, Oh My!

The halls are crowded as we make our way to the dining hall—it's thirty-five minutes before first period starts, and apparently everyone in the school tries to eat during the same half an hour period. Which makes sense. I mean, if I'm not worrying about bizarre fang marks or trying to fit in at a new school, I don't want to get up one second sooner than I have to, either.

Still, now that I know, everything feels even weirder than normal. People move by us, jostling Macy, bumping into me, or even skirting us entirely the same as they did yesterday. But today, all I can do is look at them and wonder. Vampire? Shifter? Witch? *Dragon?* It's so strange, like falling into the pages of a fantasy novel...or a horror movie, depending on how this all goes.

As we walk, I kind of assign monsters to people based on characteristics they exhibit, but I have no idea if I'm right or not. For example, the really athletic ones who bound down the hall with all the energy, I figure must be wolves. But Jaxon moves hella fast when he wants to, so I could be completely wrong.

I want to ask Macy, just to see if any of my guesses are right. But it seems rude to whisper about people's ...species? Identity?

Whatever I'm Supposed to Call It? in the middle of the hall where anyone can hear. Or, for that matter, to whisper about it at all.

But at the same time, don't I kind of need to know? Like, if I cut my finger in front of a dragon, I figure it won't matter at all. But what happens if I do it in front of a vampire? Do I need to run, or is everything going to be okay?

And why are vampires even in the dining hall if they drink blood? I mean, I saw Jaxon eat that strawberry at the welcome party, but he didn't touch any of the food at breakfast yesterday. And now that I think about it, neither did any of the other guys.

And if Jaxon does drink blood regularly, where does he get it? Where do any of the vampires get it? I mean, short of kidnapping a fully stocked bloodmobile every day—which seems an impossible feat anywhere, let alone in the middle of freaking Alaska—where do they get the blood?

More importantly, do I really want to know the answer to that question?

Also, I've seen Jaxon and Lia outside during the day. I mean, it wasn't super sunny, but it was definitely not pitch-black, either. So does that mean the whole *vampires can't be in the sun* thing is a myth? If so, there are a lot of stories throughout history that got it wrong.

It's so confusing. Like, supremely confusing, especially since there's a part of me that still thinks Macy and Mekhi are just messing with me. I mean, yeah, I saw what she did with that teacup, but still... Witches? Dragons? Vampires?

Can I just say that I'm *really* beginning to miss my alien theory?

Especially when we step in the cafeteria and—surprise, surprise—everyone is looking at me. Per usual. I thought it was because I was the new girl. Now I can't help but think it's because I'm the *human* girl. Which then leads to thoughts about whether or not any of them are thinking about eating me.

Do wolf shifters eat humans? Or is it just vampires? What about dragons? What do they eat?

I really hope human isn't on their delicacy list. Then again, wishing hasn't gotten me much in the last month. I can't expect it to get me this, either.

"You know what?" I tell Macy as we make our way to the buffet table at the front of the dining hall. "Maybe I should go back to the room."

"What's wrong?" She searches my face with a concerned frown. "Are you feeling dizzy? Or weak?"

"I'm feeling…out of place."

"Oh." Understanding dawns. "They're the same people you went to class with yesterday. The same people you had a snowball fight with the day before that."

"The same people who have been watching me since I got here. I thought they'd be over it by now, that they'd get used to me. But they're *never* going to get used to having a human here."

"I hate to be the one to break it to you, Grace, but the stares you're getting these days have way more to do with Jaxon than they do with you."

I don't bother to hide my confusion. "What do you mean?"

"I mean, he's a big deal here. Obviously. And he's shown an interest in you. Which makes *you* a big deal. It also makes you the person eighty percent of the female population wants to murder."

"Because they're jealous, right? Not because—"

"Yes, Grace." She rolls her eyes. "Because they're jealous. They want to be where you are."

"Bandaged up and sore, with a weak ankle and a vampire bite in my neck?" I joke.

"Exactly," she deadpans back. "Now, can we please get in line? It's chocolate croissant day, and they go fast."

"Of course." I gesture for her to precede me. "Who am I to get between a girl and her chocolate croissant?"

"A question every guy in the place asks himself at least once on Wednesdays," a familiar voice says from right behind me.

"Hi, Flint." I turn to him with a little bit of a forced smile. Not because his being a dragon makes me like him less, but because his being a dragon *FREAKS ME OUT.*

"Hey, New Girl." He looks me over. "Gotta say, I'm not a huge fan of your new look."

I touch the bandages self-consciously. "Yeah, me neither."

"I bet." He reaches out, rubs a reassuring hand up and down my non-damaged arm. "You don't look so good. Why don't you go sit down and let me bring you a plate?"

"You don't have to do that."

"I know I don't *have* to. But I still feel guilty about the whole *falling out of the tree* thing. This will help me make up for it." He gives me a beseeching look.

"What do you have to feel guilty about? You saved me from getting hurt worse." For the first time, I wonder if the reason he didn't get hurt at all is because he's a dragon. If so, then I'm glad he isn't human, glad that he wasn't in jeopardy because of me.

I look up at him with his incredibly handsome face, his glowing amber eyes, his charming grin, and wonder if I'm seeing the dragon or the human. Or maybe I'm seeing both. Who knows?

And then he raises his brows at me, and I wonder why it even matters when Flint—whatever and whoever he is—is my friend.

"Thank you again for that, by the way. I really appreciate it."

"Stop it, Grace. You wouldn't even have been up that tree if it weren't for me."

"I think we're just going to have to agree to disagree on this," I tell him.

"Fine. We'll agree to disagree…as soon as you let me bring you breakfast." He gives me his most charming grin, the one that would probably knock my socks off if I hadn't seen Jaxon first.

But I did see Jaxon, and now he's pretty much all I *can* see, vampire or not.

I start to argue with Flint some more—I'm sick of people treating me like an invalid—but we're holding up the line. And since the last thing I want to do is make an even bigger spectacle of myself, I just give in.

"Fine. I'll take a chocolate croissant if you can get one."

"Oh, I'll get one," he assures me.

"I have no doubt. And some fruit, if there is any."

"Sure. And what do you want to drink?"

I grin. "Surprise me."

His eyes darken, and for a second, something flashes in them. But before I can figure it out, it's gone, and the lightness is back. And so is the teasing as he says, "Believe me, I intend to."

Then he grabs both my shoulders and turns me around. "I'm sitting over there." He points toward the end of the center table. "There're a few extra seats. Why don't you head that way, and I'll be over as soon as I get our plates?"

"Sounds good." I do as he says, stopping just long enough to let Macy know where we'll be sitting.

Flint watches me the whole time, but I figure that's because he doesn't trust me to actually sit down. What he doesn't realize is that when the alternative is standing around awkwardly waiting for him while everyone looks on, it takes all my self-control not to run to a seat. Preferably in the back corner of the room.

Especially when I see Mekhi and Luca heading my way, dark frowns on their usually relaxed faces. I think about waiting for them, but I don't really want to hear what they have to say. And I don't want to explain to them why Macy and I decided it would be okay to come to the dining hall—at least not in front of most of the student body.

So instead of waiting for them to catch up, I do what any girl who doesn't want to deal with a boy would do—I take off toward another boy's territory. In this case, the table where Flint and his friends are sitting.

It may not be the bravest or brightest move, but it's definitely the path of least resistance. I'm not ashamed to admit that I could do with a little less resistance and a little more easy in my life. Especially today.

I'm pretty sure it would have worked, too—the Order and Flint dislike each other *that* much—except for the terrible wrenching sound that splits the air directly above me just as I get close to Flint's part of the table.

42

Good Thing Pancakes Aren't on Today's Menu

It's a horrific noise, and I glance up, trying to figure out what could possibly be making it, just in time to see the biggest crystal chandelier in the place pull free of the plate holding it to the ceiling. I have about half a second to think, *Oh shit*, and then someone is there, slamming their body into mine.

The hit knocks the breath out of me—or maybe it's the subsequent slam, face-first, into the nearest wall that does it. Either way, it's a struggle to get my breath back, especially since there's a long, lean male body pressed against my back, his arms caging me in on either side.

I realize that at the same time there's a gigantic crash. For a second, all I can hear is the tinkle of glass as it shatters and flies, hitting everything in its path. The boy behind me grunts and wraps himself more tightly around me, and that's when I know. I may not be able to draw a full breath yet, but there's enough oxygen in my body for my brain to function again. And my newly functioning brain registers one thing above all else—that the guy currently wrapped around me is *Jaxon*.

"Are you okay?" he demands as soon as the glass stops flying.

I don't answer him—I can't. My lungs still aren't working at full capacity yet and neither is my voice.

I try to nod, but that's obviously not good enough for him because he's whirling me around, his hands skimming over my body as he orders, "Answer me, Grace! Are you all right?"

"I'm okay," I finally manage to gasp out. But that's when I get my first good look at him and realize that while I may be okay, he very definitely isn't. "You're bleeding."

"I'm fine." He shrugs it off. "Does anything hurt?"

"I'm not the one who's injured." I run a light finger over the right side of his face, pausing at the bloody parts. "What are you even doing here? I thought it would take a couple more hours for you to get back."

His dark eyes smolder at me—and not in a good way. "Obviously."

I don't know what to say to that, and he doesn't look like he's in the mood to listen anyway, so I reach into my purse (score one for vanity) and pull out the tiny first aid kit I keep inside it. It's a habit I picked up after my parents died in the car accident—ridiculous, since it would have taken more than a first aid kit to save them, with their injuries. Still, Heather's mom suggested it when I was freaking out right after they died, and for whatever reason, it calmed me down. Today's the first day it's actually going to come in handy, though.

"Sit down," I tell him, and when he doesn't move, I put my hands on his chest and gently push.

He doesn't budge.

"Please," I ask, moving a hand up to cup his uninjured but scarred cheek. "You're hurt. Let me take care of you."

For long seconds, he still doesn't move, just stares at me, unblinking. It sends chills down my spine—I don't think I've ever seen Jaxon this furious. Which…fine. He can be as angry as he wants as long as he lets me treat his wounds. "Please," I say again, and this time I accompany it with a little shove to his chest.

He still doesn't say anything but slowly, grudgingly, he allows me to guide him to the nearest chair.

Macy makes it to me right around the time I get Jaxon settled. Tears are pouring down her face as she throws her arms around my neck. "Oh my God, Grace! Are you all right?"

"I'm fine, I'm fine," I tell her even as I try to disengage from her hug. What is wrong with her and Jaxon? Can't they tell that he's the one who's hurt? Maybe it's not a big deal when vampires bleed; I don't know. But it's a big deal to me.

I pull an antibacterial wipe out of the pack and press it gently to his cheek. He doesn't wince. In fact, he doesn't move at all—just stares stonily ahead. Still, I clean the wound carefully, making sure there's no glass in it, before squeezing ointment onto his cheek and following it with a Band-Aid. I have a moment of wondering if he needs the ointment—can vampires even get infections? But he doesn't stop me, and neither does Macy, so I figure even if it's not necessary, at least it won't hurt anything.

By now, adults are swarming the dining hall, teachers checking for injuries and trying to clear students out of the room as quickly as possible. It's a surprisingly quiet affair, one I don't pay much attention to as I move on to the jagged cut on Jaxon's arm.

I'm pretty sure it looks worse than it is, considering he hasn't bled much and it's already clotting. I wonder if maybe their venom isn't the only thing with a quick coagulant in it. Still, I clean it as thoroughly as I did his cheek. I have to admit I'm a little surprised no teacher has come by and tried to bundle him off to the nurse, but maybe there are people with worse injuries and I just don't realize it.

It's not until I finish bandaging his arm and step back that I realize there's a very good reason no one has tried to take Jaxon for medical attention. It's the same reason that the room is so quiet despite everything that's happened.

The five other members of the Order have surrounded us.

They're several yards away, but they have definitely formed a perimeter around Jaxon and me, one that no one but Macy has been able to get through. Not that many people are exactly trying. Flint's getting into it with Byron, who isn't budging, but other than that, everyone else is standing back. Watching and obviously waiting, though I'm not sure for what.

It's an eerie feeling to know that they're expecting something that I don't understand, and it has my stomach dropping and nerves skittering along my spine. I assume it's because I've done something wrong, but what was I supposed to do? Just leave him bleeding?

"I'm…sorry." I say it haltingly as I'm packing up my first aid kit. "I guess I shouldn't have done that."

"Don't apologize," Jaxon growls as he stands up. "And don't duck your head like that. No one in here has the right to say a damn thing to you."

"I just wanted to help. And to thank you for saving me."

"I wouldn't have had to save you if you'd been in your room, where you were supposed to be. Where I told you to be." He grinds the last sentence out between clenched teeth.

I take offense at the *where I told you to be* part of his statement, but considering he's still shaking a little bit, I decide not to make an issue of it. Yet. Instead, I explain, "Macy and I were hungry. Plus, once we figured out the mystery of the bite, we figured it would be fine for us to come down to breakfast. It turns out the nurse—"

"Chandeliers don't fall on their own," he tells me. "And neither do tree branches."

"The tree branch didn't just fall. The wind was out of control."

"There are at least two hundred people in this room alone capable of making that kind of wind. And almost that many capable of dropping that chandelier." He's speaking softly now, so softly that I have to strain to hear him, even though he's right in front of me. "I keep trying to tell you, but you won't listen. Someone is trying to kill you, Grace."

43

What Doesn't Kill You Still Scares the Hell Out of You

At first, his words don't register. And when they finally do, it takes a few more beats for me to remember how to form my own words.

"Kill *me*?" I finally whisper back to him as my stomach plummets and a chill works its way down my spine. Or I should say, I *try* to whisper because it's pretty hard to keep my voice super low now that the squeak is back.

I would be embarrassed, but to be honest, I feel like I've got a lot to squeak about. It's been one hell of a morning, and the hits just keep on coming. "That's ridiculous," I tell him even as I wipe my suddenly damp palms against my skirt. "Why?"

"I don't know yet."

I take a deep breath, try to get my racing heart back under control as I struggle to think through the panic slamming through me. It takes a minute, but I finally get the anxiety to recede enough that I can answer, "It doesn't make sense. I'm harmless."

Especially at this school. I mean, I'm not a threat at a regular high school. I'm sure as hell not a threat at a school where a quarter of the residents can shoot fire and fly.

"There are a lot of words I'd use to describe you, Grace.

'Harmless' isn't one of them." He glances around the room, eyes narrowed, whether in thought or warning, I can't be sure. "And if *I* know that, so do they."

"Jaxon." I wrap my arms around my waist and rock back on my heels a little as I try to convince him to see reason. As I try to convince *myself* that his words don't mean anything. "You can't really believe that. You're just upset at the near miss. You're not thinking clearly."

"I always think clearly." He starts to say more, but then something over my shoulder draws his attention. His eyes narrow to slits that have my heart racing all over again.

I turn and follow his gaze, only to find him staring at the rope that ties to the chandelier so it can be lowered for cleaning. Or should I say what's left of the rope, because even from here, I can see that it's in two pieces.

"It broke," I tell him, but there's an uncertainty to my voice when I say the words. Because how often does one of those ropes actually break? "Sometimes ropes—"

Jaxon interrupts me with, "Your uncle's here," and a small shake of his head.

"So? I want to talk about this."

"Later."

Before I can voice another objection, Uncle Finn closes in.

"Grace, honey, I'm so sorry it took me this long to get to you. I was out on the school grounds." He pulls me into a hug and holds me tight.

Normally, I'd find it comforting—the way he feels and smells so much like my dad. But right now, all I can think about is the look in Jaxon's eyes when he said someone was trying to kill me. His face was completely blank, completely unreadable. But burning deep in his eyes, where most people don't get close enough to look, was the most terrifying rage I've ever seen.

I don't want to leave him alone with it, don't want to let him stay trapped in his own head. But no matter how I pat Uncle Finn's back and assure him I'm okay, my uncle doesn't seem to be letting go any time soon.

"I can't begin to tell you how horrified I am that this has happened to you," he says when he finally pulls back. His blue eyes, so like Macy's and my father's, are sad and shadowed. "Once is unacceptable. Twice in two days..."

I guess I should count myself lucky he doesn't know about me falling out of that tree a few days ago. Three near-death experiences in a week are a lot for anyone.

Then again, when I think of it like that, suddenly Jaxon doesn't seem so paranoid. And maybe I don't seem paranoid enough.

"Well, let's get you out of here," my uncle says. "We hadn't planned on you going to class today anyway, but I would like to talk to you before you go back to your room."

"Oh, sure." I can't imagine what there is to talk about—I mean, what is there to say except *whew, close call*—but if it will make him feel better, I'm all for it.

Except every instinct I have is screaming at me not to leave Jaxon, screaming that this isn't the time to walk away from him, though I don't know why. "But can I come by your office a little later? I have a couple of things I need to do first—"

"Jaxon's already gone, Grace." I whirl around to find that my uncle is right. Jaxon *is* gone. "And I want to talk to you before you see him again anyway."

I don't know what that means, but I don't like the sound of it. Any more than I like the fact that, once again, Jaxon took off without so much as a goodbye.

How does he do it? I wonder as I reluctantly follow my uncle. How does he just disappear without my even hearing or sensing him moving? Is it a vampire thing? Or a Jaxon thing? I'm pretty sure it's a Jaxon thing, but as I walk toward the dining hall doors, I realize every other member of the Order is gone, too. They all left, and I didn't have a freaking clue.

Which only backs up what I was telling Jaxon before my uncle showed up. I'm just a harmless human—why on earth would anyone here think I'm dangerous enough to try to kill me?

I mean, Jaxon, sure. I'm surprised they aren't lined up around the castle to take a shot at him—everything about the guy screams total, complete, *absolute* power. I'm pretty sure the only thing keeping him safe is that those same things also scream dangerous as fuck. I can't imagine anyone here being foolish enough to challenge him—even Flint backed down right after the snowball fight.

Which is why dropping a chandelier on Jaxon makes sense. But dropping one on me? Come on. One bad spell, wolf attack, or even *earthquake*, and I'm a goner. Why go through the trouble of bringing an entire chandelier down on top of my head when a broken window nearly did me in all on its own?

Uncle Finn doesn't say anything as we walk to his office and neither do I. I have to admit I am surprised, though, when he turns down what has to be the least-ornate corridor in this entire place and then stops in front of the most boring-looking door. Doesn't exactly jive with my idea of any headmaster's office, let alone the headmaster of a school that's taken on the responsibility of educating students from a wide range of paranormal backgrounds.

That impression is only reinforced when he opens his door and ushers me inside the most boring room in existence. Gray carpet, gray walls, gray chairs. The only spot of brightness in the room—if you can even call it that—is the heavy cherrywood desk loaded down with piles of papers, files, and an open laptop.

Basically, it looks like every other principal's office I've ever seen—except the window coverings are sturdier and the gray carpet is a little more plush.

He catches me staring and grins. "Surprised?"

"A little bit. I thought it would be more..."

"More?" His brows go up.

"Just more. No offense, Uncle Finn, but this has to be the most utilitarian room I've ever seen. I guess I expected a witch to have more flair."

"Good thing I'm not a witch, then, huh?"

"What?" My mind boggles. "I thought— Macy said— I don't—"

"Relax, Grace," my uncle says with a laugh. "I was just trying to lighten the mood. Macy told me she spilled all the tea."

"No offense, but it's kind of hard to keep the tea in the pot when I have fang marks in my neck."

"Touché." He inclines his head, gestures to one of the plain gray chairs in front of the desk as he walks around to the back of it. "Have a seat.

"I *am* sorry you had to find out that way," he continues when we're both seated. "It's not what I wanted for you."

He looks so miserable, I want to tell him it's okay, except it really isn't. "Why didn't you tell me? Or my dad? Why didn't he ever admit that he was a—" I break off, still having a hard time wrapping my head around the fact that my dad was a real-life witch. Or at least he'd been born one.

"I believe the word you're looking for is warlock," my uncle tells me, filling in the word I'm having such a hard time saying—and believing—with a sympathetic smile. "And yes, your father was a warlock—and very powerful at one point."

"Before he gave it up for my mother."

"It's a little more complicated than that." My uncle makes a face, kind of wobbles his head back and forth. "No warlock gives up his power willingly, but some, like your father, are willing to risk everything for the greater good."

That's not how Macy described it, which makes me wonder just what my cousin doesn't know about my father. And what my uncle does. "What—what do you mean?" I ask as my heart skips a beat. "What did he do?'

For a second, my uncle looks far away, but his eyes clear at my question. "It's a long story," he tells me. "One for another day, considering you've got more than enough going on for this morning."

"Pretty sure I have enough going on for a lot of mornings," I answer. "For *all* the mornings, really."

"Yeah, you do." He sighs. "That's actually what I want to talk to you about. You've had quite a first week, young lady."

Talk about an understatement. I wait for him to say more, wait for the other shoe to drop even though it feels like a hundred have already fallen, but time passes and he doesn't say anything. Instead, he just kind of steeples his hands in front of his chin and stares at me across the desk. I don't know if he's doing it because he's waiting for me to break or if he's just trying to figure out the right way to say whatever he wants to say. I figure it must be the latter, because I haven't done anything wrong. I have no secrets to spill, especially not compared to the man who runs a school for monsters.

The prolonged silence does give me time to think, though. About all the wrong things. Including the fact that in the last week, what little control I've had over my life has disappeared completely.

I mean, seriously. Death by chandelier has to be one of the most random and bizarre deaths on the planet. The whole thing seems ridiculous, no matter what Jaxon says. But losing my parents the way I did—having them go from happy and alive to cold and dead in the space from one minute to the next—has taught me just how easy it is for life to be extinguished.

As simple as the blink of your eye, the snap of your fingers, making the wrong turn at the wrong time...

I squeeze my eyes shut as the images flood back, desperate to stem them before they fill my head. Before they overwhelm me and bury me in the grief I'm only just learning how to crawl out of.

The pain must show on my face, because suddenly my uncle is breaking the silence to ask, "Are you sure you're okay, Grace? That chandelier was huge—and terrifying."

It *was* huge and terrifying, and I'm not sure how my life has gone so completely out of control. Five weeks ago, Heather and I were shopping for homecoming dresses and complaining about AP English. Now I'm an orphan living with half an encyclopedia of supernatural creatures and dodging death on the regular. At this rate, my only hope is that the universe doesn't hold a *Final Destination*–type grudge.

"I'm fine," I tell him, because physically I am. There's not even a scratch on me—or at least, not a new one. "Just a little shaken up."

"Give me a break, kid. *I'm* traumatized, and I wasn't even there. I can't believe you're only a little shaken up." He reaches for the hand I have resting on the desk and pats it a little awkwardly. I know he's trying to be comforting, but his eyes are filled with worry as they search my face.

I do my best to make sure there's nothing for him to find there, and I must succeed because, eventually, he shakes his head and leans back in his chair. "You're just like your mother, you know that? She always faced whatever life handed her head-on, too. No tears, no hysterics, just cool, calm resolve."

His casual mention of my mom now—when I'm missing her so much—destroys me, has me squeezing my hands into fists and digging my nails into my palms in an effort to keep it together.

It helps that Uncle Finn doesn't stay there, dwelling on my mom's incredible ability to take everything in stride—something I haven't inherited, no matter what my uncle thinks. Instead, he pulls something up on the computer and prints it out.

"You really sure you're okay? You don't want Marise to check you out?" he asks for what feels like the millionth time.

No freaking way. I know Macy said she bit me so that she could mend my artery, but that doesn't mean I'm anxious to let her near my throat again—or any other part of my anatomy, for that matter. "I swear I'm fine. It's Jaxon you should be concerned about. He shielded me from the glass."

"I've already requested that Marise check him out," he tells me. "And I'll call him in later to thank him for saving my favorite niece from harm."

"Only niece," I remind him, falling into the game we've played my entire life. It's a tiny bit of normalcy in this day that is anything but normal, and I grab on to it with both hands.

"Only *and* favorite," he tells me. "One doesn't discount the other."

"Okay, favorite uncle. I guess it doesn't."

"Exactly!" His slightly strained smile turns into a delighted grin. But it doesn't last long as silence once again descends between us.

This time I can't stop myself from fidgeting—not because I'm nervous but because I want to get out of here and get to Jaxon. He looked like he was on edge earlier, and I just want to make sure nothing bad happens—to him or anyone else.

But Uncle Finn obviously takes my fidgeting for something else entirely, because he rubs a hand over his hair with a heavy sigh. Then says, "So now that the cat is out of the bag..."

"Don't you mean the werewolf?" I ask with a raised brow. "Or do you have cat shifters up here, too?"

He laughs. "Nope, just the wolves and dragons for now."

"Just." My tone is ripe with irony.

"You must have a lot of questions."

A lot? Nah. Just two or three million. Starting with the question I asked earlier that he chose not to answer. "Why didn't you tell me? You could have told me when you asked me to move to Alaska, when you came for the funerals."

"I figured you were pretty overwhelmed then, and the last thing you needed was for me to try to convince you that vampires and witches are real."

It's a fair point. But still... "And after I got here?"

He blows out a long breath. "I figured I would ease you in slowly. That first night, I had planned to let you know that things were different here than you might expect, but you had the most miserable altitude sickness. Then everything else happened, and it just seemed easier to leave you in the dark for a while. Especially when Dr. Wainwright told me that after talking to Dr. Blake, she thought we should let you get used to Alaska, and the huge change in your life, before you had to face the fact that everything you'd ever heard about the supernatural world was actually real."

"Everything?" It's my turn to lift my brows.

"Maybe not *everything*. But a lot of it, certainly."

What he says makes sense, I guess, but I'm still skeptical—especially since I haven't even had a chance to meet Dr. Wainwright yet. But how could anyone actually think they could hide the fact that this school is filled with things that go bump in the night?

I mean, when I think of Flint jumping out of a tree to save

me or Macy doing a glamour right in front of me or the shifters walking around in nothing but a pair of jeans or Jaxon…doing whatever Jaxon does, it seems impossible to imagine I wouldn't catch on. Sure, I was thinking aliens instead of vampires, but I still knew something was very, very wrong.

My skepticism must show on my face, because my uncle kind of grimaces. "Yeah. In hindsight, it was a bad plan all around. It's not exactly easy to hide the fact that vampires and dragons are real when we're in the middle of a giant turf war."

"Turf war?" I ask, because Macy has already alluded to the same thing. I thought she was talking about high school clique BS, but now that I know we're talking about different supernatural species…her warning makes a lot more sense.

And seems a lot scarier.

He shakes his head. "That's for another day. I'm pretty sure you've had as much as you can handle today—I know I have. Which leads me to the reason I've really called you in here."

It's pretty much the most awkward change of subject ever, and I almost call him on it because I know there is more to the story than he's telling me. A lot more. I'm also sure there are a lot more stories that I don't have a clue about, let alone the information that fleshes them out. But I don't think arguing with him is the way to get him to talk.

So instead of demanding answers to all my many, many questions, I bite my tongue and wait to hear what Uncle Finn has to say.

"I was thinking, a lot of really horrible stuff has happened to you since you got here."

"Not much has actually happened to me," I remind him. "Jaxon has saved me a bunch of times."

"I know he has, but we can't count on Jaxon to always be around. Stuff happens here that doesn't happen in other schools—as you've seen the last few days. What happened with the earthquake was a freak accident, and I'm sure the chandelier was as well. But it's made me think. What will happen to you if someone loses control of their powers when Jaxon or Flint or Macy isn't around to whisk you out of the way? What happens if you end up getting seriously hurt?" He shakes his head. "I wouldn't be able to live with myself."

"Do you think that's what happened? Someone lost control of their powers?"

"We're not sure, but that's the assumption we're going with right now. Some witch was trying to see what she could do and *bam*... While we've never actually lost a chandelier before, we have had crystals fly across the room. Among other things."

That might actually be the best news I've heard all day, because it means Jaxon was probably freaking out for nothing. No one is trying to kill me—someone just had an oops with their powers and I happened to be in the way. Which makes so much more sense than thinking that someone might actually be out to get me.

"Anyway." My uncle is back to steepling his fingers. "That's why I want to send you back to San Diego."

44

Sweet Home Alaska

"Send me back?" Horror slides through me like a plane on an icy runway—fast, desperate, all-consuming. "What do you mean? There's nothing for me there."

"I know." He shakes his head sadly. "But I'm beginning to think there's nothing for you here, either. And at least there, you'll be safe."

"You mean like my parents were safe?" The words are torn out of me, ragged and painful and terrified. Going back to San Diego means leaving Jaxon, and I don't want to do that. I *can't* do that, not now, when it's obvious that something is happening between us. Not now, when he's the first thing I think of when I wake up and the last before I fall asleep.

"That was a fluke, Grace. A terrible accident—"

"Accidents can happen anywhere. And if something is going to happen to me, I'd rather it happen here when I'm with Macy and you and—" I break off, unwilling to put voice to something I'm just beginning to understand myself. That somehow, in just about a week, Jaxon Vega has come to mean something to me.

But apparently, my uncle is more perceptive than I thought, because he finishes the sentence for me. "Jaxon?" he asks gently.

I don't answer. I *can't*. Whatever is between the two of us is between the two of us. No way can I try to explain it to Uncle Finn.

Then again, my lack of answer is pretty much an answer in and of itself. "I know Jaxon can be..." He pauses, blows out another long breath. "Seductive. I know how the girls feel about him, and I get it. He's—"

"Uncle Finn! No!" I all but put my hands over my ears to keep from hearing my uncle refer to the boy I'm falling for as "seductive."

"No?" he asks, looking confused. "You're not attracted to—?"

"I mean, no! Just no! I don't know what, if anything, is going on with Jaxon and me, but *we*"—I gesture back and forth between us—"are not talking about it."

"We aren't?"

"No. We aren't." I shake my head emphatically. "Not now, not ever."

"I swear, talking to you about boys is as bad as trying to talk to Macy about them," he says with a roll of his eyes. "Every time I ask her about Cam, she acts like I asked her to swallow eye of newt or something. But fine. No talking about boys. Except I do need to warn you that Jaxon is—"

"Dangerous. Yeah, Macy's already ground that into my head. And maybe he is, but he's never been anything but gentle with me, so—"

"I wasn't going to say dangerous." For the first time, there's a touch of annoyance in his voice. "And you'd know that if you stopped interrupting me."

"Oh, right." I can feel myself start to blush. "Sorry."

He just shakes his head. "What I was going to say is that Jaxon is not like any other boy you've ever met."

"Well, obviously." I do the same fang-miming thing I did with

Macy, and Uncle Finn bursts out laughing, too.

"I meant for a lot more reasons than just his being a vampire, but yes, there is the vampire thing as well."

Oh. His words set off butterflies in my stomach, though I'm not sure why. "What else is there?" I ask, because I can't *not* ask. "I know about his brother—"

"He told you about Hudson?" Now my uncle sounds shocked.

"Just that he died."

"Oh, yes." The way his face relaxes tells me there's a lot more to the story than what I know. Well, that and the fact that everyone has the same reaction when I mention that I know about Hudson. "His death left Jaxon with a lot of responsibility to shoulder—Hudson's and his own."

"I can imagine."

"No, Grace, you can't." He looks more somber than I have ever seen him. "Because being a vampire isn't like being a regular person."

"Okay. Sure. But he was regular once, right?" I think back on every vampire movie I've ever seen, every novel I've ever read. "I mean—"

"No. That's just it. Jaxon was born a vampire."

Now I'm the shocked one. "What do you mean? I thought all vampires..."

"Not all, no. Vampires can be made—in fact, most of them are. But they can also be born. Jaxon was born, as were the other members of the Order. And that means...a lot in our world."

I can't even begin to imagine what it means, because I'm still stuck on his *vampires can be born* revelation. "But how? I mean, I thought you had to be bitten to become a vampire?"

"Usually, yes. But that's assuming they want to turn you. If they don't, you just get a bite. Like..."

"Like what Marise did to me, you mean."

"Yes." He nods.

"That still doesn't explain how vampires can be born," I tell him. Part of me feels like I'm going to drown with all this new information, and part of me is kind of like…huh, okay. No big deal.

I guess after making the leap to accept that all these creatures exist, *how* they came to exist isn't nearly as shocking.

"Like other things, vampirism is a genetic mutation. Rare, exceptionally rare, but a genetic mutation nonetheless. The first documented cases happened a few thousand years ago, but since then, many more have happened."

"Wait a minute. You have *documented* cases of vampires from thousands of years ago? How is that possible? I mean, how can you prove it?"

"Because they're still alive, Grace."

"Oh. Right." Something else I didn't see coming, though I probably should have. "Because vampires don't die."

"They do die, just much more slowly than the rest of us, because their cells develop differently than ours."

Of course they do. Otherwise there wouldn't be so much bloodsucking and who knows what else. "And Jaxon is one of these vampires? One of the old ones?" The thought turns the butterflies into vultures. Which is strange. I mean, I'm totally willing to accept the vampire thing, so why does the old thing totally freak me out?

"Jaxon was born into the most ancient vampire family. But no, he's not four thousand years old, if that's what you're asking."

Oh, thank God. "So these families are the only ones who can give birth to vampires? I mean, vampires can't just be born from anyone, right?"

"It's a genetic mutation, so yes, vampires can be born to anyone. Usually, they aren't. Usually, born vampires come from one of the six ancient families, but other born vampires do happen. They're usually the ones you read about in stories, because they don't have any knowledge of who or what they are, so they..."

"Run rampant killing everyone in sight?"

"I wouldn't put it quite like that," he tells me with an exasperated look. "But yes. They are the ones who tend to make other vampires, because they don't know any better. Or because they're lonely and want to create a family. Or for several other reasons, as well. The older families aren't like that, though."

"What does that mean? They don't kill people?" I have to admit that's a huge relief.

At least until my uncle laughs and says, "Let's not get carried away."

"Oh, well, then. Jaxon has..."

"I'm not in the habit of talking about students with other students, Grace. And this conversation has gone far afield from where I intended it to go."

True, but I've learned a lot, so I'm more than okay with where the conversation has gone. Though the laugh that accompanied his *let's not get carried away* line was more than a little chilling. "I don't want to go back to San Diego, Uncle Finn."

It's the first time I've said it out loud. The first time I've really even thought it and believed it. But as the words come out of my mouth, I know they're true. No matter how much I miss the beach and the warmth and the life I used to have with my parents, going back there isn't what I want. My parents are gone forever, and nothing else that San Diego has holds as much appeal as Jaxon.

Nothing.

"Grace, I'm glad you like it at Katmere Academy. I am. But I don't know if it's safe. I thought I could protect you here, but obviously being a regular person in a school meant for paranormals is dangerous."

Considering my week, that seems like an understatement. But still… "Isn't it my decision to make?"

"It is. But you can't make it over a boy."

"I'm not making it because of Jaxon. Or at least, not just because of Jaxon." This, too, is true. "I'm making it because of Macy. And you. And even Flint. I'm making it because I miss San Diego and my life there, but that life is over. My parents are dead, and if I stay there, if I go back to the same school and the same life I had—minus them—it's going to be a slap in the face. A reminder, every day, of what I lost.

"And I don't think I can do that, Uncle Finn. I don't think I can heal there, driving by my old house on the way to school every day. Going to all the places my parents and I used to go—" My voice breaks, and I look away, embarrassed by the tears in my eyes. Embarrassed by how weak I feel every time I think about my mom and dad.

"Okay." This time, when he reaches across the desk, he takes both my hands in his. "Okay, Grace. If that's how you feel, you know you can stay. You're always welcome wherever Macy and I are. But we have to do something about all these near misses, because I am not okay with something happening to you on my watch. The day you were born, I promised your father I'd take care of you if anything ever happened to him, and I am not about to let him down."

"That sounds perfect, because, honestly, I'm not a big fan of all the near misses, either."

He laughs. "I bet. So what—?"

He's interrupted by the buzzing of the intercom on his desk. *"Headmaster Foster, your nine o'clock call is on line three."*

"Oh, right. Thanks, Gladys." He looks at me. "Unfortunately,

I've got to take this. Why don't you head back to your room and relax for the rest of the day? I'll think about how we're going to keep you safe and come by around lunchtime to talk to you and Macy about it. Sound good?"

"Sounds great." I scoop my backpack off the ground and head for the door. Once I've got it open, though, I turn back to my uncle. "Thank you."

"Don't thank me yet. I haven't come up with any ideas."

"No, I mean, thank you for coming to San Diego to get me. Thank you for taking me in. Thank you for—"

"Being your family?" He shakes his head. "You never have to thank me for that, Grace. I love you. Macy loves you. And you'll have a place with us for as long as you want it. Okay?"

I swallow the sudden lump in my throat. "Okay." Then I book it out the door before I turn into a blubbering mess for the second time in as many days.

But I've barely closed the door and made it three steps down the hall before the floor beneath my feet starts to shake. Again.

45

I Always Knew There Was Fire Between Us; I Just Didn't Realize it Was Your Breath

This one isn't bad—the ground just rumbles a little. But it's enough to make me nervous. More than enough to have me sheltering in the nearest doorway, like they taught us in elementary school. No way am I interested in any more injuries… or any more close calls, for that matter.

When the aftershock finishes a few seconds later, I pull out my phone and text Jaxon. Just to let him know I'm okay—and to make sure he is. Plus, I'd like to actually have a conversation with him where neither one of us is hurt—and half the school isn't looking on. I text him a quick, *Where are you? Want to meet up?* then wait impatiently for his answer.

It doesn't come, which only makes me more nervous.

I wish I'd gotten Mekhi's phone number this morning so I could text him, too, but I didn't, so I'm stuck, wandering the halls and waiting for Jaxon to text me back.

Not sure what else to do, I head up the stairs toward Jaxon's tower. But truth is, I'm not keen on showing up at his door uninvited again. He's the one who left me in the cafeteria, and he's the one who isn't answering my texts. I want to see him, want to talk to him, but I'm not going to chase him anymore.

This time, he needs to come to me.

Which means I probably shouldn't head back to my room, where I'll spend all my time obsessing over where Jaxon is and what he's doing instead of something productive. And I've already spent enough of my time thinking about that boy today—probably too much, considering the way he's currently ignoring me.

It's that thought more than any other that has me heading down the hallway to the library as soon as I get to the second floor. I've been meaning to go back during regular hours so I can take my time looking around—and also maybe even find some books to check out. Apparently, I have a lot to learn about paranormal creatures, and now is as good a time as any to get started. Plus, I figure my uncle and Macy can't complain I'm not resting if I spend the day curled up with a bunch of horror movie throw pillows and a good book.

Class is in session, so the library is almost empty when I get there. Which is more than okay with me—the fewer people I run into, the lower the chance of any more "accidents."

I think about starting in the mythology section, seeing if there are any books on the different paranormal creatures I go to school with. It's where I would start in a regular library, but here at Katmere, monsters are real. So would I find books about them under nonfiction? Or biology?

This whole *monsters are real* thing is going to take a lot of getting used to.

I decide to stop at the main desk and ask the librarian where I should start. And the truth is, I've been dying to meet her since I found this place the other day. Her sticker choices and gargoyle placements alone mark her as supercool in my book.

It's an impression that is only reinforced when I actually get to see her up close.

She's tall and beautiful, with glowing copper skin. Her long, dark hair is threaded with orange and silver tinsel—leftover from Halloween, I imagine—and she's dressed like a total hippie, all flowing, long-sleeve boho dress and boots. Plus, she's got a giant smile on her face as I approach, something I haven't seen much of here at the very dark and very Gothic Katmere Academy.

"Ms. Royce?" I ask when I reach the front of the desk.

"You can call me Amka. Many of the students do." If possible, her grin gets even friendlier. "You must be Grace, the new student all the fuss is about."

My cheeks go warm. "That's not quite how I would have put it, but yeah. I guess I am."

"It's good to meet you. I'm glad to get to know the girl shaking up the status quo around here. They could use it."

"They?"

She chuckles and leans forward just a little. Then, in a loud, staged whisper, says, "The monsters."

My eyes go wide at the description, and relief floods me as I think back on what my uncle said. "So you're human, too?"

"Most of us are human, Grace. We just also happen to have a little something extra, that's all."

"Oh, right." I feel like a jerk. "Sorry, I didn't mean to offend you."

"You didn't." She holds out a hand. Seconds later, a light wind blows through the library, ruffling my hair and making the magazines on the rack behind me flutter.

"Oh! You're a witch!" I turn my face up so I can feel the breeze.

"I am. From the Inupiat tribe," she answers. "With an affinity for the elements."

"The elements?" I repeat, emphasizing the S. "So not just wind?"

"Not just wind," she agrees. She closes her hand, and the wind dies down instantly. Seconds later, without so much as a flick of her fingers, the candles in all the wall sconces begin to burn. "Fire. And I'd show you water, but I'm thinking you've had enough snow already."

"I really have," I agree. "But…if you don't mind, I'd still like to see it."

She nods, and seconds later, snowflakes start falling from the ceiling directly above our heads.

Instinctively, I reach my tongue out and taste one. Then tell her, "That's the coolest thing I've ever seen."

"Keep your eyes open," she answers. "There are a lot of cool things to see at Katmere."

"I'm looking forward to it," I say honestly. Because watching her manipulate the elements actually calms me down, convinces me that maybe things aren't as scary as I fear.

"Good," she says with a wink. "Now, what brings you to my library today?"

"Honestly, I just wanted to explore some more. I was in here the other day, and I fell in love with it. You've done an amazing job."

"Books are fascinating and fun. I figure the rooms that house them should be as well."

"You've definitely made that happen." I turn and look behind me. "I mean, the stickers alone are incredible. I could spend all day reading them. And the gargoyles. And the horror movie pillows? I love it all."

"I figure what's the good of working in a place like this if I can't have a little fun with it."

"Exactly!" I say with a laugh. "Which is actually the second reason I'm here. I was hoping to find some books that would help me learn more about the different kinds of people who go to school here."

She smiles at my clumsy attempt to incorporate the first lesson she taught me in my request—that most of the people here are human, just different. "I admire your open mind. And your willingness to embrace what you've learned."

"I'm trying. I figure there's a lot to learn."

"You've got time." She reaches over and takes hold of my hands, clasping them between both of hers.

It surprises me, but doesn't offend me, so I don't pull away. Though I kind of wish I had when her eyes start to do this weird swirling thing.

It's no big deal, I tell myself. I mean, Macy did a glamour and I was totally okay with it. This is no different.

Except it feels different. It feels like she's looking deep inside of me, like she can see way more than I want her—or anyone—to.

Which is ridiculous. I mean, just because she's a witch doesn't make her a mind reader. Except just when I've got myself convinced that nothing weird is happening, she whispers, "Don't be afraid."

"I'm not," I answer, because what else am I supposed to say? That her eye thing is freaking me out a little bit?

"You're more than you think you are," she continues.

"I…don't know what that means."

She smiles as her eyes go back to normal. "You will when you need to. That's what matters."

"Thank you," I say, because what else do you say at times like these? I guess I should work up a few comebacks, since I'm going to be here for a while.

"Here." Amka rips a piece of paper off a notepad on her desk and scribbles something down on it, then folds it in half and hands it to me. "You might benefit from checking out the end of the stacks a couple of rows down."

"What section is it?" Excitement thrums through me, chasing away the disquiet of just a few moments ago.

"Dragons." She flashes a dimple. "Always a good place to start."

"Absolutely." I think of Flint and all the questions I have about him. "Thanks!"

"No problem. When you find what you're looking for, you'll know what to do with this." She hands me the piece of paper, then reaches under her desk and pulls out a bottle of water. Here, take this, too. And drink it. You need to stay hydrated at this altitude."

"Oh, yeah." I take the bottle. "Thanks again."

She just waves me on my way.

I head down the aisle she pointed to, wondering what kind of books on dragons I'll find there—especially considering it looks like I'm in the mystery section. But as soon as I get to the end of the aisle, Amka's grin makes sense, as do her directions. Because sitting at one of the round tables—with his earbuds in and a really old book open to a section with weird writing—is Flint.

Dragons indeed.

He glances up when I take a step toward him, and a look I can't quite decipher flits across his face for a second. It's followed quickly by a huge grin as he pops out one of his Airpods. "Hey, New Girl! What are you doing here?"

It's impossible for me not to smile back. "Researching dragons, apparently."

"Oh yeah?" He pats the chair next to him. "Looks like you came to the right place."

"Looks like I did." As I move to sit next to him, I hand him the note Amka gave me. "I think this is for you."

"Really?" His brow wrinkles a little as he reaches for the paper. While he reads it, I check my phone to make sure I haven't missed a text from Jaxon.

I haven't.

"So," Flint says, deliberately not making eye contact as he drops the note on the table next to the book he's reading. What do you need to know about dragons?"

"We can do this later," I tell him. "I don't want to interrupt whatever you're working on."

"Don't worry about it. This is nothing." He closes the book before I can see much of anything and slides it away from him.

I see the language on the cover, though. "Oh, hey! Is that an Akkadian text?"

His eyes go wide. "How did you know about Akkadian?"

"Actually, I just learned about it for the first time a couple of days ago. Lia was researching it for a project. Are you guys in the same class?"

"Oh, yeah." He seems distinctly unenthusiastic, which isn't exactly a surprise considering how much they seem to dislike each other.

"What class is it for?" I reach for the book. "I kind of want to take it next semester, if I can."

"Ancient Languages of Magic." He eases the book away before I can even open it up and slides it into his backpack. "So, what are you looking to find out about dragons?"

"Anything. Everything." I hold my hands up in an *I'm clueless* gesture. "This whole *magical creatures are real* thing is…a lot."

"Nah. You'll get used to it in no time."

"That makes one of us who thinks so."

He laughs. "Come on. Hit me with your first question."

"Oh, I haven't really thought of specific questions. Except… Macy says you have wings. That means you can actually fly?" My mind boggles at the thought.

"Yeah, I can fly." He grins. "I can do other stuff, too."

"Like what?" I lean toward him, fascinated.

"Well, jeez, if we're going to get into all this, I feel like we need some sustenance." He reaches for his backpack.

"Oh, sorry. I didn't mean—"

"It's all good, New Girl." From the backpack's front pocket he pulls out a half-eaten bag of marshmallows, then holds it out to me. "Want one? They're my favorite snack."

"Mine too," I tell him as I take one. "I mean, usually in Rice Krispies treats, but I'm not complaining."

I start to pop it in my mouth, but he stops me with a hand on my arm. "Hey, that's no way to eat a marshmallow."

"What do you mean?"

He just wiggles his brows. Then tosses the marshmallow up in the air and *blows fire straight at it out of his mouth.*

I shriek, then cover my mouth, half in shock, half in delight, as the marshmallow turns a perfect golden brown right in midair. Seconds later, Flint closes his mouth, and the treat falls directly into his hand.

He holds it out to me. "Now that's how you eat a marshmallow."

"You're telling me!" I take it from him and pop it in my mouth. "Oh my God, it's hot!" I say around the gooey goodness.

He gives me a look that says, *No shit, Sherlock.*

"And it's perfectly roasted!" I can't believe how cool this is.

"Course it is. I've been doing this a long time." He holds the bag out to me. "Want another one?"

"Are you kidding? I want them all. All the marshmallows, all the time."

He grins. "My kind of woman."

"Can I throw it?" I pick out another one.

"I'd be insulted if you didn't."

I giggle as I toss the marshmallow up in the air. And this time

I scream only a little as Flint shoots a stream of fire straight at it.

When it's done, he closes his mouth and the marshmallow falls straight back into my hand. It's hot—really hot—so I juggle it between my hands for a second, waiting for it to cool down. Then I hold it out to him. "This one's yours."

He looks surprised as he glances between the marshmallow and me. Then he says, "Hey, thanks," and pops it in his mouth.

We roast the rest of the bag, one after the other—sometimes two or three at a time—and Flint cracks jokes during the whole thing. When the marshmallows finally run out, my stomach is killing me—partly because I've been laughing so hard and partly because I just ate a shit ton of marshmallows. Either way, it's a good hurt, unlike so many other things at this place, so I'll take it.

I'm also thirsty from all the sugar, and I reach for the water bottle Amka gave me. As I do, I can't help wondering if she gave it to me because she knew I was going to need it. Is foresight a thing with witches? Just one more thing I need to research.

I start to open the bottle, but Flint snatches it out of my hand before I can even break the seal. "Drinking warm water is such a plebian thing to do," he teases. Right before he opens his mouth and blows a stream of freezing cold air straight at the water.

Seconds later, he hands me an ice-cold bottle with another waggle of his brows.

"Wow. Just...wow." I shake my head in excitement. "Is there anything else you can do?"

"What? Flying, fire, and ice aren't enough?"

"Yes! I mean, of course they are." I feel like a total jerk. "I'm sorry. I was just—"

"Chill, I'm just messing with you." He holds out a hand, much like Amka did when she was calling up the wind. Except Flint isn't about anything as boring as wind.

I watch in astonishment as a cluster of pale-blue flowers

blooms on his hand. "Oh my God," I whisper as I start to smell their subtle fragrance. "Oh my God. How did you do that?"

He shrugs. "I'm one of the lucky ones." He holds it out to me, and I reach forward, stroke a gentle finger over one of the flower's delicate petals. It feels like silk.

"These are called forget-me-nots. They're Alaska's state flower."

"They're beautiful." I shake my head.

"You're beautiful," he answers. And then he leans forward and weaves the stem of flowers into my curls, right above my left ear.

My stomach bottoms out as his lips come within an inch of mine. *Oh, God. Oh no!*

Instinct has me jerking back in my chair, eyes wide and breath coming way too fast.

But Flint just laughs. "Don't worry, New Girl. I wasn't hitting on you."

Oh, thank God. I nearly sag in relief. "I didn't think— I was— I just—"

"Oh, Grace." Flint half laughs, half shakes his head. "You're something else. You know that?"

"Me? You're the one who can shoot fire and ice and create flowers out of thin air."

"Good point." He inclines his head, watching me with those molten amber eyes of his. "But I'll make you a promise right now, okay?"

"Okay?"

"When I hit on you, it'll be because you want me to. And we'll both know exactly what's going on when I do."

46

I'll Get You and Your Little Dog, Too

I have no idea what to say to Flint's promise, which is probably a good thing, considering my throat is suddenly desert dry and I can't speak anyway.

Not because I want Flint to hit on me—I don't. And not because I'm offended by his words, because I'm not. But because when I look into his laughing amber eyes, when I see his infectious smile, I can imagine that if Jaxon wasn't around, I would totally welcome any move this dragon chose to make.

But Jaxon *is* around, and sitting here with Flint just got a million times more awkward.

I take a long sip of water to wet my throat…and to stall as I try to figure out what to say to defuse the situation. But before I can come up with anything, Flint's phone buzzes with a series of texts messages.

He picks up the phone, glances at the messages. And his entire demeanor changes. "Something's going down."

Immediately, I think of Jaxon. "What is it? What's happening?"

Flint doesn't answer, just scoops up his backpack and starts shoving things inside it. As he does, the note Amka sent him falls open and I can't help but read it:

"There are a thousand ways to get somewhere, but not all ways are the correct one."

I don't have time to wonder about what it means because Flint scoops it up and then barks, "Come on, let's go."

I grab my purse and follow him, dread pooling in my stomach as I try to figure out what could possibly make him react like this. "What's going on?" I ask again.

"I don't know yet. But the Order is on the move."

"On the move? What does that mean?" I'm all but running in an effort to keep up with Flint's long-legged strides.

"It means there's going to be trouble." He bites the words out like they taste bad.

Not that I blame him. God knows, I've had more than enough of that in the last few days to last me a lifetime. "What kind of trouble?" I'm right behind him when he pushes the library doors open and starts booking it down the hall.

"That's what I'm trying to find out."

I fumble my phone out of my pocket, determined to get an answer out of Jaxon. But by the time we get to the main passing area near the stairs, I don't have to. Because one level up is the Order, walking in grim, single-file silence.

They're moving fast, and though their backs are toward us, I can tell Flint is right. There's a problem—a big one. It's in their squared-off shoulders and the tenseness that runs through each and every one of them like a live wire.

I call to Jaxon, but he's either ignoring me or he doesn't hear me. Either way, it's another bad sign, considering he usually knows exactly what's happening around him at all times.

Just the thought that he's in some kind of trouble has me rushing on the stairs right after Flint, determined to catch up with them before something terrible happens.

But Jaxon is moving swiftly, too, and we end up chasing him down one hall, past the physics lab and several classrooms. He pauses for a second at the door of a room I haven't been in yet—I think it's one of the student lounges—and I call his name again. I'm all the way at the other end of the long hall, so I'm not surprised he doesn't hear me.

Byron does, though. He turns his head and stares straight at me. I'm too far away to see his eyes clearly, but the look on his face is more than a little frightening as his eyes dart back and forth between Flint and me. Then he shakes his head at me in a quick back-and-forth motion.

It's obvious he wants me to leave them alone, but that's not going to happen—at least not before I know what's going on in there. So I just lay on the speed, determined to get to Jaxon before he does…whatever it is he intends to do.

I don't make it, and neither does Flint. Jaxon walks in the room, followed by the other five members of the Order—including Byron, who doesn't look my way again.

Panic slams through me, and I run faster than I ever have before, ignoring the way my neck and arm hurt. Ignoring the way it makes me feel dizzy. Ignoring everything but the need I have to get to Jaxon, to make sure he doesn't do anything because of me that he can't take back.

I don't know how I know this is about me, but I do.

I hit the door just as Jaxon sends all the furniture in the room flying in every direction.

Next to me, Flint curses. But he doesn't move to interfere, even when Jaxon sends a guy that I'm pretty sure is Cole flying next, slamming him against a turned-over table and an upended chair in the process.

My breath catches in my throat in a strangled scream. I knew he was powerful, knew he was dangerous—everyone has been telling me so since I got here—but before now, I had no idea what that meant. But as Jaxon slams the guy—and yeah, it's definitely Cole—into the wall with a flick of his fingers, then has him dangling a dozen feet in the air using nothing but his mind, I begin to understand.

Still, no warning, no vampire lore, nothing anyone could have told me could prepare me for what comes next.

Several students rush him—other shifters, I assume since Quinn and Marc are among them—but just like in the cafeteria, Mekhi, Byron, and the others make a perimeter around him. The shifters don't seem to care, though, because they keep running straight at them in an effort to rescue the one Jaxon is still dangling about ten feet in the air. And that's when all hell breaks loose, the five members of the Order in an all-out brawl with three or four times as many shifters.

It's fast and brutal and terrifying to witness, some shifters fighting as humans, others as wolves. Teeth and claws come out, raking down Luca's back and Liam's arm as the vampires grab on to fur and send the wolves slamming to the ground. Jaxon must be the only one with telekinesis, though, because the Order is fighting the old-fashioned way—with fists and feet and what I'm pretty sure are fangs.

I turn to Flint, hoping he'll wade in, but he's just watching the fight with clenched fists and narrowed eyes.

Other students don't have his reticence, though, and they join the melee—more shifters and vampires squaring off against one another in a fight that will end I don't know how. But the ground is already littered with fur and blood. If someone doesn't stop this soon, people are going to *die*.

Jaxon must have the same thought because he suddenly drops Cole. He hits the ground hard, falling on his ass before scrambling back to his feet. At the same time, Jaxon waves his other arm out in a wild arc that stops everyone in their tracks. Some even fall over completely.

I'm still across the room at the entrance, but the power he blasts out hits me, too. And Flint. We both end up stumbling backward, grabbing on to the double-wide doorframe to keep from falling.

I know I'm just a human, but Flint isn't, and he was shoved backward, too. I can't imagine the force the people close to him felt. No wonder so many of them ended up on the ground.

I think it's over—the fight and whatever Jaxon planned on doing to that shifter—so once the power blast dissipates, I take a step forward. "Jaxon!" I call, hoping to get his attention. Hoping to make him think in the middle of all this madness.

He glances my way for one second, two, and his eyes are like nothing I've ever seen before. Not blank. Not ice. But fire. A raging inferno blazing in his gaze.

"Jaxon," I say again, softer this time, and for a moment, I think I'm getting through.

At least until he turns his head, cutting me off. Blocking me out.

Seconds later, he reaches out a hand, and Cole is once again brought to his feet. This time, though, the entire room holds its collective breath as we wait to see what comes next.

It doesn't take long for us to find out.

Cole starts struggling, eyes going wide and fingers clawing at his throat as Jaxon reels him in. Slowly dragging him closer and closer until Cole is once again standing directly in front of him. Eyes bugging out. Livid red scratches on his neck. Terror in his eyes.

It's enough, more than enough. Whatever Jaxon is doing, whatever point he is trying to make, he's done it. Everyone in this room knows what he can do.

"Jaxon, please." I say it softly, not sure if he'll be able to hear me but unable to keep silent when he's so close to killing this boy. So close to destroying the shifter and himself in one moment of careless rage.

Everything inside me tells me to go to him, to get in the middle of him and the shifter before Jaxon does something he can't take back. But when I try to move toward him, it's like I'm running straight into a wall.

Unable to rush forward.

Unable even to take one single step.

It's not me—I can move or walk however I want—but there's an invisible barrier in front of me, as strong as stone and twice as impenetrable.

No wonder Flint has made no move to interrupt this nightmare. He must have known the wall was there all along.

It's Jaxon's doing—of course it is—and I'm furious that he's done this, that he's cut me off from him and his fight so completely. "It's enough, Jaxon!" I yell, pounding on the wall because I can't do anything else. "Stop. You have to stop."

He ignores me and terror swamps me. He can't do this. He can't—

Suddenly, I lurch forward as my hand and arm slide right through the mental barricade that Jaxon erected.

"What the fuck?" Flint breathes from beside me, but I'm too busy trying to get Jaxon's attention to respond. Or pull back.

"Jaxon!" I all but scream his name this time. "Stop. Please."

I don't know what's different—if it's because I somehow pierced through the barrier or if he's reached the same conclusion I have. Either way, whatever psychic grip he's been using on Cole disappears. Now standing under his own power, the shifter nearly falls to his knees even as he drags loud, painful-sounding breaths through his abused throat and into his air-starved lungs.

Relief sweeps through me—and the room. It's finally over. Everyone is still alive. Some are more than a little worse for wear, but at least they're a—

Jaxon strikes so fast, I almost miss it, fangs flashing and hands grabbing onto Cole's shoulders as he leans forward and sinks his teeth into the left side of his throat.

Someone screams, and for a second I think it's me, until I realize my throat is too tight to make a sound. Seconds pass—I don't know how many—as Jaxon drinks and drinks and drinks. Eventually the shifter stops fighting, goes limp.

That's when Jaxon finally lets him go, lifting his head and dropping Cole into a limp heap on the ground.

The guy's pallor is frightening, but he's still alive, eyes wide and frightened, blood trickling from the fang marks on his neck, when Jaxon looks out over the room and hisses, "This is the only warning you get."

Then he turns and walks straight toward me, without so much as a backward glance.

And when he takes my elbow in a grip that is as gentle as it is unyielding, I go with him. Because, honestly, what else am I going to do?

47

The First Bite Is the Deepest

Jaxon doesn't say a word as he escorts me down the hall—and neither do I. After what I just saw, I'm too... I don't know what. I want to say "shocked," but that's not the right word. Neither is "disgusted" or "horrified" or any of the other descriptions—any of the other emotions—that someone who's an outsider might expect to feel.

I mean, watching Jaxon nearly drain that guy wasn't what I would call pleasant, but he *is* a vampire. Biting people's necks and drinking their blood is pretty much par for the course, isn't it? It feels hypocritical to freak out now just because I got to see it up close and personal—especially when Jaxon obviously had a reason for what he did. Otherwise, why go on a rampage like that? And why announce to the whole school that this is the only warning they're going to get?

I'm more concerned about finding out why he felt the need to issue the warning than I am about what he did. Especially since I'm terrified that it has something to do with me and his fear that someone is trying to hurt me.

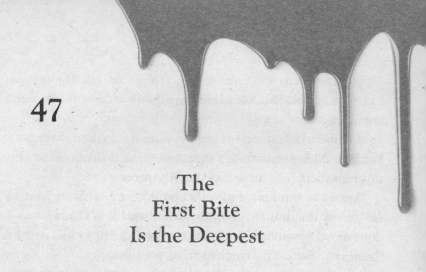

I don't want to be responsible for Jaxon getting into trouble—and I definitely don't want to be responsible for Jaxon hurting someone…or worse.

Not for the first time, my hand goes to the marks at my throat as I wonder what would have happened if Marise hadn't stopped. If she had bitten me for a purpose other than to help heal me. Would I be as laissez-faire about Jaxon's treatment of that shifter if I had nearly died the same way?

I don't know. I just know that right now, I care more about Jaxon's state of mind than I do some boy I don't know. Some boy who, if Jaxon is right, wants me dead.

As for the rest? The telekinesis, the absolute control Jaxon exerted over everyone in that lounge, including me? The obscene amount of power he wielded with just a wave of his hand? I don't know how I feel about all that, either. Except, like the violence, it doesn't scare me the way it probably should.

He doesn't scare me the way he probably should.

My injured ankle twinges a little as we round a corner—more than likely all the running I did on it earlier—but I bite down the cry of pain that wells in my throat. Jaxon's moving fast, I assume because he's trying to get us somewhere we can talk before the consequences of what just happened catch up to him.

I mean, yeah, this is a supernatural school and the rules are probably different than what I'm used to, but I have a hard time believing it's okay for one of the paranormal species to start chowing down on another one in the middle of the student lounge.

No matter how much he might deserve it.

Which is why I don't complain about the pace Jaxon sets as we quickly make our way down several hallways to the back stairs. It's as we start climbing that I realize where he's taking me. Not to my room, as I half expected, but to his. And judging from the look on his face—the blank eyes, the tight jaw, the lips pressed into a firm, straight line—he expects me to object.

I have no intention of arguing with him, though. Not until

I know what we're supposed to be arguing about. And on the plus side, I'm pretty sure no one will be crossing Jaxon again any time soon, which means maybe I can make it through a whole forty-eight hours without any near-death experiences. Not going to lie, that counts for something, too, even though I feel a little Machiavellian just thinking it.

The second we make it to the top of the tower steps, Jaxon lets go of my elbow and puts as much distance between the two of us as can be had in his little reading alcove. Which leaves me…adrift.

Nothing has changed since I was here a few hours ago. The window is still boarded up, the rug still missing, the book I tried to read while I was waiting for him still sitting in the exact same spot.

And yet it feels like everything has changed.

Maybe because it has. I don't know, and I *won't* know until Jaxon opens his mouth and actually talks to me instead of standing there next to the fireplace, with his hands in his pockets and his eyes everywhere but on mine.

I want to start the conversation, want to tell him…I don't know what. But everything inside me warns that that's the wrong approach to take. That if I have any hope of navigating what's going on here, I need to know what Jaxon is thinking before I open my mouth and say something that ruins everything.

And so I wait, hands in the pockets of my hoodie and eyes nowhere but on him, until he finally, finally turns to look at me.

"I won't hurt you," he says, his voice low and rusty and so empty that it hurts to listen to it.

"I know."

"You *know*?" He looks at me like I've grown another head… or three.

"I've never thought you were going to hurt me, Jaxon. I

wouldn't be here if I did."

He looks shocked at my words. No, not shocked. Stunned, his mouth opening and closing like a fish out of water as he struggles for a decent response. When it eventually comes, it's distinctly underwhelming.

"Is there something wrong with you?" he demands. "Or is it just that you have a death wish?"

It's my turn to pull his favorite trick and lift a brow. "Dramatic much?"

"You're impossible." He nearly strangles on the words.

"Pretty sure I'm not the impossible one in this..." I break off because I have no idea what to call this thing between Jaxon and me. Relationship? Friendship? Disaster? I finally settle on "thing," which is probably the worst description possible of whatever it is we have. "After all, you're the one who keeps running away." I'm trying to lighten up the funereal atmosphere, trying to make him smile a little. Or if not actually smile, then at least not frown so hard.

It isn't working. In fact, I think he's looking even grimmer than he was a couple of minutes ago.

"You saw what I did, right?"

I nod. "I did."

"And you're telling me that it doesn't scare you?" He looks incredulous. Suspicious. And, in a bizarre turn of the tables, maybe even a little disgusted. "That it doesn't horrify you?"

"Which part?" I want to reach out, want to touch him so badly, but it's fairly obvious now isn't the time. Not when everything about him screams boundaries. Or, more accurately, armed battlements.

"Which...part? What does that even mean?"

"It means, which part of what I just saw should I be afraid of? The part where you threw everyone across the room? Or the part where you hung someone in the air and choked him with your mind?" I ignore the frisson of discomfort that works its way down my spine at the memory. "Or am I just supposed to be hung up on the biting part?"

"I didn't realize this was an either-or situation," he growls at me as he paces back and forth in front of the fireplace. "You saw what I did to Cole. I thought you'd be appalled."

Watching him, I don't think I'm the one who's appalled here. I think *Jaxon* is—by what he's capable of and by what he's just done. Which makes my job of convincing him I'm not disgusted by him harder than I ever imagined it would be.

It also means I need to tread lightly.

"Is that the guy's name? Cole?" I finally settle on asking.

I want to get closer to him, want to shrink the gap he's put between us, but badass, take-no-prisoners Jaxon currently looks like he'll bolt at the first wrong move I make.

"Yes." He's back to not looking at me, so I wait him out, refusing to speak until he finally, reluctantly turns his gaze back to mine.

"Why are you looking at me like that?" he whispers.

"Like what?"

"Like you understand. You can't possibly—"

"Did he deserve what you did to him?" I interrupt.

His whole body goes rigid. "That's not the point."

"Actually, I think it's the most important point." I'm not going to stand here and beat him up emotionally when he's already doing a ridiculously good job of it himself. "Did he deserve it?" I ask again.

"He deserves worse than what he got," Jaxon finally spits out. "He deserves to be dead."

"But you didn't kill him."

"No." He shakes his head. "But I wanted to."

"It doesn't matter what you wanted to do," I admonish him. "It only matters what you did. You never once lost control when you were going after Cole—in fact, I've never seen anyone more in control than you were in that lounge. The power you wield... it's unfathomable."

He quirks a brow at me even as his shoulders tense, as if preparing for the next body blow. "And terrifying?"

"I'm pretty sure Cole was terrified."

"I don't give a shit about Cole. I'm talking about you." He shoves a frustrated hand through his hair, but this time his gaze never leaves mine.

I take a deep breath, let it out slowly. Then tell him the truth he so desperately needs to hear. "You don't scare me, Jaxon."

"I don't scare you." His tone is half sardonic, half disbelieving.

I shake my head. "No."

"No?"

"No," I repeat. "And I've got to say, you're beginning to sound an awful lot like a parrot." I make a face at him. "You might try being careful of that if you want to keep your badass reputation intact."

He narrows his eyes at me. "My badass reputation is pretty solid right now, thank you very much. It's you I'm worried about."

"Me? Why are you worried about me?" I'm sick of waiting on the other side of the room for him to calm down. Not when it's not getting us anywhere, and not when the need to touch him, to hold him, is a physical ache inside me.

With that in mind, I finally take my hands out of my pockets and walk toward him, slowly, carefully, deliberately. His eyes get wider with every step I take, and for a second, I really do think he's contemplating fleeing.

Not going to lie, the idea that I scare Jaxon Vega fascinates me on all kinds of different levels.

"What the fuck is happening here?" he demands after the silence between us has gone on too long.

I have no idea. I just know that I hate the way Jaxon looked when he walked up to me in the study lounge, hate even more the way he looked when he brought me into this room. Wary, lonely, ashamed, when I don't believe he has anything to be ashamed of.

"What do *you* think is happening here?" I ask.

"Now who's the parrot?" He shoves both hands into his hair in obvious frustration. "Are you okay? Are you in shock?"

"I'm fine. It's you I'm worried about."

"Me? I—" He breaks off and just stares at me, speechless, as he registers that I very deliberately mimicked his words. "I just terrorized the entire school. Why the hell are you worried about *me*?"

"Because you don't exactly look happy about it, now, do you?"

"There's nothing to be happy about."

And that, right there, is exactly why I'm not afraid of him.

I'm only a few steps away from him now and I take them slowly, under his watchful, worried gaze. "So how *do* you feel about what just happened?" I ask.

His face closes up. "I don't feel anything about it."

"You sure about that?" Finally, I'm close enough to go for it. I reach for his hand, grab on tight. The second our skin touches, he jerks like he's being electrocuted. But he doesn't pull away. Instead, he just stands there and watches as I lace our fingers together. "Because you look like you feel a hell of a lot."

He takes a step back even as he holds fast to my hand. "It had to be done."

"Okay." I take a step forward. If we keep this up, it's not going to be long before I have him pinned against a bookcase the same way he had me pinned against that chess table on my very first day.

Poetic justice, if you ask me.

"You should go." This time, he takes two steps back. More, he drops my hand.

I feel the loss of his touch keenly, but that doesn't stop me from closing the distance once again.

Doesn't stop me from reaching out and resting a hand on his hard biceps.

Doesn't stop me from softly stroking my thumb up and down his inner arm. "Is that what you want?"

"Yes." He nearly strangles on the word, but this time he doesn't move away from my touch. From me.

And while there is a part of me that can't believe I'm doing this, that I'm all but throwing myself at Jaxon, there's another part of me just waiting for him to give in.

It's the same part that's encouraged by the fact that he's barely coherent at this point.

The same part that can't help but feel—and be happy about—the small tremor running through his body.

The same part that desperately wants to feel Jaxon's mouth once again on my own and is determined not to leave here until I find out.

"I don't believe you," I whisper. And then I take the final step, closing the last of the distance between us and pressing my suddenly trembling body flush against his.

"You don't know what you're asking," he tells me in a voice that's low and tortured and anything but cold.

He's right. I don't have a clue how much I'm asking of him. But I know if I don't ask, if I don't push, I'll never get another chance. This will be the end of the discussion.

More, it will be the end of us.

And I'm not ready for that. I don't even know if there is an us, or what will happen in a day or a week or three months, if there is. I only know that I'm not ready to walk away from him—or whatever happens next. Which is why I reach for him again and whisper, "So show me."

Long seconds pass, minutes maybe, and Jaxon doesn't move. I'm not sure he even breathes.

"Jaxon," I finally whisper when I can't take the agony of waiting. "Please." My mouth is nearly pressed against his.

Still no response.

My confidence—shaky at the best of times—is about to desert me completely. After all, there's nothing quite like throwing yourself at a boy and having him turn into a human statue to make a girl feel wanted.

But I've got one more attempt in me, one more chance to get Jaxon to understand that I trust him, no matter what he did in that hall. That I want him, vampire or not.

Two months ago, I would have walked away—run away, really—prepared to hide under my bed forever. But two months ago, my parents weren't dead, and I didn't yet realize just how fleeting, how fragile, life really is.

And so I swallow my fear and embarrassment as I slide my hand down Jaxon's arm to his hand. Once more, I lace our fingers together before lifting both our hands to my chest. I press his palm flush against my heart and murmur, "I want you, Jaxon."

Something flashes in his eyes. "Even knowing what I am?"

Confusion swirls through me. "I know *who* you are. That's what matters."

"You say that now, but you don't know what you're asking."

"So show me," I whisper. "Give me what I'm asking for."

His eyes darken, his pupils blown completely out. "Don't say that if you don't mean it."

"I mean it. I need you, Jaxon. I *need* you."

His jaw clenches, and his fingers tighten reflexively on mine.

"Are you sure?" he grinds out. "I need to know you're sure. I don't want to scare you, Grace."

My knees tremble like some medieval heroine at the intensity in his voice, in his eyes. But I am not going to blow this now, not going to mess it up when I'm this close to getting what I want.

This close to having Jaxon as my own.

So I lock my knees in place, look him in the eye. And say as loud and clear as I have ever said anything in my life, "What scares me isn't you being a vampire, Jaxon. What scares me is the idea that you're going to walk away and I'm going to go my whole life without knowing what this could feel like."

And just like that, Jaxon strikes. Hands grabbing, fangs flashing, body wrapping itself around me so quickly, I barely understand what's happening. He whirls me around—my back to his front—tangles his hand in my hair, and pulls my head back.

And then sinks his teeth into my neck, right below my jaw.

48

Is That a Wooden Stake in Your Pocket or Are You Just Happy to See Me?

For one second, two, panic immobilizes me. Makes it so I can't feel, can't think, can't breathe as I wait…for pain, for emptiness, for death.

But as time goes by and the agony I'm expecting doesn't come, my adrenaline stops shooting like a geyser, and I realize that whatever Jaxon is doing to me doesn't hurt at all. In fact, it feels really, really…good.

Pleasure like molten honey pours through my veins, lighting up my nerve endings and swamping me with an intensity, a need I never imagined existed. My already weak knees give out entirely, and I sag against him, letting him hold me up with his long, lean body and firm arms as I tilt my head to give him better access.

He growls at the invitation, a deep, rumbling sound that burrows deep inside me even as the ground shakes a little beneath my feet. And then the pleasure increases, lighting me up, turning me inside out, making me tremble even as I forget how to breathe. How to be.

I press myself even more tightly against him, wind my arms up and over my head so that I can tangle my fingers in his hair. Cup his jaw in my palm. Push my skin more firmly against his mouth as my eyes drift closed.

I'm desperate for more—desperate for Jaxon and whatever he wants to give me or take from me. But he's obviously got more control than I can even imagine, because just as the pleasure threatens to overwhelm me, he pulls back, pulls away, his tongue stroking softly over his bite marks. The caress sends a whole new volley of emotions straight through me.

I stay where I am, body resting against his, hands clutching onto whatever part of him I can reach, totally dependent on him to keep me from falling as little darts of pleasure continue to zing through me. They're followed by a creeping lassitude that makes it impossible for me to so much as lift my lids, let alone step away from Jaxon.

As if I would.

"Are you okay?" he murmurs against my ear, his voice soft and warm in a way I've never heard from him before.

"Are you kidding?" I answer just as softly. "I don't think I've ever been this okay in my life. That was…amazing. *You're* amazing."

He laughs. "Yeah, well, being a vampire doesn't come with many perks, so you've got to take them where you can find them."

"Obviously." Eyes still closed, I turn my head. Raise my face to his. Purse my lips. And pray Jaxon doesn't shy away from me.

He doesn't, his lips pressing against mine in a tender kiss that has my breath catching all over again, though for very different reasons. Moments pass, and he starts to lift his head, but I hold on, wanting just a little more of him.

Just a little more of this boy who has such power and such tenderness inside him.

He gives it to me, his mouth moving against mine, his tongue stroking along my bottom lip until, finally, I find the strength to let him go.

I pull back, open my eyes slowly, and find Jaxon staring down at me, his dark gaze filled with so much emotion, I don't know whether to laugh or weep.

"No one's going to hurt you again, Grace," he whispers.

"I know," I whisper back. "You made sure of it."

Surprise glows in the depths of his obsidian eyes. "I didn't think you believed—" He breaks off as the ground rumbles beneath our feet.

"We should get under the doorway," I tell him, glancing around for the closest one.

But he just closes his eyes, takes a deep breath. Moments later, the ground settles back down.

Shock explodes inside me. "You—" My voice breaks, and I clear my throat. Try again. "The earthquakes. They're you?"

He nods, looks wary.

"Even the big ones?" I ask, and I can feel my eyes going wide. "All of them?"

"I'm so sorry." His fingers stroke over my still-bandaged neck. "I never meant to hurt you."

"I know." I turn my head, kiss his palm even as astonishment continues to ricochet inside me. How can anyone be so powerful that they actually move the earth? It's incomprehensible, unimaginable. "Does this happen often?"

He shakes his head, shrugs, like he's as baffled as I am. "It's never happened...before."

"Before?" I ask.

"Before you." He pulls me more tightly against him. "I learned control early—over myself and my abilities. I had to or..."

"Cities would crumble?" I ask, tongue firmly in cheek.

"I wouldn't put it exactly like that. But I swear, I've got it under control now. I won't hurt you again." His mouth slides along my cheek, over my jaw, down my neck.

Heat moves through me at the first touch of his lips. It makes me tremble. Makes me want.

I pull his mouth back down to mine and let the need, and the pleasure, sweep me away.

The kiss goes on and on, until we're both breathless. Shaky. Desperate.

I arch against him in an effort to be closer, then run my hands over his arms, his shoulders, his back. My fingers tangle in his hair, and he groans low in his throat. Then bites down gently on my lip, sucking at it just a little, until it feels like the Fourth of July deep inside me.

I gasp, shudder, and Jaxon uses my still-weak knees as an excuse to pull away. I try to hold him in place, try to keep his lips and skin and body on mine. But he just smooths a hand over my hair and whispers, "Come on."

He takes my hand in his and tugs me toward his bedroom.

I follow him—of course I do—but as he leads the way, I can't help but notice that his once neat reading alcove is now an utter disaster.

Books cover the floor, some lying down, some standing up, some leaning drunkenly against furniture halfway in between. The couch is upside down and the gorgeous old coffee table I liked so much is now splintered into little more than wood chips.

"What—what happened?" I gasp, bending down to pick up a few books that are directly in my path.

Jaxon takes them from me with a shake of his head, tosses them onto the bottom of the couch, which is now facing up. "I promised you the earthquake thing isn't going to happen anymore," he answers. "But it's going to take a little time for me to figure out how to control all the things you make me feel."

"*This* is learning how to control it?" I step over a pile of rubble that I'm pretty sure used to be a bookcase and try to pretend his words aren't making me melt deep inside.

He turns me inside out with a look, destroys me with a kiss. But this? This makes me feel like maybe, just maybe, he feels as much for me as I feel for him.

He shrugs. "The earth barely shook this time, and no window broke. That's definite progress."

"I guess." I swallow down the softness he makes bloom inside me and make a show of looking at the scattered wood chips instead. "I really liked that coffee table."

"I'll find you one you like more." He tugs on my hand. "Come on."

We make our way to his room, which thankfully seems to have been spared the destruction suffered by the reading alcove. It looks exactly the same as last time, complete with gorgeous paintings on the walls and musical instruments in the corner.

"I love your room," I tell him, trailing a hand over his dresser as I make my way to the drum kit. I resisted it last time, know I should resist it this time, since what has happened so far today has left us with a lot to talk about.

But it's been weeks since I've sat behind a kit, weeks since I've held a set of drumsticks in my hands, and I just need to touch it. Just need to run my hands over the skins.

"You play?" Jaxon asks as I rest my hand on the top of one of the toms.

"I used to, before..." I trail off. I don't want to talk about my parents right now, don't want to bring that sadness into my first conversation with Jaxon post...whatever that was.

He seems to get it, because he doesn't push. Instead, he smiles, really smiles, and it lights up his whole face. Lights up the whole room. Definitely lights up all the dark and sad places I've been holding on to for too long.

It isn't until I see his smile that I realize how much he's been holding back, how much he's been holding *in* for who knows how long.

"Want to play something now?" he asks.

"No." It's my turn to hold a hand out to him. I pull him toward the bed, waiting until he chooses a side to sit on before I plop down on the other side. "I want to talk."

"About?" he deadpans even as a wariness creeps into his gaze that hasn't been there since he bit me.

"Oh, I don't know. The weather?" I tease because I'm trying to be nonchalant about this whole thing. Trying to tell myself that finding out the boy I'm falling for is a vampire who can literally shake the earth really isn't that big of a deal.

He rolls his eyes, but I'm watching closely and see the corners of his mouth turning up in the smile he's trying so hard to hide.

It makes the nonchalance totally worth it, even as I scramble with trying to wrap my head around everything that's happened today. And everything that's happened in the last six days. Because there is still a tiny part of me freaking out about the fact that I let a vampire bite me—even if that vampire is Jaxon. And even if I enjoyed it way more than I ever imagined I would.

But now is not the time for me to freak out, not when Jaxon is already so on edge. So I settle for giving him a playful *don't mess with me* look even as I lay down on one side of his bed.

Jaxon lifts a brow as he watches me make myself comfortable, then stretches out next to me. I don't miss the fact that he makes sure not to touch me at all as he does.

Which is completely unacceptable. I'm trying to close the distance between us, not make it bigger. But I appreciate the fact that he's working so hard not to freak me out. I just wish he realized that I'm not the one who's freaked out here.

But since I want to get the guarded look out of his eyes, I decide to tackle that subject later. For now, I'm going with, "Did you hear the joke about the roof?"

"Excuse me?" He lifts a single disdainful brow—which means I have to work really hard to hide how googly-eyed it makes me when he does it.

"Never mind." I give him a cheesy grin. "It's over your head."

He stares at me, bemused, for several seconds. Then he shakes his head and says, "Somehow, they always get worse."

"You have no idea." I roll over until I'm on my stomach—and then scoot so the right side of my body is pressed to the left side of his. "What's the difference between a guitar and a fish?"

Both brows go up this time, even as he answers, "I don't think I want to know."

I ignore him. "You can tune a guitar but you can't tuna fish."

He lets out a bark of laughter that startles both of us. Then he shakes his head and tells me, "It's an actual sickness with you, isn't it?"

"It's fun, Jaxon." I give him the most obnoxious smirk I can manage. "You know what fun is, don't you?"

He rolls his eyes. "I think I have a vague recollection of that emotion, yeah."

"Good. What do you call a dinosaur that—?"

He cuts me off with a kiss and a yank. The kiss curls my toes, but the yank…the yank curls everything else. Especially when he pulls me over so that I'm on top of him, my knees straddling his hips and my curls forming a curtain around us.

Jaxon takes hold of a lock of my hair, then watches as the curl twines around his finger. "I love your hair," he says, pulling on the curl just to release it and watch it boing back into place.

"Yeah, well, I'm pretty fond of yours, too," I tell him, sliding my fingers through his black strands.

As I do, my palm brushes against his scar, and he stiffens before turning his head away so that I'm no longer touching it.

"Why do you do that?" I ask.

"Do what?"

I give him a look that says he knows exactly what I'm talking about. "I already told you that you're the sexiest guy I've ever seen—and that includes a lot of pretty impressive San Diego surf gods. So I don't understand why it bothers you so much if I see your scar."

He shrugs. "It doesn't bother me if you see my scar."

I don't think that's true, but I'm willing to go with it—up to a point. "Fine, it doesn't bother you if I see it, but it definitely bothers you if I touch it."

"No." He shakes his head. "That doesn't bother me, either."

"Okay, I'm sorry, but I call bullshit." To prove it, I lean down and press a series of hot, openmouthed kisses against his jaw. I don't deliberately touch his scar, but I don't shy away from it, either. And sure enough, he lasts only a few seconds before threading his fingers through my hair and gently pressing my face into the bend where his shoulder meets his neck.

Before I can say anything, though, he takes a deep breath. Then says, "It's not that I think you'll be disgusted by my scar or anything—you're not that shallow."

"Then why does it bother you so much if I go near it?"

He doesn't answer right away, and as silence stretches between us, I think maybe he won't answer at all. But then, just when I've given up, he says, "Because it reminds me of how I got it, and I don't want you anywhere near that world. And I sure as hell don't want that world anywhere near you."

49

Eventually the World Breaks Everyone

The pain in his voice has my heart thudding slow and hard in my chest.

Sure, there's a part of me that can't imagine what world he's talking about, considering I'm currently living in the middle of a fantasy novel—one complete with fantastical creatures and secrets galore. But there's a larger part of me that just wants him to know that whatever world he's talking about, and whatever happened to him in that world, I'm on his side.

I take my time running my palms over his chest and pressing kisses along the powerful column of his throat. He smells like oranges again, and deep water, and I sink into the scent of him, into the glorious taste and feel and sound of him.

His hands go to my hips, and he groans low in his throat as he arches against me. It feels amazing—he feels amazing. I've never been this intimate with a guy before, have never wanted to be, but with Jaxon, I want it all. I want to feel everything, experience everything. Maybe not now, when we're on borrowed time, but soon.

But I also want to know what's hurting him. Not so I can take it away—I know way better than that—but so I can share it with him. So I can understand. Which is why I roll off him just as things are getting really interesting.

He rolls with me, of course, so that now we're stretched on our sides, facing each other. His arm is around my waist, his hand resting on my hip, and there's a part of me that wants nothing more than to sink back into him. To just let whatever's going to happen happen.

But Jaxon deserves better than that. And so do I.

Which is why I reach up and cup his unscarred cheek, then lean forward until our mouths are so close that we're breathing the same air. "Believe me, I understand better than most if you don't want to talk about what happened to you," I whisper. "But I need you to know that if you ever want to share what happened with me, I'm more than happy to listen."

My words aren't sexy and they definitely aren't slick, but they are sincere and they are heartfelt. Jaxon must sense it, too, because instead of dismissing me out of turn, as I half expected him to, he stares at me through eyes that show more than I ever imagined.

Then he kisses me—long, slow, deep—before rolling away and sitting up, with his elbows on his knees and his head in his hands. I sit up, too, and because I can't leave him alone in this... whatever this turns out to be, I wrap myself around him from behind as I press soft, quick kisses to his shoulders and the back of his neck.

And then I say, "Tell me," because I think he needs to hear me say that almost as much as he needs to tell me the story burning inside him.

I'm not sure how I expect the story to come out—whether in fits and starts or one smooth retelling—but I do know that I never could have anticipated what he says when he finally begins to speak.

"I killed Hudson."

Shock rips through me. "Hudson? Your—"

"Brother. Yeah." He wipes a hand over his face.

A million emotions go through me at those four words—shock that isn't really shock, horror, sorrow, concern, pity, *pain*. The list goes on and on. But the one that stands head and shoulders above the others is disbelief. Dangerous as he is, I don't believe Jaxon would ever deliberately harm someone he cares about. Everyone else might be open season, but not those he considers under his protection. If I've learned nothing else in the week I've been here, I've learned that.

Which means something really horrible must have happened. What must it be like to live with the kind of power he wields?

What must it be like to live with the knowledge that one careless moment, one slip of control, and he can lose everything?

"What happened?" I ask eventually, when minutes pass and he doesn't say anything else.

"It doesn't matter."

"I think it does. I can't imagine you hurting your brother on purpose."

He turns on me then, eyes showing that yawning, empty blackness I'm coming to hate so much. "Then your imagination isn't good enough."

Fear skitters through me at the darkness in his voice. "Jaxon." I lay a gentle hand on his arm.

"I didn't set out to kill him, Grace. But do you really think intentions matter when someone's dead? It's not like you can just bring them back because you didn't want to do it."

"I know that better than most." I'm still haunted by the fight my parents and I had right before they died.

"Do you?" Jaxon demands. "Do you know what it feels like to be able to wave a hand and do this?" Seconds later, everything in the room, except for the bed we're sitting on, is floating in the air around us. "Or this?" Everything comes crashing to the ground. The guitar crumbles. One of the glass picture frames shatters into a million pieces.

I take a minute, let the shock cycle through before I try to say anything that makes sense.

"Maybe you're right," I eventually answer. "Maybe I don't know what any of that feels like. But I know your brother wouldn't want you beating yourself up over whatever happened to him. He wouldn't want you torturing yourself."

Jaxon's answering laugh is filled with actual humor. "It's pretty obvious you don't know Hudson. Or my parents. Or Lia."

"Lia blames you for Hudson's death?" I ask, surprised.

"Lia blames everyone and everything for Hudson's death. If she had the kind of power I do, her rage would burn down the world." This time when he laughs, there's only regret in the sound.

"What about your parents? Surely they don't hold you responsible for something you had no control over?"

"Who said I had no control? I had a choice. And I made it. I killed him, Grace. On purpose. And I would do it again."

My stomach churns at his admission—and the coldness in his voice as he makes it. But I've learned enough about Jaxon to know that he will always cast himself in the most awful light. That he will always choose to see himself as the villain, even if he's the victim.

Especially if he's the victim.

Pointing that out to him right now won't do any good, though, so I wait for him to say more. And there is more. If there wasn't, he wouldn't be so concerned with losing control and hurting me.

"Hudson was the firstborn," he eventually continues. "The prince who would be king. The perfect son who only grew more perfect after death."

There's no bitterness in the words, just a matter-of-factness that makes it way too easy to read between the lines. Still, I can't resist asking, "And you are?"

"Very definitely not." He laughs. "Which is fine. More than fine. Being king has never exactly been an aspiration of mine."

"King?" I ask, because when he first said it, I thought it was a metaphor. His brother the prince. But now that he said it again, in reference to himself being king, I can't not ask.

"Yes, king." He lifts a brow. "Didn't Macy tell you?"

"No." *King of what?* I want to ask, but now doesn't exactly seem like the time.

"Oh, well, here I am." He does a mock little bow. "The next vampire *liege* at your service."

"Ooookay." I don't know what else to say to that revelation. Except, "It was supposed to be Hudson? But now that he's dead..."

"Exactly." He makes a *you guessed it* clicking sound with the corner of his mouth. "I'm the replacement. The new heir apparent."

And future king. My mind boggles at the mere idea. What does a vampire king do, anyway? And is that why everyone treats Jaxon with such deference? Because he's royalty? But what does vampire royalty have to do with dragons? Or witches?

"I am, of course, also the murderer of the former heir apparent," Jaxon continues, "which in another species might cause some problems. But in the vampire world, you're only as strong as what you can defend...and what you can take. So all I had to do to become the most fearsome and revered vampire in the world was to kill my big brother."

He gives a little shrug that is supposed to show how amusing he finds the whole thing, how much he doesn't care.

I don't buy it for a second.

"But that's not why you killed him," I add, because I think he needs to hear me say it.

"I thought we already covered that motive doesn't matter? Perception becomes truth eventually, even when it's wrong." There's a wealth of pain in those four words, even though the tone Jaxon uses is completely devoid of emotion. "*Especially* when it's wrong. History is, after all, written by the winner."

I rest my head on his shoulder in a small gesture of comfort. "But you're the winner."

"Am I?"

I don't have an answer for that, so I don't even try. Instead, I ask for the truth. His truth. "Why did you kill Hudson?"

"Because he needed to be killed. And I'm the only one who could."

The words hang in the air as I try to absorb them, to figure out what he means. "So Hudson was as powerful as you, then."

"No one is as powerful as me." He isn't bragging. In fact, he sounds almost ashamed of the fact.

"Why is that exactly?" I ask.

He shrugs. "Genetics. Each generation of born vampires tends to be more powerful than the generation that came before them. There are exceptions, of course, but for the most part, that's how it's always been. It's why there are so few of us—nature's way of keeping the balance, I figure. And since my parents come from the strongest two families and wield incredible power themselves, it's no surprise that when they mated, their offspring..."

"Can literally make the earth shake."

He gives a half smile, the first I've seen from him since this conversation began. "Something like that, yeah."

"So am I right in guessing that Hudson was not exactly responsible with his power?"

"A lot of young vampires aren't."

"That's not an answer." I raise a brow, wait for him to look at me. It takes longer than it should. "And you strike me as very responsible."

He arches his own brows, takes a deliberate look around the disaster he made of the room when he was kissing me.

"You know what I mean."

"I know what you think you mean. Hudson..." He sighs. "Hudson's plans were always audacious. Always looking to give vampires more power, more money, more control, which isn't bad in and of itself."

I'm tempted to disagree. After all, if you plan on garnering more power, money, and control, it has to come from somewhere. And history has shown that taking any of those three things tends to be less than humane for the people it's being taken from.

But that's a discussion for another time, not now, when Jaxon is finally opening up.

"But somewhere along the line, he got lost in those plans," Jaxon continues. "He got so concerned with what he could achieve and how he could achieve it that he never stopped to question if he should.

"I tried to pull him back, tried to talk reason to him, but with Lia and my mother whispering all kinds of *Chosen One* bullshit in his ear, it became impossible to reach him. Impossible to make him understand that his own brand of manifest destiny was not...acceptable, especially when those plans included..." His voice drifts off for a minute, and a look at his eyes tells me that mentally, Jaxon's not here in this room anymore. He's far away in another time and place.

"Things between vampires and shifters have always been tense," he finally continues, a defensive note in his voice that I've never heard before. "We've never really gotten along with the wolves or the dragons; they don't trust us and we sure as hell don't trust them. So when Hudson worked up a plan to"—he curls the fingers of his free hand and makes air quotes—"'put the shifters in their place,' a lot of people thought he was onto something."

"But not you."

"Going after the shifters looked and smelled an awful lot like prejudice to me. And then it began to look a lot like genocide. Especially when he started adding other supernatural creatures—and even made vampires—to his list. Things got ugly."

"How ugly?" I ask, though I'm not sure I actually want to know the answer. Not when Jaxon looks more grim than I've ever seen him. And not when he's throwing around words like "genocide."

"Ugly." He refuses to elaborate. "Especially with our history."

Again the blanks in my knowledge base make it impossible to understand what history he's referring to. Instead of asking, I make a mental note to check the library or ask Macy.

"I tried to reason with Hudson, tried to talk him down. I even went to the king and queen to see if they could do something with him."

I note how he calls his parents the king and queen instead of Mom and Dad, and for a second, I flash back to the first day I met him. To the chess table and the vampire queen and the things he said about what I thought at the time was just a chess piece.

It all makes so much more sense now.

"They *couldn't*."

"They wouldn't," he corrects. "So I tried to talk to him again. So did Byron and Mekhi and a few of the others who would have graduated with him. He didn't listen. And one day he started a fight that was set to rip the whole world apart, had it been allowed to continue."

"That's when you stepped in."

"I thought I could fix things. I thought I could talk him down.

It didn't work out like that.

He closes his eyes, and it makes him seem so far away. Until he opens them again, and I realize he is even more distant than I imagined.

"Do you know what it's like to realize the brother you grew up revering is a total and complete sociopath?" he asks in a voice made more terrible by the reasonableness of it. "Can you imagine what it feels like to know that maybe if you hadn't been so blind, so caught up in your hero worship and seen him for what he was sooner, a lot of people would still be alive?

"I had to kill him, Grace. There was no other choice. Truth be told, I don't even regret doing it." He says the last in a whisper, like he's ashamed to even admit it.

"I don't believe that," I tell him. Guilt radiates off him, makes me hurt for him in a way I've never hurt for anyone before.

"I believe it was necessary. I believe you did what you had to do. But I don't believe for one second that you don't regret killing him." He's spent too much time torturing himself for that to be true.

He doesn't answer right away, and I can't help wondering if I said the wrong thing. Can't help wondering if I just made everything worse.

"I regret that he had to be killed," he finally says after a long silence passes between us. "I regret that my parents created him and molded him into the monster that he was. But I don't regret that he's gone now. If he wasn't dead, no one in the entire world would be safe."

My stomach plummets at his words. Instinctively, I want to deny them, but I've seen Jaxon's power. I've seen what he can do when he controls it and what it can do on its own when he can't. If Hudson's power was anything close—without Jaxon's morality to keep it in check—I can't imagine what might happen.

"Did you have the same power, or—"

"Hudson could persuade anyone to do anything." The words are as flat as his tone. As his eyes. "I don't mean he could con people; I mean that he had the power to make people do whatever he wanted them to do. He could make them torture another person, could make them kill anyone he wanted to. He could start wars and launch bombs."

A chill runs up my spine at his words, has the hair on the back of my neck standing straight up. Even before he looks straight at me and continues. "He could make you kill yourself, Grace. Or Macy. Or your uncle. Or me. He could make you do anything he wanted, and he did. Over and over and over again.

"No one could stop him. No one could resist him. And he knew it. So he took whatever he wanted and planned for more. And when he decided he was going to murder the shifters, just wipe them out of existence, I knew he wouldn't stop there. The dragons would go, too. The witches. The made vampires. The humans.

"He would destroy them all— just because he could."

He looks away, I think because he doesn't want me to see his face. But I don't need to look in his eyes to know how much this hurts him, not when I can hear it in his voice and feel it in the tension of his body against mine. "There were a lot of people who supported him, Grace. And a lot of people willing to stand in front of him to protect him and the vision he had for our species. I killed a lot of them to get to him. And then I killed him."

This time, when he closes his eyes and then opens them, the distance is gone. And in its place is the same resolve it must have cost for him to not only take on Hudson but also to beat him. "So, no, I don't regret that I killed him. I regret that I didn't do it sooner."

When he finally turns back around to look at me, I can see

the pain, the devastation behind the emptiness in his eyes. It makes me ache for him in a way I've never ached for anyone, not even my parents. "Oh, Jaxon." I put my arms around him again, try to hold him, but his body is stiff and unyielding against my own.

"His death destroyed my parents, and it broke Lia into so many pieces, I don't think she'll ever recover. Before all this happened, she was my best friend. Now she can barely stand to look at me. Flint's brother died fighting Hudson's army in the same fight, and Flint's never been the same, either. We used to be friends, if you can believe it."

He takes a deep, shuddering breath and lets himself sink into me. I hold him as tightly as I can, for as long as he'll let me. Which isn't long at all. He pulls away well before I'm ready to let him go.

"Nothing has been the same since Hudson did what he did. The different species have been at war three times in the last five hundred years. This was almost number four. And though we stopped it before it got too far, the distrust for vampires that goes back centuries is right up front again.

"Add in the fact that a lot of people got an up-close-and-personal look at my power and no one's happy. And can you blame them? How do they know I won't turn like my brother did?"

"You won't." The certainty is a fire deep inside me.

"Probably not," he agrees, though it's hard to miss his qualification. "But this is why I warned you away from Flint, and it's why I had to do what I did in the study lounge. They've been gunning for you since you got here. I don't know why it started, if it's because you're human or if there's something I haven't figured out yet. But I'm sure that it's continued—and gotten worse—because you're mine."

The torment is back, worse than before. "It's why I tried to stay away from you," he adds, "but we both know how well that worked."

"That's it, isn't it?" I whisper as so much of what he's said and done since I first got here finally begins to make sense. "This is why you act the way you do."

"I don't know what you're talking about." His face closes up, but there's a wariness—and a yearning—in his eyes that says I'm on the right track.

"You know exactly what I'm talking about." I rest a hand on his cheek, ignoring the way he flinches when I touch his scar. "You act the way you do because you believe it's the only way you can keep the peace."

"It *is* the only way to keep the peace." The words are torn from him. "We're balanced on a razor-thin tightrope, and every day, every minute, is a balancing act. One wrong step in either direction, and the world burns. Not just ours but yours as well, Grace. I can't let that happen."

Of course he can't.

Other people could walk away, could say it wasn't their responsibility. Could tell themselves that there was nothing they could do.

But that's not how Jaxon operates. Those aren't the rules he lives by. No, Jaxon takes it all on his shoulders. Not just the mess Hudson created and left him with but everything that happened before it—and everything that's happened since.

"So what does that mean for you?" I ask softly, not wanting to spook him any more than I already have. "That you have to give up everything good in your life just to keep things together for everyone else?"

"I'm not giving up anything. This is just who I am." His hands clench into fists, and he tries to turn away.

But I won't let him. Not now, not when I'm finally understanding all the ways he's managed to torture himself—for Hudson's death and for this new role he doesn't want but can't turn away from.

"That's bullshit," I tell him softly. "You wear indifference like a mask; you wield coldness like a weapon—not because you feel nothing but because you feel too much. You've worked so hard to make everyone believe you're a monster that you've begun to believe it yourself.

"But you're not a monster, Jaxon. Not even close."

This time he doesn't try to turn away—he *jerks* away, like a live wire has just wrapped itself around his entire body. "You don't know what you're talking about," he growls.

"You think if people are scared enough, if they hate you enough, they won't dare to step out of line. They won't dare to start another war, because you'll finish that one, too—and them right along with it."

God. The pain, the loneliness, of his existence hits me like an avalanche. What must it feel like to be so alone? What must it feel like to—?

"Don't look at me like that," he orders in a voice as tight and thin as that high-wire he was just talking about.

"Like what?" I whisper.

"Like I'm a victim. Or a hero. I'm neither of those things."

He's both of those things—and so many more besides. But I know he won't believe me if I try to tell him that. Just like I know he won't take any more comfort from me right now, not when I've just laid him open right here for both of us to see.

So I do the only thing I can do.

I tangle my hands in his hair, pull his mouth down to mine.

And give him the only thing he'll accept from me.

50

He Who Lives in Stone Towers Should Never Throw Dragons

For a second, right after our mouths meet, everything goes away. What he told me about his brother, what he told me about my being in danger, everything. For these moments, as his lips move over mine—as his tongue explores my mouth and his teeth gently ravage my lower lip—all I can think about is him. All I can want and feel and need is Jaxon.

He must feel the same way, because he makes a noise deep in his throat as his arms come around me. And then he's picking me up just a little, lifting me until the curves of my body line up perfectly with all the hard, sexy planes of his. And soon the kiss I meant as comfort shifts to something else entirely.

His hands are on my hips, his chest and stomach and thighs pressing against my own, and all I can think of is *yes*. All I can think of is *more*.

More and more and more, until my head is fuzzy, my heart is practically pounding out of my chest, and the rest of me feels like one more slide of his hands or shift of his hips will make me shatter.

Just the thought has a low, needy sound pouring out of me, a sound that Jaxon responds to with a hard, sexy squeeze of his hands on my hips. But then he's pulling away, lifting his mouth from mine, and lowering me slowly to the ground.

"No," I whisper, trying to hold on to him for as long as I can. "Please." I'm not even sure what I'm asking for at this point, only that I don't want this to end. I don't want Jaxon to go back to that cold, bleak place where he has banished himself for so long.

I don't want to lose him to that darkness anymore.

But he murmurs softly to me, brushes his lips over my cheek, my hair, the top of my shoulder. Then slowly, slowly eases back a little more.

"We won't have much longer before Foster gets here, and I want to talk to you before he does."

"Yeah, okay." I sigh, then bury my face against his chest as I take a couple of deep breaths.

He runs his hands up and down my back to soothe us both, I think, before finally settling me on the bed—with a little distance between us. "I want to talk to you about your safety."

Of course he does. "Jaxon—"

"I'm serious, Grace. We need to talk about this, whether you want to or not."

"It's not that I'm trying to dodge the conversation. I'm just saying, after what happened earlier, anyone who doesn't like me is probably going to keep it to themselves from now on. Even if they want to hurt you."

He gives me a look. "I told you, this isn't all about me. If it was, Flint wouldn't have tried to kill you on your second day here. There wasn't anything between us then, so he couldn't have been trying to get to me. Which means—"

I finally recover from the shock ricocheting through me enough to interrupt him. "What are you talking about? Flint didn't try to kill me. He saved me. He's my friend."

"He's not."

"Yes, he is. I know you don't like him, but—"

"Who told you to walk under that chandelier, Grace?" Jaxon asks with watchful eyes.

"Flint did. But it wasn't like that." Still, uneasiness stirs in my belly. It's one thing to believe nameless strangers are out to get me. It's another to think that one of the few people I call a friend here is… "Flint wouldn't do that. Why would he try to drop a chandelier on me after he saved me when I fell off that branch?"

"That's what I was trying to tell you. He didn't save you."

"That's impossible—he wasn't even on the branch with me."

Jaxon narrows his eyes in an *are you kidding me* kind of way. "He wasn't underneath the chandelier with you, either."

"So what? He got one of the shifters to half break the branch before the snowball fight, knowing it was going to be windy?"

"More like he got one of his dragon friends to start the wind that caused all the problems. That's what I've been trying to tell you, Grace. The dragons can't be trusted, and Flint absolutely can't."

"That makes no sense. Why would he dive off that tree branch to keep me from hitting the ground if he was trying to kill me?"

Jaxon doesn't answer.

My stomach tightens up as something horrible occurs to me. "He did save me from falling, didn't he?"

Jaxon doesn't answer. Instead, he looks away, his jaw working for several seconds before he finally says, "It was Cole who was responsible for dropping that chandelier, but it's a hell of a coincidence that Flint made sure you were walking in that direction instead of sitting with the witches. And I don't believe in coincidences. As soon as I prove it, I'm taking care of him, too."

The uneasiness becomes a full-fledged sickness as I remember the look on Flint's face after I thanked him for not letting me splat all over the snow. And how fast Jaxon got there after I fell.

"You're still not answering the question I asked you, Jaxon. Did Flint jump out of that tree to save me or did you somehow *knock* him out of that tree?"

Jaxon avoids my eyes for the second time in as many minutes. Then says, "I wasn't near the tree."

It's my turn to grind my teeth together. "Like that would stop you..."

"Well, what was I supposed to do?" he demands, throwing his arms up in the air with as much emotion as I've ever seen from him. "Let you fall? I figured if I stopped you in midair and brought you gently to the ground, it would freak you out even worse—not to mention leave you with a bunch of questions no one was prepared to answer."

"So you made Flint dive after me instead?"

"I threw him under you, yes. And I'd do it again. I'll do whatever it takes to keep you safe, even if that means taking on every shifter in this place. Especially any of the dragons who might have the power to kick up a wind like the one that broke that branch."

Oh my God. Flint didn't save me. For a second, I think I'm going to throw up. I thought he was on my side. I thought we were friends.

"I'm sorry," Jaxon tells me after several seconds. "I don't want to hurt you. But I can't have you trusting him or any of the other shifters when they're trying to hurt you. Especially when I don't know why yet."

"All the shifters," I say, thinking again about what went down in the study lounge. "Including the alpha."

"Including the alpha."

I don't know what to say to him right now, especially considering everything he's done to keep me safe from that very first night. Even before he knew that we were going to matter to each other. It's that thought that drives me to rest my head in the crook of his neck. And whisper, "Thank you."

"You're *thanking* me?" he demands, stiffening beneath the kisses I keep pressing into the sharp line of his jaw—and the scar he works so hard to keep hidden. "For what?"

"For saving me, of course." I pull him closer, skim my lips over his cheek and along the scar that started this whole discussion, dropping a kiss every couple of centimeters or so. "For not caring about the credit and only caring about making sure I'm okay."

He's sitting rigidly now, his spine ramrod straight with discomfort over what I'm doing. What I'm saying. But I don't care. Not now, when he's in my arms. Not now, when I'm overwhelmed by the feelings I have inside me for him.

It's those feelings that have me climbing onto his lap. Those feelings that have me straddling his hips with my knees on either side of his thighs and my arms wrapped tight around his neck.

And those feelings that bring us right back to where we were before Jaxon called a halt—with me kissing him and kissing him and kissing him. Long, slow, lingering touches of my lips to his brow, his cheek, the corner of his mouth. Over and over, I kiss him. Taste him. Touch him. Over and over, I whisper all the things I like and admire about him.

Slowly—so slowly that I almost don't notice it at first—he relaxes against me. The rigidness leaves his spine. His shoulders curve forward just a little. The hands that were fisted on the bed loosen up and wrap themselves around my waist.

And then he's kissing me, too, really kissing me, with open mouth and searching tongue and hungry, desperate hands. He pushes closer, and I arch against him, pressing my mouth into his until his breath becomes my breath, his need becomes my need.

I slide my hands under his shirt, stroking my fingers along his smooth skin and the lean muscles of his back. Jaxon groans a little as I do, arching into my touch. And then my phone goes off at the exact same time there's a heavy pounding on Jaxon's door...

The sounds break the spell between us, and he pulls away with a laugh. I hold tight to him, not ready to let him go. Not ready for this to end. He must feel the same way, though, because his hands tighten on my waist even as he presses his forehead to mine.

"You should get your phone," he says as it continues to ring. "Foster's probably freaking out because he doesn't know where you are."

The pounding on the door grows harder, more commanding. "Or he's freaking out because he knows *exactly* where I am."

"Yeah, there's that, too." He grins at me, his hands lingering on my waist for just a second as I start to climb off his lap. "You want to get the door or should I?"

"Why would I...?" Horror sweeps through me. "You don't think my uncle is the one pounding on the door, do you?"

"Not sure who else you think it would be, considering his beloved niece was last seen in the company of the guy who just picked a fight with every wolf shifter in the school."

"Oh my God." I look around for a mirror so I can fix my hair just enough that it doesn't look like I've spent the last hour making out with a vampire, then kind of stop in shock as I realize that there's nothing even resembling a mirror in here. "So are the old stories true?" I demand, combing my hair with little more than my fingers and a prayer. "Vampires really can't see themselves in mirrors?"

"We really can't."

"How is that possible?" I tuck my shirt in and make sure my hoodie is pulled down over my hips. "I mean, how do you know what you look like?"

He holds up his phone. "Selfie, anyone?" He moves toward

the door, which is practically vibrating under the force of my uncle's knocks. "Is this seriously what you want to talk about right now?"

A little bit, actually. Now that the whole vampire thing is out in the open, I realize I have a million questions. Things like how long do born vampires live—or are they immortal, like the stories suggest? Which leads me to wonder if born vampires age the same way, or is this a baby Yoda thing, where their maturation is much slower than non-magical humans? And if it is, exactly how old is Jaxon? Also, did Mekhi not come into my room today because he was being respectful or because he couldn't cross the threshold without an invitation?

There are more questions buzzing in my brain—so many more—but Jaxon is right. Now isn't exactly the time to be thinking about any of this.

"Of course not." I nod toward the door. "Open it and let's get this over with."

"It'll be fine," he promises with a wicked little grin that makes me think it will be anything but.

Especially if Uncle Finn is anything like my father. Then again, the guy's a witch and runs a school for the supernatural... so probably not that much in common after all.

"It will be whatever it is," I tell him, aiming for Zen and sounding completely out of touch instead. But come on, it's hard not to freak out when I'm pretty sure the boy I'm crazy about is going to be expelled.

Jaxon winks at me, even blows me a kiss, before rearranging his face into blankness as he throws open the door.

"Nice of you to let me in," my uncle says dryly. "So sorry you felt the need to hurry."

"Sorry, Foster, but Grace *did* have to get her clothes back on."

"Jaxon!" I gasp, my cheeks turning I can't even imagine what shade of red. "I was fully dressed, Uncle Finn. I swear."

"This is what you want to lead with after that stunt you just pulled?" my uncle demands. But before Jaxon can answer, he turns on me. "I thought you were heading back to your room more than an hour ago?"

"I was. But I got..."

"Sidetracked?" my uncle finishes for me with a raised brow.

At this point, I'm pretty sure the blush has taken over my entire body. Including my eyelashes and hair. "Yeah."

"If you're well enough to be up here, you're probably well enough to be in class, don't you think?"

"Yeah. I probably am."

"Good." He glances at his watch. "First period should be about half done right now—we are squeezing it in before lunch due to the chandelier incident...and other things." He glares at Jaxon. "You should head there now."

I think about arguing, but he's got the same look on his face my dad used to have when I pushed him to the limit. I want to stay with Jaxon, want to know what's going to happen to him, but I'm afraid if I put up a fuss now, it will just make my uncle angrier. And that's the last thing I want if he's about to decide Jaxon's fate.

So instead of demanding to stay as I want to do, I just nod and head into the bedroom to grab my purse from where Jaxon dropped it. "Yes, Uncle Finn."

For a second, I could swear that surprise flashes in my uncle's eyes, but it's gone so fast that I'm not sure I didn't imagine it. Then again, Macy doesn't exactly strike me as the biddable type, so maybe he didn't expect me to agree so easily. Or he was surprised my purse was in Jaxon's bedroom, which...I am going to choose not to think about.

Either way, it's too late to argue now, so I turn to Jaxon. "I'll see you later?" I deliberately avoid making eye contact with my uncle as I wait for his response.

"Yeah." His tone says *obviously*, even if he keeps his words simple in deference to my uncle. "I'll text you."

It's not quite the response I was hoping for, but again, I'm not in a position to argue. So I just give him a little smile as I head for the door.

And try not to panic when the last thing I hear before Uncle Finn slams it closed is, "Give me one reason not to ship your ass to Prague, Vega. And make sure it's a good one."

51

Trial by Dragon Fire

I pull out my phone on the way down the stairs to Brit Lit and find about twenty text messages waiting for me. Five from Heather, complaining about how boring school is without me, along with several photos of her in her costume for the fall play.

I fire off a text telling her how great she looks dressed as the Cheshire Cat and another one sympathizing with the boredom. I want to tell her about Jaxon—not the vampire stuff, just the cute boy stuff—but that's a subject I know I shouldn't open until I decide exactly what I can or can't tell my bestie about him. Because when Heather is on the trail for new information, she's utterly relentless.

Plus, I've never lied to her, and I don't really want to start now. I mean, logic says that if I'm going to be with Jaxon, I'm going to have to lie sometimes—I can't walk around announcing to the world that he's a vampire without us having to dodge a lot of wooden stakes and garlic. But I need to think about what I'm going to say. I'm a terrible liar at the best of times. When talking to Heather? I'll crack in ten seconds flat, and that can't happen.

Which is why I don't say anything more than I absolutely have to, even though a part of me is dying for her opinion about…oh, I don't know, everything hot-guy related.

Most of the other texts are from Macy—there are seven of them talking about what happened in the study room. She wasn't there, but the news of what Jaxon did to the wolf alpha has obviously spread. Not that I expected any different; he did it publicly for a reason. Plus Uncle Finn showing up at the tower shows just how far and fast the news traveled.

And Uncle Finn sent several texts to me as well, all of them demanding to know where I was. I don't bother to answer, considering he already found me—much to my chagrin.

The last two texts are from Flint, and I'm so shocked—and annoyed—I nearly miss a step and fall on my face. But then I remember the asshole dragon doesn't know what I know. He doesn't have a clue that I know he's been trying to kill me instead of help me.

It still pisses me off, though—the whole thing does—so I don't bother answering him. I swear to myself that I'll never answer him again, no matter what explanation he comes up with and no matter how many excuses he tries

Part of me wants to find him right now and have it out. But I've finally made it to Brit Lit, only to realize that I've totally forgotten to change into my school uniform. So I shove my phone back into the front pocket of my hoodie and head up to my room to do a super-quick change. Ten minutes later, I walk into class only to have the whole room go eerily silent the moment everyone spots me. You'd think I'd be used to that after the last week, but today, with everything that's happened, it feels a million times more awkward than usual.

But honestly, it's not like I can blame them. If I wasn't me, I'd be staring, too. I mean, come on, supernatural or not, they're still high school kids and I am still the girl who just caused a fight between the alpha wolf and the most powerful vampire in existence.

It'd be stranger if they didn't stare.

That knowledge doesn't make the walk across the room to my desk any easier, though. Even with Mekhi giving me a supportive smile.

"We just started act 4, scene 5," he tells me in a soft undertone as I slide into my desk. "You can share my book."

"Thanks," I answer, pulling a pen and a small notebook out of my purse. I have no idea why I didn't grab my backpack before heading down here, but I didn't, so this is going to have to do.

"Everyone's taking a turn reading today, Grace," the instructor informs me from her spot at the front of the classroom. "Why don't you read Ophelia in this scene?"

"Okay," I answer, wondering why I have to play the damsel in distress. Because I've already read the play, I know this is the scene where Ophelia goes mad—or at least, where the audience gets to see her insanity for the first time. I try not to take it personally that she seems to think I'm the right one for the job...

Mekhi is playing Laertes, my brother, which makes it a little easier to read the lines of an insane girl who has just lost her father and feels all alone in the world. But I still struggle to get through them, especially the lines toward the end.

"'There's a daisy: I would give you some violets, but they withered all when my father died: they say he made a good end—For bonny sweet Robin is all my joy.'"

Mekhi reads Laertes's line—obviously concerned about the state of my mental health. And by *my*, I mean Ophelia's, I remind myself as I move into softly singing my last lines in the scene—and the play. "'And will he not come again? And will he not come again? No, no, he is dead; Go to thy death-bed: He never will come again—'"

The bell rings before I finish her lines, and I stop as the rest of the class starts shoveling their books into their backpacks as fast as they can go. "Thank you, Grace. Tomorrow, we'll pick up where you left off."

I nod, then shove everything back into my purse, doing my best not to think about the death scene I just read. Doing my best not to think about my parents—and about Hudson. About Jaxon's grief over who Hudson was and what that forced him to do.

It's harder than I want it to be, especially when I realize my World History of Witchcraft Trials (and yeah, okay, now that I know about the whole paranormal thing, classes like this one make a lot more sense) is next.

It's not the class that bothers me; it's the walk through the creepy-as-fuck tunnels. Especially now that I wonder what would have happened to me down there alone with Flint if Lia *hadn't* come along when she did.

But I've got to get to class, so it's no use spending too much time dwelling on might-have-beens. Especially now that Jaxon has pretty much made me untouchable. What happened in that lounge might have been horrifying to witness, but I'm not going to lie. The fact that I no longer have to be afraid of chandeliers falling on my head or random shifters shoving me out into the snow isn't a bad thing.

And when Mekhi walks with me down the hall instead of racing off to his next class, I realize that Jaxon's protection extends even further than I thought. The threat was made—and I'm pretty sure heeded, judging by the wide berth everyone is giving me at the moment—and still it's not enough for him. Still, he wants to make sure I'm safe, so much so that he's called in other members of the Order to ensure I am.

Maybe it should bother me.

And honestly, if this was a normal school or a normal situation, it would probably bug the hell out of me to have such a protective…boyfriend? But I'm currently surrounded by shifters, vampires, and witches—all of whom play by rules I don't have a clue about. Plus, it's been less than three hours since a chandelier nearly crushed me to death. Not accepting Jaxon's and Mekhi's protection would be foolish, at least until things calm down around here.

I turn to thank Mekhi for walking with me, then freak out a little when Flint pretty much shoves his way between us. "Hey, Grace. How are you feeling?" he asks, all sweetness and concern. "I've been worried about you this morning."

"Worried about me or worried that the chandelier didn't do its job well enough?" I query, walking faster in what I already know is a useless attempt to get away from him.

He doesn't stop walking, but everything about him kind of stills when I confront him with what Jaxon told me—which tells me all *I* need to know.

And still, he tries to play it off. "What do you mean? Of course I'm worried about you."

"Give me a break, Flint. I know what you've been up to."

For the first time in our entire "friendship," anger flashes in his eyes. "Don't you mean you know what that tick told you I was up to?" he sneers.

Mekhi's face goes livid at the insult to Jaxon, and suddenly he's right there between the two of us again. "Back the fuck off, Dragon Boy."

Flint ignores him and continues talking to me. "You don't know what's really going on, Grace. You can't trust Jaxon—"

"Why? Because you say so? Aren't you the one who's been trying to kill me since I got here?"

"It's not for the reasons you think." He shoots me a pleading look. "If you would just trust me—"

"Not for the reasons I think?" I repeat. "So you actually think there are good reasons for trying to kill me? And you still want *me* to trust *you*?" I wave an arm his way in a *step right up* kind of gesture. "Fine. Then tell me the truth about what happened during the snowball fight. Did you jump out of that tree to catch me, or did Jaxon knock you out of it?"

"I... It wasn't like... Jaxon overreacted. I was—"

I let him stutter all over himself for a few seconds, then cut him off. "Yeah, that's what I thought. Stay away from me, Flint. I don't want to have anything to do with you from now on."

"Well that's too bad, because I'm not going away."

"You know, there's a name for a guy who continues to hound a girl after she tells him to leave her alone," Mekhi tells Flint after we make the turn into the hallway that leads to the tunnels.

Flint ignores him. "Grace, please." He reaches out and grabs hold of my arm. Before I can tell him not to touch me, Mekhi is right there, fangs bared and warning growl pouring out of his throat.

"Get your filthy dragon hands off her," he hisses.

"I'm not going to hurt her!"

"Damn right you're not. Step back, Montgomery."

Flint makes a frustrated sound deep in his throat, but in the end, he does what Mekhi asks. Mostly, I think, because there was going to be a fight right here in the hallway if he didn't. One where Mekhi tries to tear him to pieces.

"Come on, Grace," he implores. "It's important. Just listen for one minute."

I stop because it's fairly obvious at this point that he isn't planning on going away. "Fine. You want to talk, talk. What's so important?" I cross my arms over my chest and wait to see what he has to say.

"You want me to say it now? In front of everyone?" he snarls, looking at Mekhi.

"Well, I'm sure as hell not going to go somewhere alone with you at this point. I may be ignorant about your world, but I'm not downright foolish."

"I can't do this. I—" He breaks off, runs a frustrated hand through his hair. "I can't talk to you in front of a vampire. It needs to be alone."

"Then you're not talking to her at all," Mekhi says, once again getting between us. "Let's go, Grace."

I allow Mekhi to guide me away from an increasingly angry Flint. Which is kind of obnoxious when you think about it. He's the one who tried to kill *me* with a chandelier, and now *he's* the one who gets to be angry? Where's the logic in that?

"Damn it, Mekhi, at least do me a favor and don't leave her alone, okay?" Flint calls after us. "I'm serious, Grace. You shouldn't go anywhere alone. It's not safe."

52

If You Can't Live Without Me, Why Aren't You Dead Yet?

The irony of that statement isn't lost on me. Nor is it lost on Mekhi, if the way he snarls at Flint is any indication. "No shit, Sherlock. What do you think is happening here?"

Flint doesn't answer, and I don't bother to look back as Mekhi and I head into the tunnels. He doesn't say anything about Flint or anything else as we make our way through the first door. But the silence only makes me feel worse about what just happened. And about trusting Flint from the beginning, especially when Jaxon warned me not to.

I just wish I knew what he got out of hurting me when I've never done anything to him. *Not to mention playing at being my friend at the same time he was plotting to kill me.*

"Who knows with dragons?" It's not until Mekhi answers that I realize I spoke out loud. "They're super secretive, and nobody ever really knows what's going on with them."

"Apparently." I give him a shaky smile. "I really am sorry about all this—and about you having to walk me to class. I do appreciate it, though."

"No worries. It takes a lot more than a bad-tempered dragon to ruin my day. Besides, if I end up a couple of minutes late to

Calculus, you'll only be doing me a favor." He grins down at me as we follow the route into the tunnels.

As we make our way through all the doors, including stops for the security codes and the rest of the stuff I had to do with Flint, I'm struck by how different it feels with Mekhi. With Flint, everything inside me was screaming a warning, telling me to get the hell away from him as fast as I could.

With Mekhi, this trip into the tunnels feels normal. No, better than normal. Like walking with an old friend, one I'm totally comfortable around. There's no voice warning me to be careful, no uncomfortable shiver running down my spine. All of which tells me the bad feelings were tied to Flint and not the tunnel all along.

Still, I wait for that same voice to kick in as we go deeper into the tunnel. If not in warning, then at least a little self-congratulatory rumba for staying alive against all odds. Something that proves I'm not crazy for thinking I hear a voice deep inside myself that tells me what to do.

I admit, I've never had anything like it before, just the normal conscience-type stuff we all have when I'm trying to decide between right and wrong. But what happened the last time I was down here is different. In some ways, it felt almost sentient, like it existed away from my own consciousness and subconscious.

I can't help wondering what's actually going on. Can't help wondering just what Jaxon or Katmere Academy or freaking Alaska itself has woken up within me.

If anything.

I will say that whatever's happening, I'm at least glad the feeling of doom is gone. For now, I'm just going to accept that it is and worry about the rest when I've had a chance to breathe for a little while—which won't happen until I know for sure what Uncle Finn has decided about Jaxon.

Jaxon didn't act like he was afraid of being expelled, but that doesn't mean much. He doesn't strike me as being afraid of anything, let alone what the headmaster of his high school might do to him. But just because he didn't look worried doesn't mean Uncle Finn doesn't have the power to make him leave school temporarily…or for good.

I check my phone as we walk through the last gate into the tunnels. Still no text from Jaxon.

"Have you heard from him?" I ask as we start the long trek to the art building.

"No."

"Is that normal? I mean, does he usually check in with you or—"

I break off as Mekhi laughs. "Jaxon doesn't check in with anyone, Grace. I thought you would have figured that out by now."

"I did. I just… What do you think is going to happen?"

"I think Foster is going to give him a slap on the wrist and then move on."

"A slap on the wrist?" I don't even try to hide my shock. "He nearly killed that boy."

"*Nearly killed* and *killed* are two very different things here—in case you haven't noticed." He gives me a knowing look. "At some point, we all screw up learning how to deal with our powers."

"Yeah, but this wasn't a screwup. This was a calculated attack."

"Maybe." Mekhi shrugs. "But it was also necessary. I don't think Foster will blame Jaxon for trying to protect you. Or be shortsighted enough to send him away when he's the one standing between you and God knows what. In my opinion, the wolf alpha is more at risk for being kicked out than Jaxon is."

"School rules aren't all about me, even if the headmaster is my uncle. Besides, I thought Jaxon was the whole reason the shifters were after me. Because they wanted payback for everything that went on with Hudson?"

I mean, what else could it be? I've never done anything to any of these people, nor is there anything supernatural about me. No powers, no shifting, no sudden desire to bite people's necks. So unless they're playing a rousing game of Terrorize the Human, I can't imagine what the shifters could possibly get out of trying to kill me.

"Jaxon's operating under that assumption, which makes sense, considering they've just been waiting to find something that matters to him. Waiting for something they can take away from him."

My heart beats a little faster at Mekhi's words—and the implication that everyone knows that I'm who Jaxon cares about. It's probably ridiculous to be so excited at the thought, since if it's true, those feelings put a big red *X* right on me. But after the time I spent with Jaxon in his room today, I don't care nearly as much as I should. I want to be with him.

"So what was Hudson like?" I ask Mekhi as we reach the back part of the tunnels. Maybe it's an indelicate question to ask, but how else am I supposed to find out anything about Jaxon's relationship with his brother? I'm pretty sure he's not going to tell me.

Mekhi glances down at me, and there's something different in the look he gives me, something wary and fearsome at the same time. It's so similar to the look Jaxon had when he was talking about Hudson—minus the palpable anguish—that it makes me wonder just who this guy was. And how his presence can be so keenly felt even after he's been dead for nearly a year.

"Hudson was...Hudson," Mekhi says with a sigh. "I guess the best way to describe him would be as a light version of Jaxon."

"A light version?" That's not what I was expecting, especially after what Jaxon had to say about him earlier. "I thought he was a…" I trail off because I don't want to call the former heir to the vampire throne a monster, even though that's exactly what I'm thinking.

"Not light as in sunshine," Mekhi elaborates as we reach the center rotunda of the tunnels. "I mean Jaxon lite. He was the older brother and pretty much the prodigal son—their parents adored him. And so did a lot of other important people in our species.

"But being able to fool people into thinking you have character isn't the same as actually having character. And the one thing I know for sure is that Hudson wasn't a quarter of the person Jaxon is. Too selfish, too egotistical, too opportunistic. All Hudson cared about was Hudson. He was just good at pretending to care about what those in power wanted him to care about."

I don't know what to say to that, so in the end I don't say anything. After all, I never met Hudson, and I don't care about him in the slightest, beyond the fact that Jaxon is using his brother's death to punish himself.

But I've got to admit, Mekhi's description sounds awfully close to what I figured out reading between the lines of what Jaxon was telling me. He's beating himself to hell and back for what happened between them, but it sounds to me like he did the world a favor taking Hudson out of it. No matter what Jaxon thinks about it.

A noise sounds far behind us, and suddenly Mekhi is shoving me in back of him as he whirls around, hands raised in an obvious fighting stance. Which he drops once he realizes the noise came from Lia, who is racing up the tunnel toward us.

And by racing, I mean really booking it. Wow, she can move fast when she wants to. I mean, that's no surprise—I've seen Jaxon move, and it's a little shocking how quickly he can get to me when he wants to.

But so far, every time he moves like that, it's because I'm in some kind of trouble and he wants to get to me. The same kind of trouble that keeps me from paying close attention to him because I'm afraid I'm in the middle of trying not to die.

Watching Lia run without any safety fears for myself, though? It's intense. It takes her less than a minute to cover the tunnel we just spent the last five minutes walking down.

And when she gets to us? She isn't even breathless.

"Hey, girl, where's the fire?" Mekhi asks as she moves to pass right by us. I'm surprised at his tone, and the fact that a lot of the warmth he has when he talks to me is now absent.

Of course, she isn't exactly dripping friendliness herself when she answers, "Oh, hey, guys. Just using my free period to do some extra time in the art studio."

Mekhi raises a brow. "Since when do you use your free period for anything productive?"

She looks away, jaw working, and for a second, I'm pretty sure she isn't going to answer him. But then she shrugs and says, "I'm working on a painting of Hudson."

"So that's who it is," I exclaim, thinking back on the portrait I saw her working on yesterday. "He's really good-looking."

"You have no idea." Her lips curve in the closest thing I've seen to a smile from her. "I'm nowhere near talented enough to do him justice."

"False modesty?" Mekhi mocks. "That's not like you, Lia."

"I'd say bite me," she answers with an eye roll, "but who knows where you've been."

"Thanks, but I'm too afraid of catching rabies to ever bite you," he sneers back.

And can I just say, wow. There are enough bad vibes flowing between them that I can't help thinking I'm about to witness my second vampire attack of the day.

Apparently, when her relationship went bad with Jaxon, it went bad with the rest of the Order, too, because right now, Mekhi honestly looks like he wants to rip her throat out.

But just when I'm trying to determine how to get out of range, Lia flips him off. Then hooks her arm through mine and says, "Let's go, Grace. He's so not worth it."

"Oh, well, actually, Mekhi was just walking me to class." I don't like being in the middle of the two of them, but that doesn't mean I'm going to bail on Mekhi the first chance I get.

The warning bell chooses that exact moment to ring, and Mekhi gives a little shrug as he takes a step back. "I'm good heading to Calculus if you're good with Lia showing you the rest of the way."

"I'm pretty sure I can get her to class safely," Lia snarks, but I just smile my gratitude at him.

I like that Mekhi isn't making a big deal of the *me not being alone* thing, just kind of making sure all the bases are covered without putting up too big a fuss. Especially since Jaxon has already covered the giant-fuss department.

"I'm good," I tell him, and I mean it. Down here, surrounded by people Jaxon trusts—even if they don't trust each other—makes everything else that's happened so much easier to deal with. "You should get to math."

"Words absolutely no normal person has ever wanted to hear," he answers with a sigh. But he steps back, does a little two-fingered salute as a goodbye wave.

Impulsively, I close the distance between us to give him a hug. "Thanks for walking with me. I really appreciate it."

He seems a little taken aback by my very human show of emotion, so I pull away, worried that I did something wrong. But when I look up at him, he's got a goofy smile on his face that says he doesn't mind at all. And that's before he pats my head like I'm a prize-winning Chihuahua or something.

Still, it feels pretty good to have one of Jaxon's friends' stamp of approval, so I just grin at him and do that ridiculous two-fingered salute back at him.

He laughs, then snarls a little at Lia—for show, I think—before turning around and heading back the way we came.

I watch him for a second, expecting him to start booking it like Lia was, but instead he takes his time, moseying along like he's in the middle of one of the old Westerns my dad used to watch.

Which only makes me appreciate Mekhi more. He's willing to give Lia and me some privacy, but he's in no hurry to leave me alone with anyone. Even another vampire.

"So what's been going on with you?" I ask Lia after another glance at my phone reveals still no texts from Jaxon. And the fact that we have two minutes left to get to class.

"Pretty sure that's my line after that whole scene in the lounge today." She raises her brows in a WTF look.

"Oh, that. Um, Jaxon..." I trail off, not sure what I can possibly say about what happened.

Lia laughs. "You don't have to explain anything to me. Hudson was overprotective in the same way, doing whatever he thought necessary to take care of me. Even if there was nothing to protect me from."

I think about correcting her, maybe even telling her what's been going on so I can get her take on it, but we're almost to the cottages, and suddenly more people are around—vampires, witches, *and* shifters. And since there's more than enough gossip surrounding me right now, I figure the last thing I need to do is add fuel to the fire.

So instead of letting Lia know everything that's happened over the last few days, I just kind of shrug and laugh. "You know how guys are."

"Yeah, I do." She rolls her eyes. "Which reminds me…I was thinking you might want to get away from all that machismo for a while. Want to do a girls' night tonight? We can do facials, watch some rom-com, eat too much chocolate. Maybe even do those mani-pedis we were talking about the other day."

"Oh." I sneak another glance at my phone. Still no Jaxon. Maybe my uncle banished him to Prague—or Siberia—after all. "Yeah, I guess."

"Wow." She gives me a mock-offended look. "Don't sound so enthusiastic."

"Sorry. I was just hoping Jaxon would ask me to spend some time with him tonight. But—" I hold up my phone with a sigh. "Nothing so far."

"Yeah, well. Don't hold your breath. Making plans isn't exactly Jaxon's modus operandi." There's a sadness running underneath the bitterness in her voice when she talks about him. It makes me think that, despite what she says, she misses his friendship as much as he misses hers.

Which sucks, especially considering how much the two of them are hurting right now.

It's not my place to get involved—I didn't know Hudson and I wasn't around when things went bad between Jaxon and Lia—but I know how fleeting life can be, even for vampires. How quickly things can just end, with no warning and no chance to put everything right.

I also know how much his problems with Lia weigh on Jaxon, reminding him daily of his role in what happened to Hudson. I can't help wondering if those problems weigh just as heavily on Lia…and if maybe the two of them might finally begin to heal if they can forgive each other and themselves.

I mean, anything has to be better than this enmity between

them. She's destroyed, he's devastated, and neither of them can move into the future because they're so traumatized by the past.

Which is why, in the end, I can't resist saying, "You know, he really misses you."

Her eyes jump to mine. "You don't know what you're talking about." It's a half whisper, half hiss.

"I do know. He told me what happened. And I can't imagine how hurt you must be—"

"You're right. You can't imagine." She starts walking faster as we head up the final incline. "So don't."

"Okay. Sorry." I'm practically running in an effort to keep up with her. "It's just, I think you would be better off if you could try to connect with Jaxon a little bit. Or anyone, really, Lia. I know you're sad; I know you just want to be left alone because everything else is too agonizing to even think about. Believe me, I know that." God, do I ever.

"But the thing is," I continue, "you aren't getting any better like that. You're staying exactly where you were, drowning in grief, and until you decide to take the first step, you're always going to be drowning."

"What do you think I was doing when I invited you over for facials?" she asks, her voice smaller than I've ever heard it. "I'm tired of crying myself to sleep every night, Grace. I'm tired of hurting. That's why I thought I could try to start over with you. You're nice, and you didn't know Hudson or the person I used to be. I thought we had a chance of being friends. Real friends."

She turns her face away from mine, but I can still tell she's biting her lip, obviously trying not to cry. I feel like a total jerk. "Of course we're friends, Lia." Impulsively, I wrap an arm around her shoulders and squeeze.

She stiffens up at first, but eventually she relaxes and leans into the hug. I used to be one of those people who never let go of the hug first—right up until my parents died. Then I got so many hugs I didn't want from well-meaning people who didn't know what else to do that backing away became self-preservation.

For Lia, I go back to the pre-accident time, hugging her until she decides it's enough. It takes longer than I thought it would, which, in my mind, proves the theory that you hold on until the other person pulls away because you never know what they're going through and if they need the comfort.

Of course, my phone chooses to *finally* vibrate right in the middle of the hug, and it takes every ounce of self-control I have not to make a grab for it. But real friends are important—not to mention few and far between—so I wait it out, not letting go until Lia finally steps back.

My phone vibrates three more times, stops, then vibrates again. Lia rolls her eyes, but in a friendly way that says the storm has passed. "Why don't you answer that and put Jaxon out of his misery? He's probably terrified the shifters decided to have barbecued Grace for lunch despite his warning."

She must be right, because two more texts come in before I can pull my phone out. Lia just laughs and shakes her head. "How the mighty have fallen."

Not going to lie, my heart skips a beat—or five—at hearing her say that, even if there's a part of me that's afraid it's wishful thinking. Still, it's hard not to smile when I look at the string of texts he's sent me.

Jaxon: Told you not to worry

Jaxon: I have lived to fight another day

Jaxon: Or should that be I have lived to bite another day...

Jaxon: Anyway, come to my room tonight, whenever you're available

Jaxon: I want to show you something

Partly because he contacted me as soon as he was done with Uncle Finn.

And (mostly) because he asked me out tonight. Or as close to out as we can get here in the middle of Alaska.

Me: Sorry, talking to Lia

Me: Definitely! What time?

Me: Glad things went okay

I hesitate for a second, then text what I've been thinking since he made the pun about living to bite another day. It's the same thing I've been thinking about off and on since I left his room a couple of hours ago.

Me: I like it when you bite

I blush a little as I send it, but I don't regret it. Because it's the truth and because I've already thrown myself at the boy. What else is there but to see it through to the end?

When my phone vibrates immediately, I'm almost afraid to look at it.

Afraid I've gone too far.

Afraid I'm pushing too fast.

Jaxon: Good, because I like the way you taste

It's corny and unoriginal and that doesn't matter at all, because *swoon*. For a boy who tries to be so implacable, Jaxon's got serious game. I mean, really. What girl is supposed to resist a text like that? Or the guy who texted it, when he's also the guy willing to fight wolves and dragons and anyone else who comes for her?

Not me, that's for sure.

Lia, on the other hand, makes a little gagging sound as she reads over my shoulder. "Wow, Jaxon. Sappy much?"

"I like it." Still, I blank out my phone screen and shove it back into my pocket. No need for her to see anything else Jaxon might decide to write to me.

I tingle a little at the thought.

"So we raincheck tonight?" Lia says as she pushes open the door to the art studio. "And do facials tomorrow?"

It sounds like a plan to me. But after everything she just revealed, I can't help asking, "Are you sure? I can go see Jaxon after we have our girls' night."

"And make me the one responsible for standing in the way of true love?" she snarks. "I don't think so."

"Oh, it's not like that," I tell her, even as a part of me melts at the description. "We're just…hanging out."

"Wanna bet?" Lia asks with a snort. "Because the Jaxon Vega I've known my whole life doesn't almost start a war over a girl he just wants to 'hang out' with."

53

If This Kiss Is Going to Start a War, it May as Well Be Worth It

Lia's words are still ringing in my ears several hours later as I'm trying to figure out what to wear to Jaxon's room for our...date. Logically, I know he won't care, but I care. I haven't exactly been at my best since I got to Katmere, and just once I'd like to knock his socks off.

"You should go with the red dress," Macy says from where she's sitting cross-legged on my bed, watching me agonize over my clothes choice. "Guys love red. And that dress is killer, if I do say so myself."

She's right. The dress is amazing, but... "You don't think it's too obvious?"

"What's wrong with obvious?" she demands. "You're crazy about him. He obviously feels a whole lot of something for you or he wouldn't have nearly ripped Cole's throat out in the lounge today. There's nothing wrong with letting him know you dressed up for him."

"I know that. It's just..." I hold up her red dress for the ten millionth time. "This is a lot of dressing up."

"There's not enough material for it to be a lot of anything," Macy snickers.

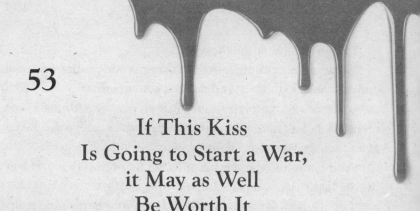

"Yeah, that's kind of my point."

The red dress is amazing, no doubt about it. And I bet it looks gorgeous on Macy. But with all its geometric cuts and angles and the absolute lack of fabric near anything important, it's about as far from my usual style as I can get. Which is fine, I guess, except whatever happens with Jaxon tonight (or doesn't happen), I want it to happen when I look and feel like me.

"I think I'm going to go with the yellow one," I decide, reaching for the dress in question. It still has spaghetti straps, but the neckline is a little higher than the red one, and it should actually hit below my knees when I put it on, versus the top half of my thighs, like the red one.

"Seriously? That's my least favorite one of the bunch." Macy makes grabby hands for it, but I move back so it's out of her reach. "I mean, *my dad* picked it out for me."

"Well, I like it. And the fact that it doesn't scream that I want to get naked with him."

"Says the girl who got up to all kinds of naughty stuff in his room today," she says with a smirk.

"I never should have told you that! And it's not like we got naked. We just made out." I take off my uniform and slip into the dress. "The dress is just to make a point."

"And what point is that exactly?" She gets off the bed and starts tugging on the skirt to help it fall into place over my ridiculous curves. "Oh, right. The point that you lust after Jaxon's sexy, sexy body."

"I thought you didn't like Jaxon." I shoot her a smug look. "I mean, aren't you the one who told me how dangerous he was and that I should stay far, far away from him?"

"And look how well you listened." She crosses to her dresser and starts opening and closing the myriad assortment of little doors on the jewelry box she has perched on the top of it. "Besides, just because he scares me doesn't mean I can't appreciate how sexy he is for you," she says in a deliberately deep and funny voice. "Plus that gorgeous bite mark he left on you? *Swoon.*"

Swoon is right. Every time I see it in the mirror, it makes me want to melt. "Everything about Jaxon is gorgeous to me," I tell her as she crosses back over to me, a pair of dangling gold earrings in her hand.

"Try not to salivate on the dress," she answers dryly. "Drool is so last decade."

I stick my tongue out at her, but she just crosses her eyes at me. "Save that for Jaxon."

"Oh my God! Are you trying to embarrass me to death before I ever make it to his room?"

"What's there to be embarrassed about? You're head over heels for him; he's head over heels for you… I say go for it."

"Can you please just give me the earrings so I can get out of here?" I demand, holding my hand out for them.

"Stay still and I'll put them in for you. The clasp is kind of tricky." She leans over and slides one of the earrings into my earhole. "Wow, you smell good enough to eat… Oops. I mean drink."

"I swear to God, Macy…"

"Okay, okay, I'll stop messing with you." She moves to put the second earring in. "It's just so fun to watch you blush."

"Yeah. So much fun," I deadpan as she struggles to fasten the second earring.

Finally the clasp slides into place, and she steps back. "How do you stay so still?" she asks as she straightens out the skirt of my dress. "I swear you're a statue. It barely felt like you were breathing while I was putting that earring in."

"Terror that you were going to slip and rip the thing out of my ear. Or poke me in the eye," I tease.

She makes a face at me as I slip my feet into the one nice pair of heels I brought with me. They're nude and strappy, so they go with almost anything. Including, thankfully, this yellow dress.

"So how do I look?" I do a little twirl in the center of the room.

"Like you're going to need another blood transfusion by the time Jaxon's done with you."

"Macy! Stop it!"

She just grins as I make my way to the door. "Seriously, you look amazing. You're going to knock that vamp's socks off."

This time when I blush, it's from excitement. "You really think so?"

"I know so." She motions for me to twirl around again, so I do. "Also, I'll bet you ten bucks that dress is going to be missing buttons when you finally make it back here."

"Okay, that's it!" I give her a mock glare as I head for the door.

But she just grins and crosses her eyes at me, all of which makes me laugh ridiculously hard. And calms me down, which I know is exactly what she was intending.

It's so strange. Before this week, I hadn't seen Macy in ten years. We were virtual strangers. And now I can't imagine going back to life without her.

"Don't wait up," I say as I make my way out the door.

"Yeah, like that's going to happen," she tells me with a snort. "FYI, I'm going to need all the details. And I mean all. So you should probably pay really close attention to everything that happens so you get them right."

"Absolutely," I agree, just to tease her. "I'll take notes. That way I won't forget anything."

"You think you're being funny, but I'm serious. Notes would be extremely helpful."

I roll my eyes. "Goodbye, Macy."

"Come on, Grace! Let a girl live vicariously through you, will ya?"

"Why don't you go find Cam? Do a little non-vicarious living of your own?"

She considers it. "Maybe I will."

"Good. And you should totally wear the red dress when you do. After all, guys love it when you're obvious."

She flips me off and throws a pillow at me that I only narrowly manage to dodge.

"Temper, temper," I tease, then hightail it out the door before she decides to throw something at me that will really hurt. Or, you know, cast some kind of spell that makes all my hair fall out. There are perils to living with a witch, after all.

My palms are sweating and my heart is beating a little too fast as I make my way to the tower room. Maybe I should have come up right after classes, like I wanted to, because all the preparation—the hair, the makeup, the dress deliberation—has done is give me more time to think.

And more time to get nervous.

Which is ridiculous. This is Jaxon. He's seen me falling out of a tree and nearly bleeding to death. He's saved my life several times since I got here. He's seen me looking my worst—why am I suddenly so determined that he see me looking my best? It's not like I actually think he cares if I straighten my hair and put on high heels.

I tell myself all of this on the way to his room—and I even believe it. But my hands are still trembling when I knock on his door. And so are my knees.

Jaxon opens the door with a sexy grin that turns to total blankness the second he sees me. Which is definitely *not* the reaction I was hoping for after spending the last two hours getting ready.

"Am I early?" I ask, discomfort suddenly racing through me. "If you want, I can come back later—"

I break off as he reaches for my wrist and gently tugs me into his room—and his arms. "You look gorgeous," he murmurs against my ear as he hugs me tight. "Absolutely beautiful."

The ball of tension in my stomach dissolves as soon as he wraps himself around me.

As soon as I smell the sexy orange and fresh water scent of him.

As soon as I feel the strength and power of his body against and around my own.

"You look pretty amazing yourself," I tell him. And he does, with his ripped jeans and bright-blue cashmere sweater. "I think this is the first time I've seen you wearing something other than black."

"Yeah, well, let's keep that between us."

"Absolutely." I keep my arms wrapped around his waist as I grin up at him. "Wouldn't want to mess up that badass reputation of yours."

He rolls his eyes. "What is it about my reputation you're so obsessed with?"

"The fact that everybody feels like they need to warn me against being with you. Obviously. I've never dated anyone like you before."

I'm teasing, but the second the words leave my mouth, I want to take them back. After all, it was only this morning he was telling me how worried he is about hurting me. Just because that fear seems ridiculous to me, considering he's never been anything but gentle with me, doesn't mean he doesn't take it very, very seriously.

Sure enough, Jaxon pulls away. I try to grab on, but there's no holding him if he wants to go.

“I hurt you once, Grace,” he says after a second, eyes and voice deadly serious. “It’s not going to happen again.”

“First of all, let’s be clear. *You* didn’t hurt me. A piece of flying glass hurt me. And secondly, I know I’m safe with you. I already told you. I wouldn’t be here if I thought otherwise.”

He studies me for a second, like he’s trying to decide if I’m telling the truth. He must decide I am, because eventually he nods, reaches for me again. And this time when he pulls me against him, he lowers his head and presses his lips to mine.

It’s different than the kiss we shared earlier, softer, gentler. But it reaches inside me all the same. Lights me up. Turns me inside out with everything I feel for him and everything I hope he’ll let himself feel for me.

But tonight isn’t about wishing for what might be. It’s for celebrating what is, so I lock that thought down deep inside me and hold on to Jaxon with everything I have. And everything I am.

The kiss lasts forever, the soft whisper of his mouth against mine, and still he pulls away too soon. Still I’m clutching at him, fingers tangled in his shirt, my body straining against his as I try desperately to hold him to me for just a little longer.

But when I finally let him go, when I finally open my eyes, the Jaxon staring down at me isn’t the one I’m used to seeing. There’s no regret in his dark eyes, no scowl on his face. Instead, he looks lighter, happier than I’ve ever seen him.

It’s a good look on him, one that has me breathless for a whole host of different reasons. I wonder if he feels the same way about me, because for several long seconds, we don’t move at all. We just stare at each other, eyes locked, breaths held, fingers entwined.

There’s a bubble of emotion inside me, and it grows with every second I get to look at him. Every second I get to touch him.

It's been so long since I've felt it that it takes me a few minutes to recognize it as happiness.

Eventually, he turns away, and the loss I feel is a physical ache inside me. "What are you doing?" I ask, watching as he rummages in his closet.

"Much as I love that dress, you need a hoodie," he answers, pulling out a heavy fur-lined one from The North Face…in black, of course.

He slides my arms into the sleeves, zips it up. Pulls the hood over my head. Then he grabs the red blanket off the end of his bed and says, "Come on."

He reaches a hand out to me, and I take it—how could I not? Right now, there isn't anywhere I wouldn't follow this boy.

And that's before he pulls back the curtains that cover his window, and I get my first look at what's waiting for us.

54

What Could Possibly Be More Interesting than Kissing Me?

"Oh my God!" I gasp, all but running to the window. "Omigod! How did you know?"

"You've only mentioned them like, three different times," he answers, sliding the window open and climbing onto the parapets before holding his hand out to me.

I follow him outside, my eyes glued to the sky spread in front of us. It's lit up like one giant rainbow, the background an incredible, intense purple while swirls of periwinkle and green and red dance across it.

"The northern lights," I breathe, so caught up in the incomparable beauty of them that I barely feel the cold…or Jaxon draping his super-warm blanket around me.

"So do they live up to your expectations?" he asks, wrapping his arms around me from behind so that I'm snuggled up in the blanket *and* his arms.

"They're even better," I tell him, a little astonished at how intense the colors are and how fast the lights are moving. "I've only seen pictures before this. I didn't know they'd actually move like this."

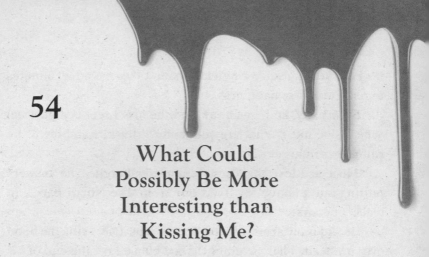

"This is nothing," he answers, pulling me closer. "It's early yet. Wait until they really get going."

"You mean there's more?"

He laughs. "So much more. The higher the velocity of the solar winds hitting the atmosphere, the faster they dance."

"And the colors are all about the elements, right? The green and red are oxygen and the blue and purple are nitrogen."

He looks impressed. "You know a lot about the lights."

"I've loved them since I was a kid. My dad painted a mural on my bedroom wall when I was seven. Told me he'd bring me here to see them one day." I can't help thinking about how he didn't get to keep that promise. And about all the other promises that were lost when he was.

Jaxon nods and hugs me tighter. Then he turns me around so that I'm facing him. "Do you trust me?"

"Of course I do." The answer is instinctive and comes from the deepest, most primitive part of me.

He knows it, too. I can see it in the way his eyes widen, feel it in the way his heart is suddenly thudding heavily against my own. "You didn't even have to think about it," he whispers, fingers stroking reverently down my face.

"What's there to think about?" I wrap my arms around his neck and pull him down for a kiss. "I know you'll take care of me."

He closes his eyes then, rests his forehead against mine for a few moments before taking my mouth with his.

He kisses me like he's starving for me. Like his world depends on it. Like I'm the only thing that matters to him.

I kiss him right back the same way, until I can barely breathe and the colors behind my eyes are brighter than the aurora borealis. Until it feels like I'm flying.

"Maybe I should have asked if you're afraid of heights," Jaxon murmurs after a few minutes, his lips still pressed against mine.

"Heights? Not really," I answer, sliding my hands through

his hair and trying to get him to kiss me again.

"Good." He moves my right hand until it's at my throat, so that I'm able to keep the blanket around me by clutching both corners in one fist. "Hold on to that blanket."

And then he grabs my left hand and spins me out fast and sharp, like they used to do in those old-time swing dances.

I gasp at the fast, jerky movement—and the fact that through it all, I can't feel the ground beneath my feet. Then scream a few seconds later as I get my first good look at the sky since Jaxon started to kiss me.

We're no longer on the parapet looking up at the northern lights. Instead, we're floating at least a hundred feet above the top of the castle, and somehow it feels like we're right in the middle of the aurora borealis.

"What are you doing?" I demand when I can finally get the words out past the terrified lump in my throat. "How are we flying?"

"I think *floating* is a better description of what we're doing," Jaxon tells me with a grin.

"Flying, floating. Does it matter?" I clutch his hand with all my might. "Don't drop me."

He laughs. "I'm telekinetic, remember? You're not going anywhere."

"Oh, right." The truth of that gets through to me, has me relaxing, just a tiny bit, the death grip I've got on him. And for the first time since we started floating, I really look at the sky around us.

"Oh my God," I whisper. "This is the most incredible thing I've ever seen."

Jaxon just laughs and pulls me back in, this time with my back against his chest so I can see everything and feel him wrapped around me at the same time.

And then he spins us around and around and around through the lights.

It's the ride of a lifetime, better than anything Disneyland or Six Flags could ever dream up. I laugh all the way through it, loving every second of it.

Loving the thrill of whirling across the sky with the lights.

Loving the feeling of dancing through the stars.

Loving even more that I get to do it all wrapped in Jaxon's arms.

We stay up for hours, dancing and floating and spinning our way through the most spectacular light show on earth. On one level, I know I'm cold—even wrapped up in the jacket, with Jaxon curled around me and the aurora borealis spread out across the sky in front and behind me—but on all the important levels, I barely feel it. How can I when the joy of being here, in this moment, with Jaxon makes it impossible to focus on anything else?

Eventually, though, he brings us back down to the parapet. I want to argue, want to beg him to keep us up just a little bit longer. But I don't know how his telekinesis works, don't know how much energy and power it took for him to keep us up there as long as he did.

"And you thought vampires were only good for biting things," he murmurs into my ear when we're once again standing on solid ground.

"I never said that." I turn in to him and press my mouth against his neck, loving the way his breath catches in his throat the moment I put my lips on him. "In fact, I think you're good for a lot of things."

"Do you now?" He pulls me closer, drops kisses on my eyes, my cheeks, my lips.

"I do." I slide my hands into the back pockets of his jeans and revel in the way he shudders at my touch. "Though, not going to lie, the biting is pretty impressive too."

I lift my mouth for another kiss, but he steps away before I can press my lips against his. I start to follow him, but he just smiles and rubs his thumb across my bottom lip. "If I start to kiss you now, I'm not going to want to stop."

"I'm okay with that," I answer as I try to plaster our bodies together.

"I know you are." He grins. "But I have something I want to do first."

"What could possibly be more interesting than kissing me?" I joke.

"Absolutely nothing." He drops a quick kiss on my lips and then takes a big step back. "But I'm hoping this comes in a close second. Shut your eyes."

"Why?"

He gives a heavy mock sigh. "Because I asked you to. Obviously."

"Fine. But you better still be here when I open them up."

"You're in my room. Where else would I be?"

"I don't know, but I'm not taking any chances." I narrow my eyes at him. "You have a bad habit of disappearing whenever things get…interesting."

He grins. "That's because I'm usually afraid if I stay any longer, I'll bite you. Now that I know you don't mind, I won't have to run quite so fast."

"Or you could just not run at all." I tilt my head to the side in an obvious invitation.

His eyes go from their normal darkness to the pure black of blown-out pupils, and I shiver in anticipation. At least until he says, "You're not going to sidetrack me, Grace. So just do us both a favor and close your eyes."

"Fine." I pout a little, but I do as he says. After all, the sooner we get past this, the sooner I'll be able to kiss him again. "Do your worst."

His laugh is a warm breath of air against my ear. "Don't you mean my best?"

"With you, I never know." I wait impatiently for him to do whatever it is he's going to do—at least until I feel his chest pressed around my back and his arms on either side of me. "What—?"

"You can open your eyes now," he says.

I do and then nearly fall over in shock. "What...?"

"Do you like it?" he asks, his voice soft and uncertain in a way I've never heard from him before.

"It's the most beautiful thing I've ever seen." I lift a trembling hand to the necklace he's holding just a few inches in front of me, brush my finger across the *huge* rainbow-colored gemstone hanging in the center of the gold chain. "What is it?"

"It's a mystic topaz. Some jewelers call it the aurora borealis stone because of the way the colors flow together."

"I can see why." The cut of the stone is incredible, each facet carved to highlight the blues and greens and purples within it so that they bleed into one another even as they stand out. "It's gorgeous."

"I'm glad you like it." He lowers the necklace until the stone rests a little below my collarbone and fastens it around my neck. Then he steps back to check it out. "It looks good on you."

"I can't take this, Jaxon." I force the words out even though everything inside me is screaming for me to hold tight to the necklace and never let it go. "It's..." Huge. And I can only imagine how much it cost. More than everything I own put together, I'm pretty sure.

"Perfect for you," he says, nuzzling the pendant aside and

pressing a kiss to my skin underneath it.

"To be fair, I'm pretty sure it's perfect for any woman." Of its own volition, my hand creeps up to hold on to the stone. I don't want to give it back. "It's so beautiful."

"Well then, you're well-matched."

"Oh my God." I groan. "That was ridiculously sappy."

"Yeah," he agrees with a little you've-got-me shrug. "And you're ridiculously beautiful."

I laugh, but before I can say anything else, he's kissing me, really kissing me, and anything I was going to say flies right out of my head.

I open to him, loving the way his lips move over mine. Loving even more the way his tongue brushes against the corners of my mouth before he gently scrapes a fang across my lower lip.

I shiver as he moves lower, brushing his lips across my jaw and down my neck. I've never felt anything like this before, never imagined that I *could* ever feel something like this. It's so much, physically and emotionally, that it's almost overwhelming—but in the best way possible.

"You're cold," he says, misinterpreting the shiver. "Let's go inside."

I don't want to go inside, don't want this magical, mystical night to end just yet. But as Jaxon pulls away, the cold catches up with me, and I shiver again. That's all it takes to have him lifting me up and all but shoving me through the window.

He follows me in, then slams the window shut behind us. I reach for him, feeling a little bereft now that we're back down here in the real world instead of dancing across the sky. But I'm finding that Jaxon on a mission is not to be deterred, especially when that mission involves something he considers important to my safety or comfort. So I wrap my fingers around the pendant I never want to take off and wait for him to do his thing.

Within minutes, he's got a new blanket around me and a cup of tea in each of our hands. I take a sip to placate him, then take another one because the tea is really, really good.

"What is this?" I ask, bringing the cup to my nose so I can sniff it a little. There's orange in it, along with cinnamon and sage and a couple other scents I can't quite identify.

"It's my favorite blend of Lia's. She brought it to me this afternoon, kind of a peace offering, if you will."

"Lia?" I can't keep the surprise out of my voice, considering the conversation she and I had this morning. I take another sip. It tastes different than the tea she made me last week, spicier, but very good.

"Yeah, believe me, I know. When I opened the door, she was the last person I ever thought I'd find on the other side of it." He shrugs. "But she said you talked to her this morning and she hadn't been able to stop thinking about me since. She didn't stay long, just brought the tea and told me she was willing to try to get back to how things were if I was."

"And are you?" I ask, joy a wild thing within me at the idea of Jaxon finding a little piece of what he lost.

"I want to try," he tells me. "I don't know what that looks like or what it means, but I'm going to give it a shot. Thanks to you."

"I didn't do anything," I tell him. "It's all you two."

"I don't think so."

"I do. In fact—" I break off as he drains his tea and then sets the cup aside. His eyes are glowing in that way they do when he wants something, and my stomach does a slow roll at the realization that *I'm* what he wants.

I set my half-drunk tea aside and reach for Jaxon, everything in me straining to be close to everything in him.

He pulls me against him with a growl, burying his face in the curve between my neck and my shoulder and pressing long, slow, lingering kisses on the sensitive skin there. I shudder a little, press closer, loving the way his mouth skims over my shoulder and down my arm to the bend of my elbow. Loving just as much the way his hand slides up and down my back over the thin fabric of my dress.

Usually, when I'm with him, I'm covered in layers of clothing—sweaters, hoodies, thick fleece pants. But right now I can feel the warmth of his palm through the thin fabric of this dress. Can feel the softness of his skin as his fingertips skim over my shoulder blades.

He feels really, really good. So good, in fact, that I just lean into him and let him touch me wherever, and however, he wants.

I don't know how long we stand like that, him touching and kissing and caressing me.

Long enough for my insides to turn to melted candle wax.

Long enough for every cell in my body to catch fire.

More than long enough for me to fall even harder for Jaxon Vega.

He smells so good, tastes so good, *feels* so good that all I can think about is him. All I can want is him.

And when he scrapes his fangs across the delicate skin of my throat, everything inside me stills in anticipation.

"Can I?" he murmurs, his breath warm against my skin.

"Please," I answer, arching my neck to give him better access.

He draws a lazy circle right above my heart with his fangs. "You sure?" he asks again, and his reticence—his care—only makes me want him more.

Only makes me want *this* more.

"Yes," I manage to gasp out, my hands sliding around his waist to hold him close. "Yes, yes, yes."

It must be the reassurance he needs, because seconds later, he strikes, his fangs sinking deep inside me.

The same pleasure as earlier sweeps through me. Warm, slow, sweet. I give myself up to it, up to him, because I know that I can. Because I know that Jaxon will never take too much blood from me.

He'll never do anything that might hurt me.

I slide my hands up his back to tangle in the cool silk of his hair even as I tilt my head all the way back to give him better access. He snarls a little at the invitation, but then I feel his fangs sinking deeper, feel the pressure of his sucking getting stronger, harder.

The longer he sucks, the deeper I fall into the pleasure, and the more I want to give him.

But slowly, the warmth I feel in his arms is replaced by a chill that comes from my bones and seems to swallow me whole. A creeping lethargy comes with it, making it hard for me to think and even harder for me to move, to breathe.

For a moment, just a moment, some modicum of self-preservation rears its head. Has me calling Jaxon's name. Has me arching back and struggling weakly against his hold.

That's when he snarls, his grip on me getting harder, tighter, as he pulls me more firmly against him. His fangs sink deeper and the moment of clarity fades as he begins to suck in earnest.

I lose all sense of time, all sense of self as I shudder and wrap myself around him. As I give myself up to Jaxon and whatever he wants from me.

55

No Use Crying Over Spilled Tea

Everything kind of fades after that, so that I have no idea how much time passes before Jaxon shoves me away from him. I hit the bed and tumble onto it, where I lay, dazed, for several seconds.

Until Jaxon snarls, "Get up, Grace. Get out now!"

There's a wildness to his voice that cuts through the lethargy, at least a little. An urgency that has me opening my eyes and trying desperately to focus on him.

He's towering above me now, fangs dripping blood and face contorted with rage. His hands are curled into fists and a deep, dark growl is coming from low in his throat.

This isn't my Jaxon, the voice inside me all but screams. This caricature from every B vampire movie in existence isn't the boy I love. He's a monster, one teetering on the brink of losing all control.

"Get out," he snarls at me again, his dark eyes finally finding mine. But they aren't his eyes, not really, and I shrink back at the soulless, bottomless depths staring out at me even as the voice deep inside me echoes his words. *Get out, get out, get out!*

Something's wrong with him—really wrong—and while

there's a part of me that's terrified *for* him, right now there's a much bigger part that's terrified *of* him. And that part is definitely in control as I scramble off the bed, careful not to make any movements he can interpret as the least bit aggressive.

Jaxon tracks me with his eyes, and the snarling gets worse as I start inching toward the door. But he doesn't move, doesn't make any attempt to stop me—just watches me with narrowed eyes and gleaming fangs.

Run, run, run! The voice inside me is full-on screaming now, and I'm more than ready to listen to it.

Especially when Jaxon bites out, "Get. Out."

The fear and urgency in his voice cuts right through me and has me running for the door, to hell with worrying if that will trigger the killer in him or not. He's already triggered and if I don't heed his warning, I'll have no one to blame but myself. Especially when it's obvious he's doing everything in his power to give me the chance to escape.

With that in mind, I stumble to the door as fast as my shaky legs can carry me. It's heavy, so I grab on with both hands and pull as hard as I can. But I'm weak from blood loss and it barely budges the first time. I can feel Jaxon getting closer, can feel him looming over me as I try desperately to find the strength to make the door move.

"Please," I beg. "Please, please, please." At this point I don't know if I'm talking to Jaxon or the door.

He must not know, either, because suddenly his hand is there on the door handle, pulling it wide open. "Go," he hisses out of the corner of his mouth.

I don't have to be told twice. I scramble over the threshold and through the reading alcove, desperate to make it to the stairs...and as far from this evil incarnation of Jaxon as I can possibly get.

It's a small alcove, only a matter of feet between me and freedom. But I'm so light-headed right now that I can barely stand upright and I sway with every step I take.

Still, I'm determined to get to the stairs. Determined to save Jaxon the pain of having killed another person that he cares about. Whatever is happening right now isn't his fault—even as messed up as I am at the moment, I can see that something is very, very wrong.

But there will be no convincing him of that if anything happens to me, no way of getting him to believe that this—whatever this is—isn't completely his fault. And so I dig deep, push myself harder than I ever have before in an effort to save myself...and in turn, save Jaxon.

I use every ounce of energy I have to make it to the top of the stairs, but I do make it. *Crawl down them if you have to*, the voice inside me yells. *Do whatever you need to do.*

I grab on to the wall, push myself around the edge of the stairs, and prepare to take my first shaky step down. Except I slam right into Lia before I can ever take that step.

"Not feeling so good, Grace?" she asks, and there's an edge to her voice that I've never heard before. "What's the matter?"

"Lia, oh thank God! Help him, please. Something's wrong with Jaxon. I don't know what it is, but he's losing control. He's—"

She slaps me across the face so hard it knocks me into the nearest wall. "You have no idea how long I've wanted to do that," she tells me. "Now sit down and shut up, or I'll let Jaxon have you."

I stare at her in shock, my sluggish brain having trouble assimilating this new turn of events. Only when Jaxon races, snarling, out of his room, does any sense of clarity kick in, brought on by the terror sweeping through me.

I'm pretty sure Lia's no match for Jaxon on a normal day—no

one is—but now that something's wrong with him, I'm not so sure.

"Jaxon, stop!" I yell, but he's too busy putting himself between me and Lia to listen.

"Get away from her!" he orders, as things start flying off the shelves all around us.

Lia just sighs. "I knew I should have made the tea stronger. But I was afraid it would kill your little pet, and I couldn't let that happen. At least not yet."

She shrugs, then says in a kind of singsong voice, "No worries," right before she pulls a gun out of her pocket and shoots Jaxon straight in the heart.

56

Vampire Girl Gone Wild

I scream, try to get to him, but all I manage to do is fall to my knees. I'm weak and dizzy and nauseous...so nauseous. The room is spinning and waves of cold are sweeping through my body, tightening my muscles and making it impossibly hard to breathe, to move.

And still I try to reach Jaxon. I'm sobbing and screaming as I crawl across the floor, terrified that she's killed him. I know it's not easy to kill a vampire, but I'm pretty sure that if anyone would know how to do it, it would be another vampire.

"God, would you shut up already!" Lia kicks me so hard in the stomach that she knocks the breath out of me. "I didn't kill him. I just tranq'd him. He'll be fine in a few hours. You, on the other hand, won't be so lucky if you don't stop that incessant whimpering."

Maybe she expects me to get hysterical all over again at that threat, but it isn't exactly a shock. As drugged and unable to think as I am right now, my mind is still working well enough to figure out that I won't be getting out of this alive. Which is saying something considering I can barely remember my own name at the moment.

"You should have drunk more tea," she tells me, disgust evident in her voice. "Everything would be easier if you just did what you were supposed to do, Grace."

She's looking at me like she expects me to say I'm sorry, which definitely isn't happening. Besides, what would that even look like? *Oops*? *So sorry I'm making it harder for you to kill me*?

Give me a break.

Lia keeps talking, but it's getting harder and harder for me to follow what she's saying. Not when the room is spinning and my head is muddled and all I can think about is Jaxon.

Jaxon, twirling me through the aurora borealis.

Jaxon, staring at me with hellish eyes.

Jaxon, telling me to run, trying to protect me even when he's drugged out of his mind.

It's enough to have me rolling over, enough to have me trying to crawl to him even though I don't have the strength anymore to push up to my knees.

"Jaxon," I call, but his name comes out so slurred I can barely understand it. Still, I try again. And again. Because the voice inside me is screaming that if Jaxon knows I'm in trouble, he'll move heaven and earth to get to me. Even if it involves waking up from a stealth-tranquilizer-gun attack.

Lia must know it, too, because she hisses, "Stop it," as she towers over me.

Which only makes me try harder. "Jaxon," I call again. This time, it's little more than a whisper, my voice failing as everything else does, too.

"I didn't want to do this the hard way," Lia says, raising the tranquilizer gun and aiming it straight at me. "When you wake up feeling like a herd of elephants is running through your head, remember you're the one who chose this."

And then she pulls the trigger.

57

Double, Double, Toil and a Whole Lot of Trouble

I wake up shivering. I'm cold...so cold that my teeth are chattering and everything—I mean *everything*—hurts. My head worst of all, but the rest of me is almost as bad. Every muscle in my body feels like it's being stretched on a rack, and my bones ache deep inside. Worse, I can barely breathe.

I'm awake enough to know something is wrong—like really wrong—but not quite awake enough to remember what it is. I want to move, want to at least pull the blanket from my bed up and over me, but the voice deep inside me is back. And it's ordering me to lie still. Ordering me not to move, not to open my eyes, not to even breathe too deeply.

Which won't be a problem considering I feel like a fifty-pound weight is crushing my chest—kind of like how I felt when I was fourteen and got pneumonia, only a million times worse.

I want to disregard the voice, want to roll over and find a way to get warm again. But flashes of memory are starting to come back, and they scare me into lying very, very still.

Jaxon, with hellfire burning in his eyes, shouting for me to run.

Lia brandishing a gun.

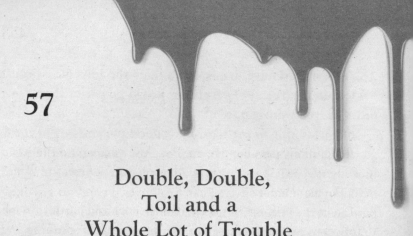

Jaxon falling over, passing out.

Lia screaming at me that everything is all my fault right before she—

Oh my God! She shot Jaxon! OmigodOmigodOmigod.

Panic slams through me, and my eyes fly open before I can think better of it. I try to sit up, determined to get to him, but I can't move. I can't sit up. I can't roll over. I can't do anything but wiggle my fingers and toes and move my head a little, though I'm still not coherent enough to figure out why.

At least not until I turn my head and see my right arm stretched out to the side and tied into an iron ring. A quick glance to the other side shows my left arm in the same predicament.

It doesn't take a genius to figure out that my legs are tied down, too, and as more of the fogginess fades, I realize that I'm spread-eagled on top of some kind of cold stone slab. And I'm wearing nothing but a thin cotton sheath, which, honestly, is just adding insult to already egregious injury.

I mean, she drugged me, shot me, and tied me up. She has to freeze me as well?

As my memories come flooding back, adrenaline surges through my system. I try to tamp it down, try to think around the sick panic winding its way through me. But with the cold and the drugs and the adrenaline, clear thinking isn't exactly easy right now.

Still, I have to figure out what happened to Jaxon. I have to know if he's alive or if she killed him. She said she wasn't going to, but it's kind of hard to trust anything she says considering her original invite for tonight was for mani-pedis and look where I am now.

Just the thought of something happening to Jaxon has emptiness yawning inside of me. Has my panic turning to terror. I have to get to him. I have to figure out what happened. I have to *do* something.

For the first time since coming to Katmere Academy, I wish I had some supernatural powers of my own. Namely the power to break through rope. Or teleport. Hell, I'd even take a shadow of Jaxon's telekinesis at this point—something, anything that might possibly get me untied and off this horrible rock.

I shake my head a little, struggle to clear the light-headed, packed-with-cotton feeling that's going on in there. And try to figure out how the hell I'm supposed to get these ropes off me before Lia comes back from whatever level of hell she's currently visiting.

Wherever I am, it's dark. Not pitch black, obviously, because I can see my hands and feet and a little beyond where I'm lying. But that's it. Only about four feet past my hands and feet in every direction, but after that it's really dark. Like really, really dark.

Which isn't terrifying at all considering I'm in the middle of a school filled with things that go bump in the night. Lucky, lucky me.

I think about screaming, but the chill in the air tells me I'm not actually inside the main school anymore. Which means there probably isn't anyone around to hear me—except Lia, and I definitely don't want to attract her attention one second sooner than she wants to give it to me.

So, I do the only thing possible in this situation. Strain against the ropes as hard as I can. I mean, I know I'm not going to be able to break free from them, but rope stretches if you pull on it long and hard enough. If I can just get some wiggle room around one of my wrists, I can slip my hand through, and I'll at least have a fighting chance.

Okay, maybe not a fighting chance. More like a teeny tiny chance. But at this point, I'm not exactly complaining. Any chance, no matter how small, is better than just lying here, waiting to die.

Or worse.

I don't know how long I tug and strain against the ropes, but it feels like a lifetime. It's probably more like eight to ten minutes, but terrified and alone in the dark, it feels like so many more.

I try to concentrate on what I'm doing, try to put all my focus into escaping and nothing else. But it's hard when I don't know where Jaxon is, when I don't know what's happened to him or if he's even alive. Then again, if I don't get out of here, I'll never know.

It's that thought that has me pulling harder, twisting back and forth with more determination than ever. My wrists hurt now—big surprise—the rubbing back and forth against the ropes chafing them raw. Since I can't do anything about the pain, I ignore it and twist faster even as I strain to hear any sound that might indicate Lia is coming back.

For now I don't hear anything but the rasp of my wrists against the ropes, but who knows how long that will last.

Please, I whisper to the universe. *Please, just work with me a little here. Please, just let me get one arm free. Please, please, please.*

The pleading doesn't work. Then again, I didn't actually expect it to. It didn't work after my parents died, either.

The chafing on my wrists has given way to intense pain—and a slippery wetness that I'm very much afraid is blood. Then again, the fluid is making it easier to turn my wrist now, so maybe bleeding isn't the worst thing that could happen in this situation. At least if it helps get me out of here before a vampire or seven show up to finish me off.

For the first time, I understand—really understand—why an animal caught in a trap is willing to chew its own foot off to escape. If I thought it would give me a fighting chance, and if I could reach my wrist, I might be tempted to do the same thing. Especially since this yanking and pulling doesn't seem to be—

My left hand slips, nearly comes out of the rope. I'm so surprised that I almost cry out in relief and maybe blow everything. Paranoid about letting a sound escape—although I don't actually think it's paranoia considering the situation I currently find myself in—I lock my jaw in place to keep the sounds of excitement and pain from spilling out into this pitch-dark room.

Ignoring the pain, ignoring the panic, ignoring everything but the fact that I am so close to getting one hand free, I twist and strain with every ounce of strength in my body, so hard and so long that it's almost a shock when my hand finally slips free from the rope.

The pain is excruciating, and I can feel blood running down my hand, slipping between my fingers and along my palm. I don't even care, though, not now when I'm so close to finding a way out of this. I twist my body and reach for my other wrist—not the easiest thing to do when I'm spread-eagled. With my legs tied as tightly as they are, I can only twist a little bit, but it's enough to reach my right hand.

Enough to maybe have a fighting chance at breaking completely free.

Slipping my fingers in between the ropes and my right wrist, I start pulling as hard as I can. The bizarre twisting adds another layer of pain to the mix, but once again I ignore it. I'm pretty sure any pain I feel now is nothing compared to what I'll feel once Lia decides to…do whatever it is she's planning on doing.

Finally, the rope on this wrist slips, too, and I manage to slide my right hand free as well. Somehow the hope that comes with that little bit of freedom makes me panic more, and it takes every ounce of concentration I have not to cry as I sit up and start fumbling with the ropes around my ankles.

Every second feels like an eternity as I strain my ears in a desperate attempt to listen for Lia. I don't know why it matters so much; it's not like I'll be able to lie back down and fake it if she shows up. All this blood pretty much negates any chance of that ever happening.

Just the thought has me doubling my already frantic efforts, yanking on the ropes and pulling against them until my fingers and ankles are as raw and bloody as my wrists.

The rope around my right ankle finally gives a little bit. Not enough to get my foot through, but more than enough to have me concentrating solely on that side.

Another minute and a half, I'm guessing, and I've got my right foot free, which leaves me to concentrate on the left foot with everything I've got. At least until a high pitched scream slices through the cold air and has pretty much every hair on my body standing straight up—especially when the scream echoes around and around me.

It's Lia, I know it. My blood runs cold, and for a second I can't move, can't think through the terror. But then the voice is back, cutting through the fear and ordering me to *Hurry, hurry, hurry.*

I start tearing at the rope, no longer caring if I dig deep furrows into my skin as I try desperately to untie it. Try desperately to escape.

"Please, please, please," I mutter to the universe again. "Please."

I have no idea where I am, no idea if I actually manage to get loose if I can even get out of this place without freezing to death when I step outside. Just the idea of being trapped here has the panic simmering right below the surface rearing its ugly head again.

One problem at a time, I remind myself. Get free from the restraints and then worry about what comes next. Everything else, no matter how terrible, is still a step up from being tied to a stone table like some kind of human sacrifice.

My breath catches in my throat at the thought, a sob welling up within me. But I push the tears back down where they belong. Later, I can cry.

Later, I can do a lot of things.

For now, I need to get off this altar or whatever the hell it is. I need to escape and I need to figure out what's happening to Jaxon. Everything else can wait.

The rope gives—thankyouthankyouthankyou—and I manage to wiggle my foot out without sacrificing too many layers of skin.

The moment I'm free, I jump off the table...and nearly fall flat on the ground. Now that I'm standing, I realize just how woozy I still am. I thought the adrenaline would burn through the drugs lingering in my system, but they must be really strong drugs. Or I must not have been lying on that table as long as I thought I was...

Still, I take a deep breath and focus. Try to see through the dizziness to figure out where I am...and how to get the hell out of here before crazy, crazy Lia finds her way back.

Another scream rends the air, and I freeze—then run. I don't even know where I'm running to, but I figure if I make my way along the walls, I'll find a door eventually. And if I'm lucky, it'll be on the early side of eventually.

But I've barely taken a step before a roar follows the scream, this one deep and powerful and completely animalistic. For a second, just a second, I think it might be Jaxon, and a new rush of terror slams through me.

Then logic reasserts itself—I've heard Jaxon sound a lot of different ways, but never like that. Never like an animal with no human qualities at all.

There's another roar, followed by the sound of something slamming into the wall. Another scream, some growls, something breaking, something hitting the wall again.

Lia's obviously in a fight, and I should take the opportunity to find a way out and run like hell. Except what if I'm wrong? What if the person making those growls and roars *is* Jaxon. What if he's as dizzy as I am and can't fight her off? What if—

I take off running toward the wall that I can hear things clattering against. It's a dumb move—the dumbest—but I have to know if it's Jaxon. I have to know if he's okay or if she's doing to him whatever she'd planned to do to me.

I knock my knees against something as I try to make it to the other side of what I'm beginning to realize is a huge room. Whatever I bumped tips over, and liquid splashes onto my feet and the long cotton shift Lia has me dressed in for some reason.

The water feels gross, squishing inside my toes and soaking through my dress, but I ignore it as I take off running again as fast as I can. To be honest, that's not saying all that much considering the drugs and my raw, wet feet, but I do my best. At least until what feels like a thousand candles burst to life all around me and all at the same time.

As their flames illuminate the room, I stop dead in my tracks. And wish with everything I have that I was back in the dark.

58

Never Do a Trust Fall with Someone Who Can Fly

At least I know exactly where I am. The tunnels. Not the part of the tunnels I've already been in, but one of the side rooms they lead to that I haven't seen before. Still, I'm sure that's where Lia has brought me. The architecture—not to mention the bone chandeliers and candelabras—is a hard decorating choice to forget.

Too bad the obviously human-bone candle holders are the least terrifying thing in the place. The same can't be said for the—at least—two dozen three-foot glass vases filled with blood that line what can only be described as an altar in the center of the room. At the center of which is a stone slab with bloodied ropes.

So, not actually that far off when I snarked about being a human sacrifice. Fantastic.

A quick glance down at my legs shows just why that "water" squishing between my toes felt so gross earlier. Because it's not water. It's blood.

I'm covered in someone else's blood.

Funny how that sets me off worse than anything else in this nightmarish hellscape. But it totally does. I manage to swallow down the scream clawing at the inside of my throat, but it's a close thing. So close that I can't stop a little whimper from doing the same.

And that's before I turn around and see a giant green dragon flying straight toward me, wings beating fast and talons extended.

Not going to lie—I freak out. Like totally, absolutely freak the fuck out—screams absolutely included. I duck down, try to make myself as small as possible as I run for the door, but I know it's too late even before a volley of flames streams right by me, slamming into the stone wall to my right.

I jump back, try to turn around, but that little delay is all the dragon needs to get to me. Talons wrap around my upper arms, pricking my biceps, as he lifts me straight off my feet and starts flying back across the room.

I struggle against his hold, trying to get him to drop me before he gets too high. But his talons go from pricking my skin to piercing it. I gasp as new pain slams through me, but the dragon gets his wish—I stop struggling, too afraid that he'll tear me to pieces to risk it.

At the same time, I'm too terrified that he'll kill me to just do nothing, so I grab on to his feet and try to pry his talons out of and off of me. I know I'll fall, but at this point it's the best plan I can come up with. Especially considering the voice inside me that's been telling me what to do for days now is suddenly, inconveniently absent.

Unfortunately, my prying fingers only make the dragon dig in deeper, and for a second, everything goes black. I take a few deep breaths, concentrate on beating back the pain. And wonder how the hell I got myself kidnapped by both a vampire *and* a dragon in *one night*.

San Diego has never seemed so far away.

All of a sudden, the dragon sweeps down, so low that my feet can practically touch the ground. We're headed straight for the huge double doors on the other side of the room—looks like I was running in the wrong direction earlier—and that might not be a problem except for the fact that they are closed and the dragon's...hands? paws? claws?...are currently filled with me.

I shrink down, brace for impact and what I'm pretty sure is my imminent death. But about a second before we fly into them, the doors burst open and we soar right through...and over a screaming, infuriated Lia.

The dragon doesn't pause, just stretches out its wings and starts flying even faster, straight down the long hallway that I'm guessing leads toward the center portico with the huge bone chandelier.

Lia's running along below us, and she's fast enough to more than keep up. And at this point, I'm really close to losing it. Because trapped between a dragon and a vampire gives a whole new meaning to the old "rock and hard place" cliché, and that never works out well for the person in the middle.

Plus, I'm getting really sick of being dragged around by supernatural creatures. I mean, sure, I want to believe this dragon—whether it's Flint or some other kid I go to school with—is trying to rescue me, but the talons currently ripping through my arm muscles tell a different story.

At this point, I'm pretty sure the best-case scenario involves me choosing between death by dragon or death by vampire. Too bad I have no idea which one would be least painful. And does it really matter considering I'll be dead at the end, anyway?

We're moving crazy fast, so we reach the center hub of the tunnels in seconds. The only problem? We're flying straight toward the giant bone chandelier, with its hundreds of lit candles, and the dragon shows no sign of slowing down. Which, fine. He's a dragon and, I assume, fireproof. Too bad that same adjective can't be used to describe me or the cotton shift I'm wearing.

Suddenly, death by vampire bite doesn't sound so bad. Not when the alternative is burning alive in midair.

But at the last second, the dragon pulls his arms up tight to his body, with me still clutched in his talons, and dives right under the chandelier. His goal is obviously to get past it while staying as high and fast as possible. But that drop in altitude is what Lia's been waiting for, because now she's leaping off the ground and grabbing hold of the dragon's tail.

The dragon roars, tries to flick her off him, but she holds on. Seconds later, she's got her arms wrapped completely around his tail and is slamming us toward the ground as hard as she can.

Which—for the record—is really freaking hard. Especially considering the dragon doesn't let go of me while we fall.

We hit the ground with a crash. On the plus side, the dragon lets go of me on impact, and for the first time in several minutes, there are no talons digging into my arms. On the negative side, I hit the ground shoulder-first and am now seeing stars of the very not-good variety.

Plus, I can barely move my left arm. A problem that's compounded by the fact that I am also still bleeding from my wrists, my ankles, my fingers, and now my arms where the dragon was holding me. And, oh yeah, I'm being stalked by a crazy-ass vampire with ritualistic murder in her eyes.

And here I thought Alaska would be boring.

Snarls and screams sound behind me, and I scramble to my knees, trying to ignore the pain in my sprained? broken? dislocated? shoulder as I spin around in time to see Lia and the dragon going at it full force.

The dragon lashes out with a claw and slices Lia's cheek open before she jumps out of range. Seconds later, she responds by leaping onto his back and yanking his wing back so hard that he screams in agony even as he twists around and shoots fire straight at her.

She dodges but gets a little singed around the edges—which only seems to piss her off more. She plasters herself low across his back and punches a hole straight through his other wing.

The dragon screams again, then blurs into a rainbow array of colors for several seconds. When the blur of color passes, he's a boy again—and not just any boy. Flint. And he's bleeding. Not as much as I am, but the wing punch obviously hurt him if the way he hunches over as he scrambles awkwardly to his feet is any indication.

He's dressed in the ripped-up version of the clothes he was wearing and has a lot more cuts and bruises on him now. Lia seems a little worse for wear from the fall, too, but she rushes him with a primal scream that has shivers running along every nerve ending that I've got. Flint meets her halfway, arm muscles bulging as he attempts to keep her flashing fangs out of his skin. Once he's got a good grip on her, it's his turn to send her flying to the ground. Then he grabs her head and starts pounding it over and over again into the stone floor.

She's fighting him, bucking and snarling and doing everything in her power to get away from him. But he holds tight as he growls something indecipherable at her. I take their preoccupation with each other as my cue to get as far from them as I possibly can, as fast as I possibly can.

I stumble to my feet, ignoring the pain and the fact that my messed up shoulder makes it impossible for me to do anything but list to my left side. But forward movement is forward movement even in this world, and I can't stay here watching Flint and Lia try to kill each other for one second longer.

Keeping one ear on the fight behind me, I start running/hobbling through the portico, looking for the tunnel that will take me back into the school's main building. The tunnel that will bring me back to Katmere.

I make it across the center of the room to the tunnel that's one to the side of being directly across from where Lia and Flint are fighting. But when I start to run down it, I'm torn between screaming for help and trying to go unnoticed a little while longer. And by a little while I mean long enough for me to stagger through the tunnel and into the school, where surely my Uncle Finn will put a stop to this madness.

Before the entire world explodes.

But I barely make it to the entrance to the tunnel that I think will lead me to the castle before Flint is on me. He grabs me by the hair and slams me face-first into the nearest wall.

"Flint, stop. Please," I manage to gasp out through the pain tearing through me courtesy of my injured shoulder.

"I wish I could, Grace." He sounds grim, defeated. "I thought I could get you out of here. But Lia's not going to let me. And I can't let the ticks get away with using you for what they want to do."

"Using me for what? I don't know what you're talking about."

"Lia's had a plan all along. It's why she brought you here."

"She didn't bring me here, Flint. My parents died—"

"Don't you get it? She killed your parents to get you here. We knew it for sure as soon as you arrived and the wolves got close enough to smell you.

"We were sure we'd be able to finish this long before we got here, but taking you and Lia out is one thing. Taking Jaxon out when we realized he was involved in the plan was another thing entirely."

I'm reeling, his words hitting me with the full force of a wrecking ball as I scramble to make sense of them. "What are you—my parents—Jaxon—how could…" I pause, take a breath. Try to breathe through the pain and confusion and horror his words stir up inside me.

"Look, I don't have time to fill you in on everything. And it wouldn't change anything if I could. I want to save you, Grace. I do. But we can't let Lia do this. It'll mean the end of the world. So you've got to die. It's the only way we can stop this thing from happening." He reaches forward, wraps his hand around my neck.

And then he starts to squeeze.

59

Carpe Kill-Em

"Stop!" I gasp out, clawing frantically at his hand with my bloody fingertips. "Flint, please. You can't do this."

But Flint isn't listening. He just stares at me with broken, tear-filled eyes as he squeezes tighter and tighter.

I'm panic-stricken by this point, terrified that he's really going to do it. That he's really going to kill me...and worse, he's going do it before I know the truth behind what happened to my parents.

"Flint, stop!" I try to get more out, try to beg him to tell me what he's talking about, but the pressure on my throat is too much. I can't speak anymore, can't breathe, can hardly think as the world starts going dark around me.

"I'm sorry, Grace." He sounds tortured, devastated, but the squeeze of his fingers around my throat never falters. "I wish it didn't have to be like this. I never wanted to hurt you. I never wanted—"

He breaks off on a scream and suddenly the pressure around my neck is gone, his fingers bending back from my skin at an unnatural angle.

I gasp, try to suck air into my starving lungs via my abused throat. It hurts, a lot, but the pain doesn't matter right now. Nothing does except being able to breathe again.

When I finally have enough oxygen inside of me to think semi-clearly again, I look around for Lia. Find her crumpled on the floor in the same spot where Flint had been beating her head against the floor with all the strength of the dragon inside him.

Convinced she isn't a threat—at least for now—I focus back on Flint who has sunk to his knees at this point. He's clutching his hands, his face a mask of agony, and for a second—just a second—I feel sorry for him. Which is bizarre considering a few moments ago he was using those very fingers to strangle me.

I beat back the sympathy and take a step away, sliding along the wall in the most unobtrusive manner I can muster. I don't know what's happening here, don't know which of the many, many supernatural forces surrounding us is responsible for Flint's suffering, but I have a pretty good idea. And if I'm right, things are about to get a million times more dicey. If I'm right, Flint is about to have a very bad—

Jaxon bursts into the room like a dragon-seeking missile, his focus completely and totally on Flint as he races across the room at an unimaginable speed. His eyes, glowing and livid and filled with violence, meet mine for a second before sliding over every inch of me as if cataloging my injuries. Moments later, he's on Flint, grabbing him by the hair and heaving him across the room into the opposite wall.

Flint hits back-first, hard enough to make the wall shake. Then Jaxon's on him, his snarls of rage filling the room and echoing off the ceiling. There's a part of me that wants to run to him, that wants to beg him to hold me and take care of me after he deals with Flint. But there's another part that can't get over Flint's words. That can't get over the casual way he said Jaxon was part of Lia's crazy plan.

It doesn't make any sense. If Jaxon was a part of her plan all along, why did she give him tea to drug him? And why did she shoot him full of tranquilizers?

No, Flint has to be wrong, I tell myself as sobs I refuse to let escape threaten to tear my chest apart. Jaxon wouldn't deliberately hurt me, and he definitely wouldn't have had anything to do with killing my parents. He wouldn't do that. He *couldn't* do that, not after everything that happened with Hudson.

Out of nowhere, Flint roars an answer to one of Jaxon's snarls, and then he starts fighting back. Jaxon's response is to send him flying once more, this time headfirst into another wall.

Anyone else would be dead after the impact Flint makes, but dragons are obviously built very different from humans—even when in their human form. Because Flint shakes off the blow then whirls around to face Jaxon once again.

But when he brings his arms up to fight, his hands are no longer human. Instead they're talons, and he punches straight out with them, aiming for Jaxon's heart.

A strangled scream escapes me, and I slap my bloodied right hand over my mouth, desperate to avoid attention even as Jaxon deflects the blow. Then he reaches out, aiming to wrap his fingers around Flint's throat the way Flint just did to me, but before Jaxon can get a good grip, Flint starts to shift.

It takes a few seconds, and Jaxon tries to stop him—or at least, that's what I think he's doing when he thrusts a hand into the magical rainbow glow that comes whenever Flint changes form. But his hand goes right through it and he doesn't grab onto anything while we both wait to see what monstrous version of Flint this new edition can add to the story.

We get our answer when he comes back into focus in his full dragon form. Tall and majestic and a sparkling emerald green, all of his power, all of his strength and determination and *fire* are focused on Jaxon.

Who doesn't even flinch. He just plants his feet and stares down a freaking dragon like it's a gecko, waiting for an attack or an opening or who even knows what.

Except Flint is apparently as patient as Jaxon, even in dragon form, and the two circle each other for several seconds.

Jaxon seems to have calmed down. His eyes are almost back to normal and his face is totally blank, totally unreadable. Which is a good thing, because—

Suddenly, the whole tunnel shakes like it's being hit by an eight-point earthquake. Okay, not so calm, I think as my already shaky knees give way and I hit the ground, hard. I expect the shaking to stop, expect Jaxon to get control of himself, but that doesn't seem to be on his agenda as the walls start crumbling and bones start falling from the giant chandelier in the center of the room.

Flint shoots a stream of fire straight at Jaxon, who throws a hand up and deflects the fire into the nearest wall. The move seems to infuriate Flint, who lets loose with another blast of fire, this one so hot I can feel it from halfway across the room. And he doesn't let up. He keeps the fire stream going even as Jaxon continues to block it.

On the plus side, the ground stops shaking as Jaxon focuses every ounce of his power on not getting incinerated while Flint focuses every ounce of his power on doing the incinerating. At first, it looks like we've finally reached an impasse, Flint shooting fire and Jaxon holding that fire at bay. But as the seconds tick by, I realize Jaxon is doing more than just deflecting the fire. He's bending it back toward Flint and using his telekinesis to slowly—so, so slowly—push a stream of it back toward the dragon.

Part of me wants to stay and see what happens, to make sure Jaxon is okay at the end of this. But the voice inside me is finally back and it's urging me to run, to get away, to leave Flint and Jaxon to their fates and save myself.

Any other time, I'd ignore the voice and stay, just in case I could find a way to help Jaxon. But Flint's words keep running through my head—about how Jaxon is a part of Lia's plan, about how Lia is responsible for my parents' deaths, about how whatever they have planned can't be allowed to happen.

I still don't know if what he's saying is true or not, but if it is…if it is, I can't count on Jaxon, or anyone else, to help me. I have to escape. And I have to do it by myself.

With that thought at the front of my mind, I start moving toward the exit tunnel. I tell myself to stand up, to make a run for it, but I'm too sick and dizzy to do anything but crawl. So that's what I do. I crawl toward the tunnel, each movement an agony for my screaming shoulder and raw, aching hands.

Thankfully, Jaxon and Flint are too caught up in their battle to notice me and my slow-but-stealthy progress. I'm hoping to keep it that way as I finally reach the mouth of the tunnel.

Just a little farther, I tell myself as I make it around the corner.

Just a little farther, I repeat like a mantra as I take a second to lean back against the wall and let the pain dissipate.

Just a little farther, I say one more time as I push myself up and off the floor.

I give myself one more second to take stock—stomach rolling, knees shaking, body hurting—and then say screw it and start staggering up the tunnel as fast as my abused ankles can carry me.

I've only gone about twenty feet when something hits me from behind, sends me pitching forward, and I hit the ground all over again. Agony slices through me as my shoulder bangs against the ground, and for a second, I'm sure I'm going to pass out.

But seconds later, the pain dissipates, and as I try to wiggle away I realize my shoulder no longer hurts. Or at least, it's no longer screaming at me like it was a couple minutes ago. I must have knocked it back into position when I fell on it. Or, more specifically, when I was pushed down onto it.

Adrenaline surges through me at the thought, and I wonder if it's Jaxon who has found me. Or if it's Flint. I want it to be Jaxon—even with everything Flint said about him working with Lia—but the roughness of the shove says otherwise, as does the follow-up kick delivered to my side.

I'm panicking now, terrified that Jaxon is hurt...or worse. What if Flint was lying? What if Jaxon isn't a part of Lia's crazy plan and I just left him alone out there?

I spin around, hands raised in a pathetic defense against what I'm sure is a fire-breathing dragon. And find myself staring into Lia's wild and unhinged eyes instead. Eyes that only get more demented when she demands, "You don't actually think you're walking out of here, do you?"

60

Some Call it Paranoia, But I Call it an Evil Bitch Trying to Use You as a Human Sacrifice

"Don't say a fucking word," Lia continues as she grabs me by the hair and starts dragging me up the tunnel. Pain—excruciating, overwhelming, *maddening*—explodes inside of me, and I clutch at my head, trying desperately to get some relief from the searing, tearing agony of being yanked around by my hair.

It doesn't work, and for a second the pain is so sharp that I can't even think. But it doesn't take a genius to figure out that Lia's dragging me to my death. If I let her get me back into that room with the blood and the altar, I'm going to die—in what I'm pretty sure is the most awful, most gruesome manner possible.

So, to hell with her warning and to hell with staying silent. Sucking in a huge gulp of air, I let loose with the loudest, most hysterical-sounding scream I can manage while at the same time digging my nails into her hands hard enough to draw blood.

Lia curses and slams my head into the wall she's been dragging me alongside. Which dazes my already not-functioning-so-great brain but doesn't get me to shut up. Nothing is going to do that, I promise myself as I scream and scream and scream, even as I struggle to free my hair from her viselike grip.

Lia's not having it, though, because this time she turns around and kicks me in the face. Not hard enough to fracture my jaw, but more than hard enough to have me reeling backward—which has the added benefit of shutting me up despite myself as everything around me starts to go black.

"Oh, no you don't, you bitch," Lia hisses at me. And this time when she hits me, it's a sharp slap on my cheek. "You are *not* going back to sleep. The whole reason we're in this mess right now is because I need you awake for this."

That's the best incentive I can think of to make myself pass out again. But unfortunately, that doesn't seem to be in the cards, since the pain of being dragged along by my hair is definitely keeping me awake. I just hope if I survive this—or even if I don't—that I'm not completely bald by the end.

We're about halfway up the tunnel now, and Lia pauses. At first I think it's to take a break—in the grand scheme of her vampire strength, I'm pretty sure I'm not making her strain much. But with her normally impeccable clothes ripped and her bloody hair matted to her face, she's not looking so good right now. Which means, maybe she's more hurt or worn out than I think.

The idea gives me hope, and I start to struggle again, but she's got something else planned, because she's definitely not resting. Instead, she tightens the hand in my hair until I stop moving, then she puts the other hand against one of the stones about halfway up the wall and pushes as hard as she can.

The wall shifts and groans, but eventually a whole section of it opens up, revealing a *super* secret passageway in this maze full of secret passageways.

It's narrow and dark and there is nothing in the world I want less right now than to be in this stuffy, airless corridor with Lia. But as she drags me to my feet, her hand still fisted deep in my hair, it's not like I have much of a choice. Especially when she shoves me inside first and then frog-marches me down this new alleyway.

We're only a few steps in when the secret door closes behind us. As it slams shut, I have a moment of overwhelming anguish when I realize this is it. I've exhausted all of my options, and now I'm going to die here in this crazy labyrinth of tunnels, the victim of a vampire who has gone totally and completely around the bend.

And there's not a damn thing I can do about it.

The realization hits me hard, and for a moment it takes me to a place beyond despair and beyond hope. Because unless something changes fast, all I can do is pray that whatever's coming is over quickly. Well, that and to make sure that I don't give Lia the satisfaction of seeing me break down, no matter what she does to me.

I have a sick feeling that's going to be next to impossible, but I'm still going to try. Because if I came all the way to Alaska to die, I want to do it on my terms, not hers.

And so, even as exhaustion sets in, I continue to put one foot in front of the other. Continue to walk closer and closer to the site of my own demise. And with each step, the hopelessness deep inside me turns to anger and the anger turns to rage. It fills up the emptiness, fills up the aching, until all that is left is a fire in the pit of my stomach. A white-hot flame that wants nothing more than it wants justice.

For myself and, more importantly, for my parents.

I'm here in Alaska because Lia wanted me here.

My parents are dead because Lia decided they needed to die.

She's played god with too many people's lives to just get away with it. I'm weak and exhausted and broken and human, but even I know that much. Just as I know she can't be allowed to continue with whatever insanity she has planned. All of which means I'm going to have to do whatever I can to take her with me when I die.

I just wish I had a clue how I'm supposed to do that.

My brain makes and discards half a dozen feverish plans as we walk for what seems like forever. Eventually, though, we must get to where we are going, because Lia jerks me to a stop. She presses her hand against the wall, and seconds later, it opens just like the wall at the beginning of this passage.

All but cackling with delight, she shoves me through the open doorway and into the room where I was tied up what seems like forever ago. It seems strange to think that it's probably only been an hour or so since I woke up spread-eagled on that cold slab of rock.

Then again, it seems even stranger to think that after all the pain and frustration I've been through in the last hour, I'm about to be tied up there again.

FML. And Lia's, too.

"Move it!" she snarls, pushing me through the hundreds of lit candles to the raised altar in the center of the room. "It's almost time."

"Almost time?" I ask, figuring that getting her talking might buy me some time to think of something. Or buy me enough time for Jaxon and Flint to find me…though I'm not sure how much help either of them will be in this situation.

Flint's answer to Lia's insanity is to kill me before Lia has a chance to do whatever crazy thing she has planned, whereas Jaxon might actually be a part of her crazy plan. Not exactly a typical selection of heroes, but my mom used to say that beggars can't be choosers, and right now I'm definitely willing to beg if it means I don't become Katmere Academy's first human sacrifice.

"The stars align at twelve seventeen."

I have no idea what that means, but as Lia and I get closer and closer to the altar, I know that I've got very little time to do whatever I'm going to do to stop this madness. Because once she gets me tied down this time, it's game over for sure.

With no other ideas and no other options, I make my legs go weak.

"Walk!" she screeches, but I ignore her as I let my head loll back and my entire body sag. Then, using every ounce of willpower I have left, I close my eyes and make the gamble that she won't kill me right here, right now. And then I drop to the ground, ignoring the searing pain in my scalp as I rip out what I'm sure is a whole handful of hair in the process.

Lia howls in outrage as she loses her grip on me.

The sound bounces off the ceiling and echoes around the room in a macabre warning that has everything inside me urging me to run, to crawl, to put as much distance between her and me as I can possibly manage. Even the voice inside me is screaming to get up, to get moving.

But even on my best day, Lia's ten times faster than I am and twenty times stronger. Outrunning her isn't an option even if I could move faster than the sad, pathetic crawl I'm currently limited to.

So instead of running, I play possum. Not running, not moving, not even breathing as she screams at me to get up. When screaming doesn't work, she tries slapping my face a few times. And when that doesn't work, she hauls me up herself, throws me over her shoulder and starts stumbling toward the altar with my head hanging halfway down her back.

That alone tells me she's in a lot worse shape than she let on. Flint obviously did more damage than I gave him credit for. Good for him.

My injured shoulder is screaming at me in this position, but

I ignore it even as I give myself permission to open my eyes for a second.

Everything looks exactly as it did when I ran from this place, including the jar of blood that's still knocked over on its side. Lia steps around the glass containers and carries me past a stone lectern that has a book spread wide open on it. I have just enough time to wonder if it's the same book she was reading from in the library all those days ago, when I have to close my eyes again and play dead—or at least unconscious—as she dumps me on the altar.

This is the best—the only—chance I'm going to have to get myself free, so I wait until she turns her back on me and starts trying to untie the knot on one of the hand restraints. Then I grab her hair and throw every ounce of my weight behind it as I push her forward and slam her head against the edge of the altar as hard as I can.

Lia howls like a banshee.

And since she doesn't immediately strike out in revenge, I pull her head back and do it again, even harder this time. Then I scramble backward as fast as my bruised and battered body can carry me.

I don't get far before she whirls on me with a growl worthy of a big cat episode on Animal Planet. It doesn't stop me, though. Just makes me push harder through the pain. This time I'm not running for the door, though. Instead, I head straight toward the lectern—and the book Lia has resting on top of it.

It takes her a second to realize what I'm going for, but when she does, she lets loose a scream like nothing I've ever heard before. And then she leaps after me, clearing the altar with a single bound and landing right next to the lectern. But she's too late.

I'm already there.

I grab the book, rip out the pages she's got it open to—plus a couple on either side just to be safe. Then nearly cry in relief when Lia completely loses her shit.

She screams and lunges for me, but I use the last drop of strength in my body to jump backward even as I tear the pieces in half.

She's on me in seconds, her claws and teeth tearing at me in a desperate effort to get her hands on what I'm pretty sure is some ancient spell. "Give it to me!" she screams as she rakes her fingers down my biceps. "Give it to me now!"

I hold on as tightly as I can, even as new blood flows down my arms. Then I do the only thing I can do to keep the paper out of her reach. I roll the both of us straight off the altar to the hard stone ground several feet below.

We land with a *thud*. Lia barely seems to notice the drop, but I'm half convinced the landing dislocated my shoulder all over again...and maybe even broke my back. Still, I've got one shot at foiling her plan—whatever the fuck it is beyond killing me as painfully as possible, so I ignore the pain as best I can and reach my hand out to one of the hundreds of candles burning around us.

And plunge the spell straight into the fire.

61

Sticks and Stones May Break Your Bones, but Vampires Will Kill You

The dry, ancient paper instantly goes up in flames, and the sound Lia makes as we watch is like nothing I've ever heard before. Crazed, desperate, inhuman, it chills me to the bone.

It also brings to light what I've known all along—that what little time I had left is now used up. And there's nothing more I can do about it.

Lia dives for the paper, grabs the remnants of it despite the flames currently devouring it. Her skin sizzles at the contact, but it's too late. Anything useful is already gone.

She whirls on me with a snarl. "I'm going to enjoy ripping the flesh from your bones."

"I have no doubt."

The voice inside me wants me to get up, to run, but I've got nothing left. I'm battered, broken, and without my parents—without Jaxon—to run to, I can't figure out why I'm fighting so hard anyway. I've foiled her plan, kept her from doing whatever it is she murdered my parents to do.

It will have to be enough.

She's on me in seconds, and I wait for the kill shot, for new waves of agony to roll over me. But instead of ripping me to pieces as I expect, she lifts me into her arms. Throws me back onto the altar.

"Do you think I need that book?" she demands, dragging me to the center of the stone slab. "I've spent months preparing for this. Months!" she screeches as she reaches down and tears a long strip of cotton from the shift I'm wearing. "I know every word, every syllable of what's on that page."

She throws herself down on top of me and grabs my left arm. It's my turn to scream as she wrenches it above my head.

She just laughs as she ties me to the metal ring I was tied to before and sneers. "Payback's a bitch."

She rips another strip from my gown, and though I kick at her, we both know it's not going to do any good. She doesn't even bother to slap me back. Just shifts her weight so she can tie my right arm up as well.

"I spent months searching for you," she tells me as she climbs to her feet. "And then after I found you, I spent weeks planning your parents' accident and planting the seeds with Finn that would get you here. Then more weeks making sure Jaxon was ready for you. And now you think you can ruin everything by burning a little spell? You have no idea."

She staggers back toward the lectern, grabs the book from where it fell onto the floor. "You have *no* idea!" she screams again, brandishing the book like a weapon. "This is my one chance, *my one chance*, to bring him back, and you think I'm going to let you *ruin* it? You? You pathetic, miserable excuse for a..."

"Human?" I interject, even as my mind runs wild at what she's suggesting. Bring *him* back? Who? *Hudson?*

"Is that what you think you are? Human?" She laughs. "God, you're even more pathetic than I thought. You think I would do all this to get my hands on a *human*? One trip to town and I could have a hundred of them without even trying."

I have no idea what she means, or even if she's telling me the truth. And still her words go through me like lightning. Still they wake up something inside me that I don't recognize but somehow feels the slightest bit familiar. Am I a witch after all, despite what Uncle Finn said? Is that what this voice I keep hearing inside me means?

And if I am, so what? There are more than a hundred witches at this school alone. What makes me so special? The fact that she thinks I'm Jaxon's mate? Or something else? Something more?

There's no time to dwell on the whole mess right now, not if she's being honest about knowing the spell. And not while the clock is ticking inexorably toward twelve seventeen. "Are you seriously trying to bring Hudson back?" I ask, and though I know Lia's crazy and that she plans to kill me, there's still a tiny piece of me that might actually feel sorry for her…or it would, if she hadn't also been responsible for the murder of my parents.

The fact that it's Hudson's death that did this to her, that made her so lost and broken that she came up with this ridiculous, convoluted scheme to bring him back…it's pathetic and heart-wrenching all at the same time.

But still, there's no way Lia can be allowed to bring Hudson back. Not if one-tenth of what Jaxon told me about him was true—and I know that it was. No wonder Flint and the other shifters were so adamant about doing whatever they had to to stop Lia, even if it meant killing me. But they were insane to think Jaxon would ever play a part in this. There's no way he would ever try to bring his brother back. No freaking way.

Knowing this makes me feel horrible for doubting him.

"You can't do this, Lia."

"I'm going to do it. I'm *going* to bring Hudson back," she answers. "And *you're* going to help me."

"It's impossible, Lia. You can kill as many people as you want, find as many spells as you think necessary. But you can't bring the boy you love back from the dead. It doesn't work that way."

"Don't talk to me about what I can or can't do," she snarls, even as she pulls out her phone and holds it out to me so I can see the time. "In five minutes, you'll know the truth. Everyone will."

I really hope that isn't true. I read *Frankenstein* last year—I can only imagine what abomination she'll bring back from the dead if her little plan actually works.

Before I can say anything, though, the main doors to the room rattle on their hinges. Seconds later, the whole wall shakes, but the stones stay in place. As do the doors.

"He's getting close," Lia says, crawling to the edge of the altar and pushing to her feet.

"Who? Hudson?" I ask, shivers of horror sliding down my spine at the thought of a resurrected vampire breaking through those doors—and then doing God only knows what? Feeding from me because of whatever Lia thinks I am?

"Jaxon," she answers me. "He's been out there for a while, trying to find a way to get to you."

Jaxon. Jaxon is out there. For the first time since I woke up strapped to this damn altar, I feel like there might be a chance to stop Lia. And to save my life. "How do you know?" The question escapes before I even know I'm going to ask it.

"Because I can feel him. He's desperate to get to you. But no vampire can enter a room he isn't invited into—even the most powerful vampire in existence. If he wants in here, he'll have to use more power than he even knows he has." She laughs, and this time there's no hiding the crazy in it.

"I hope he's suffering. I hope he knows what's happening to you in here and that it's killing him that he can't get to you. I can't wait for you to serve your purpose so you can die and finally, he'll know just how excruciating it feels to lose a mate."

It turns out that even in the middle of all this, I can still be shocked. "You're wrong, Lia. I'm not—I'm not Jaxon's mate. I don't even know what that means, but I'm sure if it were a thing Jaxon or Macy would have told me."

"It's cute that you believe that. But it doesn't matter what you think. What matters right now is that it's true. And that *he* believes it." She shrugs. "Then again, he also believes he can get around thousands of years of safeguards and break down these doors to get to you. So he could very well be delusional. Who knows?" She shrugs. "And who cares? As long as he suffers when you die, I don't care what he believes."

As if on cue, the door rattles, its hinges screaming at the pressure brought to bear on them by Jaxon's powers. "Jaxon!" I scream his name, desperate for him to hear me.

The rattling of the doors stops for just a second. "Grace! Hold on! I'm almost in!" The door shakes so much that the rocks around it start to crumble.

"Come in! You're invited in! Please! Come in, come in, come in!" I shout the words loud enough for him to hear them.

Lia just laughs. "Not your room, Grace. Not your invitation to issue. Sorry to burst your bubble."

The alarm on her phone goes off before I can respond, and suddenly she's all business. "It's time." Raising her arms above her head, she begins to chant, her voice low and rhythmic and strong, so strong.

She doesn't falter at all, doesn't stumble over words even though the written spell is long gone. Looks like she wasn't lying when she said she'd been practicing for months. Which means I really did throw myself off this altar for nothing.

My shoulder is *not* impressed.

I mean, logically, I know this isn't going to work. There's

no way she's going to be able to bring Hudson back from the dead—life just doesn't work like that. Believe me, I know.

But I'm not going to lie, when a breeze sweeps over me out of nowhere, ruffling my hair and brushing against my skin, it chills me to the bone. As does the sudden electricity in the air that follows it.

Every hair on my body stands straight up in response. Combined with Lia's odd chanting that's only getting odder, it's more than enough to have me screaming for Jaxon like the hounds of hell are after us.

He bellows in response, a primal sound from deep inside him that has me yanking on the ties around my wrists as hard as I can. It hurts—*ohmygod* does it hurt—but the pain doesn't matter. Nothing matters right now but stopping Lia and getting to Jaxon.

This time the whole wall shudders under the force of Jaxon's power. I'm facing away from the door, but I can hear the grinding of stones being pulled loose and the crash of them as they hit the floor. He's close now, so close, and everything inside me strains toward him and away from Lia's madness.

I can't believe I let Flint get inside my head, can't believe I thought even for a second that Lia and Jaxon were working together. And I definitely can't believe I ran from the only boy I've ever loved. Jaxon would never be involved in something like this. Especially if that something aimed to hurt me. I know that now.

Plus, how could I forget just how much Lia hates Jaxon? No way would she bring him in to her own personal Project Lazarus.

I really am a fool. And it's going to be the death of me.

Lia's chant grows louder, echoing throughout the cavernous room as she grabs a long, ceremonial knife from inside the lectern. I watch in horror as she slices open her wrist and lets her blood drip onto the altar.

It sizzles as it hits the stone, where it turns into a noxious black smoke. The wind picks up, starts churning the smoke into a kind of mini-tornado that has me pulling against my bindings as hard as I can even as I scream for Jaxon.

I'm beginning to think there just might be something to this raising Hudson from the dead thing. And if there is, I want absolutely no freaking part of it. I sure as hell don't want to be the catalyst that brings everything together.

Lia obviously has other plans, though, because she walks toward me with the knife. Her blood is still gleaming on the blade and I have an *oh God, please let her clean it off before she touches me with it* moment. Which seems absurd considering: One, shouldn't I be praying that she doesn't come near me with it at all? And two, what does it matter when I'm already covered in her blood, my blood, and some stranger's blood? What's a little more at this point?

Still I shrink back, pulling my legs up and trying to curl into a ball as best I can. It's not much protection—or really any protection—but it's all I've got until Jaxon manages to break through the ancient safeguards.

I expect Lia to start hacking at me with the knife as soon as she gets to me, but instead, she stands above me—arms spread wide and knife pointed directly at my midsection.

Not cut, then. Stabbed. Awesome.

I brace myself for more pain, but the knife never descends. Instead, the black smoke surrounds us, winding itself tighter and tighter as the breeze picks up and Lia finally stops chanting.

"Open your mouth!" she screams at me as the smoke centers itself directly above me.

No freaking way. She can kill me if she wants to—in fact, at this point she can feel free to do just that—because there is no way I'm opening up and sucking some noxious and terrifying smoke into me that may or may not be Jaxon's dead brother. Not going to happen.

"Grace!" Jaxon yells from the other side of the door. "Grace, are you okay? Hold on! Hold on for me just a little longer."

I don't answer him—doing so would require opening my mouth, and right now I've got my face pressed into my arm and my jaw clenched as tightly as I possibly can. No way is this going down the way Lia seems to think it will.

"Do it, or I'll kill you!" Lia screeches. "Right here, right now."

Like that's going to scare me? I resigned myself to death a while ago, so the threat of dying doesn't hold much weight at the moment—especially since I know she'll kill me once she gets what she wants anyway. So why on earth should I give it to her? Especially when it involves me turning into some kind of bizarre host for an ancient vampiric ritual?

Lia abandons the threats and throws herself on top of me as she tries to pry my mouth open with her fingers.

Don't let her do it, the voice inside me warns. *Hold the course.*

I kind of want to answer it with a resounding *no shit, Sherlock*, but I'm too busy trying to buck Lia off me.

It's not working—big surprise considering she's a pissed-off vampire with superhuman strength and I'm a human in really, really bad shape. That doesn't mean I'm giving up, though, doesn't mean—

A giant wrenching sound suddenly fills the air. Lia freezes on top of me as stones go flying in every direction. And in walks Jaxon.

"No!" Lia screams as she picks up one of the stones that landed near us and chucks it back at him as hard as she can. "You can't be here! You're not invited in!"

Jaxon deflects the rock with little more than a look. "No wall, no invitation needed." And then he's leaping across the room in a single bound. He lands next to us on the altar and rips Lia off me, sends her flying across the room.

She hits the wall with a crash but comes right back at him. Jaxon, in the meantime, whispers, "I'm sorry, Grace," as he waves a hand over me. The bindings on my wrists simply fall away. Then he's crouching down next to me, stroking a hand down my face. "I'm so sorry."

"It's not—" My voice breaks as relief sweeps through me. "It's not your fault."

His voice is bitter. "Whose fault is it, then?"

I start to answer, but—big surprise—Lia's not going down without a fight. "Look out!" I scream as she hurtles across the stage straight at Jaxon. He waits for her to get close then uses her own momentum to send her flying off the altar and across the room.

She lands with a sickening crunch of bone, but that doesn't keep her down, either. She staggers to her feet, holds her arms up, and starts that horrible chant again. The black smoke responds, circling Jaxon, circling me, cutting off our view of Lia and the rest of the room.

"What's happening?" Jaxon demands.

I don't answer him now that the smoke is right next to me again, too scared of opening my mouth to so much as make a sound.

Jaxon uses his powers to try to move the smoke away from us, but it must be the one thing in the universe not under his control. Because instead of clearing out, it winds itself more and more tightly around us, until I can barely see Jaxon, let alone the rest of the room.

Which, apparently, is Lia's plan, because as soon as Jaxon turns his back in search of an escape, Lia is on him. She leaps onto his back with a primal kind of war cry and plunges the knife straight into Jaxon's chest.

It's my turn to scream—or as close to a scream as I can get with my jaw clamped shut. I try to get to him, but Jaxon throws a hand out, uses his telekinesis to keep me where I am. Then he reaches down and yanks the knife out of his chest.

It falls to the ground with a clatter.

Blood is steadily leaking out of his wound, but Jaxon doesn't seem to even notice. He's too focused on Lia. Reaching over his shoulder, he grabs Lia by the collar and pulls her over his head and onto the ground at his feet.

I expect him to use his powers on her now, but instead he plunges his hand down, aiming straight at her chest. She rolls away at the last second, tries to kick him in the face. But he grabs onto her leg and twists it, fast and hard.

A sickening crunch fills the air, followed by Lia's howls of pain. Jaxon grabs on to her hair, prepares to break her neck and put all of us out of our misery, but before he can do it, the black smoke circles his neck and starts to choke him.

He claws at his neck, tries to get it away from his throat, but it's not letting go no matter how hard he wrestles with it.

Somehow, Lia is on her feet again. Her left leg is bent at an unnatural angle, but she's standing, arms raised as she starts that horrible chanting again. The spell only seems to make the smoke stronger as it continues to strangle Jaxon.

He's sheet white as he falls to his knees and tries to wrestle with something he can't get an actual grip on. Blood continues to seep out of his chest wound, and I know if I don't do something, Jaxon is going to die right in front of me.

I can't let that happen.

I crawl forward, hands stretched out in front of me as I search for— My fingers come across the cold steel of Lia's ceremonial knife, and I grab onto it with all of my waning strength.

It's sharp and it cuts me, but I barely feel the pain as I push myself up off the floor. And swing the knife at Lia's chest with every ounce of strength I have left in my body.

She's wide open, her arms spread out to the sides, so I connect. The knife makes a sickening squishing sound as it sinks through skin and flesh to the organs below.

She doesn't scream this time. Instead, she rears back with a strange gargle-gasp and falls straight backward onto the floor.

The horrifying rattle coming from her chest tells me I punctured a lung instead of her heart, but at this point I don't actually care. As long as she's out of commission, I'm good. Or I will be as soon as we figure out how to get the greasy black smoke off Jaxon, who honestly isn't looking much better than Lia at the moment.

If he's not strong enough to pry it off—with or without his telekinesis—I know I've got no shot. So I do the only thing I can think of, the only thing guaranteed to get the smoke to let him go.

I open my mouth and take a long, slow breath.

62

Where There's Smoke, There's a Dead Vampire

It takes a few seconds, but the smoke—or whatever that thing is—finally catches on. It relinquishes its hold on Jaxon and arrows straight for me.

Which, gotta say, is probably the most terrifyingly awful thing that's ever happened to me in my life.

But considering the alternative is standing around and watching another person I love die, there is no alternative. And so I open my arms and gather the smoke toward me. Once it's surrounding me, I take a breath, start to suck it in.

"No!" Jaxon roars.

Suddenly, I'm falling backward, *flying* backward off the altar and halfway across the room while Jaxon stumbles to his feet. He's nearly gray at this point, but he manages to stand tall as he holds his hands out in front of him. Then slowly, slowly—so slowly I think I may have a heart attack watching him—he starts to compress the air between his hands into a spherical shape.

As he does, the entire room—the entire tunnel—starts to shake. And then it starts to crumble around us.

And still, Jaxon doesn't let up. Still, he continues to compress the sphere, his hands slowly rotating in a circle as he pulls more and more energy, more and more mass into the sphere.

The smoke flattens itself out, starts streaming in the other direction, but Jaxon is having none of it. He just starts pulling harder, until stones and candles and vases filled with blood start flying across the room toward him. He takes it all, pulls it all into the sphere and then reaches for more, until even the air in the room is streaming toward him in what looks and feels an awful lot like a tornado. And with the air comes the smoke, no matter how hard it struggles against Jaxon's power.

It's getting harder to breathe as Jaxon absorbs more and more of the oxygen in the room, but I don't even care. I just drop to the floor the way they taught me in fire safety and try to breathe whatever's left down here as I watch him draw the smoke inexorably closer to him. Closer and closer and closer.

Soon even Lia and I are caught up in the energy suck, getting dragged across the floor by Jaxon's power and his indomitable will. I don't try to fight it, don't do anything that might possibly make this harder for him. Instead, I just give myself over to Jaxon and trust that somehow he will keep me safe, even from himself.

He always does.

He's got the smoke in his grasp now, floating between his hands as he struggles to condense it, to break it down into whatever he needs it to be so that the vortex or whatever he's got going on in there can absorb it.

But the smoke isn't going down without a fight. Every time it looks like Jaxon might have it contained, a small stream escapes his hold and he has to start all over again. But Jaxon has a will of iron and more power than I even imagined possible inside of him. He won't give up.

Instead, he spins the sphere between his palms faster and faster. The ceiling starts caving in, the walls fall to pieces, even the stones on the floor start to crumble. And still Jaxon doesn't relinquish his hold. Still, he continues to pull.

The oxygen in the room is getting thinner, and I'm really struggling for breath now. He must be, too, but you wouldn't know it from the way he continues to manipulate every single thing in the room.

The smoke struggles to escape one more time, but with a roar, Jaxon yanks it back inside the sphere once and for all. And then he just shuts it down, just turns off the conduit or the energy suck or whatever it is so that everything around us just settles.

The room stops shaking, the walls and ceiling and floor stop breaking apart, the remaining candles drop to the floor, and the oxygen slowly starts to stabilize. I settle back against the ground and just breathe for a few seconds, even as I watch Jaxon condense the sphere between his hands into a glowing orb only a little larger than a tennis ball.

And then he pulls his hand back and fires it straight at Lia.

It hits her in the stomach, and her whole body arches off the floor. She gives one last terrifying gasp as she absorbs the energy, the matter, the smoke. Then she looks straight at him and whispers, "Yes. Finally. Thank you."

Seconds later she explodes into a cloud of dust that slowly settles back onto the ground.

All I can think is that it's over. Oh my God, it's finally over.

"Jaxon!" I turn to him, try to crawl toward the only boy I've ever loved. But I'm weak, so weak, and the altar is too far away. Instead, I hold a hand out to him instead and call his name over and over and over again.

Jaxon staggers across the altar toward me, then half jumps, half falls off of it to the ground below, where I'm waiting for him.

He takes my hand, brings it to his lips. And whispers, "I'm so sorry," before falling into a dead faint at my feet.

"Jaxon!" Frantically, I call his name. "Jaxon, wake up! Jaxon!"

He doesn't move, and for one, terrifying second I'm not even sure he's breathing.

Somehow I find the strength to roll him over. I press a hand to his chest, feel the shallow movement of his chest up and down, and nearly sob in relief. But there's no time for that, not when he's still bleeding out from the chest wound Lia gave him. And not when he's turned a pasty, sickly white.

"I've got you," I whisper to him as I grab on to one of the ragged strips Lia actually left on my shift and rip it off. I ball it up, press it firmly to Jaxon's wound in an effort to staunch the blood. "I've got you."

Except I don't have him. Not really. Not when he could die on me at any second. He's lost so much blood—more than I have at this point—but I don't know what to do about it. If I leave him and go for help, he might very well bleed out while I'm gone. If I don't, he may bleed out anyway, since I can't seem to staunch the blood.

Desperate, I look around for any untouched jars of the blood Lia had lined up around the altar earlier today. But they're all gone now, sucked into Jaxon's vortex or spilled onto the floor around us.

"What do I do? What do I do? What do I do?" I mutter to myself as I try to get my panic-stricken and pain-addled brain to work. Jaxon's heart rate is slowing down and so is his breathing. I don't have much time to do something, anything to save him.

In the end, I do the only thing I can think of. The only thing I *can* do in this situation. I claw open one of the wounds on my wrists until it starts to bleed freely again. And then I press my wrist to his mouth and whisper, "Drink."

At first there's no response as my blood drips onto Jaxon's lips. Seconds go by, maybe a full minute, and I'm beginning to despair. If he doesn't drink, he'll die. If he doesn't drink, we'll both—

He regains consciousness with a roar. Then his hands are gripping my arm like a vise as he bites down right over my vein. And sucks and sucks and sucks.

It feels nothing—and everything—like it usually does when he drinks from me. There's pleasure, yes, but also a lot of pain as he takes in as much of my blood as he can with every swallow. Despite the pain, relief swamps me even as the room around me goes black.

There's no fighting it this time, no need to fight it this time, because I'm not alone. Jaxon's here with me, and that's all that matters. So when the next wave of blackness rises up to swamp me, I don't struggle against it.

Instead, I give myself over to it—and to Jaxon—trusting that somehow everything will be okay.

Trusting that somehow Jaxon will make sure of it.

63

A Bite to Remember

The first thing I notice upon waking up is that I'm warm. Really warm, which feels off for some reason, though I can't quite figure out why. Then again. I can't quite figure out a lot of things as I drift slowly between sleep and wakefulness.

Like what the weird beep I'm hearing is from.

Or why my right arm feels like it's being crushed.

Or why my room smells like apples and cinnamon.

Eventually, it's the second question that brings me to full consciousness, that has me opening up my eyes and shaking out my arm in an effort to get the pain to stop.

The first thing I see when I open my eyes is a woman in a black-and-purple caftan holding a clipboard and reading a little machine next to my bed. The same machine that's making the beeping noise, it turns out. And making my arm hurt, because as soon as she presses a button, the pressure goes away.

Because blood pressure is an actual thing, apparently. And so are IVs, if the needle stuck into the back of my hand and the tube it's attached to are any indication.

It all comes flooding back to me in a rush—Flint, Lia, the fight.

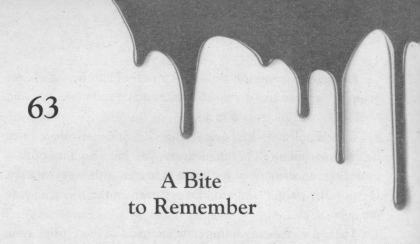

"Jaxon." I push myself up, start looking wildly around the room. "Jaxon! Is he all right? Is he—"

"He's fine, Grace," the woman tells me with a soothing pat on the shoulder. "And so are you, though it was a touch dicey for a minute—with the both of you."

Her words feel an awful lot like déjà vu—then again, a lot of this morning feels like déjà vu. After everything that just happened, it's hard to imagine that it was just a couple of days ago that I found out about vampires. And now, I've helped murder one.

And—please God—helped save one, I remind myself as I scoot down the raised hospital bed until I make it past the guardrails and can actually swing my legs over the edge. "Where is he?" I demand of the short-haired woman standing next to my bed. "I need to make sure..." I stop, because I can't even say the words out loud.

"He really is okay," the nurse assures me, her tone soothing. "In fact, he's right outside your room. I asked him to step out while I took your vitals, but other than when medical personnel request it, he hasn't left your side since he brought you in."

"Can you get him for me?" I ask after licking my dry lips. "I just need a minute with him."

I'm assuming if I'm here, then Jaxon made it out of that hellhole of a dungeon. But emotion is currently outweighing logic, and I just need to see him. Just need to hear his voice and feel his hand—his body—against mine to believe that he actually made it out.

To believe that the nightmare is finally over.

"I'll get him," she tells me. "*If* you lie back in that bed. Your pulse rate is skyrocketing, and we just got everything stabilized, for heaven's sake."

My pulse is skyrocketing because I'm panicking, I want to

screech at her. Jaxon was nearly dead the last time I saw him.

But I don't screech. Instead, I settle for whispering, "Thank you," as I lean back against the raised head of the bed. My hands are shaking, so I hide them under the covers—no need to broadcast the fact that I already feel exhausted from one little adrenaline spike.

"You're welcome," she answers. "And just so you know what's going on, you're in Katmere Academy's infirmary, where you've been for the last two days. I'm Nurse Alma, and I've been taking care of you along with Marise. Like I said earlier, you're pretty banged up and you lost a lot of blood. Plus you have a dislocated shoulder, so now that you're awake and moving around, Marise will probably be splinting it up for a while. But overall, you're in good health. Jaxon got you here before the blood loss could do any permanent damage. You're going to be fine in a few days."

I know I should care about what she's saying and I will… soon. "What about Jaxon?" I ask anxiously. "He was stabbed. He lost a lot of blood, too. Is he—"

"From what I understand, you took care of him quite well. But let me get him so you can calm down. He can tell you how he is while I call your uncle and let him know you're awake."

I watch anxiously as Alma walks through the door into the hallway. She's speaking softly, so I can't hear what she's saying, but seconds later Jaxon bounds through the door. Alive and reasonably well.

Relief sweeps through me, and I finally feel like I can take a real breath. I mean, yeah, he looks like hell—or at least, as close to hell as someone like him can look—but he's alive. And walking under his own power. That has to count for something.

As he gets closer, I realize his complexion is still a little gray, which makes his scar stand out against his cheek in stark relief. He also seems like he's lost at least five pounds in the two days

I've been asleep. Which is impossible, I know, but he looks so tired and thin and worn out—nothing like the force of nature I'm used to.

"You're awake," he says, and for a second I swear I see tears in his dark eyes. But then he blinks and there's nothing but strength there...and something else I don't even try to interpret. Not when my head is spinning and I can barely keep my eyes open.

"Come here," I tell him, holding my hands out to him. As I look down at them, I notice my wrists are wrapped in gauze and the many cuts on my hands and arms seem to be sealed with a shiny liquid bandage. I'm a mess, but at least I'm a sterilized mess.

He moves closer, but he doesn't sit on the bed. And he doesn't touch me. "I don't want to jostle your shoulder—"

"My shoulder is fine," I tell him, which isn't even a lie right now, courtesy of whatever drugs or herbs or spells Alma currently has going on with me. "So come here. Or I'm coming to you."

I kick the covers down in preparation to do just that, then wince as the motion aggravates my raw ankles—which it turns out are also wrapped. Big surprise.

To be honest, I'm beginning to feel a little like a mummy here. And an unwanted one at that, if Jaxon's reaction to me is any indication.

"Stay where you are," he barks as he takes another couple of steps toward me.

"Then get over here and tell me what's going on," I say. "Because I'm beginning to feel like I've got the plague or something."

"Yeah, that's the problem here. You've got the plague." But at least he takes my outstretched hand this time as he settles himself gingerly on the edge of the bed.

"Don't be snarky," I say as I rest my forehead on his shoulder. "I did save your life, after all. You should be nice to me."

"Yeah, and I repaid you for that kindness by nearly killing you, so you should want me as far from you as I can get."

I roll my eyes, even as exhaustion threatens to swamp me. "Are you always such a drama queen, or do you just trot it out on special occasions?"

The look of shock on his face is priceless. And so is the snitty tone in his voice when he answers, "I don't think being concerned about you makes me a *drama queen*."

"No, but taking on all the blame for what was obviously Lia's giant head trip, does." I press a couple of kisses to his neck, reveling in the way he can't stop himself from shivering at the first touch of my lips to his skin. "So chill out a little, will you? I'm tired."

His eyebrows disappear under his crazily messed up hair, and I realize it's the first time since I've met him that I've ever seen his hair anything less than perfect. "You want me to chill out?" he repeats.

"I do." I scoot over to make room for him on the bed, biting the inside of my cheek to keep from crying out as I jostle my shoulder in the process. "Now climb on." I pat the bed next to me.

Jaxon looks from my face to the bed and back again, but he doesn't move. Which makes me sigh and say, "Come on. You know you want to."

"I want a lot of things that aren't good for you."

"What a coincidence. So do I, though I'm pretty sure we'll disagree on what's good for me and what isn't."

He sighs. "Grace—"

"Don't." I cut him off. "Please, Jaxon, just don't. Not now, when I'm too tired to argue with you. Do I need to spell it out for you? I need you to hold me."

And just like that, his resistance melts. Instead of arguing, he settles back against the pillows with me and wraps me in his arms, taking care not to bother my injured shoulder.

We lie like that—in silence—for several minutes, and I don't truly relax until he rests his cheek against the top of my head and presses kisses into my hair.

"I'm glad we're okay."

"Yeah." His laugh is harsh. "Me too."

"Don't say it like that," I tell him. "We're lucky."

"You don't look so lucky right now."

"Yeah, well neither do you. But we are." I take a deep breath, let it out slowly. "We could be..." I trail off, unable to say the words.

"Dead, like Lia and Hudson?" Jaxon fills in the blanks for me.

"Yeah. And we're not, so I count that as a win."

He pauses for a minute, but then he nods. Sighs. "Yeah, me too."

"Flint?" I ask after a second.

"You don't want to talk to me about the dragon right now."

"I know," I soothe, running my right hand up and down his arm for comfort.

"He's alive, if that's what you're asking. And currently in better shape than either one of us, though he shouldn't be."

"He thought he was doing the right thing."

"Are you kidding me?" Jaxon jerks away from me, shoots me an incredulous look. "He and his friends tried to kill you on numerous occasions, then he pulled that stunt down in the tunnels that made everything worse, and you think he was just trying to do the right thing?"

"He was, bizarre as it sounds. And I mean, I'm not *happy* with him. But I'm glad he isn't dead."

"Yeah, well, that makes one of us," he mutters as he lies back down against me. "I should have killed him when I had the chance."

I hug him as tightly as my injured shoulder will let me. "I think we have enough blood on our hands right now."

"You mean I have enough blood on *my* hands, don't you?"

"That's not what I said, is it?" It's my turn to push away from him, but only because I want to be looking him in the eye when I say this. "This isn't your fault. It isn't my fault. And it isn't Flint's or the rest of the shifters' faults. It's Lia's fault. She's the one who devised this plan. And she's the one who caused everything that happened." My voice catches in my throat. "Did the shifters tell you? About my parents?"

"Flint told me. He and Cole told Foster and me everything—including why they didn't trust the witches or the vampires with what they knew."

"The vampires because they thought you might all be colluding for God only knows what reason," I guess. "But why not the witches?"

"You aren't a witch, but your family is. They didn't think Foster would be able to see past the fact that you're his niece to the danger having you here at Katmere posed to everyone."

I roll my eyes at him. "Yeah, well, I'm pretty sure the danger here at Katmere has all been *to* me and not *from* me, thank you very much."

"I should have figured it out sooner." Jaxon looks tortured.

"You planning on having that god complex of yours looked at any time soon?" I snark. "Or are we all just supposed to live with it?"

"Wow. You've been awake fifteen minutes and you've called me a drama queen and now accused me of having a god complex." He raises his brows. "You sure you aren't mad at me?"

"I'm sure," I tell him, pulling his face down to mine so I can kiss him.

But he flinches a little when my hand touches his scar, per

usual, and damn it, we've been through too much for this to keep happening. I pull away before our lips so much as brush.

"What's wrong?" He looks wary.

I sigh as I stroke my fingers along his jaw. "I know I have no right to tell you how to feel, but I wish you could see yourself as I do. I wish you could see how gorgeous you are to me. How strong and powerful and awe-inspiring you are."

"Grace." He turns his head, presses a kiss into my palm. "You don't need to say that. I know what I look like."

"But that's just it. You don't!" I reach for him and hold on tight, ignoring the pain that shoots up my arm at the movement. "I know you hate your scar because Hudson gave it to you during the most horrible moments of your life—"

"You're wrong," he interrupts.

I stare at him. "About what?"

"About everything. I don't hate my scar, I'm humiliated by the fact that I let it happen. Hudson didn't give me the scar, the vampire queen did. And the worst moments of my life weren't when I killed Hudson. They were when I finally regained consciousness on that altar and realized I'd taken too much of your blood. That moment—and all the moments it took for me to get you here? Those will *always* be the worst seconds, the *worst* minutes, of my life."

There are so many important things in what he just said that I don't know where to start. Except… "Your mother? Your mother did this to you?" I whisper as horror slithers through me.

He shrugs. "When I killed Hudson, I interfered with her plans. I needed to be punished."

"By tearing up your face?"

"It's hard to scar a vampire—we heal too quickly. By doing this, and ensuring I didn't heal, she left a mark of weakness on me for the whole world to see."

"But you could have stopped her anytime. Why didn't you?"

"I wasn't going to fight my mother, and I certainly wasn't going to hurt her any more than I already had." He shrugs again. "Besides, she needed someone to punish for what happened, someone to hurt so that she could feel better. Better me than someone who bore no responsibility for what happened."

I can't keep the horror from my face, but Jaxon just laughs a little. "Don't worry about it, Grace. It's all good."

"It's not all good." I do my best to swallow the rage that's swelling inside me. "That woman is a monster. She's evil. She's ..."

"The vampire queen." He fills in the blank for me. "And there's nothing any of us can do about it. But thank you." It's his turn to whisper as his lips brush over my hair.

"For what?" I nearly choke on the words.

"For caring." He lowers his head for a kiss.

But our lips barely have a chance to brush before there's a knock on the open door. "Sorry to interrupt," Marise says as she sticks her head in the doorway. "But now that you're awake, I want to check out my favorite patient."

I glance around the empty bay. "Your only patient, don't you mean?"

"Yeah, well, you give me a lot of business. Plus, I had Jaxon and Flint in here for at least a day. You just require a little extra attention, that's all." She grins at me.

"Yeah, well, the whole being human thing really bites around here." Deep inside me, the voice wakes up. Whispers that I shouldn't be so fast to call myself human. Which is laughable, except...except Lia's words haunt me, about how much trouble she had to go through to find me and get me here.

Which leaves me with the question of why am I so special? Even if I am a witch—and I'm not sure I am—there are a lot of witches in this school to choose from. Is it because I really am Jaxon's mate? And if I am, what does that even mean in his world? But how would she know that? And why would that matter anyway? What does who Jaxon loves have to do with raising Hudson from the dead?

Now that Lia is gone and her plan foiled, I have even more questions than I did before she died. I want to ask Jaxon if he has any of the answers, but now isn't the time to think about it, not with Marise flashing her fangs as she quips, "That's not the only thing that bites around here."

"So I've learned," I answer with a smirk.

It only takes a few minutes for her to look me over, and her prognosis is pretty much what Alma already told me. A lot of cuts and bruises that it turns out Alma—who is a healing witch—has already put a lot of effort into minimizing. And a half-healed dislocated shoulder that will need to be splinted for a couple of weeks to finish what Alma already started.

There's also the little matter of the blood transfusion, a little more than two liters, which I really wish she hadn't mentioned in front of Jaxon. But all in all, I'm in good health and will probably get to go back to my dorm room in a couple of days, if my vitals stay steady.

Or so Marise says as she exits with a little wave.

"It's not your fault!" I tell Jaxon the second she's out the door.

"It's entirely my fault," he answers. "I nearly drained you."

"Two liters is nowhere close to draining me."

"It's close to emptying you out enough that you die. Which counts as draining to me." He shakes his head. "I'm so sorry, Grace. About hurting you. About your parents. About everything."

"You didn't hurt me. You saved me. Alma said you got me here before any permanent damage could be done."

He doesn't answer, just kind of shakes his head as his jaw works furiously.

"I *gave* you my blood, because you were going to die without it." I take his face in my hands and look him straight in the eye so he can see that I mean what I'm saying. "And the truth is, it wasn't a sacrifice. It was as selfish as I could get, because now that I've found you, I'm not okay with being in a world where you don't exist."

For long seconds, he still doesn't say anything. Then he shakes his head, swears. "What am I supposed to say to that, Grace?"

"Say you believe me. Say you know it's not your fault. Say—"

"I love you."

I gasp, then let out a slow, shuddering breath as tears I don't even try to hide bloom in my eyes. "Or you could say that. You could very definitely say that."

"It's true," he whispers. "I'm so in love with you."

"Good, because I'm in love with you, too. And now that Lia's evil plan is forever over, we can try being in love when someone isn't trying to kill us."

He stiffens, looks away, and the cold I thought I'd finally managed to escape skitters down my spine once more.

"What's going on, Jaxon?"

"I don't—" He breaks off, shakes his head. "I don't think we can do this, Grace."

At his words, the cold congeals, turns my body to ice. "What do you mean?" I whisper. "You just said you love me."

"I do love you," he answers forcefully. "But sometimes love isn't enough."

"I don't even know what that means." It's my turn to glance away, my turn to look anywhere but at him.

"Yeah, you do."

I wait for Jaxon to say more, but he doesn't. He just sits on the bed next to me, arm wrapped around my shoulder, body snuggled up against mine even as he rips my heart out of my freaking chest.

"It won't always be like this," I finally whisper to him.

"That's where you're wrong. It's *always* going to be like this. The fact that I love you means you're always going to be a target. You're always going to be in danger."

"That's not what this was about." I turn to him, tangling desperate fingers in his sweater as I tell him, "You know that. You were just a complication—Lia said she wanted me. She said it was about me. Even the shifters were after me because they knew she wanted to use me to..." I trail off, more than happy not to mention Hudson's name to Jaxon ever again.

"You don't really think the shifters are going to let this go, do you? Now that Lia's gone, they may not want to kill you at the moment, but that doesn't mean they won't reconsider the first time I—or my family—piss them off. Now that they know how important you are to me, you're more at risk than you've ever been."

Maybe his fears make sense, maybe they don't. But the truth is, "I don't care."

"*I* care, Grace." His gaze is shuttered, but it isn't blank. Not this time. I can see the pain in its depths, see that saying these things is hurting him as much as it's hurting me.

It's enough to have me sliding my hands up to his face, enough to have me cupping his cheeks in my palms as I stare deep into those eyes that have captivated me from the very first moment I saw him.

"Yeah, well, you're not the only one in this relationship," I tell him as I lean forward and press soft, desperate kisses to his forehead, the corners of his mouth, his lips. "And that means you don't get to make all the decisions for us."

"Please don't make this any more difficult." He grabs hold of my hands where they still cover his cheeks, his fingers twining with mine even as he takes care not to hurt me. "I can't walk away if you make it difficult."

"Then don't walk away," I implore, my mouth so close to his that I can feel the heat of his breath on my skin. So close that I can see the tiny silver flecks swirling in his eyes. "Don't turn your back on this—on me—before we even have a chance to try."

He drops his forehead to mine, closes his eyes with an agonized groan. "I don't want to hurt you, Grace."

"So don't."

"It's not that simple—"

"Yes, it is. It is exactly that simple. Either you want to be with me or you don't."

His laugh is dark, tortured. "Of course I want to be with you."

"So be with me, Jaxon." I wrap my arms—IV cord and all—around him, hold him as close to my battered, desperate heart as I can manage. "Be with me. *Love me.* Let me love you."

For long seconds Jaxon doesn't move, doesn't answer, doesn't even breathe as despair and hope battle deep within me. But then, just as I'm about to give up, he takes a deep breath, shudders against me.

And then his hands are on my face and he's kissing me like I'm the most important thing in the world.

I kiss him back the same way, and nothing has ever felt so good. Because for right now, for this moment, everything is finally exactly how it should be.

64

All's Well that Ends with Marshmallows

"Please?"

"No." Jaxon looks at me like I'm from another planet.

I cuddle closer, bat my eyes like a windmill on high. "Pleeeeeeeeease?"

He lifts a brow. "Do you have something in your eye, or should I call the nurse because you're having a seizure?"

"Ugh. You suck." I cross my arms over my chest and pretend to pout. But after three days of being cooped up in my bedroom, recuperating, I'm not sure how much of it is actually pretending. And even though I know I won't be here forever, it's still awful. "Please, Jaxon? If I have to stare at these walls any longer, I'm going to freak out."

Jaxon sighs, but I can tell he's deliberating, so I push my luck. "Can't we go somewhere? Just for a little while? You can even carry me if I get too tired." I try the whole *eye batting* thing again, less *panicked bird* this time and more *femme fatale*. Or, at least, that's what I'm going for.

"Yeah, like I'm going to fall for that," he says with a snort.

Which, okay. He has a point. I'm not real keen on him carrying me anywhere, especially now that things have calmed down around here. But still, the boredom is real…and getting more real every moment. "Come on, Jaxon. I know you're just following directions because Marise said I'm supposed to rest for a couple more days, but I'm not planning on joining the Iditarod. I just want to walk around for a few minutes. No big deal."

He studies my face for a minute and must figure out what I've already decided—that I'm going out with or without him—because he nods reluctantly. Then stands up from where we've been stretched out on my bed for the last two hours.

"Civil twilight has set in, so I'll take you outside for a little while," he says eventually. "But not far from the castle. And you have to promise to tell me as soon as you start to get tired."

"I will. I swear!" Excitement races through me, and I spring up after him, then kind of wish I hadn't, considering my *everything* hurts, especially my recently dislocated shoulder. Now that they've set it, it's a lot better than it was, but it still aches a lot. Not that I'm about to tell Jaxon that—partly because he might change his mind and partly because I know he blames himself for everything that happened with Lia.

Which is ridiculous, but Jaxon is totally the guy who balances the whole world on his shoulders and who takes the responsibility of that seriously, even if he never asked for it. So no way am I going to let him see how sore and battered I still feel. Not when that means giving him something else to beat himself up over.

"So what do you want to do?" I ask in an effort to distract him from the fact that I'm limping more than a little.

He's watching me with narrowed eyes and an expression that says I'm not fooling him. But he doesn't say anything else, except, "I've got a couple of ideas. Why don't you get dressed and I'll run and find a few things? I'll be back in fifteen minutes."

"We can meet downstairs—" I start but break off when he

looks at me with both brows lifted. "Oooor we can meet here," I finish.

"Yeah, let's do that." He leans down and drops a kiss on my lips.

It's meant to be quick, but I can't help wrapping my good arm around his neck and pressing myself against him as I deepen the kiss.

Jaxon goes still, but there's a hitch in his breathing that tells me I've got him. Seconds later, he slides his hands down to my hips to pull me even closer. And then he scrapes a fang across my lower lip in a move he knows makes every muscle in my body go weak.

My breath catches in my throat as I open for him. As I press even closer. As I give myself up to Jaxon and the explosion of heat and joy and light that he sets off inside me with just a kiss. Just a touch. Just a look.

I don't know how long we kiss for.

Long enough for my breathing to grow ragged.

Long enough for my knees to tremble with each stroke of his fingers against my hip.

More than long enough for me to reconsider our walk outside now that things inside have gotten so much more interesting.

But eventually Jaxon pulls away with a groan. He drops his forehead against mine, and we just breathe for a while. But then he pulls away, and in a voice gone deep and growly and oh so sexy, he says, "Get dressed. I'll be back in a few."

And then, like always, he's gone between one blink and the next.

It takes me a little longer to recover. A full minute or so passes before my heart rate steadies and my weak knees feel strong enough to support me. Eventually, I get my act together and start getting dressed in the layers upon layers necessary to survive an hour outside in Alaska. My lips tingle the whole time.

Turns out, it's a good thing I hurried, because Jaxon is back, knocking on my door and letting himself in before I even have my socks on. To be fair, getting dressed takes a lot longer with a dislocated shoulder, but still. Even if I was completely healed, it'd still be impossible for me to compete with Jaxon's speed.

He's carrying a backpack, which he drops by the door when he sees me struggling to pull on my socks.

"Here, give them to me," he says, kneeling down in front of me and gently resting my ankle on his thigh.

And just like that, my breath catches in my throat again. Because if I've learned nothing else in the time I've been here, it's that Jaxon Vega kneels for no one. Yet here he is, kneeling in front of me like it's the most natural thing in the world.

"What?" he asks as he slides the socks over my feet and past my ankles.

I just shake my head because what else is there for me to say? Especially when his fingertips linger on my calf, tracing patterns into my suddenly oversensitive skin.

I must look as flustered as I feel, because he just kind of grins at me as he slides a second sock over the first before doing the same to my other foot.

I shake my head, look away before I end up melting into an actual puddle.

A couple of minutes later, after putting my boots on for me, too, Jaxon stands up and holds a hand out to pull me up.

"Have you decided where we're going?" I ask as we head for the door.

He picks up the backpack—something I've never seen him carry if he's not going to class—and says, "Yeah."

I wait for him to elaborate, but this is Jaxon. He almost never shares more than he has to. Then again, as he gives me a wicked grin, I find myself not minding too much. If Jaxon wants to surprise me, who am I to say no? Especially when his surprises are usually so, so good.

We walk hand in hand through the halls and down the three flights of stairs to the front door. Almost everyone else is in the last class of the day—Jaxon should be, too, but he's ditching—so the common areas are nearly deserted. Which works for me. I'm still not ready to face most of them after everything that has happened.

"Are you okay?" Jaxon asks as we head out into the cold—and down even more steps. Which is great. I mean, it's not like every muscle in my body aches or anything...

Still, I nod, both because I don't want him to know that I'm hurting and because the biting cold kind of takes me by surprise. Which sounds ridiculous—this is Alaska; I know exactly how cold it is outside. But it's still a shock to my system every single time.

I must not be hiding it as well as I'd hoped, because Jaxon takes one look at my face and says, "We could go back in."

"No. I want to do something with you. Just the two of us."

His eyes widen at my words, and the guarded look in his eyes drops away. For a second, just a second, I get to see the real Jaxon—a little awkward, a little vulnerable, a lot in love with me—and it takes my breath away all over again. Because I feel all of that and so much more around him.

"Then let's go."

We set out in the opposite direction that I went on my walk around the grounds that first day. Instead of going by the classroom cottages, we head across the pristine snow to the forest that takes up a lot of the school grounds.

We walk slowly, partly because the cold isn't that bad once I start moving and partly because walking in snow really isn't easy, especially when you were beaten half to death less than a week before. Eventually, though, we get to a little clearing in the forest. It's not very big—maybe the size of my and Macy's dorm room—but there are a couple of benches to the side.

Jaxon drops his backpack on one and pulls out a tall black thermos. He takes off the cup at the top, then opens it and pours something into the cup. Then he hands it to me with a grin.

"Hot chocolate?" I exclaim, delighted.

"Yeah, well, I figure you might want to lay off tea for a while."

I laugh. "You make a good point." I start to take a sip, but Jaxon stops me. Then he reaches into his backpack and pulls out a small bag of marshmallows.

"I don't know much about drinking hot cocoa, but I do know that it usually needs marshmallows." He pulls out a few of the small, homemade-looking squares and scatters them in my cup.

And I swear my heart nearly bursts, right here in the middle of a bunch of trees, as darkness slowly descends around us. Because even after everything we've been through, I'm still blown away by how Jaxon always thinks about me. About what I might like or what makes me feel good or what would make me happy. And he's always, always right.

I take a big sip of the cocoa and am not surprised at all that it's the best hot chocolate I've ever had. "So who did you talk into making this for you?" I ask, eyeing him over the rim of my cup.

He gives me a blank look. "I have no idea what you're talking about." But there's a shadow of amusement in the depths of his eyes that belies his words and makes me laugh.

"Well, whoever it is, please tell them it's really good."

He smirks a little. "I'll do that."

I take another sip, then hold the cup out to him. "Want some?"

"Thanks, but it's not really my thing." Now he's full-on grinning.

"Oh, right." Which makes a million of the questions I've been accumulating for days rush back into my head. "How does that work, anyway?"

He lifts a brow. "How does what work?"

"I saw you drink tea, but you don't drink cocoa. You ate a strawberry during the party, but I've never seen you eat anything else. Except..." I trail off, blushing.

"Except your blood?" he asks archly.

"Well, yeah."

"Vampires drink water just like every other mammal on the planet, and tea is basically hot water. You start adding in milk and chocolate and it's a different story."

"Oh. Yeah." That makes sense. "And the strawberry?"

"Yeah, that was totally for show. My stomach hurt for the rest of the night." It's his turn to look embarrassed.

"Really? So why'd you do it?"

"Honestly?" He shakes his head, looks away. "I have no idea."

It's not the answer I was expecting, but looking at him, it's obvious that he's telling the truth. So I let it go. And instead say, "One more question."

"The blood thing?" He looks both wary and amused.

"Of course the blood thing! And the *going outside when it's light* thing. I thought vampires could only be outside when it's dark."

He looks uncomfortable for a minute, but then he squares his shoulders and says, "That depends."

"On what?"

"On what kind of blood they drink. Here at the school, Foster serves animal blood. If we drink only that, we can be outside in the sunlight. If we choose to...supplement with human blood, however, then we have to wait until it's dark."

I think about his comment in my room, about how we could

go out, since civil twilight had started. "So when I got here, I saw you outside because you were only drinking animal blood. But now—" I blush, and it's my turn to shift my face away. Not because I'm necessarily embarrassed by what Jaxon and I do but because it feels so intimate to talk about the fact that he—

"You mean, now that I've been drinking your blood on the regular?"

And the blush gets even worse. "Yeah."

"Yes. I drank from you. And Cole. And then you again in the tunnels. So, no light for me."

"For how long?" I ask, because it's been days since the tunnels, and he definitely hasn't drank from me since—even though I've kind of wanted him to. But apparently me nearly dying of blood loss has him less than eager to sink his fangs into my neck any time soon.

"Until the hormonal spike that comes from metabolizing human blood wears off." When I look mystified, he continues. "It's like humans and insulin. When you eat high-carb foods, your insulin spikes and takes time to come down. When I drink human blood, my body secretes a hormone that makes it impossible for me to be in the sun. It takes about a week for all traces of that hormone to disappear. Animal blood doesn't trigger the same hormone."

I count back in my head. "It's been six days since the tunnels. So by tomorrow, you should be able to go out in the sun again."

He shrugs. "Probably the day after to be safe. And that's if I don't..."

"If you don't bite me again." A sudden surge of heat flares through me.

Now he's the uncomfortable-looking one. "Something like that, yeah."

"Something like that?" I put my cup down on the bench and

wrap my good arm around his waist. " Or that exactly?"

He looks down at me, eyes dark and just a little bit dangerous. "That exactly," he murmurs. And I know—if I wasn't covered from head to toe in piles of clothes, he might very well be biting me right now. The idea gives me a thrill I don't even try to pretend away.

"Stop looking at me like that," Jaxon warns. "Or I'm going to take you back to your room, and we're not going to do what I brought you here for."

Not going to lie. Going back to my room suddenly sounds pretty good. Except... "Why are we here?"

"Why else?" He reaches into his backpack and pulls out a long, skinny carrot and a hat. "To build a snowman."

"A snowman?" I gasp. "Really?"

"Flint's not the only one who knows how to play in the snow around here." His face stays relatively expressionless, but there's a bite to his words that has me wondering all kinds of things. Including if Jaxon could possibly be jealous...which seems absurd, considering Flint tried to kill me on three separate occasions. Not a lot there to inspire jealousy.

"Well, are you coming?" Jaxon asks as he leans down and starts scooping snow into a giant ball. "Or are you just going to watch?"

"It's a good view," I tell him, openly checking out his very fine ass—which is encased in way fewer layers than mine currently is. "But I'll help."

He just rolls his eyes at me. But he does wiggle his butt a little—which makes me laugh. A lot.

It's not long before we're both cracking up as we stare at what has to be the world's most lopsided snowman. Which makes sense for me, because I'm a San Diego girl. But Jaxon has lived in Alaska for years. Surely he's built a snowman before.

I start to ask, but there's something about the way he's staring at our snowman that makes me hold my tongue. Even as it makes me wonder if maybe Jaxon hasn't had much time to play in his life—even when he wasn't first in line for the throne.

The thought makes me sad as he looks around for stones to use for the snowman's eyes. He's been through so much in his life. It amazes me how he could have gone through all of that and still emerge on the other side, this boy who feels so much. Who cares so much. And who is willing to try to play for me.

It humbles me even as it makes me ache for him.

The ache only gets worse as I remember the question that's been nagging at me on and off since I woke up in that infirmary three days ago. "Jaxon?"

"Yeah?" Something in my voice must tip him off, because his smile fades into concern. "What's wrong?"

"I've been meaning to ask…" I take a deep breath and blurt out the question I've tried so hard to ignore. "Where did Hudson go? I mean, we saw Lia die. But where did the black smoke go? Did it die with her? Or…" I don't finish, because the thought is too horrible.

But Jaxon's never been one to sugarcoat things—or avoid them. His face turns grim as he answers, "I haven't figured that out yet. But I will. Because there's no way in hell I'm risking Hudson being set loose on the world a second time."

There's such vehemence in his tone that it hurts to hear it, especially knowing how much Jaxon has already suffered because of his brother. I hate that he's had to go through so much, hate even more that the threat of Hudson coming back will probably hang over us forever.

After all, it's hard to relax when a homicidal sociopath has it out for you…and the rest of the world.

Jaxon's obviously better at dealing with his fear than I am, though—or maybe it's just that he's had longer to live with the threat. Whatever it is, he's able to shoot me a real smile as he finally makes the snowman a face out of stones and the carrot he brought for the nose. "Come on," he says. "You get to do the pièce de résistance." He hands me the hat.

It's the first time I've really looked at it, and when I do, it makes me laugh. And laugh. And laugh.

Because maybe I wasn't being ridiculous earlier after all. Maybe Jaxon actually is jealous of Flint.

Jaxon just shakes his head at me. "Are you going to put the hat on him or what?" he demands.

"Oh, I'm going to put the hat on." I step forward and do just that before moving back to where Jaxon is standing so we can both admire him.

"What do you think?" Jaxon asks after a moment. And even though he sounds like he's ready to make a joke, I can hear a little bit of vulnerability in his voice. A tiny little need for my approval that I never would have anticipated.

So I turn back and look at our poor, lopsided, listing-to-one-side snowman and, despite the cold, nearly melt all over again. Because to me, he looks perfect. Absolutely perfect.

I don't say that, though. I can't without revealing to Jaxon that I see more than he ever imagined. So instead, I tell him the only truth I can. "The vampire hat is a really nice touch."

His grin is huge. "Yeah, I thought so, too."

He reaches for my hand at the exact same moment I reach for his. And it feels good. More than good.

It feels right.

For the first time, I let myself think about what Lia said before she died, about me being Jaxon's mate. I don't know what that means, but as he pulls me close and his warmth slowly spreads through me, I can't help thinking that maybe I should find out.

65

Why Can't a Girl Just Have an Ordinary HEA These Days?

Four days later, I finally get to start classes again—for real this time, complete with Brit Lit homework, a research paper on the causes of the Salem Witch Trials, and my very first counseling appointment with Dr. Wainwright. Plus, actual makeup work for what I missed when a psychopathic vampire tried to murder me. Which seems a little unfair, if you ask me, but who am I to complain when I get to spend every morning, every lunch period, and nearly every evening with Jaxon, who is doing an admirably good job of staying in the moment and not borrowing trouble.

We're together right now, in fact, grabbing breakfast in the cafeteria and joking around about Luca's latest dating debacle—which, even I have to admit, is a doozy.

I'm eating brown sugar Pop-Tarts—Macy grabbed the last pack of cherry ones, because she's mean like that—and Jaxon and the rest of the Order are drinking their morning rations of school-supplied elk blood out of opaque tumblers. Turns out, that's what all the big orange beverage coolers are for—feeding the vampires.

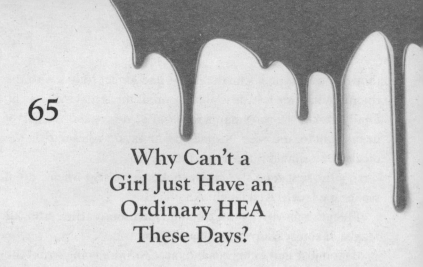

Cam still hasn't worked up the nerve to join us yet, but Macy has high hopes for him finally coming around. I'm not so sure—Jaxon's reputation has only grown more intimidating since what happened with Lia got around, and nearly everyone is giving him an even wider berth than usual. I keep telling him they'd relax a little if he smiled more, but so far he hasn't taken my advice. Personally, I think it's because he believes that the more scared they are, the safer I am.

I don't necessarily agree, but I do have to admit things have been shockingly quiet lately. No one has tried to poison me or turn me into a human sacrifice in at least ninety-six hours. It's definitely a record, one I am more than happy to ride out as long as possible.

The warning bell rings as I take my last sip of tea, and I glance up to find Jaxon staring at me, a (very) slight smile on his lips. "What's up?" I ask as I grab my Pop-Tart wrapper and mug.

"Just looking at you." He leans over, presses a kiss to the corner of my mouth. "Wondering what you're thinking about."

"You," I answer. "Just like always."

Rafael pretends to gag. "No offense, but could the two of you try to refrain from sending the rest of us into sugar shock?"

"Vampires don't metabolize sugar the same way regular humans do," I inform him with a grin. "Hence, no sugar shock."

"Now look what you've done," Mekhi interjects. "You've created a research monster. She's obsessed."

"Pretty sure it's the librarian who's done that," Jaxon answers dryly. "Every day, Amka has as least five more books for Grace to check out."

"Hey, if I'm going to live with vampires, I need to know as much about them as possible," I tell them as I stand up and tuck in my chair. "It's pretty normal to want to learn about your surroundings."

"You know what else is normal?" Jaxon asks as he bends

down so his mouth is only a few scant inches from mine.

"I have a pretty good idea," I answer, tilting my face up so that our lips can meet.

"Look at us," I whisper against his mouth a few seconds later. "Being normal."

He scrapes a fang across my lower lip, gives me a sexy look that turns my insides to mush. "Almost normal."

"I'll take that."

He grins. "Yeah, me too."

He moves in for another kiss, one that makes my head swim and my knees tremble, and I can't help but melt against him. I've never been big on PDA, but Jaxon has me breaking all the rules, and I'm pretty sure I'm doing the same for him. Especially if Lia's right and we really are mated.

Not that I've told him that yet. I mean, the boy's already terrified of this whole relationship thing. If I bring up a word like mate—something Macy spent a long time explaining to me a couple of days ago—I'm pretty sure the earthquake Jaxon generates will crumble the school.

It's Mekhi's turn to snark about how sick he is of being late to class because *some people* can't keep their lips to themselves. Jaxon flips him off, but the words must sink in, because he pulls away from me and reaches for my backpack.

"Come on. I'll walk you to class."

"You don't have to do that." I glance at the clock. "You'll be late to physics."

He shoots me a give-me-a-break look. "Somehow I'm sure they'll survive without me for five minutes."

I'm not so sure about that, but I know enough about Jaxon—and the sudden, stubborn set of his jaw—to know when to argue and when to let it go. Besides, letting him walk me to class comes with an extra perk. With him next to me, no one is going to bump into my still aching shoulder or any of my other injuries.

It's a win-win situation.

At least until we pass a small group of dragons on our way out of the cafeteria. Jaxon ignores them, and I try to, but Flint is right in the middle. And he's trying to catch my eye.

I want to ignore him, I really do. But like I told Jaxon the other day, there's a part of me that understands why he did what he did. I mean, I'm not ready to start roasting marshmallows with him again, but I can't hate him, either.

And I can't ignore him.

Instead, I let my gaze meet his for a couple of seconds. His eyes widen and he gives me the grin that's been making me laugh since my first day at Katmere. I don't laugh this time, but I do smile just a little as I walk on by. And for now, it's enough.

I kind of expect Jaxon to say something about what just happened as we weave through the halls, but he doesn't say a word. Guess I'm not the only one learning to compromise. I squeeze his hand just a little harder in a silent thank you, but he just kind of shakes his head in response.

It all feels very normal, and very right.

I know Jaxon still worries—and will continue to worry—that his being with me makes me a target. And there's a part of me that knows he's right. That I will never be safe if we're together.

But no matter what he thinks, it's not Jaxon's job to protect me. I've known from the first day that he wasn't meant to be the hero of my story. And I am more than okay with that.

Because he smiles now in a way he never did before. He laughs. And, on occasion, he even tells me a really bad joke or two. I'll take that over safe any day, especially when safety can be snatched away at any moment.

Which reminds me... "Hey, you never did tell me the punch line of that joke from the other day."

We stop a few feet away from my classroom, partly to take advantage of the now nearly empty hallway and partly in an effort not to freak my whole Brit Lit class out again.

"What joke?" he asks, puzzled.

"You know. The pirate one. Remember? What did the pirate say when he turned eighty?"

"Oh, right." Jaxon laughs. "He says..."

I never do get to hear the punch line. A flash over Jaxon's shoulder catches my attention. It's followed immediately by a noxious and eerily familiar cloud of black smoke. I start to stumble backward, to drag Jaxon with me. But it's too late. Because when the smoke clears, someone who can only be Hudson Vega is standing there, a giant broadsword in his hand—aimed straight at Jaxon's head.

The horror on my face must register, because Jaxon starts to glance over his shoulder. But the sword is already swinging. There's no time for him to even see the threat, let alone react to it.

Terrified, I grab his arms and yank him toward me. But even as he falls forward, I know it's not going to work. He's still in the blade's path. For a moment, just a moment, I flash back to how he looked last night when we were stretched out on his bed. He was leaning over me, resting on his elbow. Sleepy smile, eyes hazy with want.

His hair had fallen forward into his face, and I reached up to push it back so I could see his eyes...and, for the first time, as my hand grazed his scarred cheek, he didn't flinch. His smile didn't falter and he didn't duck his head. He didn't turn away. Instead, he stayed right there with me. In the moment.

Relaxed.

Happy.

Whole.

And that's when it hits me. Jaxon was never meant to be the

hero of my story...because I was always meant to be the hero of his.

So, in the end, I do the only thing I can do. I wrap myself around him and spin us around so that my back is to the sword. And then I close my eyes and wait for the blow I've always known would come.

0

She Persisted

—Jaxon—

"When the fuck is she going to turn back, Foster?"

"I don't kn—"

"Don't tell me that again. Don't fucking tell me you don't know." I turn on the librarian and the Biology of Ancient Creatures teacher who are sitting in front of the headmaster's desk and demand, "Aren't you supposed to be able to figure out what the hell is going on around here? What the fuck is the point of putting you people in charge of this school if none of you can answer a simple fucking question?"

"It's *not* a simple question, Jaxon." The headmaster pinches the bridge of his nose between his thumb and forefinger.

"Sure, it is. One minute, Grace was in my arms, blocking Hudson's attack." My throat closes up at the thought of those frantic, frenzied moments. Of the way she tried to drag me away, and when that didn't work, how she threw herself between—

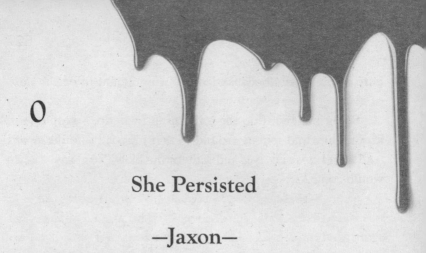

I cut off the thought before it can derail me and this entire conversation with it. Because if I think about it now, if I think about what she did… The ground beneath my feet starts to tremble and damn it, just damn it. The only thing keeping me from leveling the whole fucking school is the knowledge that I might hurt Grace in the process.

I take a deep breath before continuing. "One minute, she was there. And now Grace... Grace is..." I can't say it. I can't fucking say that she's gone, because if I say it out loud I can't take it back.

If I say it out loud, then it's true.

"She was there, Foster," I repeat. "Warm, alive, *Grace*. She was right there. And then she was—" The ground rumbles yet again, and this time I don't even try to control it.

Instead, I walk over to the corner, where what's left of Grace—my Grace—is standing. "Why can't she just turn back?" I demand for what feels like the millionth time. "Why can't you make her turn back?"

"I know it's hard for you, Jaxon." Dr. Veracruz speaks for the first time. "It's hard for us, too. But we haven't seen one for a thousand years. It's going to take time to figure out what went wrong."

"You've had four days! Four days. And you can't tell me anything more than that! How am I supposed to get to her if you can't even tell me what's wrong?"

"I think you're going to have to accept that you can't get to her," Foster says, and for the first time I realize that he looks and sounds nearly as bad as I do. "I think we're going to have to accept that she's not going to come back until she wants to."

"I don't believe that," I tell him, voice hoarse and hands clenched into fists in an effort not to lose it completely. "Grace wouldn't leave me like this voluntarily. She wouldn't leave me."

"Everything I've read in the last four days says she should be able to turn back on her own," Amka tells me. "Which means only two things are possible."

"Don't say it," I warn her.

"Jaxon—"

"I mean it, Foster. Don't fucking say it. Grace isn't dead. She can't be dead."

Because there's no way I can keep myself from breaking wide open if she is.

No way I can stop myself from razing this school to the fucking ground. And if Hudson somehow has her... If he's hurting her...just the thought of what he's capable of—and what she might be going through because of it—sends a bolt of terror skittering down my spine and twisting in my stomach. If he's harmed her in any way, I'll find him. And then I'll set him on fire just to watch him burn.

"She's not dead," I tell them again as I stare into her beautiful face. Her eyes are closed just like they were in that last second in the hallway, but that doesn't matter. I don't need to see her eyes to know how she feels about me—it's written all over her face. She loves me, almost as much as I love her.

"If she's not dead—and I agree with you that she's not," Dr. Veracruz says, "then the only other option is she's *choosing* not to come back."

"You don't know that. She could be trapped—"

"We do know that," Amka reminds me firmly. "Gargoyles can't get trapped in their stone forms. If they don't change back to human, it's because they don't want to."

"That's not true. Hudson's doing something to her. He's—"

"Jaxon." Foster's voice slices through my denials. "Do you really think Grace would change back if she thought she was bringing a threat to Katmere?" The headmaster holds my gaze, eyes somehow both solemn and fierce at the same time as I will him not to say what he's thinking—what we're both thinking. "Or to you?"

Pain slices through me, destroying me. Eviscerating me where I stand. I can barely think, barely breathe, through the agony of knowing that he's right. Of knowing that Grace might very well be suffering at this very moment—to save me.

I told her about Hudson, told her about my mother. She knows how much killing him nearly destroyed me. If coming back means bringing Hudson back with her, if it means making me kill my brother again, then there's no way Grace would do it. No way she would let me face that.

"She's saving me, isn't she?" I whisper, barely loud enough for myself to hear it.

But Foster hears it, and he braces a hand on my shoulder. "I think she might be."

There's no might about it. Because Grace loves me. She's already saved me once. I have no doubt that she'll stay locked in stone for as long as she has to. She'll stay locked in stone for as long as it takes to keep everyone she cares about here at Katmere safe.

And she'll stay locked in stone forever if it means saving me again.

My heart starts racing at the realization. My hands shake, my breath turns choppy and it takes every ounce of strength I have to stay on my feet.

I can't let her do it. I've barely made it through four days without Grace. No way can I make it through eternity without her.

For a moment, just a moment, I let myself remember all the little things I love about her. And ignore the fact that every memory breaks me a little more.

The way her eyes go all soft whenever she's touching me.

The way those same eyes narrow when she's about to call me out on my crap.

The way she laughs when she tells those awful jokes.

How do you cut the Roman Empire?

With a pair of Caesars.

That was a bad one. Hell, they were all bad ones, but that didn't matter when she giggled up at me, so proud of herself.

Fuck, I miss her.

I miss her sugar-cookie-and-strawberry scent.

I miss her softness, the way her ridiculously hot body always curves so perfectly into mine.

I miss her curls.

This time when I reach out, it's not to stroke her hair. It's to cup her stone-cold cheek the way she always cupped mine.

And tell Foster something that I desperately hope Grace can hear, too. "I'm going to find a way to separate her from Hudson. And I'm going to contain or kill him or do whatever I have to, to make sure he's never a threat to anybody ever again."

"That might not be enough, Jaxon," Amka says. "She might choose—"

"It'll be enough," I tell them. Because she loves me. Because she knows that I can't last much longer without her.

I lean forward, press my forehead to hers for one second, two. And whisper, "I'm going to find a way to stop him, Grace. I swear. And then you're going to come back to me. Because I need you. I need you to come home to me."

I close my eyes and swallow down everything else I want to say. Because it doesn't matter. Nothing does without Grace.

She has to make it back. Because if she doesn't, I'm going to shatter. And this time, I'm not sure I'll be strong enough not to take the whole world with me when I do.

END OF BOOK ONE

But wait—there's more!

Read on for an exclusive
look at three chapters from
Jaxon's point of view.

Nothing will ever be the same...

You Only Think You're a Prince If You Don't Have a Tower
—Jaxon—

I can't believe Foster did this. Just flat-out can't believe he did this. I'm spending every fucking hour of every fucking day trying to keep this whole thing from turning into a massive shit show, and Foster goes and does this. Un-fucking-believable.

"Is that her?" Mekhi asks from his spot on the couch behind me.

I look down at the girl currently climbing off the snowmobile in front of the school. "Yes."

"What do you think?" Luca chimes in. "Does she look like good bait?"

"She looks..." Exhausted. It's in the way she bows her head after she takes off her helmet. In the way her shoulders slump. In the way she looks at the stairs like they're the biggest obstacle she's ever seen in her life. Exhausted and...defeated?

"What?" Byron comes up behind me and peers over my shoulder. "Oh. Defenseless," he murmurs after a minute.

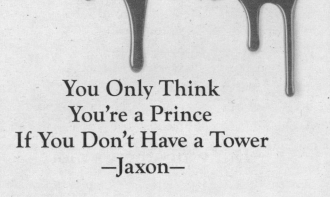

And yes, that's exactly the word I've been looking for. She looks *defenseless.* Which, no doubt about it, makes for great bait. It also makes me feel like shit. How the fuck am I supposed to use a girl who already looks like life has kicked her in the teeth about a dozen times?

Then again, how can I afford not to? Something's going on. Something big. Something fucked-up. I can feel it, and so can the other members of the Order. We've been trying to ferret it out for days, but no one's talking...at least not to us. And since we don't want to come right out and start pushing in case we send whoever is responsible for what promises to be a disaster of monumental proportions scurrying for cover, we're screwed if we don't find some bait to follow.

"Defenseless is good, right?" Liam asks in typical asshole fashion.

I shoot him a look as he grabs a thermos of blood from the mini refrigerator at the bottom of one of my bookcases. He holds a hand up in semi-apology, then explains, "I mean, it'll lull whoever's behind whatever this is into a false sense of security."

"Or it will make her that much easier for them to kill," Rafael answers. The words are careless, though his tone is anything but. No surprise there, considering he's always had a soft spot for damsels in distress. He's also the only one who's been against this plan from the beginning.

But I don't know what else to do. I can't afford to ignore whatever is happening below the surface. Not if I want to prevent another war...or worse.

I turn back to see that she's made it up the steps now, though it looks a little like she's going to fall back down. I want to see her face, but she's so bundled up, I can't get a good look at anything but the wild corkscrew curls sticking out from beneath her hot-pink hat.

"So what are you going to do?" Mekhi asks. "What will you say to her?"

I don't have a fucking clue. I mean, I know what I *planned* to say to her. What I *should* say to her. But sometimes *should* is a long way from what is. Hudson taught me that…and so did our mother.

Which is why, instead of answering my best friend, I ask, "What else do I need to know about?"

"Jaxon—" Rafael starts, but I shut him down with a look.

"What else?"

"The dragons are back in the tunnels," Luca volunteers in his rolling Spanish accent that makes everything seem not quite as bad as it actually is. "I haven't been able to figure out what they're doing yet, but I will."

"And the wolves?"

Liam gives a sarcastic laugh. "Same old assholes, different day."

"Like that's ever going to change?" Mekhi asks with a fist bump.

"It'll never change," I agree. "But beyond the usual, anything I should be aware of with them?"

"Nothing beyond howling at the moon like a bunch of criminals." Byron's still looking out the window, and I know he's thinking about Vivian. "When are you going to do something about that?"

"They're wolves, By. Howling at the moon is pretty much what they do," I tell him.

"You know what I mean."

I do. "They're not going to hurt anyone else the way they hurt her. I've got Cole's word on that."

"Yeah." He snorts. "Like there's anything trustworthy about Cole. Or his mangy pack of mutts."

It's been five years, but in vampire years, that's nothing. Especially when it comes to losing a mate.

"She's going inside," Byron murmurs, and a quick glance at the front of the school tells me he's right. The pink hat, and the girl it belongs to, are nowhere to be seen.

"I'll be back," I tell them, pulling off the red Katmere Academy hoodie I've been wearing all day and tossing it on the back of the nearest chair. After all, nothing says intimidating like a school sweatshirt...

I take the steps three at a time on my way down. I don't have a clue what I'm going to do right now—if anything—but I do want a look at the new girl. I want to see what kind of trouble she is. Because if there's one thing I do know, it's that she is going to be all the trouble.

It's a feeling that gets reinforced the second I see her standing alone, back toward the stairs and anyone who might want to sneak up on her as she looks at the chess table half hidden by the alcove at the bottom of the stairs.

And what the hell? She's been here all of two minutes, and Macy and Foster just leave her alone out here? Where anyone could approach her?

And by *approach her* I mean hassle her...or worse.

In fact, I'm not even all the way down the stairs before Baxter is sidling up to her, eyes burning and fangs flashing, just a little.

I get his attention, give him a look that tells him to back the hell off. Not because I actually care if he drinks the little human dry—and she is little, barely five foot four—but because there are rules. And one of those rules is, very definitely, don't eat the headmaster's niece. More's the pity, because she smells really good. A combination of vanilla and honeysuckle underlays the slight tang of too many hours of travel.

Makes me wonder just how she'd taste.

But since drinking her—dry or otherwise—is out of the question, I shove the thought down deep and take the last half set of stairs in one leap.

She still doesn't notice, and I can't help wondering if she's got a death wish or if she's just spectacularly unobservant.

I'm hoping it's the latter, because the former would definitely complicate things. Especially here at Katmere, where, at the moment, it feels like nearly everyone is hanging on to civilization by a thread. Myself definitely included.

I move up behind her as she picks up a chess piece and starts turning it around like it's the most fascinating thing in the world. Curious despite myself, I peer over her shoulder to see just what she finds so fascinating. But when I see what piece she's looking at—dear old Mom in all her glory—I can't help but lean in a little closer and warn, "I'd be careful with that one if I were you. She's got a nasty bite."

She jumps like I've actually bitten her instead of simply pointed out the danger. So simply unobservant, then, not a death wish. Things are looking up.

I start to warn her about turning her back on anyone in this place, but she whirls around before I can get the words out. And as our gazes collide, I lose all sense of what I was going to say.

Because fuck. Just fuck.

She's everything and nothing like I expected her to be.

She's fragile, like all humans. So easily broken—just a twist of my hand or a slice of my fangs and she could easily be dead. Problem solved, except, of course, for the shit storm Foster would unleash.

But as she looks up at me with startled eyes the color of rich, melted milk chocolate, I'm not thinking about killing her. Instead, I'm thinking about how soft her skin looks.

About how much I like the way her curls frame her heart-shaped face.

About whether the cluster of freckles on her left cheek forms a flower or a star.

And I'm sure as hell thinking about what it would feel like

to sink my teeth into that spot right below her ear.

What she would sound like when she asked me to do it.

What she would feel like against me as she offered herself.

What she would taste like on my tongue… If it's anything like how she smells, I'm afraid I might not be able to stop. And I can always stop.

It's not a realization I'm comfortable with, especially considering I came down here to check her out and make sure she wasn't going to cause any trouble when things are already so messed up. And here I am, suddenly thinking about—

"*Who's* got a nasty bite?" Her tremulous voice interrupts my thoughts, has me looking past her to the chess table…and the piece she dropped when I startled her.

I reach past her, pick up the vampire queen—even though she's pretty much the last thing I ever want to touch—and hold her up for Foster's niece, for *Grace* to see. "She's really not very nice."

She stares at me blankly. "She's a chess piece."

Her confusion amuses me—as does her determination to pretend that she's not afraid of me. She's got enough bravado that it might work on another human, but not with me. Not when I can smell her fear…and something else that makes me stand up and take notice. "Your point?" I ask, because poking the human is way too much fun.

"My point is, she's a *chess* piece," she answers, and for the first time, she's brave enough to look me in the eye. Which I like, way more than I should. "She's made of *marble*," she continues after a moment. "She can't bite anyone."

I incline my head in a *you never know* gesture. "'There are more things in heaven and hell, Horatio, / Than are dreamt of in your philosophy.'" Considering the clusterfuck we are currently in the middle of, a little *Hamlet* seems more than appropriate.

"Earth," she responds.

Which has me raising a brow at her. Not only does she know the quote, but she's not afraid to call me on my "mistake."

"The quote is, 'There are more things in heaven and *earth*, Horatio.'"

"Is it, now? I think I like my version better."

"Even though it's wrong?"

"Especially because it's wrong." She sounds incredulous and looks it, too. Which amuses me even as it concerns me. Because it means my first impression was right—she really is unobservant. Not to mention totally and completely clueless. All of which means she's going to get slaughtered up here—or she's going to cause a war. Or both.

I can't afford to let that happen…for everyone's sake. Not when I've worked so hard—and given up everything—to keep that from happening.

"I need to go." Her eyes are wide, the words high-pitched and a little squeaky.

It's the last straw, because if she can't handle a basic conversation with me on my best behavior, how the hell is she going to make it so much as a day here?

"Yeah, you do." I take a small step back, nod toward the common room—and the school entrance. "The door's that way."

Shock flits across her face as she demands, "So what, I shouldn't let it hit me on the way out?"

I shrug just before giving her an answer guaranteed to send her running for the hills. The fact that it also makes me sound like a total douche is for me to regret and for her to never know why. "As long as you leave this school, it doesn't matter to me if it hits you or not. I warned your uncle you wouldn't be safe here, but he obviously doesn't like you much."

Anger flashes across her face, replacing the uncertainty.

"Who exactly are you supposed to be, anyway? Katmere's very own unwelcome wagon?"

"*Un*welcome wagon?" I repeat. "Believe me, this is the nicest greeting you're going to get here."

"This is it, huh?" She raises her brows, spreads her arms out wide. "The big welcome to Alaska?"

The snark surprises me as much as it intrigues me—which is *not* acceptable...on any level. The knowledge has me snarling, "More like, welcome to hell. Now get the fuck out," as much as a warning to myself as an attempt to scare her senseless.

Too bad it doesn't work—on either front. Because she doesn't shut down at my warning, and she sure as hell doesn't run away. Instead, she just looks down her very cute nose at me and demands, "Is it that stick up your ass that makes you such a jerk? Or is this just your regular, charming personality?"

Shock washes over me—no one talks to me like that. Ever. Let alone some human girl I could kill with little more than a thought. With it comes a quick lick of frustration. Because I'm trying to save her life here, and she's too unaware to even notice.

I need to change that—and fast. Narrowing my eyes at her, I snap, "I've got to say, if that's the best you've got, I give you about an hour."

It's her turn for her brows to go up. "Before what?"

"Before something eats you." Obviously.

"Seriously? That's what you decided to go with?" She rolls her eyes. "Bite me, dude."

If she only knew how much I want to do just that... The angrier she gets, the better she smells. Not to mention how good she looks with flushed cheeks and the pulse point at the hollow of her throat beating double-time.

"Nah, I don't think so," I tell her even as my mouth waters

and my fangs threaten to elongate with every rapid pound of her heart.

I want to taste her. Want to feel the softness of her body leaning into mine as I drink my fill. As I drink and drink and—I cut off the thought. Force myself to look her up and down disparagingly before answering, "I'm pretty sure you wouldn't even make an appetizer."

I step closer, determined to intimidate her—determined to get her out of here before all hell breaks loose and she gets hurt "Maybe a quick snack, though." I snap my teeth fast and hard. Then do my best to ignore the way she shivers at the sound.

It's so much fucking harder than it should be. Especially when she refuses to back down like anyone—everyone—else would. Instead she asks, "What is *wrong* with you?"

And shit. I nearly laugh at that, because "Got a century or three?" That just might be long enough to scratch the surface of my answer, if I was honest.

"You know what? You really don't have to be such a—"

Behind us, everyone is circling, straining to hear. None of them is stupid enough to actually wander by too close, but I can feel them there just around the corner. Listening. Waiting. Strategizing.

Which means enough is more than enough. Time to get serious about scaring her away. "Don't tell me what I have to be," I growl. "Not when you don't have a clue what you've wandered into here."

"Oh no!" She does a mock-afraid face, then asks, "Is this the part of the story where you tell me about the big, bad monsters out here in the big, bad Alaskan wilderness?"

And damn, but she impresses me. Sure, it's frustrating as hell that she's not taking any of this seriously, but it's hard to blame her when all she knows is what she's getting from me. In fact, I'm impressed she's doing such a good job of holding her own—not many people can against me.

Which is why I respond, "No, this is the part of the story where I show you the big, bad monsters right here in this castle." I step forward, closing the small distance she managed to put between us.

She needs to know that if she's going to walk around this place challenging people like that, there will be consequences. Better that she learn it from me than from one of the shifters who likes to claw first and ask questions later.

She must read the intent in my face, because she takes one trembling step back. Then another. And another.

But I follow suit, moving one step forward for every step she takes backward, until she's pressed right up against the edge of the chess table. Nowhere else to go.

I need to scare her, need to make her run from this place as far and as fast as she can. But the closer I get to her, the more I lean toward her, the more I want to do anything but scare her away.

She feels so good pressed against me, smells so good, that it's hard to focus on the endgame. And when she moves, her body bumping into mine again and again, it's even harder to remember what the endgame is.

"What are—?" Her breath catches in her throat. "What are you doing?"

I don't answer right away—because I don't have an answer beyond, *The wrong thing. I'm doing the wrong thing.* But knowing that doesn't seem to matter when she's right here in front of me, her brown eyes alive with a million different emotions that make me feel things I haven't let myself feel in way too long.

But none of those is the answer I need to give her right now. None of them is even a thought I should have. So instead of saying what I want to say, I pick up one of the dragon pieces. Then hold it for her to see and answer, "You're the one who wanted to see the monsters."

She barely glances at the piece. Instead she sneers, "I'm not afraid of a three-inch dragon."

Silly girl. "Yeah, well, you should be."

"Yeah, well, I'm *not.*" Her voice is strained, and I start to think that maybe I'm getting through to her. Except right now, she doesn't smell afraid. In fact, she smells— Fuck, no. I'm not going to go there, no matter how much I suddenly want to.

Instead, I pull back enough to put some space between us. And to watch her freak out a little as the silence between us grows longer and longer.

Eventually, I break the silence—and the tension building between us—because I know that she won't. "So if you aren't afraid of things that go bump in the night, what *are* you afraid of?" And then I work really hard to pretend that her answer doesn't matter to me.

At least until she says, "There's not much to be afraid of when you've already lost everything that matters."

I freeze as her words slam into me like depth charges—sinking deep and then exploding so fast and hard that I'm afraid I'm going to shatter right here in front of her. Agony I thought I was long past rips through me, tearing me open. Making me bleed when I thought I had already hemorrhaged everything I had to lose.

I shove it back, shove it down. And can't understand why it's still right here in front of me—until I realize that this time, the pain I'm seeing is hers.

It's terrible and terrifying to realize that she carries some of the same wounds, if not the same scars, that I do. Knowing that, recognizing it, makes it so much harder for me to back away.

Makes it nearly impossible for me to do what I know I need to.

Instead, I reach out and gently take hold of one of her curls. I like them because there's so much life there, so much energy, so much joy that touching one makes me forget all the reasons it's impossible for me to let her stay.

I stretch out the curl, watching as it wraps itself around my fingers of its own volition. It's silky and cool and just a little coarse, yet it warms me like nothing has in way too long. At least until she brings her hands up between us and pushes at my shoulders.

And still I don't back away. I can't. At least not until she whispers, "Please."

It takes me a second—maybe two or three—before I finally find the will to move away. Before I finally find the strength to let that one, single curl, that one, single connection, go.

Frustrated with myself, with her, with this whole fucked-up situation, I shove a hand through my hair. Then wish I hadn't when her eyes immediately go to my scar. I hate the fucking thing—hate what it is, hate where it came from, and hate even more what it represents.

I look away. Duck my head down so my hair quickly covers it up again.

But it's too late. I can see it in her face and her eyes.

Can hear it in the breath that catches in her throat.

Can feel it in the way she moves toward me for the first time instead of away.

And when she reaches out, when she cups my scarred cheek in her cold, soft hand, it's all I can do not to shove her away. Not to run as far and as fast as I can.

Only the irony holds me in place—the idea that I came down here to scare her away for her own safety and now am considering fleeing for mine.

But then our gazes connect, and I'm held in her thrall, completely captivated by the softness and the strength in her eyes as she strokes her thumb across my cheek over and over and over again.

I've never felt anything like it in my too-long life and nothing—nothing—could make me break the connection now.

At least until she whispers, "I'm sorry. This must have hurt horribly."

The sound of her voice combined with the glide of her thumb across my skin sends electricity arcing through me. Has my every nerve ending screaming in a mixture of agony and ecstasy as one word washes through me over and over again.

Mate.

This girl, this fragile human girl whose very life is even now balanced on the edge of a yawning precipice, is my mate.

For a moment, I let myself sink into the knowledge, into her. I close my eyes, press my cheek against her palm, take one long, shuddering breath, and imagine what it would feel like to be loved like that. Completely, irrevocably, unconditionally. Imagine what it would be like to build a life with this smart and snarky and brave and battered girl.

Nothing has ever felt so good.

But people are all around us, watching us—watching me—and there's no way I can let this continue. So I do the one thing I don't want to do, the one thing every cell in my body is screaming against. I step back, putting real distance between us for the first time since I walked down those stairs, what now feels like a lifetime ago.

"I don't understand you." They aren't the words I need to say, but they are the ones I have to.

"'There are more things in heaven and hell, Horatio, / Than are dreamt of in your philosophy,'" she answers, deliberately using my earlier misquote with a smile that slices right through me.

I shake my head in a vain effort to clear it. Take another deep breath and slowly blow it out. "If you won't leave—"

"I *can't* leave," she interjects. "I have nowhere else to go. My parents—"

"Are dead. I know." Rage burns inside me—for her, for what she's suffered, and for all the things I want to do for her but *can't*. "Fine. If you're not going to leave, then you need to listen to me very, very carefully."

Her eyes widen in confusion. "What do you—?"

"Keep your head down. Don't look too closely at anyone or anything." I lean forward until my lips are almost pressed against her ear, fighting the instincts roaring to life inside me with every breath we both take as I finish, "And always, *always* watch your back."

Before she can answer, Foster and Macy come down the hall toward us. She turns to look at them, and I do what I have to do to keep her safe—do the only thing I can do in these ridiculous circumstances. I quickly fade to the stairs—the speed of it helping me pretend that each step away from her doesn't cut like jagged, broken glass.

I plan on going back to my room, but I don't make it that far. Instead, I stop just around the corner and listen to her voice as she talks to Foster. Not the words, just her voice, because I can't get enough of her. Not now. Not yet.

Soon enough. I'm going to have to give this up.

Soon enough, I'm going to have to stay as far away from her as I possibly can. Because if I thought it was bad for her to be used as bait, that's nothing compared to the danger of being a human mated to a vampire. And not just any vampire but one who holds the fate of the world in his hands.

It Only Takes One Hot Vampire to Win a Snowball Fight

—Jaxon—

I watch Grace head out the door with Flint and Macy and tell myself to walk away. That there's nothing to worry about. That she's going to be fine. And know, even as I say it to myself, that I'm going to follow them anyway.

Follow her anyway.

They're out in the snow now, moving slowly enough that any predator with half a mind could catch them—while walking backward on a leisurely afternoon stroll. I wait for Flint to get fed up, to try to hurry Grace along, but he doesn't do it. Instead, he walks close to her, laughing at whatever she's saying, making her laugh in return.

It's enough to make my blood boil, considering that's my mate he's trying to charm. And my mate he might very well be trying to kill. That thought does something way worse than make my blood boil. It makes every part of me freeze, every nerve in my body arrested with horror—and a rage so cold, it burns like ice.

Despite my determination to go unnoticed, I draw closer to them. Alarm bells are going off inside me, driving me to break all the rules I've held myself to for the last year. Making me do things that I normally wouldn't even consider.

Then again, the last year has been all about doing things I wouldn't have imagined. Things I wouldn't wish on anyone, even a monster like myself. And now, here I am, trailing my ex-friend through the snow as I try to figure out exactly what Flint is up to.

There was a time not so long ago that I would have trusted him unconditionally, a time when he would have done the same for me. But that was a long time ago—in events if not in actual years. And now...now I don't even trust him with a simple snowball fight.

I sure as shit don't trust him with my mate.

The three of them finally make it out to the clearing where everyone is waiting. I stay in the trees, watching as Flint moves to the center of the group. He cracks a few jokes, loosens everyone up, then lays down the most ridiculous rules in existence—I should know. We made them up together years ago. Back when I got to at least pretend that I was like everyone else.

Grace watches him the whole time. It's enough to set my teeth on edge...and more than enough to make me feel like some kind of stalker. I'm only here because every instinct I have is screaming at me that something is wrong, that my mate is in danger, but it's still hard to justify peering at her from behind a tree like some kind of creep. Especially when she seems totally absorbed in another guy.

For a minute, just a minute, I think about heading back to the school. But then Flint finishes his rules and beckons like some kind of prince for Grace and Macy to join him. They do—of course they do—and Grace reaches up and pulls on his stupid dragon hat. Flint laughs and bends his head to give her better access, and I see fucking red.

Bloodred to be exact.

It takes every ounce of control I have to stay where I am, fists clenched and teeth on edge, as I try to figure out exactly what game Flint is playing. If he's playing a game at all.

He bends down to talk to Grace, to whisper something in her ear that I'm too far away to hear—even with my heightened senses. And when his fucking lips nearly brush the small strip of exposed skin at the top of her cheek, my fangs explode in my mouth.

I'm suddenly a whole lot closer to them without having made any conscious decision about moving, thoughts of murder and mayhem blazing a trail through my brain.

I tamp them back, shove them down deep. And pretend to myself that I'm not tracking Flint's every move like a predator about to strike his prey.

"Chill," Mekhi tells me from his spot behind a tree several yards away. For the first time, I'm glad he and the others wouldn't let me come out here alone. Ostensibly, it was for my own protection—that's how they roll—but now I can't help but wonder if it's for everyone else's as well.

Fuck. I close my eyes, run a hand over my face. When it comes to Grace, I need to get my shit together…and fast. Because the universe might have decreed that she's my mate, but that doesn't mean anything if she doesn't agree. And Flint comes with a lot less baggage than I do—is it any wonder she's laughing so easily with him?

I need to move back, to give them a little more room and maybe get this damn bloodlust under control.

But then the game is on, and Grace, Macy, and Flint are running into the trees on the other side of the clearing. I let them go, determined to watch from here. But since I apparently have no self-control when it comes to this girl, my resolution lasts about five seconds before I start making my way toward them stealthily—no reason to have to explain to anyone else what I'm doing out here when I'm not even sure myself.

I skirt around a group of witches who aren't even bothering to make snowballs. Instead they're firing streams of snow at one another in what looks to be a wholly ineffectual but amazingly fun exercise in futility. At least until a witch named Violet manages to pick up enough snow to leave her opponents buried in the stuff.

They screech as they try to burrow their way out, and I'm left grinning as I slide by unnoticed. Looks like the snow spelling wasn't so ineffectual after all.

Grace is several trees in front of me now, making that arsenal of snowballs I suggested. She's laughing, and I realize it's the first time I've heard her do that since she got here. It's a good sound, a happy sound, and I grin even though Dragon Boy is responsible for it. It's nice to hear her happy.

I grab a tree branch and swing myself up the regular way. It's fast and a lot more fun than using my telekinesis to levitate. And when I climb up a few more branches to the top of the tree, it gives me a hell of a view of the action.

Some of the wolves are still in the clearing, knocking the shit out of one another with one superpowered snowball after another. The witches are dropping snow and icicles from nearby tree branches on every person foolish enough to walk under one. And the dragons are stockpiling, staying out of the action for now as they hoard snowballs like they do their jewels down in the tunnels beneath the school. It's definitely the most pragmatic approach—it won't be long before they have enough of an arsenal to take down anyone who comes near them—but I'd be lying if I said I didn't admire the witches' approach the most. Ambushing anyone who walks by with a pile of snow on their head is both ingenious and fun as hell to watch.

A nearby shriek in a familiar voice has me focusing on Grace with laser-like precision. And grinning like a fool as she tries desperately to wipe away a face full of snow. At least until Flint reaches over and helps her clear out her scarf, his hands suddenly way too close to the petal-soft skin of her cheeks. The same skin I've been dreaming about touching ever since she cupped my jaw with her hand.

And when she looks up at him with a laugh and a toss of her curls—hot-pink hat definitely included—a low growl that I have no control over emanates from my throat. Even before Flint hands her that fucking dragon hat and helps her fill it with snowballs.

The growl only gets worse when he actually puts his hands on her, picking her up and tossing her over his shoulder like she belongs there. And when he wraps an arm around her upper thighs to hold her in place, I swear I can feel his jugular beneath my fangs.

If he drops her, if he harms so much as one hair on her head, I'm going to fucking kill him. And if he doesn't…I just might kill him anyway. Especially if he doesn't get his hands off her in the next five seconds.

Relief shimmers through me as he deposits Grace safely on one of the lower branches, and I take my first real breath in what feels like hours.

Then I settle back to enjoy the show as Grace pelts everyone who walks by with snowball after snowball. She's got remarkably good form for someone who's never had a snowball fight before.

At least until a brisk wind comes up out of nowhere. Grace falters a little, and my stomach bottoms out as she grabs on to the tree trunk for support. And by the time another gust shakes the tree even harder, I'm already moving—sliding down my own tree even as I scan the surrounding area to see if the wind is natural or creature-made.

The rest of the Order is right behind me.

I'm down the tree and halfway to Grace—and about to call the wind natural despite the bizarre coincidence—when I spot Bayu several yards away. The dragon is still in human form, but he's facing Grace's tree with his mouth wide open. Everything between him and Grace—snow, trees, people—is buffeted with a powerful wind.

Fury sweeps through me. With a slice of my hand and a flash of my telekinetic power, I lift him several feet off the ground and send him hurtling into the nearest tree trunk.

He hits hard enough to knock himself out, and that's all I care about. There's a part of me that wants to stop and drain him dry for even thinking about threatening Grace, but right now I have bigger things to worry about. Namely the fact that while the wind dragon is currently incapacitated, the last of the breeze he released definitely isn't. And it's headed straight for my mate.

I take off running toward Grace, but, fast as I am, I'm too late. The wind has been buffeting the tree, and her, for too long. I can hear the branch she's on crack from here. And Flint, the fucker, is doing absolutely nothing to help her.

A million thoughts run through my head in an instant. Pulling Grace off that branch and floating her safely down to the ground. Wrapping a telekinetic hand around Flint's traitorous throat and squeezing until his fucking eyes pop out. Holding the tree branch in place until I can get there and catch her.

But as the branch gives another ominous crack, I go with the most expeditious—and easily explainable to someone who doesn't know about vampires or dragons—solution and yank Flint out of the tree just as Grace starts to fall.

He's a big guy—dragons usually are—and turns out, he makes a really good landing spot to break her fall.

Of course, Flint knows it's me who yanked him out of the

tree—knowledge that I am more than okay with him having. The second he hits the ground, he's lifting his head, looking around to try to spot me. But if dealing with Hudson taught me anything, it's the value of guerrilla warfare. Never let them see you until they're already dead.

Today is no exception as I indulge a particularly satisfying fantasy of ripping Flint's fucking head from his fucking traitorous body. And that's before my mate tries to scramble off him and only ends up straddling him instead, her knees on either side of his hips.

As she tries to make sure he's okay after he just participated in an attempt on her life.

The irony is fucking painful, especially when the jackass reassures her he's fine. And puts his hands on her hips in a gesture that makes every cell in my body yearn for destruction. It's a feeling that doesn't go away, even after Grace scrambles off him and starts alternating between yelling at him and thanking him for jumping out of the tree to save her.

And when she steps forward, looking like she wants to check out up close and personally if he's really okay, I give up any attempt at staying cool.

Screw decorum. Screw the art of surprise. Screw everything. No way is my mate putting her hands—or any other part of her body—on that jackass one more time, at least not while she's ignorant of Flint's part in her taking a header out of that tree.

I fade through the space between us, roughly the size of three football fields, in a flash. There are people milling around Grace and Flint, but the second they realize I'm here, they back the fuck up. Fast.

And then I'm there, staring down at this girl whose mere existence has changed everything, and wishing desperately that I had met her a year ago, before everything in my life and the world around us went to total and complete shit.

The yearning is so powerful that for a second, I'm barely aware of Flint.

Or my friends, who have suddenly lined up behind me in a very obvious show of solidarity.

Or the crowd, who's watching every second of the drama with greedy eyes. All I can see or hear or think about is Grace.

But then Flint moves, whether in an attempt to apologize or tell me off, I don't know. And I don't care. He got Grace up that tree deliberately so Bayu could knock her out of it, and if he thinks I'm just going to let him get away with that, then his grasp of reality is in serious jeopardy right now.

Actions have consequences, and murder attempts mean there will be hell to pay. Even if I don't yet know what kind of hell it's going to be. I do know, however, that he's going to give me some kind of answer about this debacle before we leave. Or I'll tear him limb from fucking limb right here, right now.

"What the hell did you think you were doing?" I demand when he finally has the nerve to look me in the eye.

Flint doesn't answer me right away—the coward—and I start to ask again, more forcefully this time. Except Grace steps between us before I can and whispers, "I fell, Jaxon. Flint saved me."

It's like setting a rocket off inside me. Finally hearing my name on her lips feels damn good, but listening to her defend Flint is about to make my head explode. "Did he?" I ask, reverting to sarcasm in an attempt not to tear Flint apart.

"Yes! The wind kicked up, and I lost my balance," she implores. "I fell out of the tree, and Flint jumped after me."

I'm about to question the veracity of that statement—from Flint's point of view, anyway—when Grace reaches out and touches his shoulder like he's the big, brave hero who saved her.

"What's wrong?" she asks, and it burns my ass. "Are you hurt after all?"

There's a lot I want to say to that, but I can't. Not here and not now, so once again I lock it down deep and pretend that it isn't there.

Seconds later, a small quake rips through the earth.

Behind me, Byron says my name—quietly—and I shut that shit down fast. It's harder than it should be, considering the only way I've gotten through everything I've had to do for the last year is to lock down my emotions until I forget that I even feel anything at all.

I'm not sure anyone even noticed the quake, because no one says a word. Instead, Flint shrugs off Grace's hand and says, "I'm fine, Grace." Which means he's smarter than he looks.

Except she's not buying it. "Then what's wrong?" she asks, looking back and forth between us. "I don't understand what's happening here."

There's nothing to say, so I don't answer—and neither does Flint, probably for the same reason. Grace looks confused, and everyone else around us looks like they're seconds away from rubbing their hands together with glee—even as the dragons move into place behind Flint, making sure the Order and I know that they have his back.

Like that will matter if I decide to destroy him.

Macy must sense the growing danger, because suddenly she pipes up from nowhere. "We should go back to the room, Grace. Make sure you're okay." Her voice is a lot higher than I've ever heard it.

"I'm fine," Grace assures her, once again looking between the dragon and me like she thinks I'm going to do something stupid. Which, not going to lie, I just might if we don't get the hell out of here and soon. Then she continues. "I'm not going anywhere."

And yeah, that's not going to work for me. Not when she's here surrounded by who knows how many people who want to hurt her. Or worse.

I take a couple of steps closer to Grace until I'm right behind her, so close that I can smell the warm cinnamon and vanilla scent of her. "Actually, that's the best idea I've heard all afternoon. I'll walk you back to your room."

No way am I letting her go anywhere alone.

The crowd recoils at my words. Like, I actually see people drawing back, eyes wide, mouths open, faces slack with shock. Not that I blame them. I'm acting way outside the norm now. Everyone wants to watch, but no one wants to get in my way.

Smart move. With the mood I'm in, the first person to challenge me might very well end up dead. Or at least with two very distinct marks in their neck.

It's a feeling that is only reinforced when Grace says, "I need to stay with Flint. Make sure he's really—"

"I'm fine, Grace," Flint grates out from between clenched teeth. "Just go."

"Are you sure?" She reaches out and tries to lay a hand on his fucking shoulder again. But this time I'm there between then, preventing her hand from landing. Then I step forward, moving her slowly, inexorably away from Flint and back toward school.

She doesn't object, though the look on her face holds about a dozen questions. Maybe even more.

"Come on, Macy," she says, eventually reaching for her cousin's hand. "Let's go."

Macy nods, and then we start walking back toward the castle—Macy, Grace, and me. I nod to the Order to stay where they are until the crowd starts to disperse, so that's exactly what they do.

Grace and I walk in silence for a minute or two until she

turns to me and asks, "What are you doing out here anyway? I thought you weren't going to join the snowball fight."

I don't have an answer to that, so I prevaricate with, "Good thing I was out here, considering the mess Flint got you into." I very deliberately don't look at her to keep myself from saying something stupid.

"It really is no big deal," she assures me, but there's something off in her tone even before she continues. "Flint had me. He—"

"Flint very definitely did not have you," I snap, her defense of that damn dragon setting me off like few things have in a very long time. I stop to face her, determined to make her understand. "In fact—" I break off, eyes narrowing at the flicker of pain that flits across her face. "What's wrong?"

"Besides not being able to figure out why you're so mad?" She brushes off my concern.

But that doesn't stop me from looking her over from head to toe. "What's hurting you?"

"I'm fine," she insists.

"You're hurt, Grace?" Macy joins the conversation for the first time, and I'm embarrassed to admit I almost forgot she was even with us. Then again, next to Grace, everyone pales in comparison.

"It's nothing," Grace repeats, but it's not very convincing. Especially when she continues to walk—and winces with every step she takes.

I grind my teeth together and resist the urge to make a comment about just how stubborn she is. Instead I ask, "What hurts?" and give her a look that tells her I'm not budging on this until she's honest with me.

She stares back, giving as good as she's getting. But eventually she backs off with a disgruntled sigh. "My ankle. I must have twisted it when we hit the ground."

As soon as I know what's wrong with her, I kneel down and probe her foot and ankle as gently as I can through her boot. She gasps a little, and the fact that I'm hurting her, even accidentally, goes through me like a particularly powerful current. "I can't take this off out here or you'll get frostbite. But does it hurt when I do this?"

She gasps, and I ease away, pissed off that I hurt her. Even more pissed off that I let her get hurt to begin with.

"Should I run ahead and get the snowmobile?" Macy asks. "I can be back before too long."

"I can walk. Honest. I'm okay," Grace says, but her voice sounds as pathetic as she looks.

I shoot her an incredulous look as I reach down and help her to her feet. Then, because she very obviously can't walk, I swoop her into my arms. And do my best to ignore the fact that holding her feels better than anything has in the entire hundred years of my existence.

If You Want to Feel Better, Never Ask an Evil Vampire a Question
—Jaxon—

I'm out the front door before Grace can even make it down the first step.

I know I should probably stick around, but I can't do that. Not right now. Not when she's got that bandage on her neck and other ones on her arm and cheek. And not when I know that I'm the asshole who did it to her.

I close my eyes for a second—just a second—and it all flashes back. The earthquake. The window exploding under the force of my power. The moment the glass sliced into Grace's neck.

I've never been more terrified in my life. Fear isn't something I experience very often—when you're the scariest thing in the night, you tend to not worry about what else is bumping along next to you. But watching that glass hit Grace, watching her blood spray all over the room and realizing the glass had sliced an artery... Yeah, terrified doesn't even begin to cover how I felt.

The next five minutes are a blur. I remember licking her throat closed in an effort to stop the blood, remember bits and pieces of gathering her in my arms, but fade full-out for Marise as Grace lay white and still in my arms.

I'd nearly killed her because I couldn't control myself.

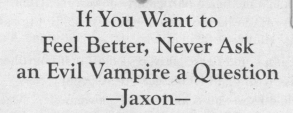

Nearly killed her just because being near her makes me feel so much that I can't lock it away.

Nearly killed her because when it comes to her, I'm weak. So weak that I unwittingly let the energy build up and nearly mated her without even asking her permission.

It's a humbling realization...and an awful one. I've spent my entire life protecting people from the terrible power and unchecked selfishness of my family. And now, three days with my mate and suddenly I'm blowing out windows, shaking the fucking earth, and nearly bonding with her without even letting her know what's going on?

What the fuck am I thinking?

But that's just it. I haven't been thinking, not since I walked down those stairs that first evening and saw Grace standing by the chess table. From that moment on, all I've been thinking about is making her mine. And now she's nearly died, twice, all because I can't get my shit together enough to take care of her—to watch over her—the way I should.

But what's the alternative to us being there together? Leave Katmere Academy—school to the children of the most influential monsters in the world—right now, when we're on the brink of yet another war? Especially when that war has been largely caused by my own family?

Or should I get Grace to leave? I already tried that the first day, all but ordering her to get the hell out because I wanted her more than I've ever wanted anything—a feeling that only grows with each day she's here. She didn't go when I told her to because she couldn't, because she doesn't have anywhere else to be.

Because she belongs at Katmere Academy, the animalistic voice deep down inside me snarls. *More, she belongs with me.*

Because she's my mate. My mate.

Even after five days, I still can't get over the wonder and the terror that one simple word engenders in me.

Every vampire has a mate, but finding them in your first two hundred years is practically unimaginable. Byron found Vivien early, but that's because they were born into the same small town in France and were raised together as friends long before they ever knew they were mates. The rest of us just have to bumble around until we find ours...and that's if we're lucky.

I haven't told anyone else about Grace, not even Mekhi or Byron, because labeling her as such puts her in even more jeopardy than she's already in. Which, apparently, is a hell of a lot, considering her mate can't even fucking protect her from himself.

I never should have gone to her room today. I should have left Grace the hell alone. But I'm selfish and I'm weak and I couldn't not see her. I couldn't not check on her, couldn't not make sure she was okay, no matter how much doing so fucked things up even more.

But that was before I saw her over Macy's shoulder, covered in cuts and bruises from the flying glass. Battered, bandaged, broken. And realized, mate or not, the best thing I can do for her is to leave her the fuck alone.

The thought has me recoiling, has the monster deep inside me screaming in rage. But that just makes me move faster, desperate to put as much distance between Grace and me as I possibly can.

There are miles between us now, and still it isn't enough. Still, I can feel her blood calling out to me, her taste like nothing I've ever experienced before. When I licked the small drop of her blood off my thumb that very first night, the taste of her nearly brought me to my knees. Last night was worse. I wanted her blood even as it spilled over me, even as I tried desperately to stanch the flow that would kill her if left unchecked.

I already know I'm a monster, but what does that need—that craving—in the middle of a life-and-death crisis make me?

Desperate? Evil? Irredeemable?

And when did that happen? When I killed Hudson? Or years, decades, before?

I keep fading, even though I don't have a clue where I'm going, as I race across the snow. It doesn't really matter, though, as long as it's far away from Katmere...and from Grace. I can't think when she's that close, her blood calling to me—one more temptation that I can't afford to give in to.

Not if I want to keep her safe.

Not if I want to keep her whole.

And I do, more even than I want to make her mine.

It's that thought that finally gives me direction. A quick glance at the GPS on my phone tells me just how close I already am to my newly decided-on destination. So close that I can't help wondering if my subconscious was guiding me here all along.

I take a quick left at the base of a mountain I once lifted a hundred feet in the air—a training exercise for twelve-year-old me—and fade another twenty miles through the snow to an ice cave whose entrance is almost completely obscured by the snow at the base of the mountains that surround it.

I pause when I reach it, take a minute to get my thoughts, and the rest of me, under tight control. The Bloodletter might be the mentor who taught me almost everything I know, but that doesn't make it any easier to go in there. The most vicious and powerful vampire in existence, the Bloodletter is an expert at ferreting out weakness. And then using it to destroy you with barely more than a word or two.

I spent twenty-five years of my life right here in this cave at the queen's insistence, learning to harness my powers. And how to use them to destroy any enemies of the throne, also at the queen's insistence. The Bloodletter made sure I could do all of that...and so much more. It's been a blessing and a curse.

When I've finally got my defenses in place, any thoughts of Grace shoved down deep inside me, I take a few long breaths. And begin my descent into the ice.

There are safeguards on the entrance, protections woven into the air and rock and ice as ancient as the Bloodletter. I dismantle them without a thought—as I was taught all those years ago. Or, more accurately, as I figured out through very painful trial and error.

The ground slopes steeply down, a narrow path carved through ice and igneous rock. I traverse it quickly, winding my way through beautiful and deadly ice formations from memory alone. Eventually, I get to a fork in the path and take the way on the right, despite the feeling of dread that overwhelms me the moment I step down it.

More safeguards, which I also undo, making sure to weave them back in place before I continue deeper into the cave. Normally, this part of the walk is done in total darkness, but today lit candles line both sides of the path. I wonder if the Bloodletter is expecting someone...or if some sacrifice has recently been made by someone seeking some kernel of the knowledge the Bloodletter so stingily doles out.

One more bend in the path, one more fork to traverse—I go left this time—and one more set of safeguards. Then I've finally arrived in the antechamber before the Bloodletter's quarters. The room is huge and also lit with candles that illuminate the brilliant ice and rock formations that line the walls and ceiling in all directions.

A small river of ice runs right down the center of the room. It's currently frozen solid, but I've seen it as running water as well. In the middle of summer and, of course, at a flick of the Bloodletter's fingers. When I was young, I used to think it was the River Styx, carting the souls of everyone who failed the

Bloodletter's trials straight to Hell without benefit of a ferryman.

More than once I threw myself into it on the off chance that a one-way trip to Hell would finally end my torment. It didn't.

I look around, take a second to collect myself one more time. And do my best to ignore the human carcasses hanging upside down in the corner, draining into a couple of large buckets on the floor. More proof that nothing has changed. The Bloodletter lures humans to the cave instead of going out to hunt. Some are eaten fresh and some are…stored for when the weather is so bad that this area is nearly deserted. It's a more efficient use of time for everyone involved, I was always told.

Right before I was punished for never fully draining my victims…not to mention leaving them alive.

I look away from the bloody carnage, take one more deep breath. And step right through an ice archway into the Bloodletter's living room.

It's exactly as I remember. The walls are painted a cozy periwinkle blue and flames snap in the rock fireplace that dominates one of the side walls. Bookshelves filled with first editions line two of the other walls and an abstract rug in shades of sunrise stretches across the ice floor.

In the center of the room, facing away from the fire, are two antique wingback chairs in brown leather. Across from them, separated by a square glass table, is a velvet sofa in dark violet.

And sitting on that sofa in a bright-yellow caftan, legs curled up beneath her, is the Bloodletter, knitting what I'm pretty sure is a winter hat in the design of a fully fanged vampire.

"Took you long enough to get through the safeguards." She glances at me over the top of a pair of half-moon glasses. "Are you going to stand there all day or are you going to come on in and sit down?"

"I don't know." It's the most honest answer I've ever given.

She smiles, pauses in her knitting just long enough to pat her short gray curls a couple of times. And gesture for me to have a seat. "Come on. I'm making you a present."

The hat is almost done, which means she started it long before I even decided that I was coming…which is not exactly a surprise, now that I think about it.

"What exactly am I going to do with a hat?" I ask, even as I follow her directions.

She grins, her bright-green eyes twinkling against the warm brown of her skin as she answers, "Oh, I'm sure you'll think of something."

I have no idea what to say to that, so I just nod and wait for her to say something else. The Bloodletter has never been fond of anyone speaking first.

Turns out, at the moment, she's not interested in talking at all. So I sit in the leather chair for almost an hour, watching as she puts the finishing touches on a vampire hat I have absolutely no interest in wearing.

Finally, when she's done, she ties off the yarn and puts everything beside her on the couch. "Thirsty?" she asks, nodding toward the bar in the corner.

I am, but a flashback to the humans draining right outside this room has me shaking my head. "No, thanks."

"Suit yourself." She gives a delicate little shrug as she stands up. "Well, come on, then. Let's take a walk."

I stand and follow her toward a second archway near the back of the room. The moment we pass through, the icy floor and walls of what I vaguely remember as my training room transform into a summer meadow, complete with wildflowers and the sun beating down warmly upon us.

"So," she says after we've walked several minutes in silence. "Are you going to tell me what's bothering you?"

"I'm pretty sure you already know."

She makes an affirmative sound, along with a face that says, *Maybe I do*. But she doesn't volunteer any information.

"How are you?" I ask after a few seconds. "I'm sorry I haven't been by in a while."

She waves a hand. "Oh, child, nothing to worry about on that front. You've had bigger fish to fry."

I think of Hudson and my mother and the nightmare of keeping the different factions from dissolving into civil war. "Yeah, I guess you could say that."

"I am saying it." She reaches up, rests a hand on my shoulder. "I'm proud of you, my boy."

It's the last thing I expect her to say. An unexpected lump blooms in my throat in response, tightening up my vocal cords until I have to clear my throat several times before I can speak. "That makes one of us."

"Don't do that." The hand on my shoulder goes from comforting to slapping the back of my head from one instant to the next. "You've done more for this race than anyone in the last thousand years. Be proud of that. And be proud of the fact that you've found your mate."

"So you do know why I'm here."

"I know why you think you're here."

I look away, only to end up staring at a patch of wildflowers in a shade of bright pink that I will associate with Grace until I take my last breath. "How do I do it?" I ask, and the earlier tightness in my throat is nothing compared to how I feel now.

I can barely breathe.

"Take her as a mate?" Her brows go up.

"You know that's not what I mean." I clench my fists and pretend this conversation isn't making me want to hit something... or throw up. Or both.

She sighs heavily. "There is a way."

"Tell me."

"Are you sure, Jaxon? Once you do it, there's no coming back from it. You can't just fix what's been torn asunder."

"I won't want to fix it." I grind the words out past clenched teeth.

"You don't know that." She waves a hand, and the meadow transforms into Grace's dorm room. Grace is curled up in bed, reading something off her phone while Macy flits around her. She looks beautiful and fragile, and I want nothing more than to wrap my arms around her. Want nothing more than to protect her from everything…even if that everything includes me. Especially if it does.

"Finding your mate is a precious thing," the Bloodletter continues. "Finding her so young is even more special. Why would you give that up if you don't have to?"

"They're already gunning for her. I don't know why yet, but she's a pawn in some plan they have to do God knows what. Overthrow the vampires? Bring about the civil war I've worked so hard to stop? Get revenge for what Hudson did? I don't know. I just know that I can't let her get hurt because of decisions I made that have nothing to do with her."

I mean every word I'm saying, but that doesn't make them hurt any less. I've never had anything that was mine in my whole life—my mother saw to that. Yet here Grace is, right in front of me. She's meant to be mine. And still I can't afford to reach for her. Not if it means risking something happening to her because of me.

"You know she'll never be safe in this world. You know they'll kill her just to make me suffer."

The Bloodletter waves her hand, and once again, we're walking in the meadow. I have to bite my lip to keep from begging her to bring Grace back, even as she answers, "I know they'll try."

"Eventually they'll succeed." I say it as much to remind myself as her. "They always do."

"Not always." She gives me an arch look meant to remind me of what happened a year ago. Like I need reminding. "Have a little faith, will you?"

I snort. "In myself?"

"In yourself and your mate."

"I have all the faith in Grace. But she's human. Vulnerable." I think back to the spurting blood, to the deep cuts on her shoulder and her neck. "Breakable."

She laughs. "We're all breakable, my boy. Part of being alive." She points a finger at me. "And your Grace might surprise you, you know."

"What are you talking about?" I ask. Then, tired of all her riddles and partial advice, I can't help demanding, "Can't you just tell me what you mean? Can't you just tell me what to do?"

"Nobody can tell you what to do, Jaxon. It's been your greatest strength—and your greatest problem—your entire life. Why change that now?"

Impatience wells up inside me, overwhelming the last of my fake calm. "Damn it! I just need to know how to break the mating bond."

This time when she smiles, there's a flash of razor-sharp incisors. "Careful how you speak to me, my boy. Just because I'm fond of you doesn't mean I won't drain you for a midwinter meal. You taste quite good if I remember correctly."

It's an old threat, one neither of us pays much attention to anymore. But I do shut my mouth because there's another threat implicit in that one—mainly that she won't help me after all.

We walk in silence for several minutes, until I'm all but vibrating with a desperate impatience, convinced I'm going to jump out of my skin at any second. Only then does she take hold of my hand.

"This will tell you how to do what you seek," she says to me, pressing a folded piece of paper into my palm and curling my fingers over it.

I want to ask her where the paper came from, but the truth is, I don't care. Not now that I have the means to save Grace within my grasp.

"Just be make sure it's what you really want." She repeats her earlier warning. "Because once you break what's between you and Grace, you can't ever put it back together again."

It absolutely hurts to hear her say that, to imagine an endless life without my mate. Without Grace. But when the alternative is watching her suffer—and die—so people can get to me, there really is no alternative.

"Thank you," I tell the Bloodletter, shoving the paper deep into my pocket.

"You're welcome, my sweet boy." This time when she lifts her hand, it's to pat my cheek. "I do love you, you know."

"I know," I agree, because in some strange way, it's true.

"And if even a crusty old vampire like me can love you, I'm pretty sure a girl as strong as Grace can, too." She winks at me before dropping her hand and stepping away. "Besides, you're forgetting one thing."

"What?" I ask, a tiny flare of hope kindling to life inside me despite my best efforts.

"'There are more things in heaven and Earth, Horatio, / than are dreamt of in your philosophy.'" She takes another step back, transforming into a winged creature I don't recognize right before my eyes.

And then she flies away, leaving me with the answer I sought and a host of questions I don't have a clue how to even ask.

Part of me wants to stick around and wait for her so we can talk some more—sometimes she's willing to do that after she feeds. But the second I walk back toward her main quarters, my phone starts buzzing with a series of texts from Grace and Mekhi.

They come in a mismatched order, though, so I head out of the cave and back into cell service range in an attempt to get the whole story. Which is when they start showing up fast and furious. As I read them, I forget all about waiting for the Bloodletter to return. I forget all about everything except getting to Grace—to my mate—as soon as possible. I need to make sure she's okay, and I need to make sure that whoever had the nerve to bite her understands just what a terrible life choice they made.

It's as I'm racing back to Denali that it hits me.

It doesn't matter who I have to fight to keep her safe. It doesn't matter what I have to do to hold on to her. Grace is my mate, and there's no way I'm giving her up. No matter what.

And what a stupid idea anyway—to sever the bond before Grace even knows it exists? This is a choice both of us need to make, and I was a total asshole to ever think otherwise.

Which is why the first thing I do when I get back to Katmere is to reach into my pocket and pull out the note the Bloodletter gave me. I don't even bother to open it before I tear it up and drop the pieces in the nearest trash can on my way up the stairs.

After all, I have a mate to see to, and nothing is going to stand in the way of that.

ABOUT THE AUTHOR

New York Times and *USA Today* bestselling author Tracy Wolff is a lover of vampires, dragons, and all things that go bump in the night. A onetime English professor, she now devotes all her time to writing dark and romantic stories with tortured heroes and kick-butt heroines. She has written all her sixty-plus novels from her home in Austin, Texas, which she shares with her family.

tracywolffbooks.com

ACKNOWLEDGMENTS

If you made it all the way to the end of this monster book, I have to start my acknowledgments by thanking you. Thank you for picking up *Crave*, thank you for reading all one hundred and fifty-two thousand words of it, thank you for letting me share Jaxon and Grace's world with you. I'm more thrilled than I can say that you have chosen to take this journey with us. Thank you, thank you, thank you.

Secondly, I have to thank Liz Pelletier, who I adore more than I can ever say. Liz, you have taught me so much about writing and myself and friendship that I don't even know where to begin to thank you. You are an incredible editor and an incredible friend, and I will be grateful the rest of my life that you chose me to take this journey with you. Thank you for everything you have done to make this book the absolute best it could be. I can't wait for the next one.

Stacy Cantor Abrams, I love that we've been working together for more than ten years now. You are an amazing editor and an even more amazing person, and I am so excited that there is more to come. Thanks so much for your unflagging enthusiasm for this book and your flexibility through all the craziness it took to make it come together. It means the world to me. I'm so lucky to have you in my corner.

Jessica Turner, thank you so much for all your excitement regarding this book and all of the wonderful ideas you came up with to market it. You are an awe-inspiring woman and a great friend, and I am so very lucky to have you in my corner. Thank you for being so fabulous!

Bree Archer, for giving me THE BEST COVER IN THE WORLD. Seriously. THE BEST COVER IN THE WORLD. From the bottom of my heart, thank you.

Toni Kerr, for the incredible care you took with my baby. Every page is beautiful and I owe that to you. Thank you so very, very much.

Meredith Johnson, for putting up with all the craziness that came with this book. Thank you so much for your help steering this behemoth all the way from my imagination to the store shelves.

Jen, thank you for all your thoughtful comments and feedback! You're amazing!

Everyone at Entangled and Macmillan, for your patience and enthusiasm for *Crave*. I'm so excited that this book has such an amazing home and such an amazing team behind it.

Emily Sylvan Kim—I don't even know what to say here. I didn't realize just how lucky I was the day you agreed to be my agent, and I thank the universe for you every single day. Thank you for always being in my corner and for always, always, always finding a way through whatever obstacle comes our way. You're the best.

Eden Kim, for being the first person besides me to read *Crave*. Thank you for all your excitement. It made everything that came after the first draft so much easier.

Jenn Elkins, for being my best friend through thick and thin for more years than we want to admit. Thanks for always being there for me and for always keeping it real, xoxoxo.

The amazing Emily McKay, Shellee Roberts, and Sherry Thomas, you are the best friends and brainstormers I could ever ask for. Thank you from the bottom of my heart.

Stephanie Marquez, for all your help and encouragement throughout the writing of this book. You remind me of all the reasons I love writing and all the reasons I became a writer to begin with. I love you so much and can't wait for what comes next.

My mom, for all your help keeping my day-to-day life running in a (kind of, sort of) smooth way. I know we're a lot, but we are so grateful that you put up with us! I love you!

And lastly, to my three boys who I love more than I can ever say. We've had a few rough and rocky years, and I just want to say thank you for hanging in there and being the coolest, most wonderful sons in the whole world. You amaze me every day, and I am so, so, so lucky to be your mom.

A lush, unique new fantasy trilogy about a girl tasked with stealing the prince's heart...literally, from *New York Times* bestselling author Sara Wolf

BRING ME THEIR HEARTS

Zera is a Heartless—the immortal, unaging soldier of a witch. Bound to the witch Nightsinger, Zera longs for freedom from the woods they hide in. With her heart in a jar under Nightsinger's control, she serves the witch unquestioningly.

Until Nightsinger asks Zera for a prince's heart in exchange for her own, with one addendum: if she's discovered infiltrating the court, Nightsinger will destroy Zera's heart rather than see her tortured by the witch-hating nobles.

Crown Prince Lucien d'Malvane hates the royal court as much as it loves him—every tutor too afraid to correct him and every girl jockeying for a place at his darkly handsome side. No one can challenge him—until the arrival of Lady Zera. She's inelegant, smart-mouthed, carefree, and out for his blood. The prince's honor has him quickly aiming for her throat.

So begins a game of cat and mouse between a girl with nothing to lose and a boy who has it all.

Grace's story continues in

crush

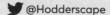

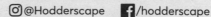